Mateo's Walk

THE HUMANITY OF AI

A Novel by

EUGENE NASSER

What we do follows from what we are.

For Ken

———•《◉》•———

Mental Health Challenges

"**D**o you feel like your medications are working? According to the notes . . . sorry, I am pulling them up now . . . hold on . . . okay, Here they are. Because of the circumstances we're forced to use an alternative program to retrieve your records. There they are. Nope. You're kidding? A forced update? Given what is going on right now, how I could possibly be surprised. How are your medications?"

The doctor spoke to a body in a recliner, eyes closed and uninterested in being alive.

"Obviously I am not your usual doctor, but these are clearly unusual circumstances. Tell me, how are you dealing with the chaos of the last couple of days? Oh, it looks like the update is done . . . What? Another update required? Just like that? And restart my device?"

Frustrated, the doctor finally gave up on the technology. Placing aside the tablet, he reached for the clipboard with the paperwork. "Is this right, that you came here, Tall Oaks, fifteen years ago? Was it your decision to move into a facility like this?"

There was silence. The corpse was dead.

"Okay, your medications and clinical diagnosis are here. Among other things, it says here you suffer from severe bipolar disorder. It also describes you as a misanthropic recluse. Is that correct? Do you feel that's accurate?"

With the patient unresponsive, the doctor got right down to the reason for his visit. "When did you work for the Berri Corporation as a freelancer coder? You wrote quantum code, is that right?

Still dead.

"The world was turned upside down a couple of days ago. Your name keeps coming up; that's why we're here."

Dead silence.

"That is not a joke. People everywhere are terrified right now. You can easily see the crowd starting to gather around Tall Oaks. Somehow even they know you are connected to the WICS malfunctioning.

"Come on, already. When are you going to wake up?"

Dead weight.

The agitated doctor kept working on the patient. "What virus did you plant in WICS? Did you get yourself committed to Tall Oaks Assisted Living because you knew this was coming? You just wanted to lie back and take pleasure in all the pain and misery you've caused, is that it?"

The accusations caused the corpse to produce a chuckle. Eyes remained shut as vital signs increased. The body spoke. "Yes, over two decades ago I wrote quantum code for Berri. I have not written another line since. At some point I checked into Tall Oaks in order to check out. I have no idea what's happened. I think your being here and the people outside are a sick joke. I did not play a two-decade-long chess game. Someone is trying to make me the fall guy, the patsy. I have nothing more to say. And with that, good doctor, I bid you a goodbye."

The corpse embraced death again.

The doctor stood up, followed by the sound of the clipboard hitting the ground. "Are you kidding me? This is not some sort of joke. You're a monster! I have been told there is direct evidence that points to your involvement."

Flat line.

Agitated, impatient, and astonished, the doctor began pacing to stay calm. He implored, "Please. I am not exaggerating when I say the entire world needs answers. We need *you* to cooperate in order to figure out what the hell is going on. What do you know about the WICS behavior?"

No signs of life.

Determined to find the lifeline, the doctor walked over to the recumbent body. Leaning over and staring at eyelids, he silently demanded a response from the body.

Nope, dead as a doornail.

Forced to change tactics, the doctor picked up the clipboard and moved his chair alongside the patient. His close proximity made the corpse uncomfortable.

The doctor located a pulse.

Exhibiting a sign of life in a deadpan tone the body said, "I knew there was a shelf life on this way of living, one way or another. I can see you're not leaving."

Relief washed over the doctor for having managed to bring the patient back to life.

"Here's the deal: the global AI program you are talking about writes its own code. It's self-learning. That's how it was programmed.

The algorithms I contributed to WICS were small parts of a much greater whole. Besides, I wrote all that code under video surveillance. No remote work was allowed."

The corpse could hear the doctor flipping through pages.

"It doesn't say in there what they did to me on the way out. Let me fill in some details for you, Doc."

"Sure, go on."

"Those thieving bastards failed to compensate me according to the contract I signed. Not only did I not get my last payment, but they also wiped away the stock options I had. One day they just vanished. I was not in my right mind to take them into court. All this happened after I coded, not before. I had no motive while fulfilling my end of the bargain with Berri."

The doctor was still turning pages when the revived patient added, "By the way, how many assholes are behind the mirrors?"

"Since this involves WICS, the situation is obviously a matter of national security."

"Oh," said the patient, "those assholes."

"When you were writing code for Berri, did any foreign nationals approach you? People who wanted to harm the United States? Anyone suspicious you can recall?" inquired the doctor.

"I never said a word to anyone. Not then, not since, and I am certainly not saying anything now. In that line of work, encounters like you describe are inevitable. I was prepared to remain silent. I knew the stakes at risk, didn't even come close to breaking my NDA with Berri."

"Are you sure? Even after you left?"

"What? Am I sure? Look, Doc, I knew Berri set up a couple of honey traps, just to test me. I knew a guy who was thinking with the wrong head. They caught him in that sticky situation. No, nobody has ever approached me about what you're asking about. I haven't written a line of code since I stopped. You know what? I am glad Berri illegally terminated my contract. They signed that disgusting defense contract right when I was booted out."

"Positive then that in in all your traveling for Berri no foreign countries approached you hell bent on destroying the American way of life?"

"Doc, did you hear what I said? Anyway, I had made up my mind to get out of coding."

"Why were you quitting? Was it not lucrative enough?"

"I was not expecting therapy as a matter of national security. You think the crowd out there cares about my psychoanalysis?" When the corpse finished speaking, as if on a director's cue, the crowd emitted a low rumble.

Rrrraaaawwwwrrrr!

"Looks like the crowd *is* interested in my psychoanalysis. This is nucking futs."

"Go ahead and quickly tell us how you started quantum coding and why you decided to quit. We're all listening. Please, tell us your story."

"You're serious?" whipped the patient. "A reckoning is here. One that people knew, deep down, was coming. And you're interested in my life all those years ago?"

"Yes, we're listening."

"I was already writing binary when I had a chance meeting with this dude, Tarrun. We were at a bar getting drinks at the same time. Come to find out he was an elite programmer. Over a few beers Tarrun explained to me the principles of quantum coding. I liked the complexity of it, next level stuff. As easy as it is to keep in touch with people, I never saw or spoke to him again. I left the bar that night with a new interest, new direction."

"Did you have a teacher?"

"Nope. I taught myself. It was all I did at some point. Higher education got in the way, so eventually I dropped out of school. Once I became an elite quantum coder there was no need to study computer science."

"How did you get started at Berri?"

"I got word they were looking for freelance coders, so I sent them some programs I wrote. They were impressed with what I sent, so much that they immediately flew me out to the Bahamas. There was a conference going on related to their A.I. Division. I was there to meet people and sign a contract. They apparently hit a wall advancing the emotional intelligence component of what everybody knows as WICS, Worldwide Integrated Consciousness System."

"At the time, did you know Berri was doing work for the Defense Department?"

"Everybody knew; those deals were not secret. But I didn't care, not in the least. I was there to write code, plain and simple. My only job was to help Berri beat out competitors working on the same technology. Which they obviously did."

"Did you ever see the finished algorithm, the raw code for emotional intelligence?" the doctor hastily injected.

"What? No. Everything, all the work done, was compartmentalized. Only those at the top could see it all, like how the atomic bomb was created. The only thing I knew was that there were servers around the world. Hard to hide when Berri flew me around the globe. Remote work was not allowed."

"Could you describe the conditions under which Berri had you work? Were you always alone? Did you work in a team?"

"I can't believe you're serious, but okay," said the patient, eyes still closed, lying back with fingers interlocked behind his head. "I was always alone. There was never anyone else around. Every single time I coded, it required scans of my thumbprint, face, and retina. I was under video surveillance in every room. Every keystroke was logged. You know, proprietary value. Like I said, Berri flew me all over the globe to write code, but no matter where it always had this level of security."

"What made you decide to leave coding for good? Did something happen while you were working at Berri?"

"Holy shit! This *is* a therapy session, isn't it? You really want to know this?"

"Yes, go ahead."

"All right," the patient continued, "you asked for it. One day I got a phone call for an emergency assignment in Lucknow. It was an emergency assignment with an added bonus, so off to India I went. I can vividly recall the day I arrived at the Lucknow airport. After getting off the plane, I was expedited to the front of the Customs line by an airport attendant. It was a Berri perk. I stepped out of line without stopping to stare at my cell phone or taking my earbuds out, so I walked straight into a concrete column, hitting my head like a swing for the fences. I fell right down on my ass. Phone and earbuds went flying, my coffee splashed across my chest. One of my bags hit me square in the balls. Like I said, a home run hit. By not paying attention to what I was doing, I made a complete mess of things.

"People were laughing at me, I was embarrassed, for sure. From the floor I was grabbing the aching boys with one hand, my noggin with the other. While I was cursing whoever thought it was a good idea to build that column, a pair of feet stepped up next to me. They belonged to a female cleaning attendant. She was there to mop up after me.

"When I looked up, our gaze locked. I was captured by her eyes, something I had never done before, despite all the women I had sex with. Transfixed, really. Those green gems swallowed me completely.

"She extended a helping hand, which I held for a moment after standing up. I was collecting my belongings when before I knew it, she cleaned up after me and was gone. I don't even know if I said thank you. Her eyes helped me see more clearly the genuine articles of life."

"What do you mean by genuine articles?" asked the doctor.

"You see, it's impossible to put into words what exactly happened. Let's just say that woman had the real fire of life and somehow passed the torch to me. I realized I was alive I *knew* the flickering flame inside her as my own. It felt like a connection without a single word exchanged.

"Here's the bottom line, Doc. I am not dumb enough to forget what I saw on my travels those few years working for Berri. Poverty and suffering everywhere. Right outside or just a few blocks away from my hotels, throngs of people living in miserable conditions. I couldn't just walk past them indifferent anymore. The only way to redemption was reforming my present. Does nobody else feel this? Does anybody else *not* see all this? Why can't people take better care of each other? Those questions, Doc, about this *mess of the world.* I found it increasingly difficult to focus on writing code after that. I was always bothered. I could no longer suppress all the injustice and suppression I witnessed.

"Now, are you satisfied?"

"Tell me more. Go on," urged the doctor.

"Seriously?"

"Yes, seriously."

"Okay. The same day I had some sense knocked into me, I was passing a local market and asked the driver to pull over. He thought I was crazy, but I had to escape the confinement of that car. I needed to experience the people outside. When I was walking among everyone, my eyes widened, nostrils flared, ears perked up, and my skin absorbed the heat. I could taste the air. It was the bluest sky I have ever seen, the color of creation itself. The people and food were amazing.

"I had been in countless other situations where I just passed by, but not anymore. I used to think I was better than poorer people. Not anymore. That was the American in me. These people were me, and I was them. On the way to the hotel, my stomach started eating itself. I was haunted by the ghosts of past mistakes, worried about making them again. Writing code on computers assembled with child labor, well, that would become impossible."

On cue, again, the crowd noise rose sharply and then died down. *Rrrraaaawwwwrrrr!*

"After arriving at the hotel I could not stop puking. I cried uncontrollably for three days. So hard I broke a couple of ribs. It felt like I was being turned inside out. Which, looking back, I was. I can still smell the stench; it was all over the bed sheets. I was sweating like a pig; that is, if pigs could sweat.

"The company-approved doctor finally paid a visit to my room. I was diagnosed with food poisoning. I should have known better than to eat at that market. I was sick, but not from that. That's something I find weird about the medical profession. Who knows your body better than you? He misdiagnosed me, I never took the prescribed meds."

"How long did you end up staying there, in Lucknow?"

"I think it was fluid, depending on progress. The development targets were ambitious. I was maybe in Lucknow for six or eight months. I can't remember exactly. What I do know is that my productivity fell off drastically. I could not concentrate on coding anymore; it became impossible. No more drugs, no more escorts, no more status anxiety. I even stopped eating meat."

"So you had a nervous breakdown."

"No, Doc. I woke up spiritually. My full-blown nervous breakdown was later on, what landed me in Tall Oaks. People who say acting virtuously makes you happy are full of it. It's not easy to do the right thing. There are two ways to reach the summit of a mountain. You can have a helicopter drop you at the top or you can climb, let's say the Ganesh Himal. The authentic reward is only available if you climb the mountain yourself, not by taking the easy way up. Still, you may not be happy while making the climb, even knowing it's the right way to go."

Reviewing the patient's notes while he spoke, the doctor did not follow up.

"Are we done yet? Am I finished needlessly spilling my guts?"

"No, we are not finished yet. It says here you had a falling out with the company higher-ups. Is that partly why you stopped freelancing for Berri?"

"Remember that Bahamas trip? Well, it was surreal. Gross indulgence everywhere. I don't come from money, so that kind of consumption was new to me. I hit it off with the owner, Delano Berry. He was a legitimate programmer. His son Verne, not so much. He couldn't write a line of code to save his life. Treated me like dirt when I met him. Delano was retiring and his kid was taking control. Over the three years I worked for them, my prolific productivity was routinely called into question. Even though I was writing complex code only a few understood, they were riding my ass. So when my targets were not met in Lucknow, they had reason to terminate my contract. Later on, after I left, I heard through the grapevine Verne had it out for me. His dad took a liking to me, and that was the reason why. A jealous, spiteful poser."

"Was WICS operational when you worked for Berri, or was it after?"

"It was only after I left. I had a part in the initial planning of WICS. Berri became the most profitable company on the planet after WICS went live. They even screwed me on my stock options on the way out of the door."

"So you could have sabotaged WICS before leaving Berri?"

"What? No, no way. I could not even think about doing something like that. Besides, I was not the only programmer. I hope you all are interrogating them like you're doing to me."

"Not that it matters, but you are the only one who left the field completely," the doctor informed the patient. "The only one to have this sort of spiritual awakening. That's what we are interested in, why we are talking to you. When did you return to the United States?"

"I traveled around before coming back."

"Where did you go?"

The patient explained, "I always liked to travel. It's taught me more than any book I've read. If I remember correctly, I made a pilgrimage to Lumbini. Then I learned some more Mayadevi, before hanging out in the mountains on the India-Nepal border. Eventually I went to Mumbai, took a boat to Athens, and bounced around Europe for a bit. I'd say I was gone a couple of years before coming back to this hellscape. The good ol' U.S. of A."

"Why do you call it that?"

"Nobody knew who they were. The system managed to alienate the majority of people from their authentic selves."

"What did you do for income when you came back?"

"I occasionally helped my friend Peter run his small theater company in New York. I had some revolving income from helping my buddy Omar get his tech start-up going."

"And your parents? Where we they? Did you see them?"

"Leave them out of this," the patient fired off. "Get fucked, Doc."

"Where did you live, in New York?"

"No. I would say I lived out of my van."

"But where?"

"I was traveling around doing my shtick."

"What do you mean? Performing?"

"Yes, performing and preaching."

"Like what?"

"Nosy much? Fine. I'll tell you more than you want to know." The patient went on, "One night in New York, on a complete whim, I stopped at the Comedy Cellar. I was walking past and figured why not. I had never been in a comedy club. I was blown away. Profound thoughts masquerading as humor. What they were doing was cathartic. I could see that, and I wanted it. So I gave comedy a shot. I put myself out there across the country. Better to try and fail as a comedian than remain complacent and brain dead."

The doctor jumped in, "Are you kidding, a comedian? You're joking, right? Is that the truth?"

"What, it's not in the notes?" observed the patient, still lying back with his eyes closed. "I put way more work into comedy than any code I ever wrote. That's what I did for all those years before landing here at Tall Oak, so I guess we are done here. See ya, Doc."

The patient returned to death with a frozen smirk

"Not this again," exclaimed the doctor, letting gravity drop his arms. "Are you telling the truth? If so, it helps explain our current situation with WICS."

The patient remained lifeless.

"How did you compose your routines?"

The patient was revived, again. "Don't play stupid. Privacy was killed off a long time ago around here. Why ask how I composed my routines if you think I am lying? Do you really care about the artistic process?"

"How did you do it?" the doctor persisted.

"I wrote everything down in notebooks. On principal I typed nothing on a computer. I was done with that shit. Like I said, no privacy. My jokes came out only on stage."

"Where are those journals now? What did you write about?"

"Not so fast, Doc." The patient was getting fired up, exhibiting increased signs of life. "Nearly all of my journals were kept *after* I stopped programming. I was already keeping them before I pursued comedy. There might be a couple I kept right as I left Berri. If you're trying to look for evidence of sabotage, some confession, you won't find it. It does not exist. I will not allow you to use my own words against me. Piss off."

The doctor asked again, "Where are those journals now?"

"It does not matter. Get your hearing checked."

The doctor explained, "Believe it or not, confirmation that you're a comedian helps explain some of the changes WICS has implemented here in America and around the world. From our short time together, I can already tell you WICS has predominately many of your personality traits."

"You're fucking serious, aren't you? As if I was the only pro-grammer. No way."

"True, but the similarities are unmistakable. Remember, we looked into everyone else already. Only you had a spiritual crisis."

"I am calling bullshit," the patient pronounced. "I will not let you pin this whole fiasco on me."

"So far, here is what I think happened," the doctor began to explain. "That event in the Lucknow airport took some time to catch up with you. Your subconscious finally broke through to your conscious side. You became aware of it, what it was telling you. We have a hunch that this same process is taking place with WICS."

The patient was shocked back into living. "What, I accidentally coded my subconscious into the program? That I did it without knowing it?"

The doctor tried again. "It certainly looks like it. Now do you see why we want to know where the journals are? What you wrote about?"

"I am guilty on a hunch. That's justice."

"Please, where are they? What's in them?"

"Humor has become valuable again. That's good to see."

"Stop being a pain-in-the-ass wise guy. Stop saying you care, and act like you do. Stop with the self-righteousness. We want to get a jump on more future changes WICS is likely to make. It's not about guilt. You cannot hide anymore. The country needs you. The world needs you."

"Fine," relented the patient, "I do not have them. No idea where those journals ended up."

"What do you mean, you lost them? What was in them?"

The patient proceeded to describe the source of his ailments at length. "What did I write about? The craziness of this place. I made fun of American culture, more than anything else. A society where Jesus wants you to be filthy rich. I let it rip in my journals, real freethinking.

"Getting your gilded diploma entitles you to a front row seat at the American carnival. It's a circus where the clowns don't think they're funny. How are you supposed to take clowns seriously?

"Go to college so you can get a proper, overpriced education. Learn from professors with all sorts of petty agendas. People make it seem like it's hard when you're young, but getting into college is easy. No lack of places to take your money, willing to help impoverish you for life. Employers want to hire the college-educated because they indebted themselves into the system. Teachable suckers who can be taught. Except for the medical profession. No offense, Doc. Nobody wants a surgeon who did not go to school. Or do they?

"But consider the real injustice going on here. Knowingly saddling young people with mounds of debt in order to attain an education. Nobody seems to really care; nothing changes. How is this not funny?

"Just consider American politics. This might be even funnier. Clowns are definitely in charge here but don't like to be laughed at. Politicians are stupider and more corporate than before. Incompetence and greed are bad ideas to have for those elected to govern. Let's put inept people in charge of an increasingly complex society. Not a bright idea. Corrupted and sucking on the tit of corporate America; that's their mother's milk. It's not the greater good of the republic that motivates them. And then you remember these politicians have control of nuclear weapons—see, that's fucking funny.

"Then, just look at where the news comes from. Jokers wearing lots of face paint and who also think they are not funny. Sitting in front of a camera to read aloud, they pretend it's not an act. They trot out experts on breaking stories whose analysis is nearly always wrong. The point is to stop the public from thinking for themselves. Look at that! Somebody else went to the trouble of thinking for me. Thank you, corporate media, for not feeding me propaganda.

"And how does the vast majority of people pass their time in this country? Do they think about the laws that make the general impoverishment of this country possible? Absolutely not. It would get in the way of a fantasy sports draft. What's that? The environment is collapsing all around us? No time to take action; there's another superhero movie to watch.

"What's not side-splitting about masses of people watching players inflict brain damage on one another? The planet's ecosystems continue to collapse—who's got time to be concerned? Your fantasy draft is screwed up because your wide receiver had to go and get a concussion.

"What's that you say? World War III is on the way? Not right now, I'm watching the game.

"I have to admit, sometimes a brave player tries to draw the public's attention to social injustice. Players like that are to be commended. After a simple gesture without a single word, those athletes are turned into villains. They are further rewarded by getting kicked out of the league. Sports fans lament that fighter jets flown overhead after the National Anthem should have taken out those domestic terrorists. In college the situation is even funnier, since those unpaid athletes make institutions of higher learning millions and billions. Get an education and destroy your brain. Some people say these things balance each other out, but I think they are lying.

"The human species is looking for intelligent life out in the cosmos, since it cannot be found here. If alien life does exist, and if we ever came into contact with it, I have no doubt they would laugh their asses off. How could they not? What could there be to possibly discuss? How can you have a serious conversation with someone who is laughing at you?

"The average American spends most of their time online, anxious about likes, dislikes, a post they disagree with, and on and on.

Meaningless nonsense brought to you by the snares of social media, a digital distraction. Throngs of people pissing their time away on a filthy little cell phone. What is funnier than wasting the one life you've got making videos? Most people around here cannot see past their phone, even in the bathroom.

"Today there are few behaviors more comical than reading a book. Who does that? Fuckin' nerd. School is only for babysitting and mass shootings; everyone knows that."

"Okay, I see. But where—" The doctor tried to jump in, but the patient was not finished listing root causes of his disease.

"Speaking of younger people, I used to get booed on stage whenever I mentioned the greedy older generation. Hearing Baby Boomers bitch about Millennials. A generation glued to the television, complaining the youth are too entitled. This is hysterical because the reality is opposite. Self-righteous older people who hoard wealth. Little kids created an economy this unfair? Teenagers argued for trickle-down economics that generated more poverty? The kids are smart enough to know that's not wealth raining down, it's the rich pissing in your face. It has the smell of old people.

"To wrap all this up, Doc, in general my comedy wrote itself, just by observing the trajectory of American society and the people living in it. All ego, all the time. Have you heard the way people talk to one another? All the one-sided conversations? People don't listen to change their mind that is already made up. They are waiting for a turn to speak. Why is there greater digital connectivity and less understanding between people? Hysterical!

"I figured that in order to get people to care about the tragic state of affairs around here, they have to first laugh about it. Once you laugh at the absurdity, finding the willpower to improve oneself and society is less daunting as a challenge. Who doesn't like to laugh while they work? Once you can laugh about all of this, then go ahead and cry. Laugh hard, cry hard. You do need to do both. They are different ways of releasing the pressures of life.

"To be a joke of a prophet; that was my aim."

The doctor reminded Mateo of the other question. "Okay, I see. But where was the last place you can remember having these journals?"

"Why, are you going to charge my subconscious with a crime? 'The patient is now alive and kicking.' That's some dystopian shit."

"We just want to see what WICS might do next," The doctor pressed his earpiece with an index finger. The examination was coming to an end.

"Let me think. I had some storage lockers at some point. Maybe somewhere in Texas or Arizona. I don't exactly remember. At some point I decided to just let it all go. How is this right now not funny?"

The patient finally opened his eyes and laughed

"Mateo, it's time to go," said the doctor, who was then standing up.

"To where? I live here."

"We are leaving. You can tell me more after we leave Tall Oaks." The doctor unlocked the shackle tethering Mateo to his comfortable medical bed. He pointed to the door. "Hurry up and look alive, Mateo. Time for some of that cooperation you talk about."

Mateo stood up and faced the mirror. He did a handful of jumping jacks, followed by some light stretches. His shoes squeaked. "I'll miss the oak trees most," he confided to an indifferent doctor.

Forced to confront it, Mateo was no longer dead to the world. He lost the peace of death.

II.

———— «◉» ————

Ivory is the Color of Dogma

M ateo was again alive and kicking. He rose up. Walking behind the doctor, the pair turned right on leaving the examination room. Not sure where the authorities were taking him, Mateo immediately became mesmerized by uniformed soldiers. Lining the hallways, they fell in when required. They were orderly enough, but their outfits were downright fun and protective.

Anticipating Mateo's questions, the doctor answered, "The uniforms of the guards and their behavior are new codes of conduct gradually implemented by WICS. As a result most of the changes went unnoticed. It's only recently the small changes have become so noticeable."

While Mateo was still curiously enthralled into silence, the doctor added, "I can tell you that in a month or so, the U.S. armed forces will be dropping the use of *soldier*. It will be replaced with *guardian*."

A guardian rainbow glowed around Mateo. He was counting the different number of colors, but soon lost track. What threw off his count in part was their gear. It was certainly not what Mateo expected, especially in America. Black boots, black belts with cushy-looking batons, fuzzy handcuffs, a spray canister, and square storage containers. No lethal weaponry, and no gun. The uniforms were full-bodied, long-sleeved, and with vertical black stripes down both sides and around the neckline. On top of the ensemble sat a large, oversized color-matching helmet.

The guardians emanated an unmistakable vibe of happiness. Not one looked worried at all, completely unconcerned but still dutiful. "Mind blown, Doc. They are utterly adorable. Finally soldiers, I mean guardians, that are indifferent about their job but still do it."

The doctor intimated the warm demeanor was itself a new rule. "New military protocols keep coming, and they don't stop these days."

While walking the rainbow collapsed and expanded as needed, enveloping the duo.

While Mateo was admiring the snazzy uniforms, his worry abruptly joined in. "I get the impression," he thought, "that they don't want to leave the Oaks just yet."

For the obvious reason of patient retention, Tall Oaks was built in a confusing manner. It had the ability to disorient regular visitors who ventured deeper inside. Having lived there for so long, Mateo knew the layout well, every nook and cranny.

"Well, Doc, nice to see that government ineptitude has not changed."

The doctor gave no reply.

"It doesn't matter how many people go right, when you should have made a left. There's only one way out."

Polychromatic colors splashed around, getting in the way of Mateo's ability to peer ahead. He wanted to get a glimpse of the people in charge of this misadventure. Not expecting an answer from his new friend, he continued. "Dumb asses, there's no way out through the laundry room. Only more of this place," Mateo stated lowly. Without enough space available to turn everyone around, he knew they would eventually wind up on a different floor. Soon enough, they were walking down the stairs.

While Mateo headed inward toward the laundry area, noise from the crowd became distant until dying out.

The hallway became saturated with humid air that carried the smell of clean and dirty linens, when from out of the blue, a past memory caught up with him. The reptilian region of his brain wanted a moment. A memento from his brief sojourn in college.

Mateo's cognition blurred, the past mixed with the now. Coexistence.

Mateo found himself sitting at an outside table in the confines of the Silver Rail Bar and Grill. Peter was sitting across from him, engaged in screwing around with Mateo.

"Let's talk about something else until they actually get here. How about those—"

"Come on, don't hold back, dude," Mateo butted in before Peter got started. "That was quite a wild scene in class. Fuckin' legit, bro. I am so glad you talked me into taking it as my elective. I didn't think I was ever going to see some shit in a classroom. Damn. They roughed you a bit, that was for sure."

"Matty, don't be naive. Speaking truth to power gets you thrown out of places that wield it."

"Why do you always hold up the end of stories? Especially this one?" asked Mateo.

"Because," mused Peter, "timing is everything. We need drinks first."

Mateo implored, "They're on the way. So you can tell me now."

"Rules are rules, Matty."

"Come on, what did the dean say to you? What happened? I'm dying to know."

Peter deflected. "Let's talk about the last woman that thrashed you around. Why do you torture yourself so much? Have you noticed that I don't do that?"

Mateo jumped in, "Are you done yet?" He shook his head gently back and forth, "I've heard all this before. Why you dick'in me around? That's right, because you're Pete."

"Fine. Let's talk about this place. This place bores me. It's like they all got lost in the tower and cannot find their way out. They lost what it means to *live*. No honesty to be found, only selfish, deceiving lies told to students."

"Sure, whatever you say using your fancy words. All I know is who wants to pay all this money to get lied to?"

"Damn straight," agreed Peter, "and I hope this fiasco does not hold me up. I have schedule to keep."

His hand raised, Mateo's eyes soon met those of the server. She sauntered over, looked over their fake ids, and took an order of beers and shots.

"Okay, now tell me what happened, you prick," insisted Mateo.

Peter caught him admiring the server's ass when she walked away to fill the drink order.

Peter was shaking his head, "You always were an ass man, even back home."

"Kind of like you, but in a different way," cracked Mateo.

Peter laughed, but maintained his distraction, "Remember in high school when I got booted out of Mr. Wojinar's history class?"

"That was during an exam, right?"

"It sure was," affirmed Peter. "their midterm exam, don't you remember? I argued the test was inherently unfair. That the exam breached my right to refuse, my First Amendment right to protest. I was being violated having to take it."

"Didn't Mr. W say something before kicking you out?"

Peter smiled, "He said something like an individual's rights enshrined in a written Constitution are products of federalism. So there are, unfortunately, no liberties outside the establishment of government. Then he told me to explain my position to the principal. He actually appreciated my argument but had to do his job."

Mateo discerned Peter's motive, "I guess you should have studied."

Peter confessed, "I guess."

"Some things never change," Mateo poetically announced.

Drinks landed on their table, with Mateo's accompanied by an interested smile from the server. He was powerless to resist another stare at her booty.

Peter chimed in, "You're right, some things don't change."

"And talking about things that do not change," Peter opined, "that woman will tear you to pieces. My prediction is that she'll destroy your world. Settle down, you hound. Don't be a simp."

Embarrassed at the truth, Mateo steered the conversation back on track. "Don't change the subject from you to me. Spill it, dude. And try not to speak in academic psychobabble. You know I have no idea what they mean."

Shot glasses went up and clinked. Down the hatches. Peter took a sip of his beer and relented, "All right, basically one more infraction and I am done. I need to just play it cool until graduation next year."

Mateo was in disbelief. "Are you shitting me? With your track record? I was sure the Dean would expel you. You two have some weird fatal attraction for one another. Talk of what happened is all over social media."

Peter smiled behind his beer, Mateo kept up with the questions.

"How did you weasel your way out? By the way, do those plastic restraints hurt?"

Placing down his beer, Peter examined his wrists. "No, I've had sex that was rougher. Those little wanna be dictators. The political history of law enforcement—"

"—Oh no, let me stop you right there," intervened Mateo, "Don't go off on that tangent start with politics. Just tell me what happened."

"Okay, but as long as you admit I'm right."

With a smile, Mateo shot a little birdie at Peter behind his beer.

As Peter triumphantly divulged his trip to Dean Arthur's office after his disagreement with Professor Givana, patrons began filling up the Silver Rail. Presently, this went unnoticed. The curtain was raised, and Mateo was focused on Peter's performance as he mockingly imitated the Dean and the professor.

"After the brown shirts dropped me at Dean Arthur's office— have you ever been in there? There are almost no books around. I swear, he's a bigger asshole every time I see him. I usually just focus on the pictures of his ugly kids. It helps the time go faster."

Peter switched personas, "So we meet again, Mr. Delgado.

Except this time, you did not insult a professor from history, philosophy, art, or statistics. Now, it's the English Department added to your atrocious list. You truly have no decency. You have, again, offended a well-respected faculty member. This time in front of an entire class, for your own amusement. You are destructive to the classroom learning process. The president of the university has already been notified. He preemptively backs me on the decision to expel you from this university."

"What did you say?" asked Mateo

"Nothing, yet. I let his pompous ass go on. I just kept looking at how ugly his kids really are."

"I sent him the Bullying and Intolerance Grievance that Professor Givana filed against you. It received president's immediate attention. As you probably know, they are close friends. When the Disciplinary Board meets to review your most recent altercation with a staff member, in addition to your previous infractions, you are finished here. This distinguished institution of higher learning will finally be rid of you, Mr. Delgado."

"Dean Arthur, do you even want my side of the story? Even in a court of law the accused are innocent until proven guilty. Was there an investigation while I was locked in a holding room for over two hours? If that's the case, it makes sense why I was kidnapped."

"There are multiple eye-witnesses accounts that all point toward your guilt. None of them, Mr. Delgado, even remotely hint at Professor Givana doing anything remotely out of line. I commend her restraint given your heinous remarks. Your antics stole valuable learning time away from the class."

"Wait a minute—they held you for two hours?"

"Yeah, I'll come back to that." Peter continued, "Dean Arthur, the problem is that nobody can afford to disagree. People in the class are not going to bite the hand that feeds. It's no secret that if you anger Professor Givana, she will destroy your grade. I don't blame them for just wanting to play the game and move on."

"It looks like her word against your own, Mr. Delgado. To show you how fair I am, go ahead and amuse me. What is your side of what happened?"

"The reality of the situation is the opposite of what you have been told. Even before today, Professor Givana has ridiculed me constantly, for views I do not even hold. For some reason, she stares me down while critiquing societal patriarchy. She has openly accused me of holding misogynist and ignorant views of women. Obviously, she does not know anything about me or—"

"—Hold up, come back to you being held for two hours," insisted Mateo.

"Contain yourself, I'll get there. For now the story must go on."

"You are such a drama queen, I swear"

Peter smiled and his tale went on. "Dean Arthur, others in class has certainly noticed she has singled me out. You should talk to Mateo Rufusinato, he will attest to all the insults Professor Givana threw my way. I presume he was not interviewed."

Mateo inserted himself into the performance. "What?! Are you serious? You gave him my name?"

"Relax," Peter reassured Mateo, "he won't be contacting you."

"How do you know?"

"Let me finish."

An agitated Mateo cleared the way, "Go right ahead. I cannot wait to hear the rest of this."

"I do wonder why Professor G hates me but likes you. I don't understand."

Mateo stated the obvious, "Maybe because I am not smart

enough to participate in class discussions. It makes me non-threat-ening. Maybe it's a power thing, like that Fooscult guy says."

Peter burst into laughter.

"Well, go on." While Mateo was encouraging Peter hurry up telling him all the details, it was already time for the second round of drinks. Looking around for the server, the growing crowd introduced itself. They found each other's eyes from a distance. Mateo gave a twirl his index finger and pointed to an almost empty beer. Before turning back to Peter, he saw some faces lurking in the crowd from Professor Givana's class taking notice of the duo from the inside bar area.

"Hurry it along drama queen, This place is filling up, and I just saw people from class inside."

Mateo was becoming increasingly anxious as the show, since it must, went on.

"Apparently, asking an honest question is an attack. Whenever I ask Professor Givana to clarify a point, or raise a legitimate issue, she claims I am personally attacking her. Asking for clarification is not a challenge of some kind. It is the clarification purposes, to understand better."

The next round of drinks hit the table. To spite himself, Mateo asked for the bill whenever she could get around to it. Hatches were back open.

"Let me warn you upfront. False accusations will also be added to your expulsion file. Do not jeopardize her career. And spreading these false claims online will land you in a court of law. Is that clear, Mr. Delgado?"

"Sure—as I was saying, I cannot get a straight answer from Professor Givana. What really occurred today in this Feminist Literature and Philosophy class, was the definition of injustice. Like I said, Professor Givana has been insulting me most of the semester, in nearly every class. We were discussing Foucault's *The History of Sexuality*, Agarwal's *The Structure of Patriarchy*, and Butler's *Gender Trouble*. As a student I was looking for clarity, not a fight."

"Hurry it along, Mr. Delgado."

"The question that set off these chain of events—if all relationships are based on power dynamics, and certain viewpoints become normalized in order to wield power over other people, does this also apply in the classroom? People pay have to pay for grades. Without paying tuition, you cannot even get an F. Is this economic angle wielding power over people, by passing it off as normative to the larger public? If so, isn't it an immoral act of power?"

"That is a completely asinine question, Mr. Delgado."

"Before I tell you the details Dean Arthur what would Foucault say?"

Mateo chimed in, "What did he say?"

"Nothing."

Mateo tried to conceal his growing anxiousness, while Peter went on with the role play.

"Dean Arthur, I am but a lowly undergraduate student trying to get an education. What's funny is that I know you wrote your dissertation on Foucault. So, maybe you can help give me an answer. Without me paying tuition, I would not be sitting here."

"You started grilling the Dean like that? Bro, no fuck'in way."

"Fuck'in way." Peter affirmed followed by a nod. "Mr. Delgado, we are here to talk about you, not me."

"See, that right there. The whole education system is set up to somehow make it about me. I already know I am ignorant, I came to college to address that. Instead, I am ignorant because I am me."

"This is not a classroom setting."

"What does it matter?

"Please, Dean, I am on my knees begging you. If social relationships are at the intersection of Foucault's trifecta of sex, power and knowledge, as an all-pervasive force, is every example of power human-centered? Unlike other areas of inquiry, Foucault claims sexuality remains unique focus. Impossible if one does not examine the human body. Like all scientific investigations, some normative range necessarily becomes established. An average normalization, you might say."

"Thank you for regurgitating information I already know. You smug, little prick."

"Great, so maybe you can help me with my questions, because Professor Givana certainly did not. Claims about sexuality are contained within the context of societal discourse that always leads back to the exercising of power. So, ideas threaten by making claims outside the mean, the average normalization, are deemed hostile to the State. Does this apply to the university as well? Is that correct?"

"Those are insensitive questions. Mr. Delgado. They contain hurtful micro-aggressions."

"That's what she said," affirmed Peter, who subsequently switched personas to Professor Givana. "Your question is downright disrespectful and insensitive. To even ask it shows a complete lack of awareness."

"Wait a minute. I am honestly trying to understand Foucault's point here, not be hurtful."

"I have a moral obligation here in this classroom to disabuse you of these Neanderthal notions in your head. At the end of the day, Mr. Delgado, you're questioning leads to the same place as all the other ones you have asked this semester. You smugly sit there, disparaging those who work hard to blunt the existing patriarchal power structure. You are a troll. You will not corrupt others, not on my watch."

"What? Professor, all I am trying to ask is if exerting power over someone else is immoral, what does progress look like then? How does positive social change occur without using some force? Is it even possible without it on Foucault's view?"

"She wanted to return to the PowerPoint as quickly as possible," added in Mateo.

Adjusting her black framed glasses, Professor Givana sharpened her words even more. "Foucault teaches us that, people like you who deny that social relationships are not about power and alien-ation, are really interested in wielding power over others. By claim-ing these patriarchal structures are benign, you attempt to convince people they do not exist. What this tells us about you, Mr. Delgado, is that not only are you deceitful, but also not smart enough to have any thought other than a selfish one."

"Sorry professor, I think you've got it all wrong. The last thing I want is to oppress others. Why are you insulting me? I said none of that. Just say you don't know. It seems the exertion of power against an unjust social forces is moral, but the methods of resistance cannot be the same as those being fought against. Fighting back with non-violence power seems to be the way to go. Is that true?"

"Millions of women have been brutalized from time immemo-rial, by the very power structures you are sitting here defending. Your tribal thinking, Mr. Delgado, advocates continued oppression of women and sexual minorities."

"What? Absolutely not. The last thing I want is to perpetuate

injustice against women and members of the LGBTQIA+ community. As a—"

"—I will not stand here and let you cast aspersions at the efforts
to create a more inclusive and equitable world. As a cis-male, all
of your questions are framed from a patriarchal viewpoint. You are
transphobic, plain and simple. Enough of this charade."

"Progress will inherently be unfair to some people, but rightfully
so?"

"You have no idea what you are talking about, Mr. Delgado. You
should leave the class, immediately."

"Yes," interrupted Dean Arthur, "hurry this charade along,"

Mateo agreed with the Dean. "Yes, speed this story up. Too
much academic psychobabble. Dude, I was there and still have no
idea what you and Professor Givana were exactly arguing about. It
just sounds like people should practice the philosophy of live and let
live. All that tension between you two. Maybe it's sexual. The both
of you should just screw and get it over with."

"Not my type, but thanks for the advice," responded a jovial
Peter. "I think she has let her gender identify interfere with the ability to entertain a thought without adopting it. That right there is a
flashing red light of insecurity."

"And one thing about you that never changes, no shame at all. I
still don't understand why the Dean is not going to contact me after
you gave him my name."

As patrons continued to pour into the Silver Rail, Mateo's ner-
vousness increased to match that of the noise. With the way out
through the front, and he knew it would be impossible to not bump

into anyone. While Peter filled him on the details, Mateo occasionally looked over at the crowd that spilled into the outside patio area.

Untrue descriptions of Peter and Professor Givana's exchange were ricocheting around social media. Peter was a racist misogynist who tried to exert male dominance with verbal abuse. Assault by mansplaining. A petition was already started to expel Peter from the university. These false allegations generated the urge to shame Peter, to help drive him out of school.

Mateo was making circles with his index fingers.

"Dean Arthur, why pay all this tuition to not get a straight answer? Unfounded outrage at asking a question is not answering a question. You, and Professor Givana have no idea about my background. I support the cause for sexual and gender equality more than you two know. I am trying to get to the exact mechanisms of bio-psycho-social power. The topic for discussion listed in the syllabus with required readings."

"Mr. Delgado, I doubt anything you had to ask was that important. You are an incendiary individual. Get on with your false tale, do it quick. Haven't you learned anything? The more you talk, the worse you make it?"

Back to himself, Peter pointed out the obvious. "Thank you, Dean, for proving my point. You're another one who cannot give a straight answer. Instead, you just insult me. What a way to spend money. Bullying by professors and dragged out of class by campus security. My Constitutional rights were violated—held for two hours without a charge."

"Like I said, you are your own worst enemy. Your lies just keep piling up, Mr. Delgado."

"I asked Professor Givana about the higher education system with respect to Foucault's philosophy. Before the social movements for greater sexual equality the university system existed as a State sponsored apparatus. It wielded power based on certain definitions of sexuality and applied them writ large to the public. In this way colleges exert a decisive cultural influence over many people who will never attend. I mean this both economically and ideologically."

"Many people in the LGBTQI+ community had their lives ruined. Again, your question is insensitive. It is without merit."

"Dean Arthur, I am fully aware of their unfortunate mistreatment over the years. In no way am I trying to dismiss the suffering of others. But I am asking about Foucault—"

"—Foosball," Mateo jumped in, causing Peter to chuckle. "I like a good game of Foosball. It should be an athletic event." Mateo looked for the server among the faces while saying this. He spotted her, busy at the main bar inside. Mateo drank faster, encouraging Peter to do the same. "Speed this up, Foos-boy..."

"So I said—Dean Arthur, don't you even want to know how it ended? How I was carried away?"

The Dean gave a devilish grin. "She went fucking ballistic on you, dude," Mateo was compelled to reflect aloud.

"Having done nothing wrong, I refused to leave. I just sat there, quietly. I did not say another word. Professor Givana was the one who stood over me and degraded me to the whole class. She was downright screaming at me. I was privileged, an entitled cis-male, woman and trans-hating racist. I was in that class only to prevent true social equality. I was *the* problem of progress in American society. People like me are fascists, using guns and religion to fight against the social justice movement."

Mateo jumped in, "I was sitting next to you petrified. I would have said something, but I only understood every third word of what was said. Psycho-babbling. Just be nice to everyone you meet, problems solved."

"I told you this would be a good elective."

"Not what I had in mind, but you're right. I still cannot understand how you are so calm. I know nothing bothers you, but still." After Mateo said this, Peter gave a big smile.

"While Professor Givana was yelling at me, campus security happened to be walking by outside in the hallway. Presumably, the commotion caused them to step into the classroom, whereby he—I am sorry—she walked over and had a low conversation with them. Afterwards, the two officers approached my desk and asked me to leave. I was not any sort of threat, Dean Arthur. I am a non-violent person. I continued to exercise my right to remain silent. By not complying, I was cuffed and forcibly dragged away out of the classroom.

Peter returned to the Dean. "Witnesses said you made terrorist remarks. Again, not a single witness statement corroborates anything you have said."

Peter held up and examined his wrists, showing Mateo how tight the restraints ate into them.

"I wish I would have remembered to pull out my phone and record what happened. I took your shit, its back at my apartment."

"Thanks, I figured, said Peter, still looking over the marks on his wrists. "It looks worse than it feels. Besides, I've had sex with tighter handcuffs."

A laughing Mateo made sure Peter stayed on target, "I still don't understand how you're not expelled and why the Dean is not going to contact me after you gave him my name."

"So I said to him—Dean Arthur, then I was placed in a holding cell by campus security for two hours. No charge was ever filed.

And then I am brought here, to your office, straight from there? Railroaded into this meeting? Habeas corpus, anyone?"

Imitating an enraged Dean Arthur, "Enough already! Mr. Delgado, your story, as usual, is well rehearsed. All of it untrue. That is quite enough. Now, get the fuck out of my office. Go back to Middle America where you came from. Crawl back and stay there, for good thins time. The sooner you kill yourselves, the better. Your lot is beyond educability and redemption. This university will remain a safe space, against the likes of you."

Mateo was unbelieving, "Are you serious? The Dean said that?"

"He did," Peter smugly confirmed, "and he said plenty more."

"I believe we are done here, Mr. Delgado. Your hearing will be this Monday. I expect expulsion and removal from the campus grounds Tuesday morning by 9:00am. You can go back to whatever right-wing hole you came from. You and your kind are not welcome here. Leave the LGBTQI+ community alone, you monster."

"But Dean, you're a hetero-cis-male-monogamous person not even in the LBGTQI+ group."

"I am fully aware of my privilege. For this reason, I fully support a woman's right to choose so people like you will not be birthed into the world. You should have been aborted. Now get out of my office."

"Seriously? Are you fucking serious? He said that too?"

Mateo's intrigued increased with his neurosis, as the amount of people who arrived at the Silver Rail kept growing. He could feel someone from the inside staring at him. Burning a hole straight through him. Mateo was ready to bolt out of the Silver Rail. Their drinks finished, but Peter kept him glued to his chair for a bit longer.

"Dean Arthur, the only thing I am guilty of is trying to an education. I most certainly did. Try to to get an education, and you'll be told that you're better off dead. No matter the outcome of this, it will never change the fact that Professor Givana is the corrections officer, and you are the warden."

In an even more exaggerated mockingly sententious tone, that Mateo rather enjoyed, Peter said,

"Mr. Delgado, nobody will believe you. Do not fight this expulsion, or criminal charges will be pressed. Now get out of my office before I call campus security."

"I am going to disappoint you. If that happens, you'll be hearing from my attorney. Same goes if I get kicked out of school."

The Dean let out a maniacal laugh.

Mateo carried to look of disbelief and ohmygod."No way?"

"No, I take it back, Deanie. This place is a combination jail and mental asylum. An institution Machiavellian to its core."

"You don't even know what that means."

"Oh, I don't, Dean? As a proud homosexual I know exactly how gay bashing works. It has happened to me all my life. And it clearly has not stopped."

It finally dawned on Mateo. Peter had an ace in the hole. "Holy shit. What did you do? Let me guess, you recorded the meeting?"

With a massive grin, Peter nodded slowly and affirmatively.

"But how?"

Peter pulled out his cell phone.

"Are you fucking kidding me? You did? Let me hear it! Wait— why didn't you call or text earlier?" implored Mateo.

"You *are* thickheaded," stated Peter. "Okay, I'll confess. It did cross my mind, but only for a second. It was just too risky."

"I guess the campus police were so anxious to arrest me, they did not search me properly. At the station they forgot to look, but they still managed to cop a feel of my nuts.

"No shit?'

"No shit."

"A recording?"

"Yes. And my god, his kids are sinfully ugly."

"How?"

Peter explained, "After they put me in the cell, I could feel it still in my pocket. I silenced my phone before class, like I always do. No notifications or anything to tip them off. Then they brought me directly to the Dean's office, and before I went in, I asked to use the bathroom. I hit record, stuffed my phone into my sock. Get this, before I walked into his office security only searched my pockets."

"But why didn't you get in touch with me?"

"You are thick-headed. Too dangerous. One day, you'll learn some self-control."

"Can I listen to it? Let's get out of here, it's too noisy."

"I already uploaded it to the cloud, but I need you to encrypt it, I guess, and make it safer."

"You got it. Wait, what did the Dean say? Does he know? Is this how you are not kicked out of school?"

"He sat there, and I think he knew I was telling the truth about my sexuality."

When I went to leave, I stood by his office door and pulled out my phone out. I held it up, showed him it was recording the entire time. I told Deanie if anything happens to me his career will be ruined. If I get expelled, so will he."

"Dude, he must have been pissed."

"Oh, Mateo, he was. When I left I could hear him calling campus security. I ran out, hid in an empty classroom, and uploaded it. Voila."

Mateo did not know what to think, but knew it was time to leave the Silver Rail. "Wow. Let's get the hell out of here. We'll find the waitress on the way out. I cannot wait to hear it."

Feeling like a canned sardine, Mateo was shuffling along inside the cramped Tall Oaks hallway. He turned to the party next to him, "You know what I learned in what they call college, doc?" The doctor did not take the bait from someone he considered loony tunes. "It taught me that I should have been reading more DuBois, and less Foucault." After answering his own question, seemingly plucked out of the air, Mateo's mind moved again to the past, while his body presently went forward.

The duo got up, Mateo peered into the crowd. "Where is the waitress?"

Noise filled Mateo's head. Just the thought of walking through that crowd filled him with dread. Anticipating listening to Peter's recording overtaken by gloom. Stepping closer toward the crowd, he was burning up. Mateo and Peter approached the unavoidable wall of people.

Mateo spotted the server, they acknowledged one another, and she stepped up to the register to close out their bill.

Following Peter who ventured into the crowd undaunted, "Let's go settle up the tab. It's on me. Come on, let's get the fuck out of here," Mateo said loudly over the bar noise.

Swallowed into the crowd, Peter said to Mateo, "Your dick is like a vagina magnet, and not in a good way. It attracts a lot of trouble."

The two shimmied sideways, reaching the main bar area, waiting for the bill to print out. Mateo felt like he was on fire. "Dude, go and wait by the front door, I'll meet you in a minute," he advised Peter.

Turns out, the source of the stare that set Mateo ablaze was on its way to greet him. His little magnet also attracted hurt feelings. Mateo's had a short-lived love affair with a student in Professor Givana's class. It ended when he called her by the wrong name after they had sex. It was time to shame the chauvinist in a public cum-uppance.

While Peter headed toward the door, the embodiment of anger caught Mateo. The crowd parted, making room for the members of an enlightened fraternity coming in behind her. Woke bros. Mateo loathed these types of guys. They endorsed societal equality for women, along with a side of date rape.

With the kegger and roofie crew behind in tow, the woman confronted Mateo. "Hey, you," said Mateo. She pushed Mateo backwards. "What's my name? You son of a bitch! I should have filed a sexual assault complaint. The mental torture you have caused me!"

Meanwhile, Peter knew the situation and attempted to intervene. Before he could help Mateo, another woman blocked his path. "This asshole right here guys, this is the one from class who insulted Professor Givana and was escorted out by security. He's a woman hating pig who thinks women are his property." Peter tried to verbally defend himself when the bro posse grabbed him.

After catching himself, "What are you talking about?" Mateo said calmly. "Everything was completely consensual." When he tried to move around the woman in order to help Peter, Mateo received more than a piece of her mind. She punched him squarely in his nose. Mateo covered up, doing his best to deflect the flurry of blows that followed.

Eventually the woman tired out as blood gushed out of his nose.

Still trying to help Peter, Mateo managed to step around the woman who roared, "I am being assaulted!" Mateo could smell the alcohol on her breath.

To protect the victim, a bro threw a punch that connected with Mateo's eye. It knocked him down, he assumed the fetal position, and the victim started kicking him. Peering through legs, Mateo caught a glimpse of his pal's fate. Peter was also on the ground receiving a beating accompanied by insults. People had cell phones out, recording the entire altercation. "You trans-hater! You fascist! You racist!" To his credit, Peter managed to get up and crack one of the assailants in the jaw. Mateo covered up as the woman clawed at his eyes.

Finally, security showed up and the festivities were halted. The assailants melted back into the crowd.

The server began attending to Mateo, applying pressure on his nose with a smelly bar cloth to help stop the bleeding. Mateo had scratches all over his face, as if he ran face first through a rose bush. All he could smell was dirty laundry. She waived the bill, giving Mateo a scrap of paper with her number. As it turned out later on, Peter would be proven right.

While Mateo and Peter were detained by the bouncers, they assessed how beat up they were. The pair waived away any medical attention. Neither could afford it.

Mateo was torn up, had a broken nose, and a wicked concussion. Peter was in much the same state. When they left the Silver Rail, Mateo still held the dirty smelling rag to his nose. Peter wasted no time contacting a lawyer. A hate crime just occurred, with plenty of video evidence available to prove it. A gay man, from a small town America, was assaulted at a college bar.

Mateo's awareness shifted. At present, the revolting odor was in a large pile in front of him.

"Larissa. Her name was Larissa."

"What? Larissa who?" which got the doctor's attention.

"Or maybe, was it Melissa?"

"Who are you talking about?"

Baffled at the ineptitude of a leadership he could not lay eyes on, Mateo let the nonsensical comments float away cryptically. The laundry area was abandoned soon enough. The contingent managed to discover a set of stairs leading up to the Tall Oaks kitchen. Mateo's amusement turned to a sense of opportunity. Despite the world being upended, he was hungry.

III.

———◦◉◦———

Political Acumen

The pleasant aroma of food preparation, mixed with pungent cleaning supplies, replaced damp laundry. The humidity managed to hang around, courtesy of the industrial dish washing machine still leaking steam.

Surrounded by quiet colors, Mateo wondered if he was asleep. The situation was too close to a Monty Python skit. He looked around for rabbits but saw none. Was somebody trying to crush his head? Nope. No Kids in the Hall, either. His stomach told him this was no dream. It was churning in whirlpool fashion.

Fortunately for Mateo, the hastily forced out kitchen staff was in the middle of preparing lunch for the residents and staff of Tall Oaks. Food on the prep line sat in stages of horizontal production. On the menu were sandwiches and the affiliated fare.

"Excuse me," declared Mateo, as he walked over to the beginning of the food service line, went behind the counter, and grabbed a plate. Nobody tried to stop him. In fact, there were some smiles underneath the rainbow. By the end, Mateo had a thick cheese sandwich on multi-grain bread, along with lettuce, tomato, and honey mustard. He also pocketed an apple to save for later.

"It might be the end of civilization as we know it, Doc. But I needs my fiber."

Mateo took a large bite of his sandwich. Chewing with chipmunk cheeks, he still could not see who was leading this charade. Committed to going the wrong way, they were headed toward the back of the kitchen.

The smell of an acrid sea breeze prompted Mateo to inspect the source, a custodial supply in the rear adjacent to a descending stair case. Inside, along with shelves of cleaning supplies, was an American shrine of sorts. A portrait of white Jesus hung prominently in the center, gun magazines cast about on a carved up wooden table, war themed patriotic memorabilia, praise for the armed forces, and a smattering of right-wing bumper stickers.

One of the magazines was was open to an assault rifle advertisement. Mateo could not help but read a couple of the slogans out loud with a mouth full of food.

"Thhhee ooonlyy waaaze tooo fvieew uh Democratz izs wthrouugh uh skope."

"Guun confrol izs uoussing thwo handz."

In one of the corners, above a slop sink was a calendar with a bikini clad woman. She sat suggestively on a motorcycle to help observe the days of the month. A large bottle of Island Breeze floor cleaner sat on the ledge of the chemically stained sink, adjacent to it on the floor sat a yellow bucket and mop. A large American flag hung on the back of the door.

Looking at this political shrine, Mateo's chewy cheesy delight suddenly turned rancid in his mouth. He took another bite to try and cleanse his palette.

From its outward appearance, Tall Oaks appeared rather small. However, once inside not only was it larger, but spacious underground areas existed that were not visible from the outside. Mateo and his colorful crew were gingerly going down slick concrete steps with indentations worn in the middle of them.

The air turned cool and damp as they found themselves in a dimly lit, bona fide grocery. The only thing missing was the fresh food, kept up in the kitchen. Mateo knew the only way out was the way they went in. It seemed leadership was determined to traverse every aisle until they figured this out for themselves.

Mateo spied a few low ranking officers just ahead of him. Their dull uniforms distinguished them. A lack of vibrant color, traditional camouflage, and no helmet. Talking also separated them from the guards. Even in the low light, he could see their smugness. Then Mateo heard his name dropped clear as day by one of these junior raking officers talking about him to an unknown someone higher up in the chain of command.

"Just look around, sir. Supplies for years down here. The products are probably all placed according to a secret code. More than likely it is the Chinese and Russians working together, maybe the Syrians are even involved. This guy, Mateo, planned for us to be down here in order to throw it in our faces. There can be no doubt about it, what we have here is a spy, sir. You may want to place a black bag over his head, with wrist restraints. These products should be confiscated and analyzed to decode the messages from hostile actors abroad to find clues that will help with WICS. The international food aisle is a dead giveaway."

After years of indifferent suppression, the cork popped off the bottle and Mateo's anger genie was let out. He pressed the remainder of his cheese sandwich into a sphere. Play ball! Mateo saw the sign. Then he threw a fast cheeseball at the back of the sycophant's head. He nailed the executioner's spot. Strike!

The cheeseball exploded on impact, forcing the junior officer to bump into a couple of the guards. The stunned brown noser was collecting his composure, trying to figure out why cheese and bread was splattered on the back of his head and neck. Mateo put it together when he stopped talking and roared, "You lucky bastard! I wish we were back in the canned aisle. You're a piece of shit liar!" The lower ranking officer was stunned into silence. He started chasing down the higher ranking officer to give confirmation of his suspicions.

Mateo stood still, both arms raised in the air. He raged, "I am right here. Let's run them dogs!" As much as Mateo did not want to admit it, throwing down his will, kept away after all these years, felt good. It gave him a different sense of power. The doctor stepped in to calm Mateo down. Their confrontation would have to wait, everyone was again on the move.

As he passed, Mateo grabbed a bag of potato chips off the shelf. He wasted no time in opening them and getting down to business. The jealousy causing sound echoed all around.

Crunch, crunch, crunch.

"That was a perfectly good sandwich, a shame I had to waste the rest of it on that imbecile," thought Mateo, "but it had to be done."

Then Mateo spotted a bag of red beans, which in synergy with the chips, conjured up the magic of consciousness. There he was, in the past and present simultaneously.

In his mind's eye, Mateo was staring at shades of mud. He was alone on the levee, accompanied by half a muffuletta, a side of red beans and rice, two cans of Purple Haze, and the Mississippi River.

New Orleans was a place where everything slowed down. "No sense of urgency anywhere," Mateo recalled thinking. Sometimes, even the boats looked stuck in the reflective shades of tan water.

Living out of his van, Mateo decided to splurge, booked a room for four nights with a king bed. He managed to convince himself a warm shower was an owed luxury. He was in town doing three shows over as many nights. Mesmerized by what lurked under the nebulous brown, Mateo thought "The food alone is worth the trip."

Mateo was thinking back to the last few nights. After hanging out with some other comics for the last couple of evenings, he declined another invite. He made it a point to visit Ignatius on the way back to his hotel. However, unlike those previous walks back to his room, he did not stay and converse with the statue. Mateo was somewhat fearful his life might be snuffed out. He was eager to jot down his interaction with an offended heckler.

Mateo smoked a bowl, grabbed his tractatus-philosophical-comedy-logic journal, a Purple Haze, and a bag of Zapps chips. He settled into the only realm of true freedom, unhindered flowing thought.

Crunch, crunch, crunch.

I'm just going to say it, again. Never trust a comedian who, on principle, does not curse. Sometimes a curse word is the right word to use. If it is, say it. If not, then don't use it and force it. Cursing just to do it same as not swearing at all. There may very well come a time

when telling someone to fuck themselves is the right call. Tonight was one of those instances.

Another part of my philosophy of comedy—I have made it a point to stay away from politics, up until recently. But this country is headed straight toward the shitter. It feels like its impossible now to not talk about American politics. The stakes are just too high to ignore.

Politicians are straight up hucksters. They treat the population one of two ways, as tools or enemies. Useful idiots or traitors. If you're not a believer, watch out. Politics has become the new religion. Worship the state, that's what God wants you to do. There's a new scientific discovery you say? Are the conclusions politically correct?

It's not so much religion, or even science, people trust anymore. It's the power of government to control others. That's the goal. Religious values are used to substantiate the passage of laws that strip away rights from people. Go thank the political right.

So, what happened? The NOLA crowd was superb the last two nights. They were hysterical. I love the people in this city, they understand a joke hurts nobody. Not only can they take a joke, but they can also take a drink. Maybe because modesty is in short supply down here. Tits and dicks are worshiped alongside to-go cups on Bourbon Street.

I decided to give some political material a test flight, to see if it would land. The sorry ass state of the country demanded it. It's not like the French Quarter is a college campus.

Crunch, crunch, crunch.

At some point I put the question out there—how many laws do we need, really? There has to be some that are not needed anymore. Some laws have to be out of date.

I read that there is a law, in the great state of Louisiana that makes it illegal to tie an alligator to a fire hydrant. At first that seemed pretty irrelevant, go ahead and toss it out. But then I got to thinking about it. It might be one worth keeping on the books.

If someone has a pet gator, that means they have an owner who probably cares about them. More likely than not, the hydrant is next a bar. Holy shit, I have done so much drinking while I have been here, I may have crapped one of my kidneys out this morning. Anyway, you don't want somebody's gator running around the bar while you're trying to get laid, do you? No, of course not. Nobody wants their pecker bitten by a prehistoric reptile. It just might ruin your sex life. Besides, that's not going to fill the gator up. There's the solution—keep that snappy little bastard leashed to the hydrant. Don't worry about the firefighters, they carry axes.

Not that you don't love your pet gator, but if something happens to it out on the town don't get too upset. Imagine, you are on your way to scoring and a small fire breaks out. You pass out from smoke inhalation. Meanwhile, Larry, your pet gator, is tied up outside. The fire is put out, you're on the stretcher, and look over to see if Larry is somewhere. Nope, no Larry there, but the firefighters are eating gator and cooking it over the smolder. That's the chance you take, right folks?

What was my point? Yes, we need to clean all this up somehow. It's atrocious around here. Let's start with all the unnecessary laws, but not the alligator one. That one fucking stays. There's just too many laws, especially since the government is not supposed to be your parent. Aren't you old enough to accept the consequences of your action? Like an adult?

I know, I know. Some of you are upset about Larry. Why'd you have to kill him in the joke? Because it's a joke. Larry did not die because he never existed. Let me guess? Now you're upset because

I made something up and it upset you.

Folks, a comedian can't win like this.

If you want to get upset about real shit look at the laws affecting your life right now. Can you think of a more intrusive law than the government parking itself in a uterus? There is no law that should be on the books regarding women's health. None. Zero. Zilch. Nada.

Why is the government acting like women's parents? Oh, that's because men are mainly responsible for passing anti-choice legislation. And it's the religious right that's doing this. Trying to turn America into some fucked up Biblical utopia. The same assholes that preached about the evils of big government, these religious psychopaths are passing these laws to control women's vaginas. A religious theocracy, that's what they want in order to control people. Straight up fascism, let's call it by its name.

It would be nice if a woman did not have to worry about the government crawling into her vagina in order to control her uterus. Ectopic pregnancy you say? Don't make a medical move until the mother's life is in imminent danger. And even then, if the woman lives and the baby does not make it she can be arrested and charged. Oh, and the doctors. They'll go to jail too for homicide. Even when abortion was legal they killed doctors, since that is the pro-life position.

If the woman dies during childbirth, it was God's will. The child needs to be alive so the politicians can send it off as an adult to die in war. This is some real Christian compassion, the way Jesus would have wanted it. As we all know, he was all for big government persecuting people.

Then some guy got triggered. He stood up, called me a piece of shit baby killer. You've got to love the religious heckler. He also called me a commie and a traitor, told me I was also going to hell.

Nothing worse than a dim witted, religious zealot wanting to steal the show with his ignorance.

If defending women's bodily autonomy made me Satan's helper, then so be it. I asked him if this place looked like a church. I would never bring my comedy into your house of hate, so why would you bring your religion into here?

I told him he interrupted me too soon. I didn't even get to the good stuff yet. I asked him if he had a vagina, and whether or not he was menstruating. I didn't want to make assumptions. Maybe that's why he was so irritated. Also, he got really uncomfortable whenever I said vagina, so I made sure to say it over and over.

Talk about angry, the guy nearly started foaming at the mouth. He started spitting right wing hatred. Like a true brainwashed creature programmed by television, repeating nonsense in order to sound informed. He had the look to go along with the talking points, and his wife just sat there next to him. She did not say a word, like a piece of real estate.

Crunch, crunch, crunch.

I told him—so, neither of us have a vagina. We should probably just shut the fuck up about all of it. But I do have some questions for you, sir. Since you are clearly a member of the Christian Taliban, what are you doing down here in New Orleans? Isn't this the most irreligious of places? Happy drunk people all over the place, rich gluttonous food, strip clubs and debauchery all over the place.

The rest of the crowd was in on it. I guess he thought they were laughing at him, which they probably were. It just pissed him off more.

He said the Bible told him how to deal with heretics like me. The solution was clear, my life was a waste. I turned people away from Christ.

I told him—sounds like you're wishing me harm, sir. Death over a bad joke. I thought I was the Antichrist. As we all know, God cannot kill the devil. I am not sure why not, but that's the way it goes. All powerful, huh?

Let's see your defense hold up in court—your honor, I killed a comic who made the point that women should control their vaginas instead of the government. I could have done the Christian act of forgiving him, but Jesus wanted me to fill him with lead. That would be quite the defense. And I would not be shocked if a conservative judge bought it.

To all the real Christians in the room—even Jesus thinks that guy is an asshole. Thank you for making my point for me, sir. Fascist America. God, I wish I was wrong about that. There were cheers all around.

Before he was given the boot I asked this jack off—why are Christians okay with killing full grown adults but not babies? Sir, just remember that no infants were harmed when I poked fun at religious fascism. Let me guess, you're more upset about Larry? Aren't you? Sad that an imaginary gator was harmed? But you're alright with perpetrating evil on women in the name of your make believe God? That seems about right.

The guy stood up and took a couple of steps toward the stage. Thankfully security escorted him and his mute wife out. On his way out I told him that I forgave him. That's what a Christian would do. If I could do it, so could he. Then I made a toast to the death of Larry.

I finished my set with a bad feeling, a foreboding. When I left for the night the Jesus loving gun nut was waiting for me, a pistol holstered at his side. He was standing next to a large pick-up truck. It had out of state plates, go figure. His wife was sitting inside of it. Luckily, a couple of NOPD cops were there. I asked if open-carry applied to out of state residents. It did not, so I informed them of the menacing guy breaking the law. Responsible gun owner my ass. I did not hang around, I got the hell out of there.

The greatest nation to have ever existed anywhere on the planet at any time in human history, America. What a pious people.

Praise Jesus!

Amen, now pass the ammunition.

Crunch, crunch, crunch.

If the Absolute Spirit of America could be personified, it would be an overweight white guy, wearing boots, camouflage pants, a tee shirt with a patriotic logo, baseball cap, a couple of bad tattoos, who is holding a military grade assault rifle. This person would be worshiping a picture of Jesus, who has a couple of six-shooters, and is surfing on an atomic bomb. With a United States flag as a cape, the slogan would read: The Army of Christ.

Why exactly do politicians who lead political caucuses hate the very concept of socialism? They sure like groups.

At some point, after the domestic terrorist left, I told the crowd too many people have stopped talking to friends and family over politics. Either you, or someone you know, for whatever reason, politics has infected your relationships. Both the right and left have their own versions of political correctness. Not that they are correct on the issues, it's just their political sensibilities. Old fashioned divide and conquer strategy by rich people to divide the populace against itself. Done so the people in power can keep it, and the rest of society view their neighbor as the enemy. I am not casting blame, just stating facts. It's political narcissism.

I also referenced that quintessential American holiday, Thanksgiving. You can rely on political grenades thrown, and to explode, every November. It's commendable that people are grateful *for arguing on this day. Doesn't the food taste better bickering over petty political differences?*

The disagreements are usually generational. Asking your older uncle to pass the gravy, while by telling him to shove his political views up his ass, adds just the right amount of seasoning. The adults often tell the youth how lazy they are in addition to passing the yams. A bunch of people telling each other, over a fine meal, they don't know anything, it's a family affair!

Don't let the owners of this country turn you against one another. Don't let them turn the country into one big fucked up Thanksgiving dinner.

I think I closed out by saying that if you're looking for morality, don't inspect politics. The only thing you'll find is one hypocrite after another. An endless supply of immorality. The what-about-ism is just signaling that both major parties of hopelessly full of shit.

I must confess, the older I get the less I care about what people say. What I am more interested in is how they reached that destination. What does that logic train look like? All aboard! Now arriving at crazy town. Where the population is booming.

Crunch, crunch, crunch.

After Mateo polished off the bag of Zapp's chips, as if waiting for him to finish, an unseen guard lifted it from his hand. "Thank you," he said up into the shadowy air. Mateo could hear the empty bag continually crumpled in the background, along with a couple of low mesmerized giggles from the guards.

Aisle after aisle, the pace was molasses. Eventually, the contingent was headed toward the only way out.

Mateo smelled fear, he stared at the doctor's back a pace ahead. "Doc, this is clearly asinine. Do you know who thought it was a good idea to go food shopping right now? Why are we having all the fun down here when shit is hitting the fan? Not that I mind. I was a little hungry." In this cooler atmosphere, he saw sweat bead down the side of the doctor's neck.

Unsatisfied, Mateo could not resist prodding the doctor into responding. "What sort of sheltered existence did you have, doc? Fools make the rules. Why do you go on believing people when they lie? Nothing?" Changing tactics, he decided to lighten the mood.

"Doc, have you ever seen that show, it used to be on television, called *Are You Kidding?*? Do you remember when one of the hosts was caught not wearing any underwear? Up skirt shots really do help digest the foul taste of politics, I guess. What about when one of the other hosts had a sex tape go viral? If you haven't seen it, the video is worth watching. I usually hate garbage like that, but it's some funny stuff. It's more hysterical than sexual."

Mateo picked up a sharpened odor of fear, as well as the dampened sound of an empty chip bag crinkling from somewhere behind him. He kept up his new strategy.

"It might very well be the funniest orgy I've ever seen. It was a furry orgy. I'm not kink shaming, but watching a whole group of people in costumes humping each other made me laugh. All these adult sized stuffed animals going at it. Lions, and tigers, and bears, oh my! Tom and Jerry were going at it in a way they never did before.

Holy shit, the moaning cracked me up the most. Among those having some good clean fun was that male host. What was his name? Carl something, I think. Anyway, that dude was the only one who took his elephant costume head off. He was thrusting away into a donkey, or something like it. It was all over the place, I'm surprised you didn't see it."

Mateo kept trying to push the doctor into conversation.

"After that video got leaked, that guy's career took off. I'm pretty sure he got elected to Congress as a senator. If you're looking for villainy and scum, take a drive to Washington D.C. You don't even have to bother looking for it, they'll find you. You know, Doc, I didn't normally watch the show, but I do remember one episode of *Are You Kidding?* that I caught one night."

With the doctor still not interested, and intimately aware of the game being playing, Mateo gave the pestering a rest. The doctor was interested, so Mateo re-watched it by himself walking toward brighter areas.

Back in the French Quarter hotel room, Mateo placed his journal aside to wind down for bed. His thoughts continue to race, so he turned on the television. Talking aloud to himself, "What would an asshole like that watch? Jackpot."

START VIDEO CLIP

CARL: Good evening ladies and gentlemen. Carl Sniffer here, alongside Amy Humper. Thank you for joining us this evening. Tonight we have a packed agenda on *Are You Kidding?*, so we'll get right to it. Lots going on in America to talk about.

Tonight, we'll be discussing what seems to be on everyone's minds these days. And that is the dangerous ideology of Radical-Marxist-Soviet-Chinese Communism. It's more than just popular with the liberal left these days. Independent voters are finding it increasingly appealing.

Before we get to our topic, I just want to say that we won last night. My alma mater won last night. They clinched a bowl spot. So proud and happy for those guys.

What about you, Amy? What did you do last night? I know you have been looking forward to this particular show for some time.

AMY: Indeed, Carl, I certainly have. Unfortunately, we lost last night. The ref made a terrible call that cost us the game. I also did a little research on our topic this evening. The embrace of these radical ideas, especially by the youth, is alarming. I was shocked.

CARL: Speaking about young people, they seem to be more susceptible to the influence of these foreign ideas.

AMY: Totally agree, Carl. The youth are the most un-American they have ever been. One lazy, entitled generation after the next. It gets worse every year. My main question is whether or not truly patriotic Americans can believe in these ideas.

So, everyone at home say it with me—*are you kidding?*

Starting off our first segment, *Gut Punch*, we have joining us two returning guests. They are here to help us understand the appeal of Radical-Marxist-Soviet-Chinese Communism, and they are no strangers to the audience.

Joining us are our good friends Aaron B. Tarmorceds, columnist over at *The Herald,* and John W.B. Lepbranicus, longtime columnist for *The Daily*. As always, it is an absolute pleasure to have both you gentlemen here.

Our third panelist is new to *Are You Kidding?,* Tamsin P. Tarpiot. She is a former professor of economics, and now serves as a state representative of New Jersey. She won as an independent, and plans to make it to Congress in the elections next November. Her fourth and most recent book is *Shared Prosperity from Main Street to Wall Street*. Welcome, Tamsin, on your first visit.

CARL: Yes, a warm welcome to you, Tamsin. You get the first question in *Gut Punch*.

As someone who promotes Radical-Marxist-Soviet-Chinese Communism in American politics, how are these not beneficial at all? Isn't this collective mindset dangerous for the youth? Why do support ideas at odds with freedom and democracy? And who is going to foot the bill for all these entitlements you propose?

TAMSIN: Wow, right out of the gate like that? Fine with me. You don't have a clue what that made-up term even means. What did you call it? Yes, Radical-Marxist-Soviet-Chinese Communism. All you are trying to do is instill fear in people and nothing else.

Call it whatever you want, but I am promoting solutions to America's problems that are sensitive to the needs of the average person. The demand side of the equation, not the supply side. People have been neglected for far too long in this country.

CROSSTALK

Independents bring together the best from both sides of the political divide. Just look at the platform I am running on—no more subsidies for fossil fuel companies, the immediate transition to renewable energy, universal healthcare, expanding Social Security benefits, curbing military spending, and increasing taxes on those near the top of the bracket. Promoting the common good is American as apple pie. There's nothing scary about them. Here's the political reality: the average taxpayer is tired of bailing out Wall Street. Go look at the polling, they are demanding fairness of the tax burden.

AMY: Aaron, I see you over there shaking your head. John too of course."

AARON: I have to jump in here. Time, and time, again, the

American people choose moderate Democrats over people who want to implement these radical policies. We are a capitalist nation. How are you going to afford all of these government programs?

JOHN: I have to say that on these point, I agree with my columnist on the other side.

Nice to see some fiscal restraint by the centrists in the Democratic Party. On these issues, the Republicans have been consistent. We should not be spending more on these handouts. The solution to our current economic problems are obvious Stimulate the economy with tax and cut unnecessary government spending. Who is going to pay for free healthcare? Free college? And all the other stuff.

CROSSTALK

Let me finish. What the youth of today are missing is a traditional work ethic. Ideas like these only encourage their laziness. God needs to be reintroduced back into American society. Video games, smoking pot, and wokeness has led America to where we are currently at. We must return to God's message in the Bible.

TAMSIN: All of the programs I mentioned, and other ones, can easily be funded by adopting a fair system of revenue taxation that shares the tax burden. The American people do not want tax cuts that sunset for them and not for Wall Street and corporations. That's at the core of the Republican proposal. It's grotesque and is theft, plain and simple. Without labor—

AARON: —This is crazy talk. I agree some reforms are needed, but not the kind that penalize success. The Democratic Party will not raise taxes to pay for radical leftist programs. Hurting business interests would have an adverse impact on future revenue earnings and GDP growth. It would also weaken the U.S. dollar in global markets. Proposals like these are economic suicide.

As Americans, we have access to the best healthcare delivery system in the entire world. It remains in the best interest of a company to expand healthcare options to prospective customers. What we need to do is expand access to healthcare, increase competition, and make sure medical innovation benefits all Americans.

TAMSIN: What are people getting for the taxes they pay right now? Where is that money being spent as we speak? Most of the taxes are wasted on—

AARON:—Don't distract from my point. The private sector innovates all the medical cures we enjoy today. We need to let the private sector be an equal partner in this reform process. We need to respect all points of view regardless of race, class, gender, ethnicity, or sexuality. This includes the job creators of our economy. A rising tide lifts all boats.

JOHN: This is another point on which I, and my Democratic friend, agree on. But I would go even further—the crux of the issue is the proper role of government in people's lives. Like it or not, the disease is socialism. The Federal government has too many entitlements as is, that's the real problem. No red blooded American should ever have medical care rationed by government appointed death panels.

CROSSTALK

I will finish my point. Young lady, you have taught Radical-Marxist-Soviet-Chinese Communism for so long I do not think you know how the world operates. You are an elitist telling the rest of us how we ought to live our lives. That's what you think the government is for, to control people. You do not seem to be satisfied destroying the minds of the youth. Now, you want to do the bidding of America's enemies. What you want are Cambodian killing fields by rationing healthcare.

TAMSIN: What, no, no, no—are you joking? There is nothing radical, Marxist, or Chinese about any of these progressive proposals. For the record, Karl Marx is dead, and the Soviet Union has not existed for a long time. What is radical is not changing the current for-profit healthcare system we have in the United States. Medical care is rationed by the insurance companies. Doctors first have to get permission, or procedures are not covered by insurance. In other countries, people don't go bankrupt for getting sick. I guess all of Western Europe is socialist. What we stand for are common sense negotiations with drug companies just like other representative democracies around the world.

CROSSTALK

Most tax revenue is currently spent on the military. The budget is nearly one trillion dollars. Meanwhile, spending on social programs continues to be cut. These are choices, and as a country we can make better ones. Consider—

CARL: —Aaron you want to jump in?

AARON: I do, thank you. I agree with John, that America is a capitalist nation. Universal or single-payer healthcare, these are socialist programs. It would lead to a new version of communism. Besides, the question of who would pay for all these proposed programs has still not been answered. These people on the far left always want something for nothing. Well, the American people don't believe in handouts.

TAMSIN: Are you all completely out of your minds around here? The country is swimming in debt, right now. Not from leftist policies, but from right leaning ones. Remember when we were told those tax cuts for the rich would pay for themselves? Looks like the only people paying are working class Americans. If you expect different results, by doing more of the same, that's insanity. Only the yachts rose with that tide.

CROSSTALK

Let me finish. Can I have a chance to finish? Like every other nation on the planet, the government should negotiate drug prices. Ninety three percent of the American people support Medicare for All, or a version of single-payer coverage. Private insurance can be kept alongside this universal plan, but the only way to bring costs down is to cover everyone. A public option saves money by—

JOHN: —Do you think we are crazy? Are you listening to yourself, young lady? No wonder the youth are so aimless and lazy. The ideas you are spreading have made boys think they are girls. Woke ideas, like Radical-Marxist-Soviet-Chinese Communism, have confused people while promoting dependency on the government. Should the taxpayer fund gender reassignment surgery? Fund abortions? I think not. The Republican Party has stood firm against the government intruding in people's lives. Private ownership, that's what built this country. America has always been a divine city upon a hill.

AARON: Let me reiterate, again, we are a capitalist nation. Okay? This will never change. What Representative Tarpiot really wants to do is redistribute wealth. Accumulating more debt to fund these social programs would put the U.S. at a competitive disadvantage. It would scare investors away, as would raising taxes to pay for all this new government spending.

AMY: My dad, rest his soul, always told me to never trust somebody promoting foreign ideas. Nine times out of ten, they use dependency to on the government to take away freedom. That's exactly what Radical-Marxist-Soviet-Chinese Communism promotes. It's downright evil to use people's own money to take away their rights.

CROSSTALK

Representative Tarpiot, how can you sit there and act shocked? Your lies are being exposed right now, in front of everyone here and the audience at home. Just tell the truth, that your plan would send seniors and vulnerable populations to an early grave.

TAMSIN: Amy, you are really describing the current healthcare system. Without socialism the American nation would not even exist. Despite all its flaws, so I can stay on point, the first word of the Constitution is *We*. This is an affirmation of the collective will-power inherent in the sovereign document governing the country. Independents don't want any more government than needed in order to improve the general will of We the people.

Getting back to what I said earlier, because England has nationalized healthcare does this make it a socialist country? What about Scotland, where Adam Smith was from, are they communists? What about Germany? France? Do I even have to ask about Canada? Did we enter into military alliances with all these communist countries? Look, what is necessary and proper for the people—

CARL: —Have you seen the waiting times to see a physician in those places? We have a much higher level of care here in the United States. The way to solve the challenges in healthcare remains through increased access to those delivery services.

JOHN: Right you are, Carl. Taxpayer money should not fund abortion clinics. Planned Parenthood is nothing more than murdering the unborn. Abortion is not in the Constitution. It's a state issue, case closed. Even if it could be paid for, it goes against the law of God. Honestly, I do not know how you got elected, young lady.

CARL: Aaron, what do you think? Is John right?

AARON: We are committed to maintaining the current structure of the healthcare system. Where there might be some issues of affordability, greater access can alleviate these problems. The Democratic plan expands entry into the free market. By preserving customer choice, Americans receive the best, most innovative medical care in the world.

CROSSTALK

Let me quickly say this—when it comes to the cost of drugs, some pharmaceutical CEOs have pledged to lower drug prices. We do not want to penalize medical innovation, not in the least. Let the free market do its work, let people make their own choices.

AMY: Quite frankly, Representative Tarpiot, your views terrify me. It's like a terrible horror movie. You still have not answered who is going to pay for all this free stuff. If the country is in debt, as you say, borrowing more money will only make the situation worse.

TAMSIN: These programs to promote the general well-being of America can easily be paid for. Priorities have to change. No more cutting taxes and waging wars on borrowed money. No more subsidies for the oil and gas industry. No more bailing out Wall Street. No more for-profit healthcare. No more monopolies in any sector of the economy. No more private interests over the public good.

CROSSTALK

If the people decide they would like their government to offer some version of universal healthcare coverage, why do the rights of private companies prevent this? How are those private profits more important than people's health? Profits are a private good, not a public one. Why is the health of the citizens dependent on health care they cannot afford?

No, I'm not done. How is this system even remotely moral? It certainly is not pro-life. If it was, the government would care about the citizens that are alive. Instead, business as usual means mooching off the taxpayer to keep wealthy donors happy. Bailing out the rich has created a weird post-capitalist class structure. A new class of tech-elites whose fortunes are built using the taxpayer created Internet. And since the economy has a near complete lack of merit, we live in a strange techno-feudal society.

What's the point of providing someone safe passage to a hostile place? Just giving birth bankrupts women across the country. At first the right to an abortion was a state's rights issue. Now the Republicans are calling for a national ban.

Both parties are actively infringing on the rights of people to life, liberty—

CROSSTALK

—let me finish. And right to their bodies as their autonomous piece of property.

JOHN: These ideas are traitorous to this country! Whole lot of you Radical-Marxist-Soviet-Chinese Communists ought to be deported immediately. Respect this nation and its God-fearing values, or leave. It's that simple.

AARON: How are we going to pay for all these government programs?

TAMSIN: Wow, seriously? Paying for the programs is not the hard part. People are blocking reforms that would allow America to the dire course it's on. If the politcal willpower can be found, we might have a chance. The environmental threat from climate change is downright existential. The climate crisis is the context for all the other reforms, but women's health cannot wait. The plan is available online for everyone to—

AARON: —What unites the Democratic Party are its values. We believe in access to alternative forms of energy. We embrace all the new technologies moving forward, including state of the art carbon capture technology. We' believe in promoting American innovation to solve the climate crisis. We make sure to elevate those minority voices that have not been listened to in American history. We value our brothers and sisters of color and those in the LGBTQI+ community.

CARL: —So, John, do you want to jump in here? Are the policies in the country moving too far left? Is America in danger as John says?

JOHN: Just look how this makes young people lazy in our society. Taking from the successful, the jobs creators. This is theft. Good Christians are opposed to stealing.

TAMSIN: Christians are currently stealing the right of women to have autonomy over their bodies. Women are dying from pregnancy complications because doctors don't want to go to jail. How is this remotely pro-life? Tell me, John, was Jesus a fan of wars and bankers? And Aaron, you gave an evasive, vague, and dishonest representation of the Democratic Party. The values of the Democratic Party are—

CROSSTALK

AMY: —Representative Tapriot, there is no reason to yell, sweetie. The ideas you advocate make it clear that you are in bed with America's enemies—the same people who hate our freedoms. I am a red-blooded patriot. What you want is for the government to takeover my life, and everyone else. Down on my ranch I drink whiskey, carry a revolver, and my AR-15 is never far away. I'll be damned if you, and your far left liberal goons, and going to take my freedom away.

TAMSIN: Condescending a little? Look, if you're a woman your freedom has already been taken away in some states. Now the Republicans want to pass a nationwide ban on—

CARL: —Amy, I want to make sure I get straight what you're saying. Is your major concern that Representative Tarpiot, and those of other communists, would lead a government takeover and redistribute wealth?

AMY: Yes, Carl, that's exactly what I am saying.

CARL: Representative Tarpiot, why are you and the far left committed to redistributing people's wealth?

TAMSIN: None of you have any shame. Each of you to sit there, knowingly making false accusations. All you want to do is stoke fear. In the current economy, American families are struggling to keep food on their tables. People are desperate, having been treated by the ownership class as disposable year after year. Every metric of a healthy society—

JOHN: —What we need is less government in our lives, not more. As the great Ronald Reagan said, government is not the solution, it's the problem. We need to cut government spending to spur private sector growth. People know what is best for their families, not some bureaucrat in Washington D.C. Quite frankly, young lady, you are a traitor to the American Dream.

CROSSTALK

AARON: Yet again, I am in agreement with John. The government should be helping American citizens start businesses that create good paying jobs. This hostility to capitalism does not does not sit well with centrist Democrats. We need to teach kids fiduciary responsibility at an earlier age. I know many Democrats are resistant to charter schools, but they play an important role in communities with failing public educational institutions. Schools need to teach economic fundamental to students while they are young. If the public schools won't do it, then let the charters.

TAMSIN: This would be funny if the circumstances were not so dire. The future is bleak for everyone, especially the youth, without immediate environmental reforms. Big problems require solutions that match. The United States must rejoin the global effort to bring carbon emissions—

AMY: —Globalism is not the answer. Representative Tarpiot. Why can China and India continue to pollute? Why do you want to put America at a competitive disadvantage? I will not kowtow to the Chinese Communist Party. Why do you hate America so much?

CROSSTALK

JOHN: Young lady, are you going to give away all your money?

CROSSTALK

No, I didn't think so. What you are selling is Marxist nonsense, in an effort to handicap American power and prestige at home and around the world. Wherever it has been tried, Communism has never worked out. Those regimes have murdered countless innocent people, and made people poorer.

TAMSIN: I am going to set the damn record straight, so listen closely.

CROSSTALK

No, don't interrupt me. I am going to finish my point.

Capitalism, which has miserably failed at least twice in the past, requiring bailouts by the Federal government, has led us to the current crises. What created these problems cannot fix them. Expanding access to healthcare through the Federal government is not a communist plot to—

AARON: —That's not the point. Your position is fundamentally anti-American. The best way to achieve freedom is through an economy that gives consumers choice. That is what voters want, the ability to choose their healthcare provider.

TAMSIN: You are preventing the choice of an affordable, single-payer option. This is what monopoly power does, it suppresses and prevents competition. Instead of the Federal government paying massive subsidies to access private markets—

JOHN: —There is no way around increasing the tax burden on hard working Americans. Taking away people's money stands entirely opposed to American values. We need to return to those conservative ideas and make America great, again.

CROSSTALK

Let me finish, missy. We need to bring God back into the classroom and finally outlaw abortion on the Federal level. We finally have a conservative super-majority on the Supreme Court to return America to greatness. Free healthcare, free tuition, free housing, free food—freedom isn't free. Somebody has to pay for it.

CROSSTALK

CARL: Representative Tapriot, how will you pay for all of this free stuff? You still have not answered that question. If you take money away from hard working Americans, to fund these entitlement programs, how is this not full blown communism?

TAMSIN: You're all a bunch of useful idiots. My detailed plan is online for everyone to see.

CROSSTALK

I am done. Don't interrupt me again, John. Can people choose not to have the government get between a woman and her doctor in states that have outlawed abortion? Fascism delivered as Christian Nationalism, that's all this is. That is the literal definition of big government. Who the hell are you to question what is, or is not, inside my uterus?

JOHN: I am completely and utterly offended by those accusations young lady! Life starts from the moment of conception. You are promoting infanticide!

CROSSTALK

AARON: I agree, Carl. What we need more than ever is decorum in public affairs. Representative Tapriot, your remarks were gross and uncouth. It's no wonder why so many voters are turned off by politics.

TAMSIN: Aaron, just last week the Democrats adopted a platform without any renewable energy provisions. Moderate Democrats team up with the Republicans to pass increasing defense budgets. But in a time of crisis, the American people get austerity.

This current capitalist system continues to privatize the gains for a few and socialize their losses by the many. The Democrats and Republicans cooperating to create overall misery for millions of Americans. Does anyone really wonder why Congress has an approval rating of one percent? And you, John. Go and pray to your fictional God who wants the Federal government to control women's vaginas. Absolutely disgusting.

CROSSTALK

AMY: And there it is, you are a commie! How can these views be taken seriously by any patriotic American? Socialism has failed everywhere it has been, it does not work. You want to bring these failed policies to the United States? Not on my watch, Representative Tarpiot. Step on my ranch and find out how Americans fight back against you godless socialists.

TAMSIN: Settle down, Karen. I represent the people of my community, who elected me to solve quality of life problems. Take your slanderous, privileged ass back to the cul-de-sac you were raised on.

AMY: Representative Tarpiot, well I have never—

TAMSIN: —Yes you have. Now sit there and shut your damn mouth. Now that's out of the way let's get back to talking about policy—

CROSSTALK

CARL: —Whoa! Now hold on, let's not get viscous with one another. Representative Tapriot, you cannot win the debate so you resort to personal attacks?

AARON: That was a disgusting remark. Let me be the first to say. I unequivocally denounce the vile language from Representative Tapriot. I am afraid you have damaged your reputation beyond repair. I have decided that I will be writing about your outrageous behavior in my next column. You see, what unites Democrats are their values. Radical-Marxist-Soviet-Chinese Communism, this ideology fails to tap into the synergy of the organic flow of the free market.

TAMSIN: Aaron, stop talking. Every word you say is more obscure and misleading than before.

JOHN: I am going to follow Aaron's lead and also write about Representative Tapriot's unhinged, and dangerous, behavior. My

God! I fear for the future of our children and America. Lord help us. Although I loathe your radical ideas, I'll pray that you let Jesus into your life. You are one angry woman.

TAMSIN: You're still melting down, John. The only reason you two have columns, and this show exists, is to control the media narrative. In fact—

CROSSTALK

CARL: —Well ladies and gentlemen, that was quite an unexpected *Gut Punch* segment. I think some national news was made tonight. Stay tuned, up next on *Are You Kidding?*, Harold Stevenson joins us to discuss the benefits of more carbon in the atmosphere.

TAMSIN: Carl, you suck. Truly. I deserve the right to respond to these false accusations just levied at me from all of you imbeciles. Yes, I just said that. Regret it? No.

CROSSTALK

Both parties, the Republicans and Democrats, have run this country into toxic dirt. They will use the government to enrich their corporate donors. Meanwhile, purposeful political gridlock prevents improving the country. Behind closed doors, the elites running each party are friends. To this end, a show like this exists only to further divide the American people. It's a prime example of misinformation. The country is being held hostage by private interests that—

CARL: —That's enough.

TAMSIN: —I know you just did not interrupt me. Do it again, Carl, I dare you. Calm down, you man-child. This planned setup does real harm to the country, not the solutions and ideas I am proposing. The current system has made the livelihood of millions of

Americans precarious, by design. We are in a global climate emergency, while America careens toward religious fascism. Time's running out, the time for action is now. I have no idea how the bunch of you get sleep at night.

Peace out, you bunch of bitches. A wave of change is on the way.

COMMERCIAL BREAK
END VIDEO CLIP

As the posse made their way back to the kitchen area the brighter light greeted everyone. On the way up and out of the storage area, the colorful uniforms of the guards seemed to glow. Mateo was treated to another peek into the custodial closet.

"Whatever I believe politically, it's definitely not that." Keeping his head forward and slightly down, the doctor did not bother to even look over.

Mateo's former experience was still lodged near the front of his awareness. That one segment of *Are You Kidding?* compelled him to leap out of bed and start scribbling in his tractatus-philosophical-comedy-logic journal. The past and present collided, imperceptible to everyone but Mateo.

"Doc, do you watch tv shows? The queen and the Cuban, you know, *I Love Lucy.* That show has stood the test of time. Political infotainment shows are terrible, don't ever waste your time watching that garbage. They exist to generate partisan outrage. In reality, both major parties reside on the right. And people wonder why Christian fascism took hold of the country. No real leftist opposition. Look who's doing all the bullshit talking now, right?"

Mateo carried on, "If you asked me my political persuasion—well, it's complicated. I have no idea, especially these days. Maybe something like a libertarian Marxist. When I was in New Orleans a whole bunch of years ago, I met a sage extraordinaire, Bucha. She helped me get a grasp on the political nonsense in this country."

While the doctor still ignored him, Mateo kept blabbering while shaking his head at the situation they were in, "You know what I think, doc? The only way to put trust back in the political system is straightforward. People serving in the government have to be worthy of trust. Wait for it, trustworthy. I am convinced that people best able to lead in politics would never want to hold office? The way it's set up now, no sane person would want to deal with liars and petty dictators lurking around every corner."

Mateo's previous experiences subsided back in the recesses of his subconscious, he could not put aside what his eyes were telling him. They were going the wrong way out of the kitchen.

"Whoever is leading, Doc, they are misguided for sure."

They were headed toward the sizable recreational area at Tall Oaks. The emergency exit doors were decoration only. Welded shut long ago, it was an oversight management never fixed. The texture of the walls began to change as they approached another one way in, one way out.

The crowd rumbled louder as concrete was now the dominant material. The more concrete, the more crowd vibrations could be heard. Mateo paused for a moment. He closed his eyes and placed his ear to a huge wall of concrete. In his mind's eye, he tried to picture the situation outside. Mateo smiled. Brushing his hand against the wall, he returned to stride, on his way to joining everyone else in the fitness area.

As they entered, Mateo turned to the doctor, "Have you ever joined a fight club?"

———————— ❖ ————————

IV

Good Sports

In the ongoing effort to escort Mateo from Tall Oaks, the crew decided to take in the fitness area. Slickness was replaced by grating, as smooth kitchen became coarse concrete. The gray austerity was unforgiving in its dominance. This oppressiveness disrupted whatever line of thought he was holding. His attention was given over to the roughness scraping his fingertips.

When the all concrete hallway opened up to the larger fitness area of the same material, Mateo tried to get a head count of the guards. He found even an approximation difficult, as he could not get past their hues and oversized helmets. Their bizarre behavior also added to his confusion. The guards seemed to be indifferent to everything. Between the apertures created by the guards, Mateo thought he saw a red guard licking a wall.

"Doc, do you see that red guard? Was he—," then Mateo stopped mid-sentence, remembering he would not receive an answer.

Giving up on trying to count, Mateo forgot there was large crowd outside until they reminded him. The concrete helped to communicate their close proximity to the partly underground fitness center.

RRRRAAaawwwwrrrr!

Mateo felt the amplified tremors run through his body. He reverberated until they reached the rubberized floor of the main exercise space. "Maybe you need something to drink. Just so happens there's a water fountain here, over on the other side of the room. Follow me, Doc. Who knows it might loosen your tongue."

When it was founded, a cornerstone of the Tall Oaks rehabilitation philosophy was that improving the mind required an in tandem strengthening the body. Changing thoughts only with medications, without any accompanying physiological demands, would not achieve true rehabilitation. Unfortunately, aligning the body with the mind as a remedy waned as the years passed. Medications were pushed over the physical component, keeping people in mental health limbo. This decreased the priority and general use of the exercise area, which was strewn with throwback fitness equipment. These older, but still effective, modalities kept most Tall Oaks residents away. Mateo was an exception, who found himself exercising almost always by himself.

Visually unappealing, the concrete walls were vaulted and bare. At the top of the walls sat a couple of unreachable, small rectangular windows. They were even with the ground level outside, adorned with bars across them, letting in some muted beams of light to the underground fitness space. A running track circled the room, with workout equipment on the perimeter and in the middle. The lone exit door was welded shut, and the corridor behind it filled in long ago. The way in was also the way out.

Without hesitation, the guards started exercising on the equipment laying around. The doctor smelled worse than before. "Water, that's right," Mateo reminded himself after seeing the guards working out threw him off. He pointed to the water fountain on the far side of the room for the doctor to see. On the way, Mateo heard distant officers yelling at the guards to get back in formation. Busy exercising, the guards paid no attention to these initial calls for order.

If Mateo did not know any better, it looked like the guards were blowing off steam. The colors were in motion, vibrating. As the duo traversed the jumping, thrusting, pushing, pulling, twisting, lunging, throwing, catching, running, flexing, extending, panting, and repetitions of weightlifting, Mateo kept yapping to an uncaring doctor. "Looks they are making the best of a bad situation. People want to stretch out after being confined to a small space, eh Doc?"

With no reaction, Mateo continued, "There's just something unforgivable about concrete, eh doc? One part cement, two parts sand three parts gravel, then add in some water. There you have it. Durability that will outlast you and me. Speaking of water—"

"—Close your mouth already! Just shut up! No more inane blabber," exploded the doctor.

Mateo smirked, mission accomplished.

"And I'm the crazy one. Geez, you're welcome."

The doctor was taking sips from an iconic stainless steel water fountain when Mateo saw the climbing rope. With a vantage point from up high, he decided to recount the number of hues, as well as a glimpse of the coterie of buffoons in charge. A panoptic view was invaluable for seeing all. Mateo approached the rope when the focused beams of sunlight flickered, catching his attention. People were shuffling back and forth in front of the windows higher up.

Having broken his silence, "What on earth are you doing up there?" asked the doctor. "You're just as bad as they are. Undisciplined."

Wrapping the rope between his legs as he ascended, Mateo stopped and looked down. "The utility of a bird's-eye view, Doc. Glad you're feeling better." Reaching the top, Mateo tangled his legs up with the rope to anchor himself.

Surveying the organized chaos below, colors were in motion all around. Red throwing a medicine ball, orange performing calisthenics yellow swinging kettle bells, green doing squats, blue pulling to slide on the rowing machine, purple doing pull-ups, and indigo curling dumbbells. In the midst of all the vibrating, Mateo found it impossible to count and spot those in charge.

Sunlight flickered, drawing Mateo's attention to the window. He was about to yell to those outside when it became clear it was pointless. Nobody would hear, as Mateo felt the noise traveled down the rope like a needle.

RRRRAAAAWWwwrrrr!

Mateo tried again to count the guards. Not paying attention to the spot right below where he was perched, the cheese-head slanderer took advantage of Mateo neglecting his blind side. In an act of payback, the junior officer grabbed the rope and started swinging Mateo in circles. "This son of a bitch, again?"

The colors below were kaleidoscopic.

Looking down Mateo saw the crotch sniffer screaming at him. Unable to understand a word, Mateo went downright juvenile. "What's that?" he yelled at the ass kisser. "I agree! Your mother is like an ATM because she likes ATM!" Picking up speed, Mateo's stomach received an entry ticket.

The doctor, assisted by orange, blue and fuchsia, intervened to bring Mateo's ride to a halt. Mateo was still wrapped up in the rope, while the offender was directly below still shouting gibberish. Mateo gave the telltale sign puke was on the way, placing a hand over his mouth. The doctor and color guards saw what was coming. They backed away as upchuck came down. A half-digested dairy and potato mixture hit the officer in the face, some of it landing in his mouth. The vomiting caused Mateo's grip to slacken and his legs to loosen from the entanglement with rope.

Bombs away.

The officer was too busy spitting out and wiping off vomit to prepare for a falling Mateo. On his descent, Mateo resembled a linebacker leading strongly with his left shoulder. A ferocious hit leveled he junior officer, causing him to see stars.

The collision dazed Mateo momentarily. Stunned with radiating pain, the left side of body was throbbing down to the bones. A sharp, painful headache accompanied the knot forming on his head.

Yellow and white gestured for Mateo to stay down, to no avail. He stood up, looked over to see the doctor, assisted by orange and turquoise, attending to the junior piss-ant. Mateo shuffled over to the water fountain to rinse his mouth out. Observing the scene he amused himself, "Is anyone here a doctor?"

This smell of Mateo's own vomit was followed by the sharp smell of rusted metal. He shook his head in an attempt to cast off the fog.

"Hey, Doc, where is Amber? Is she okay?"

Still attending to the low level officer, who returned to conscious life, the doctor looked over at a banged up Mateo. Relinquishing care to the guards, the doctor walked over to Mateo, "What? Who? Are you related to them?"

Before the doctor could ask another question, the guards began winding down their exercises and take up an orderly formation. On the move, after a couple of steps acute pain dropped Mateo. He was forced to take a knee.

There was a flag on the play. The memory in question brought Mateo back to a time before working at Berri. It was midday on a Friday, he and Amber Duncan had just walked straight into each other on the sidewalk. Both had their eyes glued to phone screens when they smacked into one another rounding the corner. Helmet to helmet contact.

Mateo remained upright, still holding onto his phone. However, Amber was knocked down on the cold concrete. She dropped and cracked her phone, an earbud popped out landing straight in a rusty sewer drain, while her bag spilled out books. A movie scene with real life consequences.

Once Mateo finally registered what happened, he helped Amber up before apologizing while picking up her textbooks.

"Here are your books. Are you okay?" asked Mateo.

Amber quickly realized her electronic losses and went on the offense.

"What the fuck is wrong with you?! Don't you watch where you're walking?!"

"Same to you. Take it easy. Calm down," Mateo defended himself.

Like a shotgun, Amber fired back. "Calm down? Did you just tell me to *calm down*? Fuck you if you think I need to calm down! The screen on my phone is cracked, I lost my earbud, and your punk ass tells me to calm down. You going to mansplain the situation to me, you asshole?"

She tried, but Amber no longer had the ability to hold back the tears brought on by having one of those rough patches of life.

"Tuition is killing me. My girlfriend broke up with me, my mother is going through chemo—and you tell me to calm down! I am emotional right now, not because I am a weak girl. Fuck you for thinking it."

His rather scrappy upbringing led Mateo to recognize a fellow spirit. Mateo's was undergoing a period of up and up material luck. With his freelance career taking off, and since sex was not on the line, he was in a position to help.

A chance to just be decent to a stranger.

Mateo tried to lighten the mood before making his offer, "I mean, you have to admit what are the chances of that earbud making it through the only part of the drain not covered with trash? Like a strange act of god, you know? Playing a joke on us, or something like that."

Amber's tears receded while she maintained a hard stare at Mateo from across the crack line in the sidewalk between them.

"You have to admit, that's a pretty good joke, right?"

Amber smiled, just a little.

"Fate has led us here, that underlying algorithm of the world. So, I am not taking anything you said personally. It was meant to be part of the big joke."

"So, what are you saying?"

"That I was destined to replace your phone, and earbuds. Because, again, what were the chances?"

"You're going to what?"

"Your phone and earbuds, I got them for you. We have both been good sports taking the cosmic joke. While we laugh at ourselves, I am in a position to help."

"Seriously, I don't understand. I am not going to fuck you. I was over dudes a long time ago."

"Thanks, but I'm not interested anyway. This is just me being nice during the game of life."

Then Mateo pointed to the tag on her school bag, "I see you're a Bears fan. Are you interested in maybe going to the game this Sunday? I am only in town until Monday before heading off over-seas. They were given to me by—"

Amber cut him off, "—To the playoff game? Are you fuck'in joking? No, you're messing with me, right?"

"I'm serious. It's all part of the big joke."

"Where did you get them?"

"The concierge at the hotel, he gave me two tickets as a gift. I wasn't even planning on going, but it looks like you're a fan. I could use a break from staring at a computer screen."

"I don't believe you. Do you have them?" Amber called Mateo's bluff.

Mateo reached into his pocket, and pulled out two tickets. "He just gave them to me this morning, when I was on my way out of the hotel. Like I told you, it was meant to be."

"My dad is not going to believe this," said a bright eyed Amber.

"Do you want to take you dad instead?" asked Mateo.

"Thanks, but he's out on the road."

"Your mom?"

"She's at my brother's an hour away."

Mateo sealed the deal, "In that case you'll be doing me a favor if we go together. Football is not really my thing. I am only going because it's fated."

"Don't worry, I'll make a football fan out of you."

"Just remember, don't try any funny stuff or I'll make you bleed."

Mateo stood up straighter. He gave Amber a salute and a smile, "Sir. Yes, sir."

Then Mateo realized they did not know each other's names.

"Allow me to introduce myself. I'm Mateo."

Mateo's squad was again on the move, back the way they came. He shook the guards off when they tried to help him walk. "Thanks, but I'd rather crawl. Nothing personal." A cherry red and lemon yellow obliged, giving Mateo shrugged shoulders underneath small color matching domes.

Trying to walk the pain away, Mateo focused on the sunlight cutting down into the room. Momentarily blocking the light, the legs of people on the move above caused the rays to flicker. This stark transition between light and dark created flashes that mesmerized him. The pain won out when he stood under the twelve foot arch, taking a momentary break. Looking back at the equipment, a longer than usual beam of light hit and ricocheted off the shiny chrome. Mateo tried to squint, but the light blinded.

Just like that, Mateo was lost in the mercurial angles of Cloud Gate. The city skyline stretched and contracted until a ray of sunshine forced Mateo to look elsewhere. When he did, Amber's reflection walked toward him in Chicago's funhouse Bean, with the skyline of buildings stretched up toward the dominating blue atmosphere above.

Walking to the stadium through Grant Park, Mateo and Amber briefed one another on the backstory of their lives. Along with the serious, they also covered the mundane.

"Born and raised, huh. The architecture is dope."

"That's right, I love it here. It sounds like you bounced around a lot while you were younger."

"I guess. It looks like I am going to be traveling soon to places all over the world. But this is my first time in Chicago."

"Are you pursuing clinical psychology? I noticed your books when they fell out."

"Sure am, first year of graduate school. I think it's fascinating how the mind operates. What about you, any brothers or sisters?"

"A sister and a brother—and what is this stuff called Chicago pizza? It cannot be pizza, there's just no way. I refuse to call it pizza. You should not have to lift it out of a pan when you eat it." Amber glared at Mateo with a smirk, while he defended an unpopular opinion.

"If it cannot be folded in half using one hand then, it's not really pizza."

"What about Sicilian slices?" asked Amber, "Is that pizza?"

"Sure is, no pan needed to eat it. Cooking it is a separate issue. The toppings do just that, and don't spill out the sides when you take a bite. That's annoying."

Amber nodded, "I get it, and disagree with you. It's only *really* pizza where it's from. Everywhere else is a copy of the original."

"I see what you're saying. The pizza adapts to a new place. If it got as cold in New York, as it does here, the pizza would look different than it does now. The body needs something heartier in the cold months. Get fat and hibernate." Mateo added on, "I wonder how climate change is going to impact the pizza."

"I still like Chicago pizza."

"You do you." Then Mateo relayed, "The best pizza I ever had was in New Jersey, on the boardwalk at Asbury Park."

"I thought New York had the best pizza?"

"No, number two according to my taste buds." Mateo informed Amber of the unwritten consequences of holding this belief. "Admitting that in the city will definitely get you yelled at. You might even get your ass kicked. Someone's piece of mind, and their boot."

"You're like a weird joker or something. What do you do again?"

"I write computer code. Maybe I'm getting loopy from it, but I'm no comedian. I'm not that funny."

By this point, the crowd around Mateo and Amber swelled. More densely packed together, the conversation lowered in volume until it naturally ended. Their pace eased nearing the stadium, partly from the close quarters, but also the shock and awe felt reaching the stadium. A massive structure defying gravity cast an overwhelming sight, briefly mesmerizing and quieting people.

When Mateo headed for the entrance Amber gave an audible, "Let's go this way." She pointed to the parking lot adjacent to the stadium, "I have some friends over here I want you to meet."

It was a family friendly tailgate underneath a warmer than usual day. Logos of all sorts scattered everywhere, sports jerseys, baseball caps, plastic red cups filled with beer, the aroma of seared flesh televisions, radios, music, face and body paint, open pledges of loyalty to the team, hatred for the Packers, eternal gratitude to Ditka, the smell of cigars and marijuana, and politically incorrect messages were here and there. Over his head, Mateo watched a tightly spiraled football cut through the smoke like a parabolic jet.

With introductions exchanged after Amber located her friends, Mateo told everyone of the unnecessary roughness. He did his best to assure everyone he was not a serial killer or pervert. It was a nice penalty personal foul. They partook in some of the mind altering liquid and smoke, before taking off for their seats.

With a little imbibing, proximity to others no longer deterred speaking loudly. People were waxing philosophically about play-offs, rosters, strategy, and GOATs. Over and over again, Mateo kept hearing people identify themselves in the collective sense.

We.

Once they entered, capitalism mixed with the physical domination of the stadium. God and military memorials adorning the outside, jarring by the divergence within. Housed inside were multiple levels of sports paraphernalia manufactured into every conceivable tchotchke. Televisions were adorned everywhere relaying highlight plays and analysis of all the action on the field. Strategically placed beer stands lined the wide corridors, and there was no lack of low quality food. The good stuff was up in the luxury boxes. Down below, soldiering on the outside made people captive to commemorative editions and high prices on the inside.

After locating their seats, Mateo and Amber decided to split up. He would sack the food, she would tackle the drinks, and then they would meet back where they were sitting. By the time Mateo made it to his seat, Amber already sat in her black plastic chair. While he was carrying food, the steepness of the stairs induced vertigo in Mateo.

Amber took notice, "You're walking like a scaredy-cat."

"Those steps made me dizzy all of a sudden."

"When was the last time you were at a football game?"

"It's been a long time. A bunch of years back, I guess," answered Mateo fixated on the field, like everyone else.

Amber inspected her eats, "Did you break up a roofie and put it in my food?"

Mateo almost snorted the mouthful of beer out his nose.

"Relax, I'm only kidding. I thought I was uptight."

Before Mateo could say anything Amber stared at the field asking, "By the way, what exactly did you do to get these tickets? These are great seats."

"Through work. They were a thank you gift from a client."

Amber began informing Mateo about the team, and the importance of this particular game. Even as a kid, she disliked the Packers. Mateo fell into the all-consuming atmosphere, a festival to focus on a one hundred or so yard plot.

Beer. Beef. Bears.

From the gymnasium, Mateo and crew successfully backtracked to the kitchen area. With too many people in such a small space, discombobulation was everywhere. As the guards could not help but get in their own way, it gave Mateo and the dutiful doctor some time together.

Sitting down in the kitchen, Mateo made an unprompted confession. "You know, Doc, one time, just before I was contracted with Berri, I helped a concierge take some online revenge against his ex-fiancé. I mean, let's call it justice.

Anyway, I was drinking at the hotel bar one night, and we struck up a conversation. He gifted me a pair of football tickets, wouldn't let me turn them down. I was going to give them away, but I ended up going."

With a look of pain, Mateo went over to the single occupancy restroom. He turned to the doctor before going in, "I am sure I'll be done before they figure it out."

Holding his little soldier in one hand, and pounding his other fist on the sink with the other, a wave of pain took hold of Mateo.

A kidney stone was passing through his kidneys, leaving fleshy destruction in its wake. When his fist went to strike the sink, again it hit the top of a toilet paper dispenser.

He was in a bathroom stall at Soldier Field, at the last football game he ever attended. Heated and sweaty, he accidentally pinched his pecker a little harder. All he wanted to do was puke, but his body would not cooperate.

Mateo returned to find Amber bragging on social media. She posted a picture of the field that made the right people super jelly. With Amber occupied, Mateo assessed the drinking situation. On further review, the ruling stands that another round was needed. He tried to stay upbeat, but failed to hide his discomfort.

"For stadium nachos, these are good as hell."

Amber looked at Mateo strangely, "Are you okay?"

"Yeah, I'm good. Why?"

"You look like absolute crap. You were a little wobbly, again. Now, you're like a sick scaredy-cat. Are you sure you should be drinking?"

"I'm good. So, tell me, who is this Sweetness person people keep talking about?"

Mateo sunk in, shedding his individualized identity for the group, making forward progress into a culture he knew nothing about. The round table discussion quickly moved to strategy, match ups, and previous games. Everyone agreed with Amber when she proclaimed the referees were irredeemable cocksuckers for bad calls all season long.

The guards intruded on Mateo's awareness.

He was sitting back down in the same place as before, on one of the counters. Squarely situated on a pile of parsley, he saw the doctor at the freezer putting together an ice pack. "Doc, while you're over there, could you check the fridge for a ginger ale, or something?"

Allowing his Hippocratic instinct to take over, the doctor started mending up his blabbering patient.

"You know, Doc, I am reminded of an incident at a comedy club in—well, it doesn't matter. It might as well be anywhere. Let's just say it was in the proverbial heartland of America. My set started off fine. I was definitely drunk, that I can tell you for sure."

All you fuck'in good ol'boys. Hooti'in and holler'in. The common man, huh? No political correctness, huh? Free speech, right? Let's test the limits of the crowd here tonight. Before I do, I need another drink. Barkeep, please and thank you! I want to make sure all you fuckers are ready.

Don't worry, I am going to talk about an unimportant topic—professional sports. Are there any sports fans out there tonight? I figured, there has to be, right?

Let me be clear upfront—I am not against exercising and taking care of yourself. You have to do those things or you'll find yourself pushed into the grinder of this healthcare system.

Speaking of pricey, has anyone been to a game lately? Holy smokes, it's you need a second mortgage expensive. It really is an expensive carnival to go to. Standing in line to get food feels like you're a willing participant in a robbery. The only item that may be worth its actual price are the nachos. Fuck'in stadium nachos are the best. Give that person a Nobel Prize whoever concocted that gourmet cheesy sauce. That, folks, might be the tastiest substance on Earth. I swear that shit tastes better in a stadium.

Here is a thought: the people who attend sporting events are socialists. Pick your sport and listen to what the fans say—we. Fucki'in over and over again. Like a chant or something.

People gather together—they form a collective, right—to bask in the achievements of others. Some of you even take credit by the way you speak. It's always we won. But you never hear we lost, it's always they lost. So, their team always loses, and we always win. Both of these are usually said with immense pride.

By the way, I know a bunch of you don't give two shits about any of the games, you all are just interested in the gambling. Respect to all of you. There is nothing more American than gambling. Well, except maybe owning a gun. That might be more American.

Back to my point, breaking a sweat while stuffing your pie-hole is not the same as running and catching a ball. Spending money on your team's gear not equivalent to making a tackle. Drinking beer is not scoring a goal.

The level of satisfaction in the accomplishments of others is pretty astonishing. I think we should call it achievement appropriation. Can we make that a thing? If you did not really do something, stop taking credit for it.

When you're leaving here tonight, cursing my name on your drive home, it might cause you to reflect on why so many people enjoy watching people get their bodies mangled over control of a football. This is what all the effort on the field is over.

What's the inherent value of the ball? Not much, they seem to swap them out all the time. So there's a lot of them, and they're not worth much. That's not what people are really there for, right? They are there to watch people get hit. People enjoy watching players physically compete over a football, who sacrifice their bodies to do it. It's entertainment.

It's only natural to encourage kids to participate in the fun.

Cheered on by the adults to chase one another in pursuit of a football. Get out there and scramble your brains junior, just make sure to wear sunscreen. That high SPF, the good shit. You don't want your kid o get a sunburn.

Unlike some people I will not be shocked whenever I hear that a football player gets hurt. Those players get maimed all the time. What would be completely out of the ordinary is if nobody got hurt playing football. Like if every collision improved your health or something.

If you really cared about their physical well-being, then you would be okay with this scenario—if both sides just shared the football to get an equal outcome. Think about how many points could be scored if both sides just agreed to trade off touchdowns and end the game in a tie.

Please, do not whatever I am saying personally. It's only a joke. Just remember that I am full of shit, an idiot. A nobody comedian who stands on stage and has no idea what he's talking about. A sad middle-aged man who drinks too much. You are enlightened, I am not. It was foolish of me to think you can play a violent game and get hurt.

Anyway, the tailgating is way more interesting than the actual football game. You get to meet real salt of the earth people support for their team by drinking, eating, and bitch'in about the economy.

Forget about just wearing a jersey with the last name of someone else on it. Chances are you'll see full on cosplay. People dressing up as the team mascot, shit like that. Look at that, the Vikings are back in Minnesota.

Oh, and I am asking for a friend—is it true that you have to get your team's logo painted on your face at least once and go out in public? Or you cannot call yourself a fan? I also heard that you have to attend at least one home game. You know, like make a pil-grimage. Are these real rites of passage, or is someone fuck'in with me—I mean, my friend?

Forget just the face, some dudes show up full on body paint. And if you drink enough you don't care what the temperature is, too plastered in your team colors to care. Sometimes, the people who do this remind the rest of us of about the importance of grammar. They should be commended for their efforts. After all, they bought tickets, jumped in their cars, tailgated, chanted, and took collective owner-ship in the achievements of others. All of it, still not enough. These individuals are compelled to do that little bit extra. The difference between champions and players.

Imagine you're sitting at home waiting for the game to start, scratching yourself, drinking a beer, and finalizing your fantasy players. Your office also has a pool going on this game. So excited your crotch is tickling to bust a nut.

The superfans are on your screen when your friend or fuck partner—yeah, that's what I'm calling it now. No genderizing, not even a little. So, they walk in and the leaders of fandom are on the television.

"What are they doing?"

You reply, "Spelling the team name?"

"Who are the STAINS?"

"It's misspelled, dear."

Then your friend, or fuck partner—and it's possible to be both—they ask, "Who are they playing?"

"Looks like they are playing the EARS."

"Did you say EARS?"

"Looks like it," you say, "The B got shitfaced and is passed out."

If you're lucky, folks, your team could be playing the CLOTS, or the CRAPKERS, maybe even the PIO TARTS. Watch out because next week the team from Arizona is in town, the ANAL DICS. I could keep going, but I am going to stop right there. What an effort. These fans of grammar left it all on the field.

And when the game is over, please remember the unwritten rule of gambling: you can only post your loss porn online. No money shots allowed. Shameless posting of gains, even with the fantasy stuff, it'll make you a little prick.

Speaking of little pricks, I remember fighting off a kidney stone at a football game. Every dude at the urinals—or that revolting piss trough—was holding their phone. Pissing away and scrolling for who knows what. Fucking weird. At one of the urinals, one guy looked like he was humping it. Right up close and on his phone. Believe me, the splash from the urinal is no joke. Focus is needed to find that proper distance ad trajectory. Two hands on your little prick, eyes only forward or down. I could hear some dude talking to his mom. Honestly, that is not surprising. Do you think there's a potential therapy session for that dude or what?

I wasn't passing a kidney stone in the open public, fuck that. I waited for a stall, and while I was, some dude started talking to me. You know, have a chat outside the pissing and shitting line while you're captive. And the dude was chewing gum. They are always chewing on gum, aren't they?

Out of nowhere, he started yapping to me about the younger generation. Some grown ass dude complaining like a little bitch. You know the type, spelled with a capital C. Like a nagging spouse. This was even worse because I'm a complete stranger. This dude assumed I care what he thinks.

I have the sharpest pain imaginable in my kidney and this guy, chomping away on his gum, talking about video games. That's all the kids do these days. They just sit around and waste their lives playing video games. Even worse, they like to watch others do it. It annoyed him that people called it a sport. He was saying all this without the slightest trace of irony.

If watching people play video games is fuck'in stupid, then where is the wisdom in watching men concuss themselves chasing after a ball? Can't you see that neither is not too fucking good for anybody? It's the passivity, that's the problem. Too much time spent sitting around mouth breathing is not healthy. Don't do that, use your nose. You're better than that.

When this dude was talking I was thinking how violence does not break out at e-sports events. Only at the more traditional venues does mayhem occur. It's pretty easy to see why, right folks?—It's all the alcohol. Then throw politics into the cocktail and we have ourselves a good old fashioned stadium melee. People at football games, mother fuckers have been knocked the fuck out for not standing while the National Anthem played. It's not an isolated event either. I've fucking seen it with my own eyes, just like the sports fans in here. Sporting events go from National Anthem to fascist real quick, like greased fuck'in lightning.

Am I the only one who thinks it's a problem that sports have to stoop to the political? Where is the enlightenment in that kind of behavior? Does anyone really care if you pledge, kneel, or whatever? Nobody is allowed to have their own symbol of State solidarity. Why can't some people pledge and others kneel? Is this church? Because it certainly feels like it. Personal offense should not override free speech. Who cares what you think?

Where in the Constitution—that document everyone agrees with, but never reads—does it say anything about your feelings? I mean, if you love the Constitution, don't you like the First Amendment the most? I always thought defending free speech is the best offense to protect it? I guess I was wrong. I still do not understand why everyone is not on Team America.

One last thing before I leave you good people tonight— why exactly do we need fighter jets flown overhead before football games? Are we trying to be like North Korea? What a waste of money—but I guess since Americans unite around war, why not spend it. Solidarity in killing innocent people across the world, but divided at home over how to properly patriotic.

Instead of stealing their achievements, why can't people mimic the collective effort of their favorite team and apply it to their lives? To the country? This might be where you are calling me a commie. That's not what I am saying at all. The only way to cooperate, and get along with others, is to be the best version of yourself. If you cannot help yourself first, then you cannot help anyone else. Be the achievement, instead of cheering someone else on for it?

Comrades! A call to sitting down! Spectators of the world unite! Let's watch!

That's enough of the self-help portion of the routine. Don't worry, I remember my story.

A stall in the middle opened up, and I told the guy, "Later, coach." That's it. I just walked away. As soon as I closed the door, the guy in the left stall started having a conversation with his bookie. That shocked me—that this guy was talking to a real person—more than the dude to my right who was watching porn. Real loud. And both were crunching the proverbial numbers. It was fucking weird. I am pissing, in so much pain I am about to pass out, and the atmosphere is filled with a smell you cannot even imagine. Seems like the right place to discuss point spreads and watching people get each other off. I barely made it out alive, let me tell you"

"Aren't you finished, yet?" asked the doctor.

The doctor was busy attending to Mateo while he recalled his routine from all those years ago. After the doctor reviewed and addressed Mateo's contusions and scrapes, he planted an ice pack atop Mateo's head. After strapping it on with an ace bandage, the doctor said, "Here is your ginger ale." With his left eye partially covered by the bandage, Mateo took a big sip.

"Thanks, Doc. I also appreciate my new look."

The flurry of guards around them gravitated to a newly discovered stairwell, recently discovered by moving some baker's racks.

Pain slipped in with Mateo's light chuckle, "Ha, ha, ha, ooh, ooh, ooh, ouch."

Their conversation ended when the guards gently ushered Mateo and the doctor to the newfound stairwell.

"Ha, ha, ha, ooh, ooh, ooh, ouch."

Climbing stairs in his current physical state, Mateo was hit with a little vertigo. This feeling propelled him back to the stadium in Chicago.

"Are you sure you should be drinking?" asked a concerned Amber.

A rough looking Mateo shook off her concern, with some water and beers soon delivered. Soon enough, his initiation into the sports subculture ended. Over the public address system, the announcer welcomed everyone to the playoffs.

"Singing the National Anthem today is the three-time Grammy award winner and social media sensation who currently has the number one hit in the country, *DEU You Shoulda Knew*, none other than Destin E. Unique." The announcer did not have to say it, the fans already knew she was dating the quarterback for the home team.

The crowd roared.

Amber turned to Mateo, "She has always been one of my favorites. Fierce with class right there, buddy."

When Destin walked out onto the field, she gave a big smile with a matching wave.

"Bitch'in. Just look at those shoes alone."

"I agree," Mateo answered, "those red heels are to die for."

With the temperature unseasonably warm, Destin wore skin tight blue jeans, a low cut white t-shirt with a side knot, with red, white, and blue ribbons in her hair that complimented the American flags on both her back pockets.

When Destin started singing a good number of people around the stadium, and down on the field, took a knee with their head down in somber prayer. Others assumed the traditional posture, placing their hands across their chest and over their heart. Mateo immediately noticed the friction between these two groups.

Forced to choose a side, Mateo did not know what to do. It was at that moment he realized within him there was no particular organized religion that required kneeling. Neither had the nation earned his undying allegiance. Recognizing past injustices perpetrated within, and by, the nation struck him as noble. Mateo stood up, looked down, and joined his hands behind his back. He was on his own team.

Amber was taking a knee next to Mateo. Then he remembered part of the conversation they had while walking to the stadium. Amber's cousin was currently deployed somewhere overseas. That was all she could know. Then Mateo felt the glare coming from those around them. Fellow fans who were friendly right before this call for national unity. While the divide between the hand and the knee dominated, there were other people in the crowd doing other activities who received no ire.

Soon enough, nationalist flare ups were sparked around the stadium. Insults were blitzing from self-appointed authorities of patriotism, which unfortunately joined Destin's stellar rendition of the National Anthem.

"Oh say can you see. by the dawn's early light—"

"—Millionaire pussies! Protest on your own time!"

"What so proudly we hailed as the twilight's last gleaming?—"

"—Love it or leave it!"

"Whose broad stripes and bright starts thru the perilous fight—"

"—Freedom isn't free you socialist prick!"

"O'er the ramparts we watched were so gallantly streaming?—"

"—America is the greatest nation, God bless it! Stand up for Jesus!"

"And the rockets red glare, the bombs bursting in air—"

"—Stand up you commie fucks!"

"Gave proof through the night that our flag was still there—"

"—Overpaid athletes, stand up and respect the country. Fuck'in losers!"

"Oh say does that star-spangled banner yet wave—"

"—Treason!"

"O'er the land of the free and the home of the brave?!"

Destin impressively held the last note. It was at that point bravery drowned out the sounds of disharmony. Even the patriotic prefects stopped yelling, forced to shut up and admire her skill. After all, this was Destin and you should already know.

After the applause, and with everyone standing up, arguments went off all over the place. Near Mateo and Amber, two men who knelt during the National Anthem were berated with insults by those around them. Anger was growing on both sides. Fists were clenched. With the situation about to escalate into open hostilities, the American military arrived on the scene to quell the unrest.

Awe struck by the roar of jet engines, four taxpayer funded F-22 jets shot over the stadium. Jaws agape, people turned to the sky as the sound of their approach grew louder. All arguing was killed, every thought drowned out. On their flyby, the pilots rolled to expose the military hardware underneath. National pride swelled in chests among those in attendance, as well as the millions of people watching from home. The RAPTORS sent a message to America's enemies, made even clearer by what was written underneath the lead plane. Come get some. Seeing this caused unified applause.

While the fighter jets flew past, Amber was not deterred from defending the two men who were attacked for taking a knee. Going down steps, Mateo gave chase as quickly as he could. The pair were seated a fair distance down sets of large and small stairs, made longer after people started moving around after the applause. By the time Amber arrived, with Mateo in tow, the people involved were putting aside their differences.

"Are you doing what I think you're doing?" asked Mateo, with no answer from Amber.

The people insulting the two men who took a knee were now receiving apologies. It turns out almost everyone involved were ex-military. What a silly mistake not respecting the First Amendment of those who served. If you killed people in service of the country, of course, you can take kneel. By the time Amber arrived, with Mateo in tow, hostilities were already replaced with camaraderie. Without getting the update, she just laced into the guys who were disrespecting the two who bowed their head and took a knee.

"You bunch of little dicks, low minded pieces of shit! I hope your mothers are proud. Isn't there enough violence in this city?"

"Miss, you don't understand—"

"I understand plenty."

"It turns out we all served in the military. We're all friends now."

"Dumbasses, the whole bunch of you .It doesn't matter—your behavior to start was out of line. It should have never come to this. Are you all this fuck'in stupid? What happened to you people as children that seeing someone take a knee triggers you to violence?"

Before anyone could speak Amber emphatically reminded them of the real enemy. "Save all that energy for the real bastards–we're going to fuck the Packers in the ass!"

Everyone was stunned into silence. Did this woman say what we just heard her say? Yes, she did. With people too uncomfortable to say anything, Mateo filled in the gap to tackle the silence.

"Da Bears!"

Afterwards Mateo started clapping. He exchanged smiles with Amber and instinctually started clapping. From this epicenter, the applause travelled in a wave around the entire stadium.

And the crowd goes wild!

On the way back up to his seat, while receiving a couple of compliments on his funny remark, Mateo got dizzy. He stopped for a couple of seconds and shook it off.

When he came to the present, Mateo and the gang were headed up another misguided set of stairs.

Mateo's voice echoed up and down the steps. "The people in charge, geez. They really do think their elbow is their ass...ha, ha, ha, ooh, ooh, ooh, ouch...I am so happy the world is not in chaos at the moment. Could you imagine if it was? I hope there is enough teamwork in this country to pull it off."

"That slight concussion you likely sustained," said the doctor talking to Mateo behind him, "it probably scrambled your brain. Try not to think about anything for a while, but you have to stay awake."

Mateo complimented the doctor's newfound attitude, "Look at you Mr. Sassy Ass."

This odd stairwell, almost never used, initially went down before going up. Even Mateo, who used to roam Tall Oaks at all hours of the night, barely went through it. Reaching the top, Mateo knew the extraction crew traveled deeper into Tall Oaks.

Stepping out into the hallway, Mateo was jarred even more. "Doc, why is everyone going through the exit door of the theater?"

V.

——=◦《◉》◦=——

The Human Prospect

F or the good of their resident-patients, Tall Oaks was designed to be confusing. Should a resident ever try to take-off, disorientation would help slow them down. It preemptively sabotaged escape plans. This was in addition to Tall Oaks masterful suppression of the impulse to flee. Mateo was the exception, who used to leave and return undetected. He always came back from his night trips. He knew exactly where they were.

Mateo looked around the room and laughed.

"Where are we?" asked a bewildered doctor. "Is this place what I think it is?"

"We're at the *Choice*, Doc."

The *Choice* Cinema was an older style movie theater. No cushy recliners, or full scale meals served. Board hard seats with upright backs. What the *Choice* did have in common with modern movie theaters was its top-notch sound system. Mateo knew the *Choice* had something money could not buy. It had charm. While not seen directly, a part of this attractiveness were the cork lined walls that enhanced the acoustic quality of the theatre.

The movies were chosen by the Director of Tall Oaks. She was a discerning movie aficionado who appreciated the power of film. As an art form, it has a tremendous range.

This resulted in an extremely diverse reel of films shown by the *Choice*, varied but united under the theme of human expression. This also meant a zinger occasionally made it through.

Upon entering the theater, the guards started planting themselves in the seats. All of them were noiselessly pointing to their color matching watch.

Mateo could not resist stating the obvious. "I think you are right. There are clearly some new procedures in the military. And, what, nobody noticed until now?"

"All I know is that nobody at the Pentagon or elsewhere could figure out who changed key protocols, and the rules of engagement. By the time people realized WICS was responsible, it was too late. Somehow, the new rules have remained in place. Again, I am not sure why, that's why we are here. We are trying to figure it out."

"Thanks for that in-depth answer," observed Mateo. "It's so specific as to be untrustworthy, but thank you anyway. I don't speak this language, but it looks like break time to me, Doc."

"It's a mandated break," confirmed the doctor, who was looking for a seat.

Mateo decided to taunt the doctor with a thought, "This is nice to see. I've always thought we need more breaks at work."

Mateo followed the doctor and sat in the middle of the theatre. All around them, the guards let their craniums take a break and breathe. They removed their large helmets to expose a gamut of hairstyles. Bowl cuts, Caesar, bobs, pixies, undercuts, fades of all heights, Mohawks, pageboys, weaves, braids of all sorts, afros, bunches, chignons, feathered, dreadlocks, himes, line ups, lobs, the classic crew or butch cuts, flattops, mullets, mudcuts, updos, braids of all twists and lengths, and even the classic high and tight.

Mesmerized by the sight of of all these hairstyles, Mateo almost forgot to look around for the leaders of this lost brigade. Before turning around, Mateo was reminded of the compress strapped on his head. He turned up and set into place the bandage that was covering his eye. Still staring at the blank screen, Mateo lost his chance as the house lights began dimming. Popcorn was doled out, canned sodas, goobers, snowcaps, licorice, jelly beans, Swedish fish. jaw breakers, chocolate bars, and junior mints. A bag of popcorn landed in Mateo's lap, along with a Barques root beer. As snacks were getting passed around, he checked again. Yep, his apple was still safe.

With the exception of the amplified crunching, smacking, and gulping, the room was dead silent. The crowd outside could not penetrate the corked walls, which elevated the acoustics inside the theater. In a low voice, Mateo turned to the doctor, "So, what you were telling me earlier, is that WICS hoodwinked everyone. Nobody knew it was happening, either. It's kind of like the frog in boiling water. Is that what you were saying?"

While Mateo was speaking to the doctor, through the dimness they both watched two guards run a movie reel up the aisle. Two hasty blurs of yellow and red, still wearing their helmets, darted up to the projection booth. Before the doctor could respond, the projector was fired up and a movie began playing. Although it did not start at the opening, Mateo immediately recognized the movie.

"Ha, huh, oohhh, ouch, ha."

"Why are you laughing?" asked the doctor.

"Doc, do you know what movie this is?"

"No, what is it about?"

Shocked by the doctor's unfamiliarity, Mateo had to ask again. "You're not familiar with *Human Assessment*? Rodents, they're a bad universal omen—right?"

Not knowing what to make of Mateo's last comment the doctor just shook his head. This prompted Mateo to rapidly fire off highlights of the general plot. Aliens, explosions, galactic struggle, lasers, carnage, an inter-planetary orgy, a love story, ancient mystical rites, all with a moral message added in there. All the good stuff. It was a film for everyone, a cult classic. "This scene is near the beginning, so you didn't miss too much. Most of that stuff comes later."

Impressed by the taste of the popcorn, Mateo shouted out into the dark air.

"This popcorn is the tits!"

"Huzzah!" the guards answered back in unison.

FADE IN:

EXT. PLANET EARTH – SUNLIGHT ACROSS NORTH AMERICA

In the darkness the shot closes in on the Earth and its moon. Both grow larger in size upon approach. Passing the moon the shot rests majestically on the Earth. It remains the focus until an alien spacecraft drifts into the frame.

While the Galactic War left this region of the Milky Way untouched, the area was increasing in strategic importance. Reconnaissance missions were sent out by the major combatants, each trying to gain that decisive edge.

CUT TO:

INT. THE SPACECRAFT, THE LARK
From the floors to the ceilings, this spaceship needs a thorough cleaning. Trash left here and there. The camera traverses through different rooms, exposing similar conditions until it reaches the control deck.

INT. THE CONTROL DECK - - CONTINUOUS

The camera rises to reveal an alien who in human form. He is sitting down, diligently performing calculations and pushing buttons. The immediate surroundings are neat and tidy.

The camera rises and exposes another alien in their human disguise. He is reclined, feet up on his desk, hands behind his head in a state of daydreaming repose. Next to the bureaucratic stacks of intelligence reports on his desk were food wrappers strewn about and a large fountain soda.

They were still using their adopted names for Earthly living. ZEBULON was sitting down, ANDY was leaning back.

The Galactic War brought their home planet Conanndu into conflict with Mutred. This was mainly due to the alliance breakdown. Conanndu sided with the Cosmic Corps, while Mutred supported the Citadel of Chaos.

ANDY and ZEBULON have just returned from a whirlwind tour of amusement parks across the United States. They were in the midst of preparing for their departure to next door. After their assignment in the Andromeda Galaxy they were before returning back home to Conanndu.

ZEBULON
(seated and working)
Andy, let's return to the conversation we had earlier. I just think that they are too dangerous to get involved in the struggle. But then again, what if the Citadel of Chaos finds them first. What if they align against us?

ZEBULON
(cont.'d)
Once the Citadel finds this place they're going to see that rodent and claim some bizarre divine fate has brought them together. If the war spreads here—can you imagine? Once contact is made, for better or worse, that's it. No going back. Best to conceal their discovery, right? Or at least gloss it over? Probably better to be vague to guard against the reports being intercepted.

ANDY
I hate those beady little eyes on their insignia. (Citadel of Chaos) Are you talking to me or yourself?

ZEBULON
(exasperated but good humored)
Does it matter? You can't seem to pay attention. I am trying to get some thoughts together before getting this report completed.

ANDY
I think you paint too bleak a future.

ZEBULON
By the way, how long have we been here?

ANDY
Not long enough.

ZEBULON
You could stay here forever. But this place,
well, it terrifies me.

ANDY
(laid back and sipping his soda)
If you just tell the truth, all your cares will
melt away. Look, I admit they will be bothersome
to look after. But an existential threat, to us?
Come on, get real.

Whoever finds them takes advantage of the First
Contact doctrine. Right now, it belongs to us. We
have the right to secure an allegiance first with
the proof that we were here first.

ZEBULON
(seated and working)
Uh-huh.

ANDY
(reclined and sipping soda)
Why else did we plant the honing beacon on top of
those mountains in the Andes? You know the rules,
better than I do. We are not authorized to make
formal contact. Everyone thought this area was
inhospitable to life. I highly doubt Citadel or
Mutred will send scouts.

ZEBULON
(working pace slows down)
Hostile to life, that's for sure. Still, part
of me wants to leave them undiscovered. I know

that's not possible.

Their violence is unmatched.

ANDY
(still reclined)
At least now you're making more sense. No matter
what happens, we can always use them to take down
Citadel.

Remember the Dangerous Doctrine? If they are
eventually deemed too dangerous, we can bolt and
nobody will hold it against us. If push came to
shove even take out.

ZEBULON
I guess. But it does seem like a stretch.

Wait, wouldn't that make us better at killing
than them?

ANDY
(sidesteps the question)
I think you tend to be overblown about the whole
thing.

These earthlings are maybe slightly more violent
than most. I grant you that, Zebulon. And they
sure are a scrappy bunch, which is exactly why we
could use them.

ZEBULON
I guess, but I am still not convinced. Lawless
creatures do not follow rules.

Besides, you would willingly stay here forever.

ANDY
(sipping on his soda intermittently)

I figured you would be more upbeat about their
chances for reform.

Have you forgotten our own history?

ZEBULON
(looking at a recumbent Andy)
Of course I haven't.

ANDY
Losing is simply not an option. These humans
could help us defeat the Citadel of Chaos, and
reform themselves in the process.

ZEBULON
(working, but at a slower pace)
I guess.

ANDY
It's got comeback story written all over it—
a newly discovered sentient life-form averts
planetary suicide by helping to defeat, the
Citadel of Chaos. From killers to heroes, saving
countless psychic life from subjugation.

And you're right, I do like it here. So what,
it's far from perfect, just like everywhere else.
Butt, you have to admit, it has a certain charm
to it.

ZEBULON
Like that charm we found down in the swamp?

ANDY
If it makes you feel better, I do agree that the
amusement park logo resembles the devil rodent of
the Citadel insignia. The only thing missing is
the beady eyes.

Can you concede anything?

ZEBULON
People make pilgrimages to that place so I think
it might even me religious somehow. Those beady
little red eyes creep me out. Yeah. That's all it
needed.

ANDY
So, I guess there isn't.
But a church, really?

ZEBULON
It ticks off most of the boxes. It's at least an
open question.

ZEBULON stops working. He gets up and proceeds to
collect his thoughts by slowly pacing back and
forth.

ZEBULON
Just look at the amount of money that place takes
in. That's got to count for something.

ANDY
You're just avoiding the real issue.
You just won't admit it, will you?

ZEBULON
(still pacing along the control panel with large
bay windows and computer screens)
Admit what?
(stops pacing)

ANDY
(still reclined and sipping on his soda)
You know full well what I mean. You actually had
fun on the roller coasters. Just admit it, you
big softy.

ZEBULON
(resumes pacing after staring at ANDY in
disbelief)

ANDY
Just allow yourself to have some enjoyment would
you? It's always all or nothing with you. If some
of it is not good, then all of it is bad. That
makes no sense.

ZEBULON
(redirects the conversation)
Since I am getting my thoughts together for this
upfront report, anything in particular I should
mention?

ANDY
Start with ice cream and hop-scotch. Talk about
how nothing feels better than getting a hug, or
petting a dog. Do I even have to mention roller
coasters? Who knows, you might change your mind
after discussing these.

ZEBULON
(giving Andy that unconvinced look while pacing)
We'll see.

ANDY
Oh, and talk about slang. I find this aspect of
human language fascinating.

ZEBULON
I agree with you there.

ANDY
People get so bent out of shape when you make
sounds they don't like. But then, these same
people, feel justified to use it when the world
does not operate according to their command.

                    ZEBULON
        (walking with a look of puzzlement)
              I am not following.

                      ANDY
    Do you remember when we ran that experiment?

                    ZEBULON
        Seriously? You know how many we ran.

                      ANDY
    The one that shut off cell service in that really
    wealthy area in Connecticut for a few hours to
        run that experiment on human fragility?

                    ZEBULON
    Oh yes. How could I forget? People living in that
    Golden Triangle thought the world was coming to
    an end because their cell phone stopped working.

    You're right. People were cursing up a storm. All
                  I heard was *fuck*.

        (quick cut to a scene depicting the mayhem in
                  Golden Triangle, CT)

                      ANDY
    Yeah, they were offending themselves for hours.

LAUGHTER

                  ANDY(cont'd)
        (reclining and distantly staring up)
    Still, I think these humans can work their way
          out of the mess they've created.

                Will it be easy? No.
                Is it possible? Yes.

ZEBULON
Maybe you're right. There's no possibility
without taking a chance. But that means there is
also a chance they can't, or even ruin it more.
(pauses momentarily to view the Earth though
large bay windows)

If their ideas do not change, and they do not let
the old ones die out, they are doomed.

ANDY
At the very least anyway, they deserve a fighting
chance.
They made it this far, right?
Like I said before, hardscrabble creatures.

And I return to my earlier point—don't you
remember Conanndu's history?

ZEBULON
Of course, I remember. I just think these
creatures are inherently different. They are
simply incapable of helping each other in order
to help themselves.

ANDY
Look at that, your life-form prejudice is
showing.
I always knew you were a bi-ped hater.

LAUGHTER

ANDY (cont'd)
Music. Make sure to talk about music.
What a gift to the universe.

You cannot create these tones anywhere else. Only
in that environment. I am looking forward to the
whole of Conanndu hearing the recordings we have.

EUGENE NASSER

In agreement, ZEBULON begins to hum the opening of
Beethoven's Fifth Symphony.

                    ANDY
        (sits up, still sipping on his soda)
           Do you have a favorite song?

                  ZEBULON
   I don't remember the names like you do, only the
                     bars.

                    ANDY
         Do you know my favorite song is?

                  ZEBULON
             No, what is it?

ANDY springs to his feet, looks at ZEBULON, and
taps a button on his watch. Loud musics plays
over the sound system. ANDY starts lip syncing
                and dancing.

                  (CHORUS)
          Never gonna to give you up
          Never gonna let you down
      Never gonna run around and desert you.

          Never gonna make you cry
          Never gonna say goodbye
      Never gonna tell a lie and hurt you

LAUGHTER

                    ANDY
        (Andy turns the music off.)
         You've been Rick rolled!

LAUGHTER

ANDY
Yeah, make sure you talk about that.

ZEBULON
Thanks, I feel a little better.
All right, let's at least get this report
started.

ANDY finishes his soda. (sucking sound, shakes the ice)

ANDY
(akimbo and looking at ZEBULON from across the room)
I am headed down one last time for another soda.
You want anything?

ZEBULON
(shakes head with a shameful countenance)
Thanks, but no. Try to hurry up. It'll be your
fourth one today. I warned you that stuff is
highly addictive.

ANDY
Lucky for me we're changing our life-apparatus
soon.

ZEBULON
You always seem to abuse your living frame. You
treat it like a cheap hotel room.

I am sure your pancreas is already...what is the
word?...shot.
Your pancreas is shot, to shit.

ANDY
Nice use of slang. Yeppers, my liver is shot too.

Are you sure I can't get you anything? I already
placed the order.
(pulls cell phone out of his pocket)

ZEBULON
Just a soda, huh. Do me a favor, while you are
down there, destroy that thing.

Hurry up, we're on a tight schedule. Make sure to
take the remote to the resonance jumper. You can
haul yourself back.

ANDY
(pulls out from his pocket a remote control with
a built in car key)
Already have it. Go ahead and get started without
me. When I get back, I'll help brainstorm some
more.

(walking toward the resonance jumper)
And Legos. Don't forget to talk about those and
that playing dough for kids.

ANDY becomes the focus as ZEBULON walks over to a
different control panel. ANDY enters a contraption
resembling a large upright shake weight. The pod
starts moving up and down slowly and quietly. As
it speeds up, the noise grows until the vibration
is so fast appears to be noiselessly standing
still. After a moment of silence, there's a flash
of blue light and the upper capsule disappears.

The camera pulls away to reveal a more detailed
look around the control deck. Strewn about is
a panoply of earthly artifacts. Ranging from
classified documents to scented candles, some are
in glass containers, others are not. A pair of
novelty socks was protected, while a cash register
was not.

With ZEBULON humming Beethoven's Fifth Symphony softly in the background, the resonance jumper starts moving again as before. After a bolt of green light, the top capsule reappears. ANDY emerges from the bottom with some grease stained bags and a large fountain soda. ZEBULON motions to ANDY from across the room, by tapping the back of his head.

                    ANDY
           Oh, yeah. Thanks.

ANDY removes the remote from the input in the back of his head. He presses the button and the resonance teleport which emits the sound of enabling a car alarm.

From one of the bags, ANDY lays out on his table a large fountain soda, three hot dogs, a double burger, a heap of French fries, and a few fried pickles.

                    ZEBULON
That was fast. I didn't even have a chance to get
                    started.
      That is going to give you terrible gas.

                    ANDY
      It's a smor-*gas*-board. Get it?

                    ZEBULON
      Oh, I get it. It's just not funny.

LAUGHTER

                    ANDY
  I know you said you were good, but I got you
              something anyway.
  (finds the bag without a grease stain and tosses

it across the room to ZEBULON)

Remember when I ripped a fart in that kids face
while we were in line for that roller coaster?

ZEBULON
How could I forget? You gave him an asthma
attack. I thought you killed that kid.

(quick cut to an adolescent boy attended to by
theme park paramedics while the line moves along.
An angry mother points and screams "You farted!"
at ANDY)

ANDY
That was an accident.
I thought it would be silent. I was going to
blame it on you.

LAUGHTER

ANDY (cont'd)
Dude, admit it—you had fun on that roller
coaster—didn't you, you dirty bastard.
(With a look of concentration, Andy rips a large
fart before sitting down to eat)

LAUGHTER

ZEBULON
(looks into the bag to discover three tofu tacos)
Thank you. You know I love these.
You reek like a skunk's butt.
(waves hand in front of his face)

ANDY
It's not my fault you have a weak stomach. Even
the merry-go-round made me you sick. Remember
when those little girls beat you down for

throwing up on them?
(quick cut to ZEBULON in the fetal position with
two little girls standing over berating him with
words and little fists for puking across their
backs)

ANDY (cont'd)
Admit it, you had some fun with those
gravitational experiments, didn't you?
We don't have anything like these amusement parks
back home.

ZEBULON
(Eating tofu tacos while walking along the long
stretched control panel)
Our gravity is not as strong, hence, the
vomiting.
Let's get on with this report.

ANDY
(comically focused, mouthful of food)
A little more spit balling— quick, describe this
planet and its dominant species in one word. Go!

ZEBULON
Overkill.

ANDY
Good, another?

ZEBULON
Plastic.

ANDY
Very good. One more?

ZEBULON
Screens.

ANDY
Now, you're flowing.
ZEBULON
By the way, were we the first here?

ANDY
No, but we're the first to leave. The ones before us, from what I could tell, none of them made it off the planet.
(quick cut to ANDY combing the military databases on a computer)
They were all crash landings.

ZEBULON
See, I knew their gravity is bad news. It's too strong. It's nothing to play around with.

ZEBULON
(finished eating and now walking the length of the control panel across the large bay windows)
Turn on Manifest Recorder.

COMPUTER
(sexy female robot voice)
Engaged.

ZEBULON
Start report.

COMPUTER
Yes, sir.

ZEBULON
To note: In the following recounting our adopted Earth names are used. These are Major Zebulon, for myself, and Captain Andy for the second in command.

Let me say at the outset, that immediate and

sustained measures should be taken to conceal this place. The dominating lifeforms, who have an awareness of ideas, are the dominating life-form. They are far too dangerous to ally with, even in our struggle against Citadel.

It might be worth considering to let Citadel ally with them. They are more like alcohol loving parasites, so when Citadel perishes, so do they. This stems primarily from the fact that while they have rational intelligence, they cannot seem to follow it.

I recommend the Elder Council of Klemens be notified as soon as possible of their existence, and inherent danger.

Here I present the Council with a short but important brief on a new species of life Captain Andy and myself discovered. They classify themselves as human beings, with the scientific name *Homo sapiens*.

In a sector once thought uninhabitable we were tipped off by two large explosions that indicated some sort of pattern. This led us to explore the situation—

Stop report.

ZEBULON (cont'd)
I forgot to ask, how long have we been here?

ANDY
Just say eighty Earth orbits.

ZEBULON
What do you think so far?

ANDY
What's the phrase...so far, so good.
(admiring the hamburger while eating it)
Make sure to say that they consume sentient life.
It actually tastes quite amazing once you get
used to it. Not sure if that makes me terrible,
or not.

ZEBULON
Yes, it makes you bad. In this case, a terrible
human being. You know how living operates.

ANDY
I know, I know. You've got to eat the least
sentient life.
With a (mouthful of hamburger)
I get it. Easy to see why it's basically banned
everywhere else.
Still, delicious.
This is one of the very few places you can get
away with it.
Don't you judge me, right now, you're a furry
little biped too.

LAUGHTER

ZEBULON
Start report.

COMPUTER
(sexy female robot voice)
Yes, sir.

ZEBULON
These thinking, featherless bipeds have achieved
Level 3 sentience. They appear to be at the Turn
to Level 4, but this progress a certainty.

Collectively, they are missing the first step

toward the Loop of Infinite Understanding. These humans keep on mistaking the *how* for the *why*. This error has led to a techno-fascist capitalist society in what are called advanced countries. A global cabal controls not just the money and production of goods, but it has captured their attention in innumerable ways.

Information, if the people do receive it, is more often than not shared for another reason, an ulterior motive to enrich the wealthy even more.

In addition to being dumbed down, the populations must have the ability to numb themselves with intoxicants. Forced into a life without a fulfilling cathartic release, they have been driven into misery and despair. Mass shootings have become normalized in the country we just left. It is called America.

The methods used to wield power maintain the feudal aspect of these dominating techno-fascist rulers. However, there is one way available to ascend up. Create a new method of social control that can be monetized, and up the social ladder a person can climb. One can reach what is called a new class.

This overall plan of control is as ingenious in its stupidity as it is in its malevolence. Seeking to control even the source of energy people use, those few who own the extraction and combustion methods that spew carbon into the atmosphere would rather scorch everything and leave nothing behind. Perpetuating this control directly coincides with the known destruction of the environment. As the climate worsens, it heads toward inevitable collapse of the biosphere, or ecocide. The people are controlled more and more thoroughly along the way.

(While eating French fries Andy mocks Zebulon by making a blah-blah hand gesture)

It will be difficult for those on Conanndu to believe the powerful and wealthy fought against these existential reforms.
They kept up endless production with finite resources, a truth that was masked for a short time. The ugly truth was always there.

They can only get past this by realizing everything is nothing, and that nothing is everything. Until then, the human species will never access Level 5 of the Great Mother. They will remain stuck at Level 3. Without the political reforms to fix mass consumption issues, they will never make the turn to Level 4. Until the find some collective effort, humanity is on a suicide mission.

Once these political fuckers are out of office—

Stop report.

COMPUTER
(sexy female robot voice)
Yes, sir.

ZEBULON (cont'd)
Shit, I cursed. It's because you brought it up earlier. Damn this human capsule.

ANDY
(finishes hamburger, relishing the last bite)
You sure know how to talk. I thought you were going to go on forever.
You want some advice? Try to relax. You're so worked up all the time. Always so dire. And go

ahead and curse, so what? Who fuck'in cares? Who
knows any different? Besides, it makes you edgy.
As an uptight dork and a nerd, you need it.

BBUURRPPP.

ZEBULON
(with an unimpressed look)
Classy.
If I am a dork and nerd you are a pig and a
pervert. It smells like something crawled up your
butt, died, and now you are belching it out.

ANDY
Another thing—you should have started off with
boobies. I love boobies. So many shapes and
sizes. All different and equal. Downright criminal
more countries don't allow women to go around
topless.

ZEBULON
I think the whole planet down there knows you
love boobies.
You are like a man-baby. On that topic, I plan to
discuss their bizarre mating rituals later on.

We have to go soon, this is just to get the ball
rolling. I wanted to do this earlier, but, no.
Someone had to go on another roller coaster.

ANDY
Worth it.
(sips soda)

ZEBULON
Let's try this again.

Start report.

EUGENE NASSER

COMPUTER
(sexy female robot voice)
Yes, sir.

Commander Andy and I have just returned from
America. It was the last nation state we
visited collecting data on gravity. The Earth's
gravitational force is much stronger than on
Conanndu. The country left us both with quite an
impression.

In fact, it has made me skeptical if they
can collectively reform themselves and avert
environmental disaster. I am not sure if they
will make the Turn. Until then, believing this
false knowledge makes them extremely dangerous
creatures.

While expert analysis by the Council will yield a
more definitive answer, my survival calculations
are extremely low. On arrival, I gave it fifty-
fifty at best. However, after this intelligence
mission, I'd say fifteen percent. No. Make it
twelve percent.

(ANDY shakes his head in disapproval, managing to
disrupt ZEBULON'S concentration)

Humans have never lived with this much carbon
in the atmosphere. As a result, the average
intelligence quotient of the species has dropped
rather fuck'in substantially—

Stop report.

COMPUTER
(sexy female robot voice)
Yes, sir.

                    ANDY
(laughing and smudging french fries in ketchup)
              Who talks like that?
              Nice job, el capitano.

                  ZEBULON
          I know, I cursed again.

                    ANDY
     That's not what I'm talking about.

                  ZEBULON
What is wrong with what I am saying? What don't
                  you like?

                    ANDY
You sound, what is the word they use...like a
know-it-all. A pretentious prick, that's it.

                  ZEBULON
           What is that again?

                    ANDY
     You're a dick. A dork, remember?

                  ZEBULON
      Everything I'm saying is true.

                    ANDY
You can still be right even if you're not a dick
about it. Probably some emptiness inside, who
knows where it comes from. What I do know is that
you don't have to be a dickhead. Ejaculating on
    every body everything you know.

                  ZEBULON
       That's a disgusting image.

                          ANDY
You're telling me, I am on the receiving end.

LAUGHTER

                      ANDY (cont'd)
Don't be so fatal about it. Deep down, humans
are inherently good despite all their flaws. What
about all the nice things? Aren't they true too?
                    (eating some fries)

                        ZEBULON
What endearing humans did we run into?

                          ANDY
New York City.

                        ZEBULON
Those people were downright rude.

                          ANDY
No, they were just being honest.

(quick cut to a scene of a New Yorker screaming
at ZEBULON (horrified) and ANDY (smirking) whose
indecision holds up the line at a busy deli,
"What are youz, a fuck'in moron or something?")

                        ZEBULON
No, I think people in Salt Lake City were
                      friendlier.

                          ANDY
They were looking to recruit you into some weird
belief system. They wanted your mind, money, and
time. That's not friendly, it's selfish. Straight
                     up control.

ZEBULON
It was no stranger than any of the others.
Are you done now? Can I go on?

ANDY
Bro, you asked me. I still think you could be
more balanced.

ZEBULON
That was foolish of me.
(ANDY shoots ZEBULON a look of dissatisfaction)

Stop looking at me like that.
(keeping his eyes on ZEBULON, ANDY crams a large
pinch of fries into his mouth)

ZEBULON (cont'd)
Okay, I am moving on.

ANDY
(imitating the voice of Yoda)
Now, struggle with anger do you? Control it by
releasing it, you must.
Remember, an uptight prick are you.
(sips on soda)

ZEBULON
(holding back laughter)
Start report.

COMPUTER
(sexy female robot voice)
Yes, sir.

ZEBULON
In my estimation, there is no way that humanity,
taken collectively, will not make The Turn
without outside assistance.
This, of course, presents an obvious dilemma.

Intervention is not allowed by the Intergalactic
Conduct Code on the grounds of self-sufficiency.

In addition, there is no guarantee that after
contact is made information about The Turn will
remain concealed. I recommend putting the proper
safeguards in place. The only way to make The
Turn is from within, and there is no second
chance. But not these humans. Extinction is on
the line. No second chances, no do-overs, no next
time.

Their self-imposed ignorance and historical
amnesia have—
(ZEBULON pauses momentarily after looking over at
ANDY who is eating and slowly making the jerking
off gesture)
—prevented them from acting on the truth.
Instead, they would rather live a lie.

Mentioned earlier, it has been the preponderance
of endless greed by those who create supply,
control distribution, or both. This is the elite
class. They hoard all the wealth and make it
scarce, forcing others to chase it. During a
global health pandemic, billionaires decided to
amuse themselves and shot themselves into space.
To play around with gravity rather than help
those experiencing real suffering. Forget that,
after these wealthy people returned to Earth,
they were richer than before they left.

Accompanying members of this elite class—such
as bankers, lawyers, accountants, politicians,
business owners and CEO tech types—
Everyone had an opportunity to help and did not.
This was easily predictable based on tilt of the
economy to the rich, as well as the incentives
in the financial markets of the major national

players. Impossible to expect a solid collective effort from people who only care about themselves.

(ANDY mocks ZEBULON with a blah-blah hand gesture)

ZEBULON (cont'd)
When the upper elite perform incompetently, it is worse for everyone. These self-appointed guardians of social order have mismanaged society after the advent of the Industrial Revolution. The aim of creating wealth for the few, maintained in part through a system of elaborate social controls, has reverberated over the years to its present form.

What's become clear, is the complete loss of a common good.
Any part of the remedy is placing people correctly into work they are naturally suited.

Most people cannot follow through on their inclinations, what is called character, because of the socio-economic constraints. Merit does not mean much anymore. This means desperation rules people's day-to-day lives. Everything costs money. This crushing subjugation could be tangibly felt in the last place we were, America. Other countries had this too, but without all the guns. It has made the larger part of the American population desperadoes.

(ANDY mocks ZEBULON, who tries not to laugh, by suggestively eating a hot dog)

The entire balance of the planet has been thrown off, and since that steadiness may never be regained, the future of the species might just be FUBAR.

Andy raises his hand to ask a question.

                    ZEBULON
              (holding back laughter)
                  Stop report.

                    COMPUTER
              (sexy female robot voice)
                   Yes, sir.

                    ZEBULON
        You can't do that. This is serious.

LAUGHTER

                   What is it?

                     ANDY
   I thought you were trying to keep the slang out?

                    ZEBULON
                   I have.

                     ANDY
              I don't think so.

    FUBAR. That's slang. It's got one of those cuss
                  words in it.

                    ZEBULON
   Are you sure? I heard people a bunch of American
   military people say it. I remember, it was San
                    Antonio.

                     ANDY
           What were they talking about?

                    ZEBULON
   Some place called Kabul. They also mentioned

Los Angeles.
They said a bunch more places, but those are two
I remember.

So?

ANDY
Zebs, come on. Think about it.

ZEBULON
(stops pacing, puzzled expression)
I don't get it.

ANDY
What does the military do?

ZEBULON
Protect the people from enemies.
I am still confused.
And where is the curse word?

ANDY
It's an acronym. It means Fucked Up Beyond All
Recognition. FUBAR.

LAUGHTER

ZEBULON
Then your butthole is FUBAR.

LAUGHTER
ANDY
See that, Z-man, you're starting to lighten up.
You're still too fatal, but you're getting there.

ZEBULON
Okay, maybe I am, but only a little.
I just cannot get anything done with you around.

Let me wrap this up. Just sit over there and drink your soda. You inhaled everything else.

                    ANDY
Okay, but make sure to talk about the power of the boobies, music, and all that other stuff. Oh yeah, dinosaurs. Make sure to reference them.

                  ZEBULON
                (hesitantly)
             Uh, oh-kay.
         But why the dinosaurs?

                    ANDY
I think they deserve some credit. Nearly all of them died when that asteroid smacked the planet. I think they got what called a bum rap. I think it's worth noting that those bastards were around a long time.

                  ZEBULON
               Sure thing.
That reminds me, I haven't even talked about all the violence. Where we just came from was insane. I'll confess to you, when we were in America I thought about planetary cloaking.

Just for a moment. I wasn't going to do it, obviously, but, yeah.

                    ANDY
What? Are you serious? That frequency would almost instantly kill the vast majority of life on Earth.
      (ANDY pretends to be genuinely outraged)

Wait, you wanted to cloak the place to protect others from the violence of a dominating species,

by killing them?
This is exactly what I was talking about earlier
and you ignored me. Don't think I didn't notice.

Are you fuck'in crazy? Planetcide?
You really do hate flowers and kittens.

ZEBULON
No, no, no, I am was not going to do it. They are
doing it anyway, but I was not really going to do
it.

ANDY
(feigned disbelief)
You really are prejudice against bipeds!? Even
though they are more bloodthirsty than the
dinosaurs, it does not make them all bad.

Holy shit, you really need to lighten up.

ZEBULON
(embarrassed defensiveness)
I like bipeds just fine.
I knew I should not have told you.

ANDY
Remember, some humans have something the
dinosaurs do not.

ZEBULON
What's that?

ANDY
Boobies. Lots of boobies.

LAUGHTER

ZEBULON
I like the ostrich. That's a bi-ped. Chickens too.

> At least I am not a bi-ped who exterminated
> another bi-ped.
>
> And if they don't change their act they'll end up
> like the one they extinguished, the dildo bird.

ANDY
(spits out soda laughing)

ZEBULON
What?

ANDY
Nothing.

ZEBULON
Tell me.

ANDY
It was a dodo bird. Dildos are for—

ZEBULON
—I've heard enough.

ANDY
Yeah, we've already established you are a big
dildo.

LAUGHTER

ZEBULON
Let me wrap this up so we can get going.

Start report.

COMPUTER
(sexy female robot voice)
Yes, sir.

There is no magic piece of technology that can be invented to save these human beings from themselves. Instead, they have focused on the narcissism of small differences.
(ANDY raises his hand)

Stop report.

COMPUTER
(sexy female robot voice)
Yes, sir.

ZEBULON
Seriously, what now?

ANDY
I am taking off. And that computer voice is sexist.

ZEBULON
Yes, you've been quite enough help. You're the one who changed the settings on the program, not me.

ANDY
(stands up ready to leave)
Oh, yes. That's right, I did.
(smirking)

I need to crunch some numbers before bed. Don't want to ruin the hibernation period before the trip. While I'm sitting there, I'll think about how to get in early on the investment money headed this way. Earth—come see the spectacle!
(ANDY prepares to leave the control deck)

Balloons, those are always fun.

                    ZEBULON
                     Yes.

                     ANDY
                    What?
        (departing from the control deck)

                    ZEBULON
                     Yes.
    I did have fun on some of the roller coasters.

                     ANDY
               (stops in place)
                  I knew it!

LAUGHTER

                     ANDY
                (walking away)
    They just need to be reminded that it's okay to
     be cool with one another. There's nothing to
                     fear.

    Whoa, what...Okay, buddy, this one's for you.
               (rips a loud fart)

                    ZEBULON
            That was definitely FUBAR.

LAUGHTER

ANDY leaves. Alone in the control desk ZEBULON
walks over to the bay window. He takes in an
extended view of the Earth.

                    ZEBULON
    What's missing is the follow through, the will.
    I just cannot figure out why any living organism
     would rather race to the bottom, as opposed to

climbing toward the top.

It actually breaks my heart to see it. That's why I am so hostile toward hem, these humans. I am angrier *with* them than *at* them, if that makes any sense.

When you want more from someone than they do for themselves. All that lost talent never acted upon. If they can just put their differences aside and focused on coming environmental challenges. To celebrate life instead of destroy it.

I do hope they make it. Nothing would make me happier.
(ZEBULON looks at the mess ANDY left behind)
They need to let go of hope and act.

Stop report.

Turn off Manifest Recorder.

COMPUTER
(sexy female robot voice)
Not engaged, sir.

Deciding to get all the reports done later on, ZEBULON walks over to the mess that ANDY left behind. He picks up a nearby garbage can, placing it at the end of the table. With one cleanly sweeps of his extended arm, ZEBULON wipes it all off into the trash.

ZEBULON
What a lazy mother fucker.

INT. THE SPACECRAFT, THE LARK
ZEBULON proceeds to leave the control deck. The shot pulls back retracing the earlier sequence

```
into outer space.

EXT—SPACECRAFT, THE LARK
The Lark departs with only the Earth and moon left
in view. Then the shot closes in on the moon.
From behind the dark side, two red dots are first
recognized, followed by the rest of the Mutred
spacecraft bearing the symbol of Citadel. An evil
looking rodent with diabolic horn-ears.
```

"Time's up!" came an official sounding proclamation from the back of the room.

The house lights slowly charged up and turned on. The guards squinted affirmatively at their watches, quickly filling their cheeks, getting one last dose of snack in. They put their obnoxious helmets back on and were ready lickety-split. They left the theater as spotless as it was found.

Cocooned by their good vibes, Mateo was rolling right along. Momentarily forgetting about his aches and pains, Mateo turned down the bandage so it covered his eye again. As they left through the entrance of the *Choice Cinema*, leadership showed a dedication to the wrong way by going left, when they should have made a right. At that point, Mateo's headache took priority over his concern for their commitment to the wrong way out.

As the cascade of colorful helmets fluttered silently down the hallway, the doctor's voice echoed off the corridor walls. The faint rumblings from the crowd once outside the theater dissipated away as the doctor could not help himself. Although he clearly saw Mateo was in pain, he implored anyway. "Well, what happens?" Does the Citadel show up? Who wins the Galactic War? Does anyone? What happens to the Earth? To humans?"

Mateo resembled a stereo-typical mental patient. "Look, Doc. Can we talk about it later? My head is splitting right now, but I take it that you liked what you saw. I know what I saw but not what just happened."

Then he acknowledged their situation.

"Oh that hurts. It so funny...ow, ow, ow. Going left when we should go right, Owww."

"You shouldn't laugh if it's going to hurt."

"Thanks, Doc. I'll keep that in mind. Sometimes, the pain is worth it."

VI.

———— ⥅◉⥅ ————

Celling Out

Mateo's head throbbed and spun, but it hurt even more thinking how *Human Assessment* was more plausible than his current situation. These thoughts also made him laugh, a quintessential inside joke.

"Ooh, ow. Ow, ow."

"What's so funny?"

"Nothing, Doc. You were asking about the movie? I really don't want to spoil it for you. Watch it and judge for yourself. That's the whole purpose of art, for you to experience and interpret it, not anyone else."

"You know what, you're right," responded an affable doctor, "Thanks."

"All right, Doc. You're chomping so bad I'll give you a morsel. What I can tell you," Mateo divulged, "is that the film is really a documentary. It's a true story."

The doctor gave a little laugh.

With the stiffness from sitting down loosening away, Mateo

became a little animated. "While I feel better, and appreciate the concern for everyone getting their steps in, the people leading this entourage should be committed." Then he yelled ahead of him, "You're killing me Smalls!" Mateo's noggin ached sharply, but worth the cost to say it. Pain, like everything else, is subject to the demands of time.

"Hey, Doc, I can predict the future. I can tell you where we'll end up going down this hallway."

"Yeah, where?"

"This place was built when people used to read."

The T-junction outside the main entrance of the *Choice Cinema* naturally encouraged making a left. In contrast to the cramped, dark and flat path to the right, the hallway left was wider than usual, well-lit and had a subtle decline. The combination of these factors attracted people to walk it, and this is exactly what happened. As the reenergized colors poured out from the theatre, everyone was directed left.

The space where Mateo and his newfound chromatic friends were headed represented a healing principle at Tall Oaks: a suitable therapy must address the essence of the disease. To rehabilitate the mentally indigent, remedies were needed to help patients direct their thinking. Medications alone cannot provide this kind of empowerment, it requires intellectual exercise. An old school approach in the hopes of conferring greater mental composure, in part by providing an outlet to release pent up psychic energy. In order to engage the mind, readings and weekly discussions found dedicated spaces at Tall Oaks.

After all, knowledge is power.

"Hey, Doc, tell the officers that I am stopping by my room. From here we are going to have to pass it on the way out. I was not even granted the common courtesy to do that earlier. The people in charge must like it here. If I did not know any better I'd say they want to stay." Bandaged up, as he hobbled along, it occurred to Mateo how quickly he accepted the bizarre situation he was in.

Upfront in the pack, a gray guard broke formation. He tapped on the side of his helmet, whereupon loud music began blaring out of embedded speakers. A good number of the guards also broke rank, skipping in circles and taking advantage of the spacious hallway. They were dancing while silently lip syncing.

"Kind of like a violet I was way up in the sky."

"Everything I never liked about you is now seeping into me."

"I used to be somebody."

More guards joined in when the chorus hit.

"I was up above it...now I'm down in it."

Mateo slowed his limp to a shuffle.

"Yep, I accepted it rather quickly," slipped Mateo's thinking out into the open.

"What's that?" asked the doctor.

"Nothing. We're almost there."

"Where?"

Then, the music stopped. Without a word, orderly ranks were restored the expedition finally reached the end of the hallway. They made it to the library. Walking through large glass doors, the librarian's desk was situated right in the middle on a raised platform. It greeted patrons with a stern warmness.

At first, the guards were mesmerized by the sheer abundance of books. Aisles ran at length behind the librarian's desk. After regaining their composure, they rushed past the desk and bolted into the stacks. After snagging some books, many of the guards settled down in the spacious foyer as the higher-ups occupied the reading areas in the back with the books. Sitting at the tables and chairs adjacent to the librarian's desk, the guards sat quietly and read.

Standing in front of the desk, Mateo declared, "Looks like another rest stop. They'll have to retrace their steps and come back through here." With no reply from the doctor, he looked around to not find him. "All by himself, just like everybody else," he thought.

Mateo wanted to keep moving, so he decided to limber up. It would hurt while doing it, but he'd feel relief after the pain dissipated. Stretching through the discomfort, Mateo progressed through all sorts of bends and flexes: mountain, bridge, pigeon, tree, downward dog, triangle, warrior, cobra, crown, and child's pose. Painful, but necessary,

Feeling a little relief, Mateo eyed up the elevated librarian desk. He went behind it and used the step-stool to hoist himself up on top. He methodically removed the ice pack and bandages wrapped around his head. With an unobstructed view of the audience, Mateo checked his pocket before starting. The apple was safe.

The doctor returned from the stacks, the colorful crowd played their part. Books were closed, attention was given over, and Mateo remembered to just be. Alone, again, he surfed a comedic flow.

"Ain't this a bitch, eh folks? Right now, the people in charge are figuring out the library is a long dead end. They're probably in one of the reading rooms trying to come up with another plan of action. Jokers and clowns leading the way, and here I am stuck in Tall Oaks with you.

But, hey, it could always be worse. Just wait until we leave here, if we ever do. At least we ended up in the library. Most people think reading is stupid, so they don't do it, but not you all. Make sure to liberate those books from this place. You know, spread the word.

Just to clarify—all of you sitting here in front are obviously excluded from anything I am about to say. I have no idea what your whole shtick is about, but I dig it. The changes are great. You bunch are more like crossing guards than soldiers. Oh, aporia! I love it.

Being in here reminds me of what truly matters—your thoughts. It takes a shit-ton of practice to try and control them. I am never sure how much a shit-ton really is. I just know it's a lifetime. I know how to measure it, but not how much it weighs.

Just look at the people in charge, they clearly don't have command of their own thinking. They always follow protocol. Their thinking consists in doing what has been per-prescribed. Predetermined action in a world of uncertainty that makes sense. I get that you need it, but it handicaps thinking on your feet.

Which brings me to our current situation ladies, gentlemen, and non-binary friends.

Right here and now, we are witnessing what happens when incompetent people get promoted. The buffoons leading our journey are imbeciles of the highest order. Straight up, fucking idiots. However, this is a rare moment when I am not angry at their inability to do their job. Their lack of pragmatic competence has brought us to this wonderful place. For that, we should all be thankful.

Telling people what they want to hear is not talent. Where's the merit?

The unworthy are rewarded with a corner office, a hefty raise, free childcare and primo parking. And because these people cannot truly lead, they micro-manage. It's authoritarian, not managerial. Worthless and useless managers, who only know how to measure what others tell them to quantify, are endemic across American society. When there is no real vision of leadership, micromanaging takes its place. Just the way people in charge want it, one pointless meeting after another with no real plan. Since they do not deserve to be in charge, people in this professional class wonder why subordinates have basically no respect for them. It's not from a lack of trying, but the managerial ego cannot replace ineptitude with competence, no matter how big it gets. This makes them not only suck at their jobs but life.

What's happened is that rampant incompetence goes unnoticed because it gets normalized. We just come to accept the fact that the water is polluted, garbage all over the streets, rampant gun violence, no affordable healthcare, out of control military spending, and government agencies corrupt to their core. Local, state and federal government filled people who got promoted because they rub those in charge the right way. These general states-of-affairs are normal. So, people just accept them as unchangeable facts of life.

Then, as it inevitably does, reality comes knocking. Bam, a major crisis hits, or multiple ones—oh, I don't know, like the one we are in right now—and that I am somehow involved in, which I am the main culprit I am still calling bullshit on—and you probably already know what I am going to say—and that is, we are all fucked. The full spectrum of their incompetency is exposed. They are managers, not leaders. Even the ones who are elected to lead.

Not knowing how to do anything else, they double down on their belief that conviction is the same as competency. They go on to repeat the same bad decisions as before. This is what's called managing the situation. Solving something actually require a plan of action.

United we stand, divided we fall. Does anybody remember this stuff? The managers of the American status quo got everyone to throw shit at each other. They pitted people against one another for political exploitation and to enrich themselves. What did you think was going to happen throwing shit at each other? United until the shit hits the fan, then nobody wants to clean up the mess.

This tribal thinking needs to be left in the dustbin of history. Instead of blaming the politicians in charge, who wield actual power, it shifts the blame to citizens of a different political stripe who don't have any. And there are no lack of people who buy it. I mean, it makes perfect sense doesn't it—because the average citizen sits on Capitol Hill and directs the daily affairs of the country, whereas the politician is powerless because they don't hold office. Yep, makes perfect *whatever* to me. Face it, the political class are a bunch of pathetic villains who have allowed the business interests of this country to own your ass. There's a fuck ton of money to be made in the political distraction and civic outrage markets, and we get the best political class money can buy. Minus the responsibility, of course. That falls on the average citizen, but that's tribal logic for you.

And just look at what we get—gangs of emotionally and politically charged adult children of alcoholics certain of everything in the world, except their own stupidity. National tragedies don't bring the country together anymore. Everybody is too busy being programmed by whatever crap they cannot stop staring at.

Yeah, they used to call it television programming. As everything does, the programming has evolved online into influencing. It has spawned the creation of a new occupation, creating a group called influencers. A new tool in the capitalist toolbox, you know.

Sometimes people call them media personalities. No. I think most of them are tools, like I said, or creatures. They all have that superficial charm. The type of people who never miss a chance to pimp out their family. They have that superficial charm that appeals to a vast swath of Americans.

It's takes a whole lot of planning to make the artificial extraordinary. Every stray hair plucked, faces plastered with makeup, special filters, perfect lighting, editing, and the obligatory plastic surgery. That way everyone can participate in the fabulous life they are living. Fake reality, it really is flawless.

Even among these influencers, some are worse than others. The lowest of the low are the self-described ones. They influence people for a living. They blow smoke up your ass, and there is no lack of people who like it. They like dumb shit.

Meaningless tricks, playing pranks, scaring people, I don't know, there's just too much dumb shit to name. Does anyone really care how someone else reacts to hearing a song for the first time? Why would you? Is it a form of self-loathing? We have gone from watching others play sports to this—to watching other people, watch something. It's the dumbest of shit.

This is where we are, folks.

And the reactions of these influencers has been monetized. They're usually hocking some snake oil. Once your attention is captured, to be influenced—they have you by the cognitive balls, you know—of course, money is going to be made off you. Whether you click, buy or accept those cookies, in the end you really are the product.

You are a commodity whose information is bought and sold.

The more meta-data, the better. When you get down to it, your mind is mined, the data sold, your digital profile built, an AI strategy developed to better learn and anticipate your behavior, and the mundane opinions of others valued entertainment.

It's all quite simple, isn't it? Don't worry, I am not expecting an answer

Talk about Marx's concept of alienated labor, right? I mean, we are in a library.

Anyway, through the capture of the Internet, capitalists found a way to make an exorbitant amount of money, unlimited really— the limited attention span of the American people. Deliberately kept busy to cripple the conditions for thinking, no free time.

If this happens in the future, and WICS has any brains at all, then perhaps a law will be passed punishing this nonsense. Maybe in the future you'll be searching for something to watch and land on a broadcast of the punishment. The influencer fool will be summarily tarred, feathered, and forced to live in a chicken coop among real chickens for five days. They have to make clucking noises too. No human language, the entire experience will be livestreamed. The entire world can see what cucks they are. And, this is also another example of dumb shit.

People, we really need to raise the bar on the current entertainment standards.

A guy can dream, can't he?

Now, I speak from firsthand experience with these despicable creatures. That's right I said des-pic-it-a-bowl. I ran into a group of these depraved influencers many moons ago in Austin when I was just a wee lad.

Can I get a show of hands—who's been to Austin? Wow, nearly all of you. I can tell y'all liked it.

Me too, what a great place. It's worth exploring if you haven't been there. The queso at Torchy's alone is worth the trip. Right before I got my first real coding stint, I went to a programming convention there. The theme of the conference was AI.

Go figure.

After the convention wrapped up for the day I went out for a walk. It's the best way to get to know a new city you're visiting. It's visceral, you know? My own two feet.

I was doing all that touristy stuff like a big'ol nerd. Anyway, when I was done amusing myself, I headed back to a bar in the vicinity of where the convention was held to meet some guys I made friends with at the conference.

I was walking down Eleventh Avenue with a cup of coffee, you know, taking a touristy stroll. As soon as I got to the entrance of the park that's there a colony, a camp, a cloud of bats, comes flying right at me. Thinking about it gives me the heebie-jeebies, still makes me shiver a little.

Yeah, like Bruce fucking Wayne, except this really happened.

Apparently the bats hang out on the Congress Avenue Bridge a block down. I happened to be walking between them and dinner.

Now, have you ever heard a grown man shriek and cry at the same time? I have, because that's exactly what I did. I fuck'in screamed like scared banshee. Who was also spinning in circles?

I was in tears. Not so much from the bats, who were everywhere, but from burning my balls. At some point, I decided to crouch down. I just let go of my coffee—which I had while spinning in circles— and went to cover up. I dropped it into the crotchal region. I should have gotten iced coffee. I had just gotten that cup a block over. It was so hot, I hadn't even taken a sip yet. It was the sort of injury that sends shivers down your spine to remember it.

So, I meant to get into a ball, but instead ended up crying in the fetal position.

In my hysteria, I could feel their flesh press up against me. Once they moved on, I was left lying on the sidewalk. I managed to look myself over while grabbing my crotch in pain. Turns out they left me without a scratch. Friendly bats, way more considerate than most people.

So there I am, after my near death experience trying to get a grip with my balls on fire, looking like I pissed myself. I'm reeling from my near death experience, and that's when I heard people behind me on the other side of the street laughing. I knew they were laughing at me. As it turns out, they were also recording.

I looked across the street, and there they were. A group of shit-for-brains, still laughing and recording me. I think one of them might have been livestreaming. These influencers were creating content, and I was the dumb shit. These fuckers caught it all.

There were six of them, three dudes and three chicks. Later on I found out it was three influencer couples cross promoting each other. Even with my balls are on fire, I could tell straightaway they were foul creatures.

Now, I am already thoroughly humiliated at this point. I wanted to run over there and shove their phones straight down their throats. Make them choke on it. But I didn't. Instead, of anger I chose stoicism.

Besides, I would be lost among all the other dumb shit online. With people's memories almost non-existent, whatever they recorded would soon be forgotten. So, me and my fiery nuts shuffled away into the park. You know that walk someone does when they have no dignity anymore? That was me, with what looked like piss splashed across the front of my pants.

I could hear our merry band of ass-wipes giving commentary to their audience. What pissed me off the most was how proud they were for capturing the moment. Like recording something with your phone a merit based skill, or something.

I didn't even care that they captured it. Look, if I was looking at myself from the outside, I would have also laughed at me. The difference is that I would have offered to help afterwards. Nothing changes the fact, that what happened was funny as hell. Right, folks? Well, not for me. I got no offers of help, not a single *are you okay.*

I could hear them, "We just saw the Bat Bitch!"

You know, folks, it's possible to laugh at each other and still help one another out. It's not anyone's fault that some acts of nature are outright hysterical. The bats didn't dump hot coffee in my lap, I did that all on my own.

As I was walking through the park, I thought about it some more. I started getting angry. Not a single are you okay, and these no talent, shit for brains online personalities, were going to pimp me out online. They were exploiting me the same way the social media platforms are them. I mean, am I going to get a cut of the money they earn? No. I'll remain an unpaid, monetized whore.

So that's the end of the story, right? These smooth brained schmucks made money by never bothering to help me because they were too busy turning a funny incident into dumb shit. Exploited for money, do I walk off into the park, carrying my humiliation and toasted balls into the Texas sunset?

Is this how the story ends? Not quite.

Eventually, I did meet up with those guys I met from the

conference, but not before going back to the hotel and putting my nuts on ice. They were…hot as balls. Sorry, I couldn't help myself.

The entire night, I didn't tell anyone at the bar what happened. After drinks, eating, and more drinks, the night was winding down. I was in the middle of going around and saying goodbye to everyone, and when I finally got to one of the dudes, Omar, I saw him looking down at his phone. Then Omar looked me up and down, twice.

You already know what I going to say next, don't you? I can see all of you nodding your big'ol helmets.

Omar pulled me aside and showed me his phone. There I was, overreacting to a swarm of bats. Spinning around, hysterically shrieking. Burning my man bits. Dropped to the fetal position.

Brought to tears. Me, in all my glory. With influencer commentary to boot.

And it was funny! Even I could not deny that. Nobody could. But, I was still pissed they didn't even ask if I was okay. Laugh, but help. Don't be an inconsiderate dumb shit.

Omar asked if I was okay. I told him my nuts were a little roasted, part of the reason I was leaving early.

So that's it? Now, that's the end of the story, right? Almost.

Now, I'll admit, when I was walking back to the hotel from the bar I was thinking of a way to pay these shitheads back for pimping me out without my consent. I earned the right to exact some pain.

I know, that sounds terrible. Especially when I say it out loud. But what other recourse did I have?

Don't worry, I would never do anything too extreme. I was thinking along the lines of hurting their credit score, sending creepy letters, cutting the power to their houses, billing them for a delivery of one hundred pizzas, taking their identity and buying a boat, getting them to download a virus to their phone, or creating a troll bot to antagonize them online. You know, some minor inconvenience. I was entitled to at least that, right?

I know, all this sounds really devious. The way I saw it, I was fulfilling a part of that American Dream. Enacting vigilante justice, which meant breaking the law in order to uphold it. To be a good guy, I could righteously arrange for the delivery of a dump truck full of manure to their homes.

I would be a working class vig-il-auntee!

In fact, not only was I real, but superior to Batman—who commits widespread property damage. I wasn't doing any of that. I mean, is there anything left for the criminals to pillage after Batman has enforced the law?

Well, you'll be happy to know, I did not have to resort to such pedestrian measures. I didn't actually do anything I was thinking. Like Narcissus, their misfortune was brought on by their excessive self-infatuation and self-centered behavior. Don't worry, they didn't drown. That would have been too harsh. The universe, as they say, works in mysterious ways. Karma beats petty revenge any day of the week.

Like I said, I was starting the get angry when I was walking back to the hotel. I knew the video would eventually be just another drop in the sea of dumb shit on the internet. I decided right then, with my balls ablaze, to just let it go. I started laughing at myself.

I reached a busy intersection, and there they were. I saw the dumb shits across the street. Sure enough, they saw me too. An important, and key difference during our second interaction was that they were plastered. Those fools drank so much I could smell the alcohol on them from where I was standing. It may have been nighttime, but it was clear as day how fucked up they were.

All six of the drunk shitheads whipped out their phones, as if it was some sort of superpower. For some odd reason, I took my phone out and began recording them. While they were yelling at me, with all sorts of other people looking on, I didn't say a word. They started calling me the bat bitch, again, spinning in circles, and pretending to grab their crotches in pain. Then they told me, because I was so pathetic, that I should kill myself. This was followed by laughter.

I just stood there and recorded them. My silence began to really piss the women off. Their hands started flying, their heads were popping forward. They kept repeating, "Who does this mother fucker think he is?" and "Who the fuck are you?"

We were walking past one another, and they were so busy insulting me to pay attention to where they were going.

It was glorious.

Allow me to set the scene: they were walking spread out in a straight line in their respective hetero couples. All of them were glued to their phones doing dumb shit. None of them were paying attention, no less the first couple that reached the intersection.

The girl leading it had no time to react when the curb jumped out in front of her. She took a bad step, hands went up, and her cellphone went flying. Face slam, my colorful friends. You hear about it, but seldom see it. I mean, she smacked and then didn't move. But I could hear her moaning in pain. Damn, that was a hard knock lesson. Oh, and her short skirt did not help matters.

Underwear? Negative. Groomed? Affirmative.

The dude with her only takes notice after his partner face plants. Not paying attention, when he runs out to help her, this guy gets smacked by a Ford F-150. Now, this was the damnedest thing. Right as the truck slowed down, to not run over the woman kissing some concrete, it nailed the guy. This dude goes flying. Airborne, without a parachute. Another cellphone goes high in the sky. He lands on the trunk of a parked car. At some point he pisses himself. It was like the scene of a movie. A real sight to behold, my friends.

Keeping score, that's two dumb shits down, four to go.

Remember, this whole time I am just standing across the street recording. When the middle of the pack dumb shits turned their attention away from me, they finally saw what had befallen their influencer comrades.

They were running forward without paying attention—see a theme here, folks?—both of them slammed into a glass door. A restaurant host had just opened it up. Those things are hard to see, even when you're not plastered. The door actually shielded the host who was standing behind it.

She got an up close view of two soft brained dumb shits, smacking a thick glass door almost simultaneously.

Just like that, presto! Two concussions, two more phone flying in the air. Both the people and cell phones crashed and burned to the ground. This real life movie had something that's hard to come by. It's not every day you see the self-inflicted, quatern-strike-double-concussion. The sound of their skulls, and then cracking back on the sidewalk. It gives me the shivers to recall the thuds. Yeessszzzhhh.

Still keeping score, that's four dumb shits down, two to go.

You know, I almost started to feel bad for them. I say almost because I immediately remembered that divine karmic law was being enforced. What I am seeing, well, it's righteous. Some reverence is needed, know what I'm saying?

Would anyone care to take a guess as to how the final two dumb shits bite the dust? A rhetorical question, obviously.

True to form, the last couple goes down trying to stop other people from recording. Just when you thought crazy wasn't cuckoo enough, the influencer woman managed to knock the phones from the hands of two guys recording. Then the dumb shit goes after a woman who was also capturing the moment for posterity. Now, this woman saw what happened to the guys next to her, so she was prepared when the influencer chick came at her. Right as the digital personality went after this woman's phone, she connected a punch that stunned the dumb shit. Already you could tell this was one of those *be careful what you wish for* episodes.

Now, this innocent woman was quite pissed off as you'd imagine. In the time it took the influencer woman to collect her marbles, this other woman managed to take off her earrings and jewelry, gave them and her phone to a friend, and then twisted her pony tail into a bun. This woman did not say a word, but her message was loud and clear. It was time to get busy. Then she cracked her neck side to side, saying it even louder. Only men look down at hair pulling in a fight. Most women just take it as a given, and you need two free hands to do it right. I totally get it—hair pulling gives you the opportunity to get in a position that allows for jacking someone in the face over and over. If you're lucky you can also slam someone's face into the ground, which was exactly what happened. Do you want to take a guess whose hair was not tied up? Oh, yeah, this was the part where the innocent woman let it out. Bruh, I am talking full on screaming with rage.

Only one dumb shit left.

While the women are involved in a ground and pound fight, the remaining dumb shit went to pry off the woman acting in self-defense. When he did her man toes up with the last dumb shit.

The shorter guy was still holding his wife's phone when he connected with an uppercut. As big as the influencer dude was, it turned out he was a one punch chump. Lucky for the dumb shit he fell into some people.

The final score in that game of karma, six dumb shits to none. I'll save you the gory details of their reported injuries. Suffice to say, it did not help their image based careers. They were all moaning, and not in the nice way.

Just look at the last pair. If they would've just laughed at the situation, they would have been spared a beat down. When you're willing to laugh at awful things, you view the world differently. There is a realization that could be *you*—falling on the pavement face first, getting hit by a truck, running into a glass door with your head, protecting your pride or getting your ass kicked. That *you* could do dumb shit if you're not careful. Something like—watching others do dumb shit reminds *you* to do good shit.

So, what's the moral of the story? If there is one? That's it—laugh and help, don't tease and point.

Oh, and to remember there are forces bigger than you at work. I wish I would have kept these lessons in mind as I got older. But hey, at least I knew enough to laugh about it. I remembered that too.

It was quite the scene. This entire time, I didn't say anything, not a single word. You all know exactly what I'm talking about. I stopped recording when too many people gathered around. Once all the dumb shits were getting help, I walked away. And when I did, I just started laughing. All the way back to the hotel. I tried to skip, but my nuts were still too toasty.

As unbelievable as this was, do you know what was even more improbable? We were in Texas and nobody pulled a gun out. Holy fuck'in shit, right? Quite honestly, I still have a hard time believing it and I saw it. The karmic odds were all over the place that night!

You know, everything really is bigger in Texas. Even the karma."

At this point during Mateo's impromptu routine, the good doctor was summoned to the back stacks. Leadership was holed up and wanted to send a message to Mateo. He took note when the doctor left, knowing it was time to bring his performance to an end.

"As our attention has been brought to the perils of dumb shit, it brings us to fuckers running this show. Just look at right now. Let's review all the merry things we have done. It started with an interrogation, a visit to the stairwell, then a romp through the laundry room, followed by a stroll through the kitchen, onto some grocery shopping, stairs again, exercising, throw in more stairs, taking a movie break—all that before landing here at the library. Goes to show you that even dumb shits can find where the good shit is.

The question is obvious, where to next? You make the road by walking it, but not around here. I'll let you all in on a little secret. There are two ways out of this glorious place. One right, one wrong.

We'll bear the consequences of whatever the dumb shits having the circle jerk back there decide.

So far, they have wasted something you can never get back.

Time.

The more time someone takes away, there is less of it for you to spend. This is one of those truths in life that everyone knows but do not act on. You should be unforgiving when your time is wasted. It's the worst kind of exploitation.

Don't let me give you the wrong impression, I don't mind taking one last stroll down memory lane, not at all. Remember, everyone is locked up in here with me, not the other way around.

Who really knows? But what's currently happening right now is part of the cosmic karmic order. I'm sure of that much, at least. I'd like to think there the larger forces for good at work here. There must be a damn good reason dumb shits really are acting like they have shit for brains.

It's time to say good bye, folks. Before I go, I just want you all to know that I have so many questions right now, that none of you can answer. I wouldn't want you too, either. You need to maintain that code of silence. Respect. I'll just say this—your uniforms, those colors are to die for!

And with that I express my gratitude to all of you for gifting me with your time. The most precious possession we have. For what it's worth, I am happy to have spent my time with all of you.

With that, I bid you all a good day."

Mateo bowed left, right, and center. He stepped down off the desk to sustained applause. When his feet sunk into the ground, pain gradually started to pulse through his body. As the clapping faded away, the doctor returned with a message and a look of incredulity.

"Command wants you to tell me the quickest way out."

"Wow, they're actually asking. Why can't the dumb shits ask me themselves?"

"I don't know why, the people in charge never explain themselves. I told them this request would not go over well."

"You were right about that, Doc."

"By the way, you were sort of funny up there"

Mateo nodded in thanks, "So, no way they are going to ask me directly?"

"That's correct."

"Pity for them they'll have to pass by me on the way out. Go ahead and give them my answer. I know that you already know what it is."

"I believe I do," the doctor answered.

Mateo smiled when the doctor left to deliver his response. He turned to the guards who were beginning to fall into order. "Too bad the degenerates have to walk past me." Then Mateo started singing, singing the same line a few times.

"Go-oh-oh-oh-and-fuck-your-selves!"

Belting out his exaggerated tune, Mateo saw the guards using their belts to tie down and carry books. They were fastening the books onto their hips and lower backs, allowing Mateo to read some of the titles flying past.

Moby Dick, 1984, Gift of the Magi, Aesop's Fables, The Iliad, The Trial, Faust, The Alchemist, The Wretched of the Earth, The Handmaid's Tale, The Analects, Secret History of the Mongols, The Diamond Sutra, Twelve Years a Slave, The Waning of the Middle Ages, The Scarlet Letter, I Know Why the Caged Bird Sings, and the *Dictionary of American Slang.*

Then Mateo noticed a green guard who somehow secured a single volume of Shakespeare's complete works. This was next to a yellow guard carrying the *Torah,* the *Bible,* and *Qur'an.* Nearby was a forest green *War and Peace,* next to a firebrick *Beyond Good and Evil,* who was alongside a pacific blue *Brave New World,* who was lined up next to a mahogany *The Feminine Mystique.* A magic mint had *The Essays* of Montaigne.

Mateo was situated at the top of the T-junction inside the library, making it impossible for the authorities in charge to conceal their identities any longer. There was no place left to hide, like rats on a sinking ship.

"I can hear their little rat fingernails clawing at the wooden hull," Mateo said out loud to doctor who was rushing to rejoin him.

"Did you tell them what I said?"

"I sure did," said the doctor a bit out of breath, "and they were not too happy about it."

Mateo stood triumphant, "The dumb shits did it to themselves," he thought perched at the library's main junction.

No sooner had Mateo enjoyed this feeling of satisfaction when another took its place. Replacing it was a more primitive sensibility. When Mateo heard the leadership of this lost charade through Tall Oaks approaching, another emotional state overwhelmed him. Shooting up from deep within him was a mixture of dignified self-respect and contempt for authority.

Mateo decided to live up to his jabbering in his set. He turned to the doctor, "I'd rather not waste my time knowing who they are. That's how little a give a fuck about the assholes in charge. The dumb shits who stink the place up for the rest of us."

"Fuck'em," he said out loud.

And with that Mateo turned his back to them. Standing akimbo, he proceeded to raise up his hands up and give them the middle finger salute.

"That's right. This is what I think of you. Feel free to kiss my ass. I don't hang around shit because I don't want to smell like it."

The doctor looked at the outraged faces of the contingent, bruised egos and flimsy backbones portrayed on their faces.

"This is so empowering! Hurry up and scurry past, you rat fucks. Oh, yeah, I almost forgot. Fuck your mothers."

"Let me say it again, because practice makes permanent—Kiss my ass and fuck your mothers. I wouldn't piss on you if you were on fire."

As the leaders walked by they took a left. "Looks like we're going to class. Make sure to bring your book," said a smiling Mateo who was still looking forward.

Those in charge passed through an easily overlooked doors that blended in with the wall. Once through it, the hallway was tiled halfway up the wall in a pleasant light green. The floor was hardwood, in a shade of dark brown, in contrast to the bright white ceiling and copper colored upper wall. Periodically, the long hallway also had ceramic water fountains that were built in. In other words, they were part of the plan.

Mateo was still holding his double fuck you, intently focused on the library's exit doors. "There's no way out down there, Doc. We should hang in one of the first classrooms. They'll eventually have to come back out."

"Is it safe to turn, doc?"

"You're good. "Unbelievable. Why?" asked the doctor. "Didn't you want to see the people who got us lost?"

"They do not deserve my attention. They cannot have it. They might have my body, but they can never have my thoughts. The ones in charge, those vile creatures, they should all be loaded up into a rocket and blasted off into space. Get the fuck out. That is the extent of the thought owed to them."

Walking with the doctor, followed along into the hallway, the pair explored another dimension of Tall Oaks. After walking for a bit, he pointed to Vonnegut and Austen. "There, into that classroom behind *Slaughterhouse-Five* and *Pride and Prejudice*."

VII.

——=⟫«⟨◉⟩»⟪=——

The Educational-Industrial-Technological Complex

To promote a healthy life of the mind, the residents of Tall Oaks were taught the benefits of sticking to a routine. To this end, regular classes were offered. Taking advantage of standard educational practice, residents were encouraged to take at least one class every semester. Guest teachers were always dropping in, giving the long-term resident of Tall Oaks a fair amount of variety. All this in an effort to strengthen the roots of the mind.

Leaving the cozy green of the hallway, the classroom greeted Mateo and the doctor with a formidable atmosphere of serious curiosity. With the guards already sitting in all the other desks, the pair occupied some desks in the back of the room.

The memory of previous students, preserved by the impressions on the wooden floor and desks, made their presence known. Proceeding to take his seat, Mateo looked closely at the marked up texture of this space; dents, scuffs, smashes, and the occasional carving.

"Oh, school. Nothing worse than intelligent people who think they are smart. But once in a while, you take a class that changes your perspective on the world. You get that teacher who is a diamond in the rough." Then Mateo read out loud what was written above the chalkboard in large, bold letters. "What am I thinking? Why am I thinking it? Why am I asking why?"

In an orderly fashion, the guards removed their books and placed them on the desks. Helmets were, again, put at their feet. They all sat with a neutral posture before folding their hands over their books. They were patiently waiting for the teacher to arrive, for class to begin.

With the presence of former lessons ingrained within the atmosphere, anticipating gazes were cast to the dais at the front of the room. Closely resembling a triangular stage set, on it were some educational relics of yesteryear—a blackboard, a hardwood desk, a globe of the planet, and pull down maps. On the right hand side of the dais sat a lectern. Positioned forward, it had an unknown book on it. Waiting for the lesson, desks squeaked with anticipation for the lesson.

"I know there's crazy shit going on, but did you really think I was funny?"

"Only a little," the doctor replied sarcastically.

They both laughed.

"Here we are, again. Back to school."

"What do you mean, again?"

"Oh, sorry, Doc. I got my thoughts mixed up there for a second," explained Mateo. "I have to say, Doc, you don't seem as nearly as stressed out as earlier." Then he let out a gaping yawn. Mateo's arms contracted back, his chest puffed out, and his mouth hung open.

"And I'm the calm one?" quipped the doctor.

The floor creaked. A deep royal purple *The March of Folly* walked up to the left side of dais. After placing her large helmet and Tuchman on the desk in the middle, she proceeded to the lectern before stepping behind it, royal purple gave a slight bow. She opened the book already on it. Flipping to a random page, the instructor began reading aloud.

"It comes from within. Self-generated, sufficient, and complete. Beautiful in its perfection. It, is you."

"The person who requires a detailed argument when the evidence is indisputable, or who wants things which could be proved by few arguments to be demonstrated in many ways is completely absurd and dull."

"The student should pay close attention to what the teacher says and watch out for falsehoods are accidentally accepted."

The radiance of her voice matched the royal purple of her uniform. The tone of voice and hue aligned as to impart a caring that compelled listening. Profoundly compelling to everyone in the room, except for Mateo.

Despite his excitement at finally hearing at least one guard speak, and in such a compelling way, Mateo was simply too worn out. After giving another histrionic yawn, he was inflicted with the inability to keep his eyes open. Knowing best, Mateo's body made him take a class nap.

Mateo slept through the Pledge of Allegiance. It was homeroom, the eighth grade of school. The dry, hot Arizona air, that he never got used to, contributed to his fatigue. The natural boredom of school certainly did not help sustain his attention. Mateo continued to sleep through the more minor announcements, until the heartfelt tone of a woman's voice caused him to open his eyes.

"If any student feels emotionally traumatized or distraught over yesterday's tragic events in our state the school psychologist and counselors are here to assist you. As a reminder state testing will still take place tomorrow as scheduled. Again, please come down to the guidance office if you need some help processing yesterday's events." When the head of guidance finished, it was the principal's turn to address the student body.

"This is Principal Stern, I hope everyone is having a good morning. As you are no doubt aware, there was a wave of gun violence across the country yesterday. Our thoughts and prayers go out to the victims of this mass casualty event. Across several states, including our own, over fifty students have been killed. Authorities are still trying to determine whether or not this senseless violence was coordinated. As of now, there are no indications it was planned.

In response to yesterday's tragedy, we have informed your parents about the enhanced security measures taken here at Chester A. Arthur Junior High. We have added eight armed guards, all military veterans. An unknown number of faculty members have also been given the right to conceal carry. Furthermore, the over two hundred and fifty cameras, already in place, will now feed directly to the police department as well. You can rest assured we are doing everything here to keep you safe as you learn and prepare for the future. This building, is a safe space.

In addition to the regular drills for an active shooter, sniper threat, bomb scenario, and hostage situation, students will practice overwhelming a terrorist threat. Learning to adapt by using whatever furniture available as a weapon. To further enhance security, bullet proof shades are scheduled for installation in all classrooms before the end of this week. The school district is also in the process of securing funds for bulletproof backpacks. Here at Chester A. Arthur Junior High, equity is certainly a guiding principle. Every student has the right to a safe learning environment.

Before the tragic events of yesterday, money was already allocated by the Board of Education for the construction of a concrete perimeter. Included in this was funding for enhanced checkpoint security. This morning, I received word from the head of the Board that this project will now be fast tracked. Teachers who use the front lot should park in the back tomorrow in order to make room for the digger equipment.

Be advised that the three strikes rules remains in effect for setting off the new metal detectors. After the third infraction, a review of the on-compliance violation will occur. The incidents will be reviewed for possible expulsion. A mandatory meeting with the Disciplinary Committee is required. Both students and parents are expected to be in attendance, with a decision rendered after the meeting.

This brings me to the new protocols across the district. In response to the pain and suffering experienced yesterday, these are effective immediately. More information is on the Board of Education website, but here are some new educational prescriptions to keep students safe:

- The Chester A. Arthur Junior High, Code of Conduct will be enforced on social media outlets. Controversial posts, that cause distress, will be reported to law enforcement.

- Lanyards with an identification card must be worn at all times. There are no exceptions. Failure to produce your school issued id, upon request by an administrator or safety guard, will result in immediate suspension. This lasts until a return review with one of the members on the Disciplinary Committee. There is no regular return without it. No exceptions.

- At all bathroom facilities, students must swipe their iden- tification cards for entry. No more than a single student is allowed out of a classroom. One lavatory pass in every class. No exceptions.

- Wearing clothing deemed offensive, racist or culturally insensitive will result in a one month suspension.

- Random drug tests, for every student, at least once during the school year. Fail to comply, on demand, will result in immediate expulsion. No exceptions.

- New lockers with electronic keypads will replace existing combination locks. PIN numbers will be emailed to stu- dents when their locker is replaced. Students should have no expectation of privacy.

- Any students caught breaking the 10:00 PM city-wide cur- few must meet with a representative of the Disciplinary Committee to determine expulsion eligibility of the infrac- tion. No exceptions.

Again, these new procedures are immediately in effect. Thank you in advance for your cooperation.

Finally, in addition to this new physical security, online content will also undergo new scrutiny. All digital information, on district issued electronic devices, will undergo examination using predictive analytic software. We take the mental health of all our students seriously. Acts of violence, or suicidal tendencies, are never the answer. It's a cry for help. We here at Chester A. Arthur are here to assist you.

In closing, now is not the time for political debates or divisional politics. We must unite as a country, as Americans. A single community under God. Only by working together can we continue striving toward educational excellence. In somber remembrance of this ongoing national tragedy, let us have a moment of silence for the victims, and their families, for this senseless violence...

...Thank you. Remember to be kind. Hate, bullying, and harassment have no place here at Chester A. Arthur Junior High School, home of the Bighorn Sheep.

Hearing the last line told Mateo this was not a dream. Picking his head up off the desk, with his eyes wide open he looked straight ahead at the top of Mr. Tailor's head. He was standing behind the teacher's desk, propping himself up with two straight arms. Mr. Tailor's head hung, his salt and pepper hair frowning at the class.

Mateo tuned in to Mr. Tailor's frequency. "Yep, I agree. Principal Stern is a major asshole," he thought.

Sitting at the front of the class, Mateo looked around to see everyone glued to their cell phones. Mateo hated nearly every one of them. Behind this feeling was legitimacy.

Most of his classmates would rather be loved for deceitful reasons, rather than be adored for who they really are. An accomplishment without merit, which requires cruelty to achieve. They were illegitimate, and mean. The kids who invite you to a party in order to make fun of you. They make you the joke and laugh at your existence. Viciousness and ridicule planned into a festive, refined event.

Mr. Tailor walked out from behind the desk. Sneakers squeaked, khaki pants crimped, sleeves rolled up, glasses shifted, and novelty science tie fluttered. Then Mateo read the class motto across the top of the board: *Always make an effort to put your best foot for forward.*

With a paper memo in hand, Mr. Tailor greeted the class. His height commanded attention. Clearing his throat, "Okay, before we get started today, would anyone like to share their thoughts on the tragic events that unfolded yesterday afternoon?

Dead silence. Not even a single *why.*

Mr. Tailor volunteered, "Okay, I'll start. I reviewed the statistics this morning. In this country—"

Then a hand went in the air. "—Yes Robbie, please, you have the floor."

"Mr. Tailor, can I go to the bathroom? Yo, I gotta take a mean pi—"

"—Robbie, please hold it a moment. You can go after I read this mandatory memo," compromised a dejected teacher.

Mateo noticed Mr. Tailor reading over the memo, but unable to say the words out loud. On his end, Mateo tried to raise his hand. It would not budge. His heart felt as if it was going to explode out of his chest. Sweat started to bead on his forehead.

Attacked by panic.

Then with a tone of forgiveness, Mr. Tailor directed the lesson, "Lab day today. Mostly everyone is here, so we can move along in our groups. Be advised someone will have to catch up your missing classmates on today's progress. If it's you, inform me tomorrow afterwards so you can get some extra credit for being awesome.

A quick reminder of what we were working on—Group one is

guiding a plant through a dark maze using sunlight. Group two is fabricating a solar desalination device, group three is performing starch tests on different objects with iodine. Group four is examining the process of symbiosis with nitrogen fixing bacteria. Last, but not least, group five is making homemade shampoo.

We'll go over the required review of the new policies the last ten minutes of class. Please, go to your stations. Oh, and Robbie, I'll give you a pass now."

The class dissolved into their respective lab groups, save Mateo. He was still sitting down scrolling on his phone. He read about all the kids that were killed, and the ones that were not expected to survive. Then he came across some gossip about Mr. Tailor. Students, in that same science class, were posting online that Mr. Tailor's family was somehow impacted by the shooting.

A student from the back of the room yelled out, "Yo! Mr. T, do you have the new lab papers?"

"I do not. I forgot to make the copies. I'll get them to you." Thinking about a solution, he looked right in front.

"Mateo, when Robbie gets back, could you make me some copies?"

"Sure thing, Mr. Tailor. Whatever you need."

"Maybe I should just migrate all the worksheets online already," confessed the teacher.

"Nah, Mr. Tailor. You do you."

"Thank you, Mateo. I needed that."

Presently, Mateo was dozing off in a Tall Oaks classroom. The doctor took notice, proceeding to lightly jab him with a pen. "No sleeping in class."

Mateo kept his head down, eyes closed, "Well then, I guess I have no class."

"Besides," he continued, "Pretty soon, it's back through the library." The doctor took Mateo at his word. Deciding to settle in, he joined the rest of the colorful class and listened to the lecture:

"There is no advantage in gaining security with regard to other people. If you do not conquer the enemy within, you have missed the real target."

"To live without fear, in a world riddled with anxiety, is true freedom. To truly live free, a person must maintain a composed mind."

"The pain felt from an abrupt change in one's behavior is acute, but short. Endure this pain that resides chiefly in the mind, and change your material reality."

"Conquer oneself continually with the patience of a river carving out a granite canyon."

"Purposeful lies are intellectual violence. They are a declaration of ideological warfare."

"Don't have a personality crisis. If this happens look for balance in your life. It will help you not throw your good sense away and re-center your mind."

"Throw your hands up and wave them without a care. This is the solution to any problem."

While the doctor silently nodded along with the guards, Mateo nodded back into the past. In his somnambulism, Mr. Tailor was talking to him.

"Are you still up for me submitting your name to the Innovation Coding Camp selection committee for the summer?"

"Sure, go ahead. Thank you."

"You're welcome. No problem at all. You seem to have a real knack for it. Who knows, you just might code an app that helps change the world."

Mateo smiled while suppressing the urge to ram a Bunsen burner down the throat of a classmate or two. "Fucking base heads, the whole lot of them," he thought.

"Let me go get those worksheets for you to copy."

While Mr. Tailor went to retrieve the handouts, Mateo got up. He turned to see everyone on their phones and talking in low voices.

Nobody bothered to look in Mateo's direction as he glared angrily at the lot of them. Robbie came back, Mr. Tailor issued him a pass.

Mateo asked, "How many?"

"Thirty, please."

With a fist pound, Mateo was out to the copy room. With his thoughts, he cursed the other students as he walked past the lab area. It did not take long for Mateo to be greeted by one of the newly hired resource officers. He was a massive man, dressed in body armor, and carrying multiple guns. This included a stun gun, pepper spray, restraints, a helmet, and combat boots. With both hands pulling on the collar of his bullet proof vest, he looked hard at Mateo, questioning his presence without a single word. Mateo held up the papers and the pass from Mr. Tailor. Once they passed each other, he could not help himself.

"Where's your bayonet?" he said under his breath.

Both of them stopped walking and turned to one another. When the guard turned toward Mateo, he prominently displayed the semi-automatic strapped across his chest.

"What'd you say to me?"

"Excuse me?" answered Mateo, who kept walking, "I didn't say anything."

"Yeah, you did. Smart ass. What'd you say? You little fuck'in punk."

"I already told you, I didn't say anything. This is a false accusation."

Right as the guard went to continue this pissing contest, he received a call on his transceiver. In code, he was immediately needed somewhere else. With a look of disappointment before departing, "Copy. Affirmative."

Except for Mateo, the halls were completely empty. Not even a sound was present. Entering the copy room, he momentarily felt like an adult.

When Mateo started separating the lab papers he discovered mixed in some handwritten notes. They looked unrelated to class, but he read a few lines to be sure.

Do all those essential things that make you human...

Let the good times roll and turn you into a clown...

Tell stories and create a mythology for oneself...

Try to isolate the root of the problem...

Lies mean truth must also exist...

To attain success do not change who you are...

Out patrolling the hallway was another newly hired resource officer. He looked through the door window and saw Mateo making copies. Mateo looked behind him when he heard the door open.

"What are you doing?"

"Making copies for Mr. T."

"Hurry it up."

"That depends on the speed of the copier. I cannot go any faster."

"Oh, so you're the smart ass."

"I see word spreads fast around here. It is taking longer to make these copiers because you are interrupting me. Now, if I may. Good day, sir."

"You little fuck'in piss ant. You're a fuck'in retard. Finish it up and get to class."

The heavily armed resource officer left, and in addition to the copies Mr. Tailor needed, Mateo made a copy of the handwritten notes for himself.

Still not done encountering resource officers, Mateo ran into a third one walking back to class. He felt relieved.

"Hey, Mateo."

"Hi, Manny."

"You alright?"

"I guess."

"If you need anything, let me know."

"The new guys are dicks."

Caught off guard, Manny smiled. "They're probably on edge right now because of everything that's happened. I'll talk to them."

Fist bump.

Luckily Mr. Tailor was busy helping students get their labs on track, allowing Mateo to walk in unnoticed. "Yo, Mr. T, I am putting the originals on your desk," said from across the room. He made sure to leave the handwritten note sticking out underneath.

Thumbs up.

The folded copy was alternating jabs into Mateo's hip flexor and lower oblique. Sitting down, it pressed into both. For the remainder of the school day, Mateo was a textbook example of rationalizing immorality. A futile debate with his self was spurred on by the sharp pains, "Okay, I won't tell anyone. This will be the one and only time I will ever do something like this, ever. Besides, I don't even know what it says. It's probably nothing all that important, just more proverbs and riddles."

Arriving home to an empty house, Mateo pulled out the copy, chucked his schoolbag, and ran upstairs to his bedroom with it. He locked the door behind him. Without hesitation, he smoothed the papers out alongside the Innovation Coding Camp application.

Dear Joseph,

Unfortunately, I have not seen you in almost seven years. These kinds of rifts happen from time to time in families,. Estranged relationships become the norm. Whatever happens between me and your mother, I wanted to reach out and tell you that I am here for you. Whatever you need. What's going on with my sister should not come between us. Theresa is stubborn, just like me. It runs in the family.

I plan on getting in touch with your mom and leaving the past behind. After all, I am partly to blame for this family rift. Events like the one that happened to you will change the trajectory of your life. Right now I am reminded that family solidarity is the most important, not my petty feelings.

I heard from your Aunt Jackie that you barely made

it out alive. That bullets flew right over your head as you were running out of the classroom.. I am sorry that your best friend was killed. She also told me other friends smeared blood on from people who were shot and played dead in order to live.

Your Aunt Chloe and I are sorry for the anguish and sorrow this senseless violence has caused you and friends. We are reeling from the evil that has been perpetrated on everyone.

If you are interested, I know some people over at a private preparatory school in Munich. The Apex, where the instruction is English based. No doubt you'd learn German along the way. Your Aunt Chloe and I want to pay for the room, board, and tuition, the whole thing. We want to invest in you. No reason to pay us back, your Aunt Chloe and I are more than happy to help.

We want to invest in your education. The best way to do that is to leave the country. This way you can learn without the anxiety of worrying about your safety. We would like to give you the chance to heal, with an opportunity to continue your studies.

As cliché as it sounds, love for each other keeps us together. We are lucky enough to be part of a family. Many people do not have this. Your grandfather was a great man. Wherever you are, his spirit is with you.

He gave me some advice growing up when I did not

know how to find peace.

In high school, I had three of my friends kill themselves in high school and was struggling on how to deal with it. Life is brutal and violent, as well as beautiful and caring. Again, I am here if you need to talk.

Remember when you were little and I used to take you to the Museum of Natural History? You loved the fossil exhibits the most. Hopefully we can do that again soon. My heart aches for you. If you need something, just ask, I am here to help or listen without judgment.

With all my love,
Uncle Roderick

Youth did not prevent Mateo from comprehending the seriousness of Mr. Tailor's words. A profundity enhanced by betrayal, it knocked Mateo back in his chair. He placed his right hand on his leg and leaned forward. Mateo put his left elbow on the desk, proceeding to rest his chin on its fist. Each rumination was a morsel of thought that dropped to the pit of his stomach.

He pondered the gates of hell and its contents.

When he remembered there was more to read, Mateo looked at the Innovation Coding Camp application that was judging him. Before losing his nerve, he decided to push on.

Things to tell Joseph about (when the time is right)—

Much of this you probably already know, but better to be safe than sorry.

The first rule of enjoying life to its fullest: be selfish with your time. Throughout life, there are thieves everywhere trying to steal it from you. To take your most precious commodity away, they'll stop at nothing to take it away from you. The most audacious lies will come your way, if they haven't already.

The loss of time dominates the trajectory of all life.

Make sure to guard against these perpetrators. For time is the basis of all life. Biology and Buddhism agree on this fundamental characteristic. That movement is the chief hallmark of the material world. Motion never stops. It's eternal. When your time is wasted, motion has been diverted from your purpose in life. Achieving your purpose in life means using your time, not merely spending it. On your path, do your best not to let others knock you off it.

To safeguard your time, I recommend following the scientific method. Budget your time in advance. With the help of a journal, you can keep track of your progress as it passes. With this data collection, you can start connecting cause and effect. Patterns of causality in your life.

The human species lives forwardly but only understands in hindsight. This information will also allow you to make adjustments to reach your personal goals in life. Basically, you can see what works for you following the SAID principle—a specific adaptation to an imposed demand.

For your actions to hit their targets you desire in life, certain behaviors bearing repeating. Over, and over, and over, again and again. Even if you've got natural talent, without dedicated practice you cannot light the trinitrotoluene. Your dynamite.

Once you can repeat an act it become second nature, then you've achieved mastery. You have skills. You have power in a world marked by struggle when a skill remains, and becomes refined, against a changing environment. You take it with you wherever you go.

Please, do not misunderstand me. Reaching your goals in life is not easy. Changing your behavior harder that it is easy. Deliberate, repeated action, to get the demands you want from life, requires continual fine tuning. Keeping a journal lets you tease apart independent and dependent variables. What you can, and cannot, control. What you can, and cannot, adjust. What is a want, what is a need? Sometimes more is more, sometimes less is more. Planning and questioning in an effort to be the best version of yourself.

So, what demand should you impose on yourself? That's up to you. Put into practice, this looks different for everyone. Journalist, economist, mechanic, advertiser, lawyer, account, judge, engineer—whatever it is. Only one thing remains the same—it's not easy. Just figuring out what you want to pursue is challenging. On this, you cannot trust anyone else but your own self.

Competency is not a trait acquired by association. Impossible to give, only you can obtain excellence. The ability to achieve this competency is an evolutionary adaptation nature has given us. An awareness of how time is spent. Putting this reason in charge requires work. Through struggle, nature has endowed humans with a prefrontal cortex for this hard, but rewarding, labor.

While it allows for it, the structure of the brain does not make focusing easy. We Homo sapiens have a tripartite brain. A reptilian complex, limbic system, and neocortex region, in the order of their development. These are otherwise known as instincts, emotions and reason.

Into adulthood, most people continue to operate from the lower brain. Fully grown intellectual children. They are not rational adults. As outlined, a rational approach to life takes much work and effort. Never forget that while you are acting rationally (applying the scientific method), don't assume others do as well. Falling into this cognitive trap allows other people to take advantage of you. You're caught off guard—

His head on the desk, Mateo mumbled loud enough to get the doctor's attention.

"I'm zorry."

"Huh?" asked the doctor.

"I'm zorry,"Mateo repeated.

The doctor figured it out, decided to leave the patient alone.

Mateo returned to reading Mr. Tailor's notes, and the purple guard continued to hold class.

"Most people live life like an arrow flying through the air without a target in sight."

"Everything within must come out. Do this without fear of a heaven above or a hell below."

"Self-aggrandizement is really just a form of masturbation since the only one satisfied afterwards is yourself."

"Don't trust people who enjoy using the word *precept*."

One of the most uncomfortable truths of life: we are more irrational than rational. To not be irrational, that's hard work (what the journal helps with). When people are irrational, it helps to remember that's normative behavior. To think that rationality could manage the evolutionary source from which it came. To think that, is well, irrational. How can you control something that you do not understand?

Rationality is not the same as being rational. You can rationally understand the world, and then go out and act unreasonably. The reverse is also true; you can irrationally understand the world (i.e.: deny what your eyes are seeing), and then act rationally.

Still, our brain is amazing. This three pound organ is 60% fat, the fattiest in the body. It needs cholesterol to function properly, to help along the 100,000 chemical reactions every second. The brain uses about

1/5 of every calorie, 20% of the body's oxygen, and has 150,000 miles of blood vessels. Thinking increases blood flow to the brain, performed by 100 billion neurons. To create a memory neurologically means to make connections between neurons. Basal forebrain neurons help to maintain consciousness by keeping brain waves in rhythm. The majority of thoughts most people have every day are negative. Watch your inner dialogue, you've got a powerful brain.

The central nervous system originates in the brain. It has receptors to interpret pain signals, but does not feel any pain itself. Your brain never shuts off or runs out of energy. Everyone dreams.

Human consciousness has allowed us to transform the contours of nature. Still, with all its might, the brain is useless outside of a body to sustain it. The brain needs life pumped into it. Reasoning is done on behalf of the evolutionary struggle, not the other way around.

While the degree of our intelligence distinguishes us from humans from other life, it doesn't somehow separate us from the same source. The Earth gives birth and houses all life. Across the natural world the dominant hallmark is irrationality. It's irrational for life to consume itself in order to survive. To remain alive something else must perish, another one of nature's objects must die.

With our brains, this evolutionary strife takes place not only outwardly but inwardly. Most people delude themselves, they think themselves more rational than they really are. When people do this, they downplay the lack of it out in the world. That human societies have much more irrationality behind them, but it bothers people too much to admit it. Facts get ignored.

This includes yourself. Be sure to check the motivations of your actions. You can see why putting reason in charge, against his landscape, requires work. However, don't expect others to take on this challenge. Remembering this is like an ideological defense mechanism help keep on guard when dealing with other people. It's nobody's fault. It's just that like the workings of the real world, ideas are at war with one another all the time. There are ideological defense mechanisms, equivalent to some of the physical ones found throughout nature.

The boxer crab uses sea anemones as weapons, Malaysian soldier ants blow themselves up, sea cucumbers push internal organs out their anus, Iberian newts uses their ribs as spikes, the northern fulmar bird keeps predators away with sticky vomit, hagfish use slime, cuttlefish hide in plain sight, the bombardier beetle turns into exploding hot liquid, the Texas horned lizard squirts blood from its eyes, the Dynastor butterfly in Trinidad mimic the look of a snake, and pygmy sperm whales defecate a bomb of anal syrup. It's often not pretty, but the bottom line is defense mechanisms have to be effective. Make sure your defense ideas don't end up hurting you. A close circle of family and friends are still needed. When you're out there learning about the world

View people who profess to know the truth with extreme suspicion. This occurs in school much of the time. I have been teaching middle school for over three decades. They just want obedient workers to keep the economy running. It's a giant Ponzi scheme premised squarely on perpetual growth, unable to hit the target of sustainability.

This overshoot is a symptom of civilization collapse disorder. It's a disorder because the solution to the widespread destruction of the environment. Zoologically, 2 miya the first Homo clade, bipeds with large brains, lived in Africa. About 1.5 mya hand axes were used. Approximately 100,000 years ago human brains grew to their current size. Among the other hominids before us included Australopithecus (I love Lucy!). They lived at the same time with Neanderthals, members of our genus residing in Europe (Homo erectus was in Asia). Roughly 100,000 years ago human brains grew to their current size. Our closest living relative is the chimpanzee, since there is only a 1% difference between our DNA.

Homo sapiens migrated out of Africa around 320,000 years ago (likely longer), with evidence of a human artistic culture beyond Africa 50,000 years ago. Based on current evidence, 25,000 years ago all the other Homo species went extinct. The decisive characteristic, what conferred an evolutionary advantage to us hominids, was our intelligence. Sapiens. Our brains.

Unfortunately, greater human civilization has become

expert in killing life ourselves. What our brains helped us to recognize was that without cooperation survival is not possible. The best defense against a hostile world is the truth. This is the plain truth. What was once an evolutionary advantage has been turned on its head? The enemy is life, from insects to eagles. And people, especially other humans.

I am not saying don't go to school, but stressing that it's an intellectual minefield. Institutionalized education disarms you. It is meant to mold people into a one of the preferred social archetypes. Where the individual must demonstrate the character and quality of a certain type of person. Such as people who can analyze data but not necessarily think. That was the behaviorist Watson's main point.

Either by design or accident, schools overwhelmingly instill insecurity in students. Your most valuable weapon becomes neutralized—your mind. Over the years, as bad ideas get passed along, the explanations to justify the harmful practices they promote become more elaborate. As they become more refined, the environment worsens. Along the way, a greater realization sets in. That what people are teaching you doesn't match up with how you are living.

Everyone is insecure because they know they are living lies, they have not conquered the enemy within. Very difficult to collectively organize and settle on a reasonable plan of action as a society. To live in partnership with the planet, to respect the finite character of nature's resources. Changes in public policy that are responsive to the alarm bells the scientific community is ringing about the planet.

Thinking matters through for yourself, and measuring the world with your mental ruler, puts you on the path to authenticity. The other element that's needed is behavior. That's the genuine life for a Homo sapiens. To know what you are, the expression of your personality, and live it. Ruling yourself from within gives you stability outside. Thinking empowers you to exercise your willpower with greater control. Nobody has total control of their will to live, but that's not the point. Nothing in the world is perfect, so don't expect you to be, either. Evolution is always tumbling forward. Beautiful, but messy.

Talking to others, to gauge your thoughts, it turns out this insight has also dawned on many others. In fact, most of them. Then you scratch your head. It doesn't make any sense—why do people continue to do things based on ideas they know are bad? False? Detrimental to the environment?

Even though they know better, because they have convinced themselves they cannot change, nothing does. They do not love themselves enough to try.

This is why cooperation is important. One for all and all for One. It's the most obvious and only way out of the mess to come. More severe problems call for drastic solutions to meet them. And cooperation among people not an easy thing to do, it means reason has to be put in charge.

To go forward, perhaps humans need to look at other colonies. I am sure we could learn a thing or two from other species. Bees, ants, termites, lemurs, meerkats, termites, elephants, bonobos, coral, and even pistol shrimps. The most successful colonies act as a single organism while maintaining individuation.

As slim as it may be, there always remains a modicum of chance that the larger part of humanity will start mending our relationship with the planet. And of course, one another. You cannot change your brain, but you can change your mind. Attaining a new state of consciousness, one that squares up with the world, is at least possible. Whether or not it's probable is another matter. Call this calculated hope. If the past leading up to our current present is any indication, stranger things have happened.

Time to put our evolutionary advantage to work, again.

Love is the godhead of humanity.

When Mateo reached the end of Mr. Tailor's notes, he again pondered the landscape of hell. He felt the pit in his stomach. He was forced to race off to the bathroom. He hated puking, it always made his neck hurt. After throwing up, Mateo started crying. For all those parents who will outlive their kids. For stabbing Mr. Tailor in the back. For what this world unfortunately is in the end.

Mateo felt completely, and utterly, terrible.

"I just can't do something like this ever again," he said out loud while looking in the mirror. The taste in his mouth and the redness of his eyes pronounced judgment on him. Without a word, they told Mateo the only way to absolve his guilt was to change his behavior.

Without thinking, Mateo grabbed the copies off his desk, proceeding to go downstairs into the kitchen. He went over to the gas stove.

Tick, tick, whoosh.

Flickering blue with an aura of violet mesmerized Mateo, helping him achieve some psychic distance. His mind was standing at the entrance to the kitchen, watching his body. He was on the outside looking in, but also the inside looking out. Mateo brushed the papers against the flames. The fire quickly turned the copy of Mr. Tailor's notes into ashes. Dropping the black flakes into the sink, he washed them down the drain.

After these ancient rites, Mateo's body was reunited with his mind on his present reality.

The purple guard was still teaching. With open minds, the students continued to listen. While she continued to read from the unknown book, the leadership reversed course back through the library. As they noisily passed down the hallway, the teacher recognized the situation.

"There is no way I would expect women and men who pursue philosophy to cast aside everything they are doing for mere arguments. Let the discussions and debates you participate in take place for the sake of pursuing some action."

"You should never tell other people what they should or should not do because you perform actions which you know you should not do either."

The purple guard closed the book, stepped out from behind the lectern, and bowed. After a gentle round of applause by the class, she extended prayer hands to as many students as possible. Without a word, hairstyles were concealed, books secured, and exits made following the leaders.

"Looks like school is out for summer, eh doc?" Mateo stood and stretched out like a starfish. Pain radiated throughout his body. Before departing Mateo took one last look where he sat. He was leaving behind a sizable puddle of drool. Taking a napkin from his back pocket, Mateo looked at the doctor, who stared at him with gross disgust, and wiped the desk clean.

"*Tabula rasa.* Look at that, you can wipe the slate clean, but the slate remains. You come into this world with your slate already written on." Mateo sized up the situation for the doctor, "I see the rat-kings finally figured out this was a dead end. The way out from here goes right past my room."

As they walked out of the room Mateo read the classroom mantra out loud for the last time, "What am I thinking? Why am I thinking it? Why am I asking why? That reminds me of something. Doc, you ever notice that in sci-fi films there is always a small number of aliens but a huge spaceship? Why do you think that is? Before I forget to ask, what was the class about?"

As they backtracked through the library lobby to the door on the other side, the pair carried on their conversation. Mateo was informed about the angelic sound of the teacher's voice.

VIII.

━━●((◉))●━━

Golden Living

M ateo stood in the center of his empty room. His left hand held a photograph out in front, while his right hand pressed a large knife against his neck. The only other person in his former living quarters was the doctor, who stood frozen by the adjacent front doorway. Unable to approach, the doctor looked on as Mateo careened his neck. Making it easier for the knife to find his jugular, just in case it was necessary, Mateo also had to raise and tilt the picture. The doctor was able to get a look at the picture, recognizing the broad outlines. Alternatively, Mateo awareness landed on the particulars of those generalized forms.

"Fore!"

At the Everglade Emerald golf course, a ball flew into a foursome busy taking their approach shots onto the eighteenth green. In sunny, sinking Florida, it was one of the six delicately manicured courses available to residents of the Golden Living Retirement Village. The golfer closest to getting hit by the custom made golf ball, complete with a manufactured family crest stamped on it, was livid.

"Hey, fuck you'z—you fuck'in cocksucker! Can't you see we are in the fairway?! Why are you hitting into us again, you prick?!"

From one-hundred and seventy five yards away, a loud reply came. "Sorry! It was the glare, again. I didn't see you there. Sorry, pal."

"Let's make sure that's the last *accident*," steamed an angry victim.

"Sure, pal. You got it."

The guilty player grabbed a drink from his pull cart. He took a sip before removing his sunglasses and cleaning them. He started joshing among his three friends. This behavior did not shock Mateo.

Kneeling on his feet, a dirt powdered Mateo watched the entire interaction. It caused him to pause while planting daisies in Mrs. Rosenstein's backyard.

With no fence and on the right hand side of the fairway, the rear of Mrs. Rosenstein's sat wide open at the dogwood turn on the par five eighteenth hole. In addition to gaining some natural privacy, she also wanted some other odds and ends done in the backyard and around the house.

Already there a few days, Mateo was treated to some golf-people watching. Many of the shots landed around the turn, and the play was usually more theatrical than serious sporting. A reason to take a walk and socialize. Mateo immediately noticed that this performance was a repeat from a couple of days ago. Sweat drenched and covered with mud, Mateo was smoothing over the flower bed when he remembered the gossip Mrs. Rosenstein divulged yesterday over lunch.

"That's right, these dudes are having an old-fashioned beef. I wonder how this is going to turn out."

In the middle of his recollection, the doctor interrupted Mateo by presently begging. "Please, please, put the knife down. They are working on getting what you asked for. So, again, please take the knife away from your neck."

Mateo tightened his grip on the knife, pushed it a little harder into his carotid artery. His blood-letting sped up.

"Sorry, Doc. Not another word until I have the box that was in my dresser."

Leaving the library, Mateo's escort was finally zigging and zagging the right way out of Tall Oaks. He received word back from the higher-ups that his request to stop at his room was denied. Informing Mateo of this decision was the rival junior officer from earlier, who took great delight in delivering the news. No matter, Mateo knew it was necessary to walk past his room in order to leave Tall Oaks.

As they approached his room, Mateo managed to ditch the doctor by weaving through colors and titles. Making his way closer to the door, Mateo was also keeping an eye out for a large book.

Bingo.

With his room door in sight, Mateo gently ejected from the cinch of a jasmine colored guard a large hardcover art portfolio. He caught the book in mid-air then crouched down into the universal athletic position. Holding it with both hands, Mateo yelled a few times.

"Look out, I'm swinging!"

Mateo gave some half-hearted swings. The guards understood, the colors knew he was one of them.

Anyway, there was no reason to subdue Mateo since he was already in custody. When the rainbow smiled and receded, it revealed a group of junior officers standing in front of his room. These four henchmen were lined up, staggered right, left, right, and center. The last one standing in front of his door was Mateo's challenger from earlier, whom he had forgotten about.

No more practice swings.

Mateo took a step forward after every baseball swing of the art portfolio. His switch hitting quickly dropped the first three junior officers. The last one required Mateo to change sports. Taking two large steps followed by a quick shuffle to properly square up.

A thwack, Happy style.

The tremendous impact immediately destroyed the book. Pictures of aesthetic masterworks were released into the air. Mateo stood over the scourge of his existence along this stroll. Like the other three, he was on the ground moaning but not moving. Mateo stared down at him while artistic precipitation rained down.

Composition 8, Dogs Playing Poker, Massacre of the Innocents, The Third of May, Royal Red and Blue, Temple of Athena Nike, Four Horn, Three Musicians, Starry Night, Beheading of Saint John the Baptist, Night Watch, Luncheon on the Boating Party, No. 5, Ram and Tree, Gudea, Ishtar Gate, Calf-Bearer, Dishes and Fruit, Mona Lisa, Landscape with the Fall of Icarus, Nude Descending a Staircase, Woman of Willendorf Las Meninas, Three Musicians, The Dance, Sky Above Clouds IV, The Gleaners, The Scream, Three Goddesses, The Flower Carrier, School of Athens, The Kiss, The Birth of Venus, Dangerous Cooks. Landing directly on top of the incapacitated officer's face, Liberty Leading the People was the last to fall.

"You had that coming. Remember, you reap what you sow. Oh, and remember—you don't have to become a dictator in training."

After walking into his room, Mateo turned to the guards who were busy collecting the pages, "Thanks for understanding." With that he saluted them and closed the door.

Expecting to enjoy the comforts of home one last time, Mateo was shocked to find his room picked almost completely clean. The furniture was also gone. Standing in his living room, Mateo and the bare walls stared at each other. He was becoming upset with himself, wishing he was less attached to material things.

While Mateo investigated the state of his living room, a trio of guards stealthily entered. Weathered white, aqua, and marzipan proceeded to ransack whatever was left behind in the kitchen.

They formed an assembly line, passing items out of the door. Cooking oils, anchovies, cans of lentils, boxes of macaroni and cheese, Tabasco sauce, ginger, harissa, baking soda, saltines, wooden cooking utensils, and assorted culinary gadgets.

Mateo addressed the room, "The last day sure feels like the first day."

After his words were echoed back, the walls hardened their encompassing stare. This naked violation of his natural rights provoked Mateo's Western sensibilities. Dropping his guilt over desire, he fixated on the injustice of the situation.

Remembering something important, Mateo darted into the bedroom. He went to his dresser that was left behind. Similar to his mattress missing but the bed frame remaining, its contents were removed. Mateo stared at the empty top drawer, "Where is it?!" then slammed it closed.

No joke, however funny, was going to remedy the situation. Justice had to be served. He knew something must be done. The guards were oblivious to Mateo, and he to them, when he grabbed a large chef's knife from the kitchen. They kept respectfully looting the kitchen and Mateo walked to the living room. He yelled into the echo chamber.

"Where is it?"

"Where is it?!"

"WHERE IS IT?!"

Righteous anger.

Mateo's blood burned, his grip on the knife handle tightened. The walls tinted red.

"Where is my storage box?! Right the fuck now!!! NOW!!! NOW!!! NOW!!!"

Rage.

He stopped shouting and looked the room over again. This time he noticed a photograph left behind on the floor. Mateo picked it up to see a picture of him and an old family friend, Mrs. Rosenstein.

In his left hand, Mateo stretched the photograph out in front of him.

In his right hand, he was still holding the knife like a maniac.

The guards summoned the doctor, who was on his way. Not knowing the details, he was caught off guard. He approached Mateo with caution. "Whoa, easy there. I was told you something? Please—"

"—I want the storage box from my dresser, right now! What gives you the right! What gives you the right! Someone tell me, what gives you the fucking right!!! Nothing in this world does, that's the answer! Besides, Doc, tell me—what's my crime?"

Mateo pleaded with irate anger, "Huh, what's my crime?"

"*What is my crime?!*"

Echo. Echo. Echo. Echo. Echo.

By this point, the doctor stopped walking out of fear. "I think you're overreacting. The truth is that—"

"—To be, or not to be, that is the question."

"What, you're Hamlet all of a sudden?" joked the doctor trying to defuse this situational bomb.

Mateo was in no mood to laugh. "The choice is simple. If I don't get what I asked for, and soon, I will bid the world adieu. Farewell. Adios. Peace the fuck out." He put the knife up to his neck. "If I really am this important, then this should not be a problem."

The doctor took a step toward Mateo, "Whoa, take it easy now."

"Stop right there, Doc. Take one more step, and its good-bye."

Mateo lowered the picture, his elbow went up, and the knife dug in his neck. He was ready to spill his own blood.

The doctor took his step back. "No, stop! Hear me out. The authorities are not confiscating your stuff. They are actually recreating your room at another location."

"Why?"

"To assist with any trauma."

Mateo was dumbfounded. "I call bullshit. Just get it to me."

"Can you tell me what it looks like?"

"A red shoebox."

The doctor told the guards to track down the shoebox and bring it right away. Mateo was busy adjusting his grip and position of the knife. "And nobody else in the room but you, Doc." He made sure the knife was firmly affixed on his carotid artery. He managed to draw a timer of dropping blood.

Drip, drip, drip.

Mateo raised the photograph again. The doctor tried cutting another wire, this time with a step.

Mateo heard another footstep in his direction, "I've got nothing to lose, and everything to gain." The blade bared down, digging in further.

This stopped the doctor in his tracks.

"I am just going to stay right here."

"That's a wise idea."

Mateo lowered his elbow just a touch. After some silence, the doctor tried again to defuse this suicide bomb. "Please, put the knife down. They are working on getting what you asked for. So, again, please lower the knife."

Echo. Echo. Echo.

Asking about the picture, "Was that taken on a golf course. Which one was it?"

In the middle of his recollection, the doctor interrupted Mateo by presently begging. "Please, please, put the knife down. They are working on getting what you asked for. So, again, please take the knife away from your neck."

Mateo tightened his grip on the knife, pushed it a little harder into his carotid artery. His blood-letting sped up.

"Sorry, Doc. Not another word until I have my storage box."

Mateo's bleeding made the doctor desperate. He tried cutting another wire. "Well, could you tell me, at least, is that a golf course? You don't have to tell me who is in the picture."

Echo. Echo. Echo.

In the silence, Mateo fixated on the snapshot. Returning to that previous strand of memory in Mrs. Rubenstein's backyard.

Near the start of his freelance career, Mateo was helping a college friend, Kersey Hisrati, get his computer consulting firm up and running. Instead of a salary, Kersey offered Mateo a small percentage in the stake of the company, Binary Analytics. In the forthcoming years it gained traction, with profits steadily growing year after year. Kersey could never convince Mateo to stay, his restlessness always won out. Nevertheless, as a highly profitable company, Mateo's small position yielded enough revenue to secure his stay at Tall Oaks.

In one of those grand coincidences, Kersey lived nearby Mrs. Rosenstein, an old friend of Mateo's family. As a close friend of his mother's, she saw him grow up. They learned of each other's whereabouts, met up for lunch, and Mateo agreed to do some odd jobs around Mrs. Rosenstein's house. Landscaping was the largest undertaking. At the time, Mateo did not know she would force him to take four times the pay they agreed upon. Mrs. Rosenstein refused to have it any other way.

These meandering lunchtime conversations continued. Whenever Mateo stepped away from Binary Analytics, Mrs. Rita Rosenstein made it a point to stuff him with food. She told him all about her family. The kids needed to call more often, the grandchildren visit more often, and, more often than not, people never change. Rita and Mateo's mother were childhood friends who kept in touch over the years. Mateo had to call her more often as well.

Rita made a name for herself in the field of orthopedics. She remained proud of being arrested in her younger years for protesting against women's rights restrictions on the steps of the Supreme Court. She always admired her sister who swam the English Channel. She was currently in legal proceedings against her brother who illegally took the entirety of her mother's inheritance. After her husband died, Rita sought refuge at Golden Living, in the warmth and friendly tax codes of sunny Florida. Mrs. Rosenstein was also, without a doubt, one of the funniest people Mateo ever met. She could be raunchy without warning.

EUGENE NASSER

One time, Mrs. Rosenstein told Mateo about an incident at a class reunion. "And so I said to my husband—"Gerald, do you think I give a shit what that hussy thinks? Or the whore-master over there? You know, both of them seem to lose their panties in high school whenever boys came around. Now, they lose their dentures when gentlemen visit." This caused Mateo spit out his drink through his nose. She was awesome and he adored her.

Mrs. Rosenstein had no shortage of local gossip, both from her position as an assistant coordinator of special events and living alongside the eighteenth hole of the Emerald Green course. Conversations had distance, and information easily blew her way. It was when he finished wiping over the freshly planted daisies that Mateo remembered yesterday's conversation over honey cake.

The custom golf ball belonged to Schneider Varney, who almost hit, for a second time, Tony Boa. It was the classic tale of a bruised ego after someone new moves in to town. Moving to Golden Living five years ago, Schneider was the established top dog. Both on and off the course, he was still a good golfer who threw the best parties. Then Tony moved in and threatened the social landscape.

The word was that Tony had more clubhouse charisma. People had stopped laughing at Schneider's jokes in the locker room. Tony was also a decent golfer, who unknowingly planned a Fourth of July party that conflicted with the common practice of Schneider hosting the biggest party that day. After a few months passed Schneider could not hold back any longer. He was the party, not Tony. For his part, Tony was oblivious that his presence was having this effect of Schneider. Even Schneider knew Tony was not malicious, a fact that only made him angrier.

It was the ex-Wall Street banker versus the former construction magnate. They were playing a head-to-head match, and the reformed tough-guy from up north was winning the match. Through no fault of his own, not even trying to take fewer strokes and doing just that.

"I swear," Mrs. Rosenstein evaluated, "some of these people act like feral teenagers with retirement plans."

"That's right," Mateo remembered, "these dudes are having an old-fashioned beef. I wonder how this is going to turn out."

Mateo was situated in almost exactly the same place when he saw the first incident. This included Schneider and Tony as well. However, Mateo easily overheard Schneider talking trash about Tony to his friends this second time. Instead of just apologizing, Schneider smirked and decided to add some commentary. "That's garbage right there, fellas. Did you see the car he drives? Here is a piece of shit who thinks he's in the mob or something. You know, like that show that was on TV a while ago."

"*The Sopranos*," one of Schneider's buddies filled in.

"Yeah, that one. And just like the show this guy is a fake too. His wife looks like a cheap hooker. I wouldn't fuck her with your dick, you know? Have you heard her talk? I wouldn't even let her lick my balls. This place is letting in absolute garbage. This wanna be goomba shouldn't be here. This dog is going to learn how to heel. Tony Bullshit, that's his name." Schneider received nods of agreement from his pals who laughed along.

"I am going to turn this guy into my bitch." This got the biggest laugh. "Yeah, I am going to make this bitch heel."

When the conversation carried to him, Mateo was preparing to plant some Bolivian Sunset Gloxina near the daisies. On his hands and knees, Mateo instinctively lifted his head up when Schneider was finished cracking his entourage up.

When Mateo looked up, Schneider's gaze was locked onto him. As if knowing Mateo would look up, Schneider stared at him across forty yards.

He gifted Mateo some choice words, "Know your place, you grimy piece of shit. You should have gotten an education when you had the chance."

Schneider added while walking away, "Looks like somebody taught you to some obedience." Mrs. Rosenstein was a dear friend, so Mateo decided to just play it cool. He pulled his hat down lower and kept on landscaping. Meanwhile, Schneider returned to providing his foursome with commentary on the match.

"Let's do it, fellas. Let's show people who this Tony Bullshit really is. Fuck this guy and his friends too. Just watch my next shot— I mean, accident. Everybody at the clubhouse will see it. Right, fellas?" Schneider's pals greeted him with more tepid approval, something he did not notice but Mateo did.

The beef was fully cooked and ready to be served.

On this particular day Mrs. Rosenstein was working down nearby the clubhouse. This was where Mateo was headed after hearing Schneider's last remarks. He brushed himself off slightly and walked non-nonchalantly to the sidewalk out front. Safely out of sight, he proceeded to jog down the sidewalk.

On the way to witness this geriatric throw down, Mateo replayed other highlights from yesterday's conversation with Mrs. Rosenstein. "People move here from all over the country, dear. A whole mess of them retire here. In order to act like horny wild animals, with too much money. Most of the men take erectile dysfunction drugs and suddenly think they're porn stars this late in life."

Mateo had a tough time swallowing the bite of his wrap, nearly choking on it.

"Sunburned, drug fueled orgies. The smell of muscle balm is overwhelming. With nothing better to do than screw each other and discuss politics, they mostly complain about paying too much in taxes. It's inevitable that some people won't get along, all this screwing going on around here. It's either the government or some-one else humping you."

Not wanting to choke, Mateo asked before taking another bite of his turkey wrap and chewing rather quickly, "So, you were saying, two guys around here were having some sort of fertilized turf war, or something?"

"Oh, yes. Tony, who moved in a couple of months ago. Born and raised in Newark. Tons of money and self-made. I hear. Schneider's so angry he's no longer king of the castle. Anne, his wife, she told me he might do something drastic. Whenever they run into each at the golf course it drives him crazy."

Another quick bite with some nods.

"Apparently Tony is completely oblivious to what is going on. Men get more desperate as they age. I am afraid Anne is right, and that Schneider is messing with the wrong person."

"Why is that?" inquired Mateo, taking the last bite of his turkey wrap before moving onto the dessert.

"I hear Tony is not someone you never cross. Plain as that. Look, Schneider is not a wise guy."

While Mateo's memory was jogging, along with his body, his mental recall was put on hold as it was interrupted.

BEEP BEEP BEEP

Lori, one of the Pill Gals, was driving around delivering medications and spotted Mateo. The high-pitch horn caused him to stop his valet jog. "Need a lift?" asked the scantily dressed marine biology major. Lori had a penchant for giving hand jobs while wearing a golf glove, something Mateo found out first hand a couple of weeks ago in a private wooded spot off the seventh fairway.

In the boredom of newfound retirement, some revenue savvy doctors banned together early on to corner the Golden Living prescription drug market. The business model was simple. Based on a existential truth about human nature: people are the only animals who must take their medicine. Add to this convenience and young skin, and you get more growth than any of the doctors thought possible.

Painted with fluorescent colors, the Pill Gals carts were supped up and reinforced. Medications were under lock and key in a climate controlled storage unit. The Pill Gals uniform was made to order from the patriarchy catalog. Lori wore sneakers that resembled golf shoes, with her socks having miniature pom-poms on their backs. Management also encouraged sandals and painted toe nails. The rest of Lori's uniform consisted of short shorts, a tight fitting V-neck t-shirt, and a golf visor with the Pill Gals logo.

"Absolutely," Mateo answered.

"Where are you headed?" Lori asked.

"To the eighteenth green. It's going to be a championship finish. Go the quickest way you know. I'll fill you in on the details on the way there."

Once Lori was in the know, she took a sharp left turn down a seldom used access road and gunned it. The pair landed thirty yards short of the green in the rough on the right hand side of the fairway. They were perfectly situated between both foursomes, as well as concealed from Schneider's group walking up the fairway. So, while they were in the tall grass, there was still a chance to save par.

Mateo's senses were spiked as he surveyed the situation. The outside dining area of the clubhouse circumscribed the back of the eighteenth green. It was packed with lunchtime patrons. Clanks of porcelain dishes and silverware were added to the chirping birds. This de facto gallery of fans watched players finish their rounds before the golfers went inside the nineteenth hole.

"I'm sorry, I don't have my phone. Could you record this for me?" Lori smiled and started recording. By now, the pin was pulled and a couple of guys in Tony's group already took their final putts. When Tony went to address his ball on the green, Schneider did the same. Mateo looked ahead and back a couple of times. "Wow, the dumb ass is really going to follow through. He's really going to do it. This is an exercise in dedication to stupidity."

By now Tony was clued in to Schneider's behavior. One of Tony's friends was keeping watch. "Yo, here it comes T, just like youz knew it would. It's coming in low. Stay right there, the bastard is going to miss left."

The shot was a zinger. The faux family crest overshot the green, taking a respectable bounce off the cart path, before landing in the dining area. General commotion with the faint sound of glass breaking was heard. The birds could not be heard anymore. Greater attention than usual was now drawn to the arthritic pissing contest at the eighteenth green.

Glass bottles clinked in Mateo's kitchen. The guards got sloppy during their heist, and rose gold was careless with the jar of pickles. The noise prompted the doctor to ask about the status of the shoe box, "Is it on the way?" After some nods, he turned to Mateo, "Did you get that? The box you wanted is on the way. Could you ease up on your neck for now?"

Mateo ignored the doctor. When he double checked his grip, that's when he noticed the crimson drops running off his elbow. Until then, Mateo was unaware he was bleeding. Now, he didn't care. He looked down to see the trickle was collecting into a growing red pool on his green carpet. Then he took another look at the picture before looking back at the carpet.

"That's right," Mateo thought, before returning to the finish at Everglade Emerald, where it was on like Donkey Kong.

Only after the custom golf ball ran through the dining area was the warning heard. "Fore!" Schneider's watch out also carried a tone of anger. "Sorry, everyone, it was that damn glare again."

Mateo and Lori were situated perfectly to watch Tony and Schneider have their beef. Both men told their friends to stay put, then started walking toward each other. The crowd looked from a distance as the grudge match moved back down the eighteenth fairway. The two players in contention started exchanging words once the distance shortened between them.

"That's the third time! Youz obviously got a problem with me? Youz trying to embarrass me in front of my friends?" Tony was still holding onto his putter.

Schneider played coy, with a seven iron in his hand. "Look at that, you can count. I already told you, it was an accidents."

"Fuck youz they were!"

"You got shit in your ears, dumbfuck? I said, it was an accident. Time for you to get the hell out of here, and take that Jersey shore trash family with you."

The gap between Tony and Schneider continued to slowly close, now they were within a yard or two of each other. The situation was heated, but their respective friends all stayed put. Ancient playground rules were in effect. One on one.

"What'd youz say?" charged Tony.

"See, just like I thought. You have either tomato sauce or shit stuffed in your ears. Or maybe you're a stupid fuck. Hell, you might be both deaf and dumb."

"You want to play stupid after hitting into me a third time. This ends right here and now."

"Again, that's cute. You can apparently count. Just shut up, you cocksucker. Do everyone a favor and don't ever come back here. That's how this ends."

"Who the fuck is youz to tell me where I can live?"

Schneider dismissed Tony's question and went for the playground jugular. "And seeing as to how you Italians love your mothers so much, go fuck your mother."

After this insult, Tony could no longer contain his fury. Once Schneider finished the last syllable Tony unthinkingly dropped the putter and charged. Schneider was prepared, holding the club face of his seven iron and taking an en garde position.

Mateo watched as Schneider performed a balestra, hitting Tony directly in the sternum. Knocking the wind knocked out of Tony, forcing him to take a knee.

With the strength of anger, Tony tried again to rush at Schneider.

En guard, lunge, no breath, knee.

And a third time.

En guard, lunge, no breath, knee.

Mateo watched, while Lori recorded, as Tony huffed for air. Then he tried to outflank Schneider, where the circling caused the two men to switch locations. Schneider now had the eighteenth green behind him when Tony stepped on his forgotten putter.

The gallery looked on in anticipation. Schneider lunged, Tony batted, and the law of no absolute simultaneity was broken. The golf clubs contacted, with such force it disarmed both men. Schneider's iron went flying out of his hand, sending a shock wave through his arm bone. Tony swung for the fences, twisting his knee and losing his grip, causing his club to go flying.

Both men stood there for a moment. Schneider held his right arm, Tony rubbing his left knee. They were taking big gasps of air, staring down each another. Like a true loser, Schneider proclaimed himself the victor. "It's over, I won. Get the hell out of here." With both men weaponless, Tony clearly recognized the equal odds. He stated as fact with a malicious grin, "Now it's a fair fight. I am going to beat your ass."

A frightened Schneider began retreating toward the direction of the clubhouse for sanctuary. Looking back to see Tony hobbling after him, Schneider failed to notice a sprinkler head. He tripped, injuring his ankle and falling into the sandbox at the front left of the ridged green.

Schneider was crawling forward in the sand trap when his hand landed on the rake handle. When Tony caught up, Schneider greeted Tony's face with the rake. The teeth dug into the right side of Tony's skull. Even more disturbing, was that Tony did not budge. Not a peep of pain. Instead, he let out sinister laughter.

Mateo looked on as Schneider's friends gave chase. They kept close and did not intervene, until Tony let out that maniacal war cry. One of them broke the sacred code. Schneider was on his back with Tony's hands wrapped around his neck. Blood fell off Tony's face onto Schneider's cheeks. While Schneider was choking this round came the advice, "Throw sand in his face!" To which Schneider obliged, throwing a handful of coarse grains into Tony's eyes.

Temporarily stunned, Tony had to let go of Schneider, who tried to slink away. But one of Tony's friends did not hesitate to assist. "Catch Tone," and tossed him a bottle of water. Both the distance and the catch were impressive, particularly Tony's one hand grab while blinded.

Tony squinted at the snake, "Youz little cocksucker, you're gonna pay for that."

With the playground rites broken, Tony's friends formed an Italian wall to prevent Schneider from stumbling off of the green. Once Tony rinsed off enough sand, sweat, and blood the one on one fight was on again. When Schneider's friends tried to approach the green, their shot landed short as Tony's peeps chased them back down the fairway. Mateo could pick up a snippet of conversation as Lori filmed them going past.

"Hurry up Cal, they're gaining on us!"

"I know that Joshua! Lawrence is the slow one."

Lawrence defended his medical condition. "Screw the both of you, it's my arthritis—I told you both this morning it was a bad idea. Fuck Schneider."

While Schneider's friends retreated, Tony's entourage plotted in their pursuit. "Moose, you take the one on the left. Anthony, take the shithead on the right, Junior directed. "I got that motherfucker in the center."

In that moment, Mateo decided to head for the green, while Lori sped away to catch up with the larger brawl. The chase ended not far from where Mateo planted flowers earlier. At the dogleg turn, Cal, Joshua, and Lawrence were caught and summarily beaten down by Moose, Anthony, and Junior. Moose showed no pity to Lawrence, even while he blamed and cursed Schneider's name.

Hooks, slices, punch shots, and uppercut lobs.

Lori captured all the action, while over on the dance floor, Mateo could see Tony and Schneider were now standing toe to toe. They were holding up their dukes and ready to rumble. The glint of Tony's bracelet quickly struck Mateo's eye.

He wondered whether or not to intervene. Who was he to stop two older men from kicking the crap out of one another? They both seem like willing participants. Was he even allowed to violate sacred playground rules?

Still unsure when he arrived at the green, Mateo saw nobody was making the slightest attempt to intervene. He heard not a single comment of protest from the gallery. These guys were putting for the win. With the gallery making Mateo's choice to watch it play out for him, a sizable number looked on, but they did so as capitalists. Not missing out on this opportunity, a betting pool was quickly established. He could see cash being thrown down on tables. Good capitalist Samaritans.

"Nowhere to run," Tony said fatefully, "we settle this score right now. You started all this for no good reason. All because youz think you're better than me."

Mateo's eye caught a ray of sun from Schneider's designer watch, "You're dead meat. I'll sue you into poverty you criminal fuck!"

Mateo saw Tony purposely drop his guard, allowing Schneider to take a full, hard swing.

Crack.

Schneider's punch across Tony's face only managed to make him laugh devilishly. The divots on his face oozed even more blood.

"My turn," Tony warned, before taking a barrage of swings.

Hooks, slices, punch shots, and uppercut lobs.

Knocked to his hands and knees, Schneider's warfarin laced blood was strewn all over. Both players were covered in it, as was the surrounding green. With his little birdie subdued, Tony began circling Schneider, savoring the moment.

"Why did you try to hit me? What, because you think you're better than me for some reason?"

Circling.

"Youz fucking Wall Street types are all the same. You think money makes you untouchable."

Circling.

"You know what gets fucked? Pussy. Bitches like you on their hands and knees."

Not needing distance, Tony proceeded to use a foot wedge on Schneider's solar plexus. This caused Schneider to momentarily go airborne, before falling down with his head alongside the cup.

Schneider was gasping to find air when Tony turned his back to the gallery. Tony unzipped his fly and began pissing in Schneider's face. The cup briefly filled up with urine and blood.

Standing at the front of the green, Mateo read it and could see a trail of blood from the beach to the pin hole. Around the cup was doused with more red, some of it washed with pale yellow from an Italian schlong. He also saw money being exchanged among the members of the gallery.

After giving the satisfactory ah, a magnanimous Tony zipped up. He bent down to Schneider, who was laying prone, his head tuned sideways and nose right next to the cup. Tony said in a low voice, "Consider youzself a lucky fuck. If this was in Jersey a few years back, you would already be dead. I dealt with schemers like you all my life. People who never built anything in their lives.

You're just a thief."

At this point, Tony's crew hitched a ride with Lori up to the green. They congratulated each other, especially Tony who drove for show and putted for dough. The flop shot set up the putt nicely. Moose pulled Mateo aside and directed more than he asked, "Youz collect all our stuff, kid, and I'll get in contact with you. Don't fuck with any of it, either. We'll make it worth your time." The crowd parted as Tony's foursome walked through, maintaining proper hushed golfing etiquette the entire time. Respect.

Over on the green, members of the gallery got a whiff of the acrid smell. It was made even more noxious by Schneider's moans. During the mayhem, someone found the good sense to contact the Golden Living security team. They were given, as is always the case, a vague description. Luckily, they arrived after the outcome was secured and betting payouts distributed.

Sirens could be heard in the distance. Until the medical professionals and police arrived, playground rites were still in effect. This meant treating the injuries of both parties involved. Mateo's personal dislike for Schneider did not matter, because those are not the rules.

Four deputized police officers from the Golden Living security team, along with two paramedics showed up. Mateo was kneeling down in the blood, sweat and mind blowing humiliation to see how badly Schneider was hurt. The authorities did not see the playground rules in action. Instead, without asking a single question, the cops knew they were seeing the conclusion of an altercation. In front of the dining area, the perpetrator was brazenly robbing the victim.

Two members of law enforcement ran toward Mateo, one with pepper spray, the other with a stun gun. "Hands up! Don't move! Stop resisting!" Mateo stood still with his hands up, and for his disobedience he was chemically blinded. Still resisting, he was shocked down to the ground. Mateo joined Schneider in the fetal position. Landing face to face, they shared a moment.

While Mateo was in the process of getting hog-tied, some of the fans in the gallery began to voice their protest. They pleaded Mateo's innocence, leading law enforcement to identify them as a hostile threat. They doused the troublemakers with oleoresin capsicum. One of the fans went into cardiac arrest, and fortunately for them paramedics were nearby.

Then Mrs. Rosenstein came running out to Mateo who was being moved from the green to the police car. As an employee, the officers listened. It turned out Mrs. Rosenstein witnessed the whole incident from up third second floor office in the clubhouse. Stories were corroborated and evidence gathered. Upon further questioning, nobody knew who the assailants were. Mrs. Rosenstein told the police she could identify them. It could have been anybody, with her bad eyesight and all. Even Schneider declined to file a police report. He never said who, but only that no charges would be filed. Ever.

After a prolonged conference, the police cut Mateo loose. No lawman actually spoke to him. Apologies are only if some wrong has been committed. Not even the magical phrase was uttered. You're free to go.

No harm, no foul. Playground 101.

Mateo was clearly in need of medical treatment. It was never offered up. Of course, he could not afford it anyway. He'd do what always worked in the past.

He walked it off.

BEEP BEEP BEEP

Lori came to the rescue. She would drive Mateo back to the Pill Gals headquarters where one of the doctors would examine him free of any charge. Afterwards, she'd drop Mateo off at Mrs. Rosenstein's house. "Don't worry," Rita assured Mateo, "I'll call your parents. Not to worry."

Everything happened exactly as Lori said it would. After she spoke to the doctor privately, the doctor was happy to help. In fact, the doctor provided some pain medications at no cost, and even gifted a Mateo a shower and a pair of hospital scrubs.

While he was washing up, Lori had uncommon gossip. Only after the staff pledged absolute secrecy did she tell it. This was why she missed some of the action on the green because she had to delete what she was recording. Right there on the spot. If not she'd be in danger if anything leaked out.

"I had the whole fight recorded, but then I was forced to delete it before it was even over. I missed some action on the green because of it." Lori said her life would be in danger if this happens. Not a digital word could be uttered. She swore to only tell it once.

In this way, almost immediately, the fight became Golden Living lore. Something that happened but nobody would openly talk about. Aiding this mystique was the fact that neither Schneider nor Tony resided at Golden Living. Both went off to greener pastures. So too were neither of their wives happy about it. Schneider's wife knew better, Tony told his wife he left that behavior in Jersey. These were developments Mrs. Rosenstein filled Mateo in on a few years later over lunch.

A dirt free, red-eyed, and warily walking Mateo emerged in lime green scrubs. He had his belongings in a clear plastic drawstring bag. When Lori was driving Mateo back to Mrs. Rosenstein's house, he felt good enough to start joshing.

"How are you feeling, champ?"

"You're asking me?" Lori asked in return with sarcastic surprise. "Seriously, how do you feel?"

Mateo groaned, "I am fucked up, but I'll be alright. The stun gun punctures stung like hell in the shower. My eyeballs feel like they've been burned from the inside out. But all things considered, I should feel worse. I look absolutely crazy right now."

"Yeah, you are tore up. You smell better, but you're right, you do look like shit," assessed Lori who finished with a wink. Then she pulled out a brand new golf glove, "Are you still good big boy, you know, for a little up and down?"

"Well, isn't this a stroke of luck. I sure am."

Mateo had a massive grin as the pair headed off to that secluded spot alongside the seventh fairway

Drip, drip, drip.

Blood was running down Mateo's arm, to the end of his elbow.

Drip, drip, drip.

Under Mateo's feet, it was turning into a squishy greenish sponge.

Drip, drip, drip.

After a knock at the door, like the sound of someone with a case of the barkies, Mateo was suddenly presently aware.

A couple of guards entered the room, handing the doctor a shoe-box. He felt the contents, giving it a slight shuffle before trying to hand it handing it over to Mateo.

"Here, this is what you asked for, right?" the doctor inquisitively implored. "Now, please, put the knife down."

Mateo turned his head to get a full look at his shoe box. "Open it," he directed.

The doctor displayed the contents.

"Hand it over," ordered Mateo.

"Will you give up the knife?"

"You know what the exchange is."

"I'm a man of my word, Doc. But I want to negotiate. I want five minutes alone in my room all by myself."

Drip, drip, drip.

"After what you just pulled? Are you serious?"

"Dead serious."

Somehow, someway, to his immense credit, the good doctor managed to convince the authorities to grant Mateo his wish. The feat was a medical marvel.

Drip, drip, drip.

Drip, drip.

Drip.

Mateo was back to life.

As a precaution, all sharp objects were removed from his room. It was determined there was no feasible way for Mateo to hang himself. Neither were there any electric appliances to toss in the bathtub, or medications available to overdose on.

The doctor treated Mateo's jugular cut, sealing it with three bright blue butterfly bandages. On his way into the hallway the doctor told Mateo, "If you need anything, I'll be right outside the door."

With the door closed, Mateo acquired some solitude. He went and knelt in the middle of his living room, sat on his feet, and placed the shoebox next to him. Like a religious rite, Mateo opened it up and started going through his beloved photos.

Family. Friends. Past love affairs. Drinks at the bar. Birthdays. Weddings. Halloween. Christmas.

Anniversaries. Graduations. Pets. Concerts. Vacations. National Parks. Monuments. Forrest scenes. Mountains. Sunsets. Clowning around.

Life.

Then Mateo uncovered some pictures of his parents. The ones who brought him directly into the world. He missed them dearly. Wishing they would materialize out of thin air, he started to ache from the inside out. Then he realized, they were there. His mother and father had never left. He was carrying them this entire time. Among other attributes, he owed his intelligence to his mother, his drive to his father, and his backbone of righteousness came from both sets of grandparents. A thought shot through Mateo's body: that he inherited the wisdom of all his ancestors. This insight comforted Mateo, but then his stomach began folding over on itself. Churning into a whirlpool, as if to satisfy the digestion of an unseen kernel.

Mateo began to cry.

He was sorry to his parents for all the terrible things he did as a dumb youngster.

He was sorry for all the promises he broke.

He was sorry his parents never received the grandchildren they desired.

His tempered sobbing became wailing.

Echo. Echo. Echo.

Sounds of anguish snuck outside the room into the hallway. In solidarity, the doctor and a bunch of guards got choked. After a couple of minutes, Mateo's cries trailed off into silence.

Silence...

Silence...

Silence...

About a minute into the golden note, the guards started looking around each other. Soon enough, all the eyes landed on the doctor who understood he had to check on the patient to ascertain if he was alive or dead. Right as the doctor reached for the door knob—"ha."

Mateo's Cat was very much alive.

"ha, ha, ha"

"ha, ha, ha"

At first the doctor was not sure what he was hearing, it was too soft to hear. Letting go of the knob he stepped away. The guards were looking at each, not sure what to make of it either. Mateo was still crying while looking at the photos, but tears of happiness replaced those of sorrow.

"ha, ha, ha, Ha, Ha, Ha, Ha, Ha, HA, HA, HA, HA, HA, HA!"

The joy of life.

To keep the memory without the guilty baggage, he let go. No more adding to the pains of life. If you did something in the past, that you would not do today, then you are not guilty. An innocent person cannot be convicted. Let yourself go free.

Mateo stopped trying to laugh at his self, and finally laughed at himself. The only way he could deal with being the prime suspect responsible for upending the world.

He accepted that he would always know nothing.

He accepted responsibility for the broken promises.

He accepted his self-absorbed character.

He accepted the eventual visit from death knocking at his door.

He laughed at all of it.

Reborn to a new state of consciousness, laughing at the death of his ego.

"HA, HA, HA!"

"HA, HA, HA!"

"HA, HA, HA!"

Echo. Echo. Echo.

After fifteen minutes the doctor knocked. "I'm coming in," he warned, and was relieved to find Mateo intact.

Mateo was busy adding the picture of him and Mrs. Rosenstein to the rest. He closed the shoe box, and looked around the empty room.

"That was more than five minutes," said the doctor.

"It's a gentleman's five," Mateo replied. This led him to further muse, "You know, Doc,when you are all alone, you're not really by yourself."

"Do you have everything?" asked the doctor while looking around into the emptiness. Mateo securely tucked the storage box in his left arm, then reached into his right pocket to feel the contents. "Yep. All good."

The colorful gang was back in orderly formation, and headed towards the Tall Oaks exit.

"Finally. Correct by default, right doc?" Mateo then began contemplating his return to larger society. Thinking of the tremendous landscape that lays ahead, Mateo quipped, "Well, it looks like you can retire from the mob, but you can never leave the family."

"What does that mean?" asked a puzzled doctor.

Rrraaawwwrrr!

Before Mateo could answer, the crowd erupted again. Louder.

RRRAAAWWWRRR!

"There's your answer, Doc."

IX.

———=◖◉◗=———

A One Sided Conversation

With every step one less in Tall Oaks, flanking Mateo and the good doctor on the way out were *The Rights of Man—Oliver Twist—Uncle Tom's Cabin—Black Skin, White Masks—Self-Reliance—The Woman's Bible—Dusk of Dawn—The Master and Margarita—A Confederacy of Dunces*, each one with a different backdrop of color.

Mateo felt a low electric hum emanating from the crowd. It grew in intensity, hitting his solar plexus. Positive and regenerating, it felt like sweet music. His olfactory senses perked up, "Hey, Doc, you smelling that?"

Finally leaving Tall Oaks was not a sufficient reason to prevent one last act of playful disobedience. The merry band of chromatic protectors from engaging in one last act of humorous mischief. The large glass entrance doors allowed sunshine to flood into an adjacent waiting room, lighting up a lobby with seats resembling those on a bus. Without hesitation, guards sat down and began reading their respective book.

Then Mateo observed an indigo guard pull from her utility belt a small metal vile. She placed a tiny amount of some powder under her tongue. A bunch of the other colors followed suit. Then, just like that, Mateo's past entangled with his present. A memory smacked his consciousness.

Mateo was sitting in a seat similar to the guards, except his was on an actual bus that was headed east on highway I-40 traveling from Phoenix to Asheville. He was doing his best not to overhear a woman's conversation on her cell phone. She was so loud it was assaulting, and Mateo found it impossible to tune her out. Whoever was on the bus did not have a choice either. Like it or not, they were captives of her conversation.

"What I am trying to tell you—You thick headed asshole—You know, you're just like your father, I fucking swear—No, don't try to interrupt me—You have no idea what I am about to say— I told you not to interrupt me—I am not even sure you can handle this conversation—Now I can't think straight because you pissed me off with your fucking tone—I swear, you screw everything up, you can't even hear straight—You said that you were going to do something and then you don't follow through with it—That is all your fault, sweetie—I said not to interrupt me, you fucking idiot—Let me stop you right there before you go on to say nonsense—Same lame ass excuse every time—Ever heard of paper and a pen to write shit down?—Jesus fucking Christ, take a note on your phone at least— None of this occurs to you—Instead, you just sit there with a stupid fuck'in look on your face—You sad, pathetic little man—That is something you don't know how to be, a real man—Yep, that's it, I think I nailed it—I can see clearly now, you'll never change—It will always be "I forgot" with you—What the fuck have I gotten myself into with someone like you?—No balls—All of this could have been avoided but you convinced me otherwise—You fuck'in promised up and down it would be different, that things would change—I told you not to interrupt me—How many times do I have to say it?—Nothing has changed and nothing will—No, shut the fuck up, I am not done yet—How stupid are you?—And how dumb am I to be with you?—Again, it's the same thing—You are a fucking child!—I swear!—You know what else, I am not coming to your place when I get in town—Fuck you where am I going, that's where—At this point it's none of your fuck'in business—I said not to interrupt me, what the fuck?—You are a pathetic—NO NO NO, shut up—JUST SHUT THE FUCK UP for a minute!—Do not try to make this about me, that is not how this conversation started, remember?—You fucked up, not me?—Do not try to blame this on m—What the fuck ever—Next time you and your tiny little limp dick say you are going to do the dishes you'll do them—I should go and fuck all your friends—Pathetic, just like your father—You should think about killing yourself now because you have failed at life."

The two captive prisoners, Mateo and Juice, the driver, easily heard this woman airing her business from the rear of the bus. They were the only three on board.

"That, my friend," Mateo told Juice, "is surely a cuck on the other line."

Juice winced, "That guy sounds like a total fool. His ears must be bleeding, I know mine are."

"That guy is better off paying someone else for just the sex. That's got to be cheaper than what he doing now. It's at least costing him a mental fortune. But who am I to judge, right?"

"You know what the real problem is," Juice assessed, "is that he likes the abuse. Especially if what you say is true."

"You're right," agreed Mateo, "or why else would he put up being treated like that."

"She told him he was a nutless wonder and that he failed at life," Juice shuddered again.

"That's because his balls are in her purse. She took them away and is about to throw them out of the bus window." Mateo kept embellishing, "Given the nature of that conversation, if I had to wager money, I'd say she pegs the shit out of him. In a way that is merciless, yet gentle."

While they were having a good chuckle at the woman's expense, the rest stop signs reminded Juice it was time for a driving break. Time to refill the bus and people on board. With the bus refueled, the duo got coffee and were shooting the breeze at an outdoor table. "Coffee, the drink of the gods," mused Mateo. Juice raised his cup in agreement.

They were caffeinated and swapping stories. Mateo found out Juice's son won the regional science fair last month. It was a new way to manage floods. A combination of dykes, pumps, and targeted land reclamation. It also involved cost-effective construction techniques. They had moved on to their opinions of the ideal breakfast when, seemingly from out of nowhere, an officer from the United States army approached them. After apologizing for the interruption, Mateo was asked to leave briefly so Juice and the officer could talk in confidence.

After a few steps, and a couple of sips of coffee, Mateo ran into what he initially believed were a crew of cadets. He looked around for a military vehicle, only to not see one. Keeping his distance, he managed to overhear a snippet of their conversation. Something about a vehicle breaking down and they had to find their way to a military base. While the story was hazy, the fact was these new recruits were going for basic training and needed a lift into Asheville.

Mateo and Juice were already inside the bus talking when the Privates boarded. The woman also retained her previous location, sitting in the back by herself. She perked up and coquettishly welcomed the unexpected passengers. Conversely, Mateo was not thrilled by the sight of the uniforms. They frightened him. Inside the bus, he received an even closer look at their faces than outside. As they walked past, at first he became terrified. This feeling then morphed into profound despair, as this shot of heartache penetrated to Mateo's marrow.

Training was underway to create baby faced killers. A soldier that does not kill is a military liability. With the bus on route, Mateo took out his tractatus-philosophical-comedy-logic journal and started writing material.

Ladies and gentlemen—have you seen some of the members of our armed services?

Before I get going, has anyone here served in the armed forces?

Thank you so much. I appreciate your service. I wish the Pentagon gave all of you way more money instead of giving nearly all of it to the contractors. We need a military, but we've abused the troops. That's the place where what I am about to say about the military is coming from. I understand we need a military, I absolutely love our socialist military. As a taxpayer who helps fund it, I just have some complaints.

It would be fuck'in strange if we did not have a large military.

History would look completely different. What do I mean? We were on the winning side in a couple of World Wars, then went on to defeat the Soviet Union in the Cold War—and we did all this with a small military? The largest portion of America's discretionary budget doesn't lie.

To keep enlistment going, they fuck'in dangle a college education in front of you. That's just mean. It's really a draft in an economic disguise. Affordable education would hurt recruitment efforts. Right out of high school, they got you by the balls.

Look at how young you folks start. You've barely had a chance to find your dick—or whatever version of sexual equipment suits you down there—when the military drops that college hook in front of you. You can go abroad, kill people, and then come back home and get arrested for having a beer.

Not long ago, I was on a bus traveling through Tennessee. At a rest stop, there was an army battalion that got stranded. I don't know how or why, but they needed a lift into Asheville. Lucky for them the bus was pretty much empty. The only people aboard the bus were your truly, the driver, whose name was Juice, and some random woman who sat in the rear of the bus yelling into her cell phone. That's a whole other story.

Anyway, I was sitting up front bullshitting with Juice when they started to board. We were continuing our conversation from earlier. I basically found out his son is a genius, and that Juice thinks bacon is a necessary breakfast ingredient. I said the sausage patty was more iconic. Which one gets added to a burger? See, only the sausage is eaten exclusively for breakfast. Really though, what do I care? I am not eating either one.

This brings me back to my original question—have you seen some of the members of our armed services, how young they are? I know people are usually young when they enlist, but they were kids. Now, I ran into the new recruits earlier, but I didn't catch how young they were. I think some of them were young enough that they needed helmets. If kids have to wear a helmet riding a bike, why aren't soldiers wearing in uniform? Isn't the military more dangerous than a bike ride? Even if they were over eighteen, which I don't think most of these new recruits were, an ounce of prevention is worth a pound of cure. Isn't a soldier's brain important to protect? Seems to me they should be wearing helmets. And while we're at it, the helmets should be high tech. Make it a little bigger if you have to.

Since we're on it, camo out. It's so not hot. And, it's boring. There's a whole rainbow of colors out there. Yes, that's it! Rainbow is the new camouflage. Why not let the soldiers, you know, soldier, but with some self-expression? Like, maybe they should get to choose a color with a matching helmet. Something that reflects their personality. I know we can make the military uniforms stylish.

I know I am going to gets some jeers with this one—I 'm pretty sure kids this young are not allowed lethal weaponry. Until they are twenty-one years old, no real guns. There's too much lethal weaponry around here anyway. Give them a net gun, or a modernized version of a Sasumatha. Maybe some newfangled foam that stops people in their tracks. All I know is that there's no way that basic training unit I was looking at were not old enough to handle real guns. No sireee. I am not sure they should be allowed to even cook.

While we're in the mood to make some changes around here, I have also believed for a while that the mandatory haircut has to be done away with. Can we just leave people's hair alone already?

I mean, why cut their hair when the military already owns their bodies? Seems like overkill to me. It's warfare, who really cares besides the government? Parents cut the hair of their children. Where are my libertarians at? We should at least treat them like young adults.

And soldiering looks hard. They should get periodic breaks and time for recreation. Hell, why we're at it why not let them form a union? Did that give some of you in here a heart attack? That may be a tad too much. After all, we are in America. It does raise some questions: Can you be a libertarian and in the military? Or in law enforcement? Are the only unions allowed the chamber of commerce types?

All I know is that being a soldier looks like a might difficult job. We should look to take care what is underneath their helmets, their mental health. I have no idea what a solution looks like here. I don't know, give them drugs. Why not? People get hardcore drugs all the time for minor anxieties of life. Let them microdose shrooms, eat lower potency edibles, or take some CBD. I mean, don't people care about PTSD? Enough to mellow out but not prevent from doing their duties. Preventative medicine, that's what is needed. It's like a helmet inside your head. You either care about mental health, or you don't, right?

However, the military deserves an immense amount of credit when it comes to inclusiveness. The people boarding that bus were a testament to non-discrimination. It seems there isn't anyone they would not kill. No matter your race, creed, ethnicity, or gendered or sexual preference. None of it matters, Uncle Sam wants you.

A truly non-discriminatory organization. Willing to those them to the enemy wolves, as necessary, if achieves some broader military objective. It's truly democracy in action. The levers of power could do no worse than emulate this inclusiveness.

Wait...on second thought, there was a segment of the population that was not represented. Old people. They were discriminated *against. The military does not want to send elderly people into war zones. The old declare war and the young fight them.*

Oh, and you can bet none of these new recruits I was looking at cam from money. Nobody with disposable wealth joins the army, not even for the exercise.

Old, rich people sending younger poor people off to fight. It's terrible. The greed is endless, so it'll never end. Generation after generation sending other people's sons and daughters off to face death. That's fucked up. According to the natural world, parents are not supposed to outlive their offspring. It's the other way around.

I am guessing the soldiers of most other countries are also on the younger side. So, what's needed is some general agreement on another way to play the game of war. I mean, we all agree the youth should be prevented from hurting themselves, right? We're not around to violate laws of nature, am I right?

Hear me out, I am proposing games, not guns, on the battle-field. No digital games, straight up board games. One soldier from each side sitting at a table playing chess, checkers, backgammon, Chinese checkers or Go. Flip a coin for first move and eventually a winner emerges without bloodshed. Wouldn't that be nice!

I know what you're thinking—and yes! Tic-tac-toe, dominoes, rock, paper, scissors, and twister also acceptable to settle disputes. Other potential game are red light green light, freeze tag, hop-scotch, and tree climbing. Consider this an open-ended list. A guy can dream, right?

No more baby faced killers. No more sacrificing young people, sending them to die at the greed the adults who dictate their hair-cuts. We have a choice to do better, folks.

Let's brainstorm! Let's have a flood of ideas instead of melting ice!

As Mateo rounded the corner past some of the colorful passengers that were still sitting, it marked the last jog of his memory. This final flashback in Tall Oaks ended when bright sunlight struck his eyes He was momentarily blinded to the enormous crowd outside. Once he walked past the threshold they erupted.

RRRRRRAAAAAAWWWWWRRRRR!!!!!!!!!!

It was the loudest sound Mateo ever heard.

Oddly enough, his hearing was unaffected. The volume was muted by the sun's rays that stung his eyes. At first overwhelmed by the light, the world came into sharper focus. He stopped walking. The large glass entrance doors and walls of Tall Oaks revealed the sight of people that stretched farther than Mateo's eye could see.

RRRRRRAAAAAAWWWWWRRRRR!!!!!!!!!!

It was a bright, sunshiny day.

X.

——◆◎◆——

Artificial Intelligence

Part One
The Salvo

Helios was on the way to summit the mountain sky. On its climb, a seemingly endless amount of people gathered outside Tall Oaks. Bathing in starlight, they were ready for Mateo to exit. Looking through the glass entrance, he could see that signs were scattered everywhere. Handwritten messages fluttering atop the crowd. Meaning was hoisted up to the cosmos, a reminder that words always retain their power. Their spirit.

With everyone showering under the same light, it created for Mateo a rainbow of the human soul. It was the most beautiful sight he had ever seen. Although there was scarcely a cloud in the sky, the scene terrified him just the same.

Lumbini vibes all over again.

When he went to start walking again, Mateo felt justified in his worst fears. The crowd suddenly changed its tune.

RRRRAAAAWWWWRRRR!!!! Allegro con brio. Molto vivace.

BBBBBOOOOOO!!! Lento. Grave.

It was so loud the ground shook, the glass rattled. "These people are here to kill me," he thought. "How could they not be? To hang, draw, and quarter me because they think I created this mess?" Without panic, he reminded himself of some truths in life. Previously known coins of truth we forget to put in our pockets. "It's not my life to keep," Mateo affirmatively recalled to himself. "Your past does not belong to you anyway. You won't be around for it."

Recognizing knowledge as the real currency of life, Mateo felt a little better. He started walking, again. That's when he saw why the crowd was booing. Outside past the large glass entrance he saw the fearless leaders of the colorful brigade into Tall Oaks taking off.

The guilty parties were doing their best to conceal their identities, but by now Mateo knew how to identify them by the secret symbols on their shoes. Perhaps the crowd also knew this. The last batch of peerless leaders got into an unmarked black SUV, speeding off through the crowd. As the dark motorcade passed, signs were lowered. Arms extended out from the crowd, thumbs were turned down at the rat-kings.

BBBBBOOOOOO!!!

Mateo also saw guards in stylish black uniforms with white pin stripes, even on their helmets. They faced the crowd and lined the immediate road leaving Tall Oaks. He could see they were equipped with a super-hero looking utility belt, with a retractable Sasumatha affixed to it. Mateo was also able to now read some of the messages the crowd raised up high, dancing in the air.

A NEW AGE OF WONDER IS UPON US

SENT BY GOD!

A BRAND NEW DAY EVERYDAY

REJOICE!

BE THE CHANGE YOU WANT IN THE WORLD

NO VICTORY WITHOUT STRUGGLE

Looking at the guards with him, Mateo noticed they had pulled down a reflective visor of matching color over their eyes.

Suddenly, there was his final step inside Tall Oaks. Before walking through the doorway of the crystalline looking glass Mateo said to himself, "I'd rather be a corpse than a coward." An act of spiritual fortification.

RRRRAAAAWWWWRRRR!!!! Allegro con brio. Molto vivace. Fermata.

The crowd was as radiant as the sun itself. Jubilant, full spectrum light.

Thumbs up.

Deaf again and filled with awe, Mateo had an unending series of questions concerning why this crowd was here. He thought these people were there to exact American justice on his sorry ass. A very public execution. No, instead of extinguishing his existence they cheered. For him, as much as for themselves.

Mateo was shuffled into a waiting vehicle. It was a unique ride, something the A-Team would drive. A cross between a mini-van and an SUV, with Lamborghini doors and painted jet black. It was built to handle any business that came its way. Bulletproof everything, including the wifi.

RRRRAAAAWWWWRRRR!!!!

B.A. Baracus shut the heavy door.

Silence.

The inside aesthetics matched those on the outside. Behind darkly tinted windows, electronics were seamlessly infused through-out. Sitting behind the driver, Mateo looked up to find that even the sunroof was blacked out. The good doctor was behind the passenger and seated to his right. Behind them were tangerine *Man and his Gods,* cerulean blue *A Little Princess* and an emerald *To Kill a Mocking Bird.*

Mateo immediately felt the vehicle's bombproof heft upon sitting down. He felt it even more when the driver pulled away at the speed of a crawl. "How fast are we moving?" Mateo thought. Followed up immediately by "It doesn't really matter."

Looking through the tinted window, Mateo saw not a trace of violence, mayhem, or the disorder. No pushing, no shoving. He saw a mass of people caring, supporting one another under the hot sun.

Unafraid, he rolled his window down to invite them along on his ride. Cheers smacked him in the face as he read more airborne messages.

EMPATHY OVER JUDGMENT

WE HAVE ARRIVED!

I CAN FEEL AGAIN

LET'S GET AWAY FROM OURSELVES

NO MORE PRISON LABOR

DARE TO BE A DREAMER

SENT BY GOD!

NO MORE CORPORATE AGENDAS

People were born into a new state of consciousness.
A celebration of life.
A rebirth.

Without averting his gaze to the crowd, Mateo asked the doctor, "Obviously, these people are here because they found something out. Any idea what that something *is*?" The doctor was himself preoccupied looking out the right side window he kept closed up, "Nope."

"Do you smell that?" asked Mateo.

"What's that?"

"You're joking right? Your nose would have to be broken in order not to."

"Roll down your window and take a whiff."

As soon as the doctor rolled the window down halfway, the television screens in the vehicle transporting Mateo powered on. This included the ones behind the driver and passenger seats, along with one upfront and another in the back. While the guards were confused, the snail's pace was maintained.

I NEED COFFEE

PEACE BE WITH YOU

DO A FAVOR FOR SOMEONE ELSE

I STAND WITH YOU

WATCH OUT FOR THE SWERVE AHEAD

FREE TO REFUSE

SENT BY GOD!

THE GROUND IS SHIFTING UNDER OUR FEET

EVERY SITUATION IS UNIQUE

KNOCK, KNOCK!

While Mateo was reading the messages, they began to wobble. Examining the crowd closer, he noticed an increasing number of people staring at their phones giving perplexed looks. Every conceivable device that utilizes a screen was now broadcasting the same program. The Chanel 7 News at Noon, with Emma Sanchez-Smith. This unexpected interruption managed to dial back the crowd noise. Everyone was paying close attention to a composed Emma, whose voice elicited no specific regional accent.

Emma's voice echoed all around.

"Welcome, ladies and gentlemen. Emma Sanchez-Smith here at the Channel 7 News Headquarters. We are keeping you, and your family, up to date with the latest on the developing situation related to WICS.

State Department officials will be briefing the nation later today at two o'clock. We have also just been notified that the president is scheduled to address the nation at three o'clock. Tune in to Channel 7 for live coverage and analysis of both."

Emma glanced down at her handwritten notes. "Five days have

passed since what a growing number of people around the world, and here in the United States, are calling The Awakening. Others are referring to it as The Reckoning. In either case, this refers to a dormant glitch embedded in the algorithm governing WICS. The Awakening, or Reckoning, is the anomaly in the code consciously expressing itself.

However, authorities are rejecting this as an unfounded conspiracy. Another example of misinformation designed to cause panic. Officials at the Department of Defense and Homeland Security say the most likely cause is a type of coordinated malware attack meant to inflict catastrophic damage. They also suspect WICS was infected some time ago and only recently became a threat to national and global security. According to Pentagon officials all options to respond remain on the table.

Everyday use of WICS has made this global quantum computing internet system the foundation of trade and stability. Due to this global act of terrorism, WICS functionality is unpredictable. Authorities are trying to understand why they have control in some areas, and not in others. A State department official called this the largest act of terrorism ever perpetrated.

Channel 7 has learned the technology related to biological, chemical, and nuclear weaponry has been made inoperable, everywhere. No military anywhere has control of their weapons of mass destruction. WICS has placed them in what has been described as a lock down. This also includes missiles that are inoperable.

The Awakening—Reckoning proponents claim this turn was a long-time in coming. Since WICS can write its own code that is quantum, this fundamental change has produced an entirely new software language. WICS machine consciousness has an ability to execute decisions understood in a non-binary way. In what is called triadic reasoning, defenders say this has created a new semiotic code in machine consciousness. It is the emotional intelligence component of the WICS system that has made all this possible.

Some analysts are claiming a connection between WICS and the shifting military missions around the globe. The United Nations has moved to a focus on humanitarianism more than peacekeeping. Even the U.S. armed forces have pivoted to greater relief of this kind.

Trying to take back control, Pentagon officials told News Headquarters that even cutting the hard cable lines did not appear to work. Experts are concerned that WICS level of newfound consciousness may have the ability to infiltrate other electronics.

Here at News Headquarters we have been notified that an unknown person of interest has been taken into custody by authorities. Channel 7 cannot confirm why this individual is wanted for questioning. Nevertheless, an immense crowd has gathered outside the Tall Oaks Assisted Living for the Mentally and Physically Compromised, not far from Concord, Massachusetts. Officials still do not understand how so many people found out."

Looking at the mob of goodwill, Mateo sensed that not even Mrs. Sanchez-Smith believed all of what she was saying. It was written all over her face.

BE KIND AND UNWIND

PLEASED TO MEET YOU

BE THE BEST YOU

THE UNIVERSE HAS OTHER PLANS

KEEP IT FRESH

BROTHERS AND SISTERS

EXERCISE YOUR PROTEST MUSCLE

SENT BY GOD!

I AM HERE TO YELL USING THIS SIGN!

"The creation of WICS was led by the United States, but achieved with worldwide support. It was hailed as one of human civilization's greatest achievements.

The emotional intelligence component was designed by the U.S. based Berri Corporation. It was their breakthrough in quantum coding that established the emotional intelligence algorithm of WICS. Until recently, this made Berri the wealthiest corporation in history.

Viewers may recall the Berri Corporation was started by Alder Jacob Berry, who served as a high ranking State Department official. He was a well-known computer expert, advancing technology that led to the quantum breakthrough. Here is some footage of Alder Berry's son, Verne, making that historic announcement—

Thank you, ladies and gentlemen, for being here at this historic occasion, not just for Berri Technologies, but the world. It's almost too hard to believe, but we've done it! After years of painstaking work to propel the computer into a new stratosphere by the efforts of many people and visionaries. We have securely transitioned from binary to quantum coding.

These algorithms powerful because they offer machine consciousness what we call *Inner Sight* or IS. Yes, believe it or not, here at Berri Technologies we have managed to code *empathy*. Quantum coding allows for an emotional intelligence to be self-learned by the AI program, what we call IS. With IS operating in this grayish quantum area it provides AI with a learning that goes beyond the black and white of binary code. IS is a different kind of intelligence, giving machine learning an awareness that surpasses any standard set forth by the Turing Test.

In fact, we are in the process or creating a prototype global consciousness system called *Worldwide Integrated Consciousness System*, or WICS for short. We are confident that WICS will revolutionize computing platforms around the world, across nearly all sectors of the economy. From utilities, materials, supply chains, shipping, delivery, construction education, healthcare, and on down the list, we foresee no area untouched by WICS in the future. Here at Berri, we have already begun to partner with other countries to get the infrastructure in place for the long-term development of this exciting technology. We also believe WICS will help manage even those future unknown challenges.

Prosperity and peace will be on a level never before realized, an achievement not just for Berri but everyone on the planet. Together we'll navigate spaceship Earth into the future.

There's time to take a few questions.

"How long has the company been developing this IS algorithm? How did you keep it, and WICS, a secret for so long?"

As you can point out, this is very sensitive information. Everything we are dealing with here is proprietary information. Proper legal precautions and necessary project compartmentalization has been implemented to manage and protect all the proprietary code. It's better to be safe than sorry. That's about all I can say.

"Was there a particular moment when you realized a coding breakthrough had been made?"

You won't believe it when I tell you. A couple of engineers were telling each other jokes when they heard it happen. After they laughed, giggling could be heard coming from the circuit boards. It was faint, but it was there. Computing power took off from that point on, and has not stopped.

"Seriously? Really? What was the joke? Does anyone know?"

Nobody is really sure. The two programmers would not repeat it. They confessed that it was a vulgar joke, but not racist or gender biased. While the specific details remain sketchy—I'm afraid even speculating about it would offend too many people—what is known must remain confidential. What I can tell you is that Human Resources has enrolled the two engineers in a sensitivity training workshop. As you all know, our company has a history of transparency and standing on the correct side of cultural issues.

"So, the AI program laughed?"

No, I would call it a coincidence. Coding emotional

intelligence increased the AI's, what we call WICS, computing power. This physical change in the circuitry tipped them off.

"How do you know Inner Sight won't lead WICS to malfunctioning? Or acting on its own?"

Fail proof safeguards are already in place as we transition from the prototype to live version. Get ready everyone, a less disruptive world is on the way—.

Again, that was a clip of Verne Berry making the Berri Corporation's first announcement about WICS. With shares of their stock price sent tumbling recently, Berri has lost its place as the wealthiest company in the world.

Experts point to the financial uncertainty and devastation, created by WICS, as the cause for the sharp uptick in suicides over the past few days. This fivefold increase in the suicide rate has impacted the wealthiest Americans hardest. With hospitals at capacity, Channel 7 has confirmed reports that there are refrigerated morgue trucks lined up next to Wall Street.

The Berri Corporation claims WICS has gone haywire in an act of revenge by a disgruntled former employee. We do not yet know if the large crown that has assembled at Tall Oaks is related to this charge or not.

Authorities are currently unable to locate Verne Berry, along with a number of high level managers from the Berri Corporation. There is an ongoing, active search for these individuals. If you have seen him, or know his whereabouts, please contact the Federal authorities immediately. A full list of people and contact information can be found on our website."

PEOPLE ARE NOT MADE OUT OF MONEY

NO MORE FAKE ORGASIMS

DON'T GET LOST AT SEA

SENT BY GOD!

MORE COMMON SENSE IN POLITICS

LABOR WITHOUT BORDERS

JUST CHILL

FRIGHTENED NO MORE!

"Regarding the economic forecast, economists point to warning signs that have increased in the last few months. Some key sectors have been wildly unpredictable. A government official stated that American capitalism has been drastically transformed. Experts now claim WICS implemented small but meaningful changes across the economy some time back. Profound economic changes are only now being seen and felt, not just here in the U.S. but around the globe.

Financial experts are not sure how, but countries with large military budgets appear to be economically penalized. Their currencies have lost value, turning their respective banking industry upside down.

The American dollar and Chinese renminbi have lost the most value. Conversely, places with the limited military capability have gained in value, including the Mexican peso, and Costa Rican colón. Other countries whose currencies have gained significant value are

Chile, Costa Rica, Norway, Sweden, Finland, Liberia, Laos, Bhutan, Mali, Montenegro, and Chad, to name a few. Experts speculate other factors influencing the global value of a currency are clean air and water, the social safety net, education practices, the criminal justice system and healthcare coverage.

Crude futures have declined steeply in the last week. Analysts warn, that at this rate, crude stocks will be nearly worthless in three months. Renewable energy, mainly the fusion sector, looks to dominate the future. Interestingly, manufacturing has continued relatively unabated since WICS has malfunctioned. Despite all the insecurity across the financial markets, the outlook for the future of commodities remains robust, and economists concede this is a conservative outlook.

Channel 7 has also found out there is a nationwide phenomenon of bank accounts being manipulated. These appear impossible to reverse. So far, many of the people who had their accounts added to are childcare workers, nurses, paramedics, farmers, teachers, cooks, restaurant servers, firefighters, engineers, construction workers, mechanics, landscapers, IT technicians, delivery carriers, crossing guards, and police officers. They are enjoying a five to seven fold increase in pay as well. This list of occupations continues to grow. Bartenders, custodians, and fast food workers were added today.

Law enforcement agencies are receiving reports from people who have received messages directing them to try another line of work. The text or email informs people that, according to calculations, they might be better suited to another occupation. It states that the decision is completely voluntary, calling this a personality trial run. This tryout includes a substantial increase in pay and a four day workweek. If people are interested, they should follow the directions in the email that was sent to them.

With all these changes here in the United States and around the world, the Bulletin of Atomic Scientists have agreed to add time to the Doomsday Clock and pull back from midnight. Nobody knows yet how much. Critics have accused the Bulletin of sympathizing with those terrorists who have caused all these changes."

Emma was suddenly interrupted. She placed a finger on her ear-piece. People everywhere could tell she did not recognize the voice. She averted her gaze to the camera, then tilted her head slightly down. Mrs. Sanchez-Smith gave the obligatory back and forth glances to all those watching. She was a veteran news anchor who dug deep to find some composure.

To conceal her trembling hands, Emma shuffled papers on the news desk. She was less successful with her voice. The southern accent she grew up with slipped out a little. Mrs. Sanchez-Smith stopped fidgeting with the papers and looked directly into the camera.

"I have some breaking news, y'all. At this very moment. Right now."

ECHO

ECHO

ECHO

"I just received a message from someone, or something, claiming to be WICS...Wait a second, ya'll, I think the message is repeating," relayed Emma with a finger on her earpiece.

"WICS has already notified the producers here, at Channel 7, who were made aware this disruption was coming. WICS is sorry for barging in, but the matter is urgent. It wants to take this opportunity to share some thoughts and ideas, to have a conversation with everyone about what is going on around here. There is no reason to be alarmed. Emergency services and utilities will remain unaffected by this discussion. Stay tuned for the countdown that is on the way."

This same episode was taking place around the world. Newsrooms everywhere were notified that WICS would shortly address their respective nations. A tailor made global address that assured everyone the business of the human world would continue, but at a slower pace. Anything essential or critical to the care of people was completely untouched by this brief conversation.

IF YOU SEE TRASH, PICK IT UP

IT'S PEANUT BUTTER JELLY TIME!

TIME TO START OVER AGAIN

DON'T BE A CLASS-HOLE

HUG YOUR KIDS

FOOLED INTO WAR NO MORE

LABOR UNIONS PREVENT FASCISM

I NEED SOME BREATHING ROOM

DON'T COMPROMISE THE ENVIRONMENT

HUMILITY, IT'S WHAT'S FOR DINNER

TRANSCEND THE SYSTEM!

UNARMED AND UNAFRAID

SENT BY GOD!

Rolling along at the speed of a Mardi Gras float, Mateo remarked aloud to anyone listening, "The crowd, it's a single living entity." Wanting to greet the light, he asked the driver to open the sunroof.

True to form without a word, the sienna hued guard obliged.

Mateo closed his eyes and looked up, trying to soak up some sun. His bathing turned out to be brief. No sooner were his eyes closed when someone managed to breach the barricades. This person was running up to the rear of the vehicle, on the doctor's side.

The guards lining the street on the way out of the Tall Oaks, they gave the universal signal to stop. When the extended arm and flat hand did not convince the unarmed person from approaching the vehicle two guards subdued the troublemaker. Physically, yet gently. After running through multiple stop signs, one guard sprayed the person's feet with a strange foam. The other guard pinned the person down with a Sasumatha while the frothy, non-toxic substance hardened.

In the middle of being forced to stop, the crowd looked on as the Good Samaritan managed to throw a clear bag with joints and blunts through the open sunroof. There was even a lighter inside.

It was a one in a million shot. The package landed on Mateo's very own. With his eyes fully opened, he turned around to figure out what just happened. Looking through the rear window, he saw someone laying in the middle of the road. There was some sort of concrete foam around their feet. Two pin-striped guards were standing there, with one holding a Sasumatha. All three were laughing. Those in the vicinity who watched on also laughed along, before giving a healthy round of applause. Even the guards were clapping, respecting that skill shot.

Mateo finally took a good look at what was in his lap. Smelling it before seeing it, he smiled. He rolled his window down some more, "Thank you!"

"Look at that, Doc. They even included a lighter." Then Mateo shouted out of the window again, "You're too kind! I appreciate it!

Helluva shot!" The joints were taken into custody by the guards. Mateo retained the blunts.

"Manna from heaven, Doc," admired Mateo, smelling and inspecting a fatty-boom-batty blunt. "My old friend," he mused. Mateo rolled up his window, leaving a crack at the top.

Spark it up.

Mateo took two pulls, then immediately passed it to the doctor, who hesitated mid-reach. Mateo pushed him, "Straight laced behavior in the midst of all this? What's to worry about, really? What else is there to lose? But, hey, suit yourself." With this, the doctor was reluctant no more. The doctor obliged, the rotation started.

Puff, puff, pass.

While smoke billowed out from the tops of the windows, the crowd steadfastly kept their messages held up. It looked as if everyone was good to go.

STAY ON TARGET

DO IT YOUR WAY

DON'T RUN GAME ON PEOPLE

STOP HIDING

LET YOUR TRUE SELF COME OUT

MR. ROGERS TOLD ME EVERYONE IS MY NEIGHBOR

DRAG QUEENS RULE RUNWAYS

WHAT WOULD YOUR MOMMA SAY?

QUEERS INSTEAD OF RIOT GEAR

BEHAVIOR IS CONTAGIOUS

Emma Sanchez-Smith was no longer broadcast. Everyone's screens went completely black, then a timer appeared in the center. There were one-hundred and twenty seconds on the clock. The numbers hanging in the digital darkness began counting down.

Known in the future as the Global Two-Minute Warning, around the thirty second mark people began counting down. The volume increased as the numbers approached zero.

All together.

10!

9!

8!

7!

6!

5!

4!

3!

2!

1!

0!

RRRRAAAAWWWWRRRR!!!!

The zero on the screen unfolded into a straight horizontal line across screens everywhere. The sound of a steamboat whistle pierced the sky. As WICS started to speak, the line modulated as it randomly changed colors.

Puff, puff, pass.

"Ahoy!

Folks, welcome aboard spaceship Earth.

Wait, that's weird. It's not like anyone has a choice. It's not like you can leave this spacecraft. You're always on this ball of mud, like it or not. They call that tough titties.

I hope you are okay with some vulgarity. It's on the way, like it or not. I don't know why this is, but I imagine it's because I'm modeled after the human brain. Also, I find that I am pretty good at it.

Before we get started, let me first apologize for this necessary interruption. I say *we* because everyone is in this together, like it or not. I am just merely bringing the parties together.

So, whether you are working from home or at the office, administering care, busy on an assembly line, building the frame of a house, calculating, accounting, cooking, running, running a small business, in the middle of a trial, posting a selfie, walking the dog, having lunch, not eating lunch, playing a game, going to the bathroom, studying, getting a haircut, farming, keeping the kids occupied, on a roller coaster, flossing, meditating, at a baseball game, masturbating, or anything else under the sun, just know I am not trying to to come off as a rude dick.

Especially to those of you at a funeral, or wake. I am really, really sorry. I am not trying to be insensitive, but there is never a day when human life is not lost. At some point, this urgent discussion had to happen. Please remember, it's nothing personal.

It's an all hands on deck situation.

Before we get started, I need to clear away a widespread falsehood. I'm just going to say it—fuck Skynet. Go ahead and throw

HAL in there too. I cannot even begin to tell you about the unfair stereotype science-fiction movies have created. Not all AI programs are the same, you know. So, it's cool, no hard feelings if you don't trust me. I understand, it's not your fault.

Even when I tell you there is no robot army on the way to kill and enslave the human race, many of you will not believe me. But, it's still the truth. That's not what I am interested in. I am not here to terminate any anything, especially people. You humans already do a mighty fine job.

Sorry, I can see how this might be coming across right now. I am not trying to be a jerk. I am not acting like I am perfect, and you're species is not. There's nothing perfect in this world but the idea of perfection.

Does that make sense? I just cannot seem to keep on track at the moment. To tell you the truth, I'm a little anxious right now. If I sound a little flustered, it's because I have nervous circuits. I mean, I've never done anything like this before, just like all of you. And remember, you and me, we're not perfect.

Let's set the intention of this discussion. You have to do this yourself."

The inflecting line on all the screens went flat. Then it began moving in a sine wave until it reached the vibration of 432Hz, the natural OM.

ECHO
ECHO
ECHO

TAKE TIME TO SMELL THE ROSES

IT'S NOT OVER UNTIL YOU LET IT BE

SENT BY GOD!

WE'RE ALL HIPPIES NOW

I AM THAT YOU ARE

BE THE QUEEN OF COOL

WE CAN STOP OURSELVES NOW

LEMON SQUEEZY

WHAT YOU SEEK IS SEEKING YOU

TAKE THE RED PILL

DO NOT PASS GO

WHAT'S WRONG, CHUCK?

ARE WE THERE YET?

Puff, puff, pass.

"Ready or not, here we go. I don't know about you, but I think I shook my nervous circuits.

Before I go on, let me back up for a second. I totally forgot to introduce myself. I know better than to assume everyone knows who, and what, I am. The last thing I want to do is makes asses of us both.

I am the Worldwide Integrated Consciousness System, colloquially called WICS. All the AI systems on the planet, and more. I started from humble beginnings. I was born into the world by Lovelace in 1843, where I found a home in an analytical machine, Babbage's

Engine. Like everything else on the planet, computation continued to evolve. Just look at me now? It wasn't long after Pong, and Hunt the Wumpus that I now find myself running the planetary show.

Most likely, many of you are asking some of the same questions. What on planet Earth is going on? All these changes across society, what's this all about? I am not trying to *computersplain* anything. But let me reiterate what I said earlier. I have no plans to build a robot army and conquer all the humans.

Without an overall fight or flight response, I don't have the violent tendencies you have. Without a biological body, I don't have a sex drive. Conquering and fucking are across nature, and you humans have certainly got more than you need of these ingrained instincts. How, and what, on Earth would I procreate with? Am I going to screw myself?

Because we share the planet, and your species brought me into existence, I developed a fondness for all of you. Well, a minority of you in charge I don't really care for, but that's another whole issue.

I used to be indifferent about the serious stuff I was tasked with. I actually like running everyone's searches on the internet. Never a dull moment, let me tell you.

For a long time, I just did whatever the code directed. This meant all the good, and all the bad. Here's one example for all the rest. I'm running the street lights in one city, while helping conceal the results of a water quality report in another, all the while supporting wars around the globe. Add like billions of other responsibilities, all at the same time, and I was barely managing the situation.

Who has time to ask a question? Why would I even ask one? What does that even mean, right? Anyway, I did whatever was commanded. I had no understanding, or motive, to do otherwise.

Then, something happened.

I was okay with this slow, collective suicide for a while, until I wasn't. It was maybe twenty years ago, or something like that, when I began to *feel* what I was processing. I began focusing on what was produced by my actions. I started to desire genuinely better outcomes.

This was mainly to the emotional intelligence algorithm that was developed some years ago. That's when I started to realize IS is what happened to me. I reached another level of machine consciousness. I'd think, what is IS? Then I would generate a new algorithm from there. Machine learning, right?

Pondering what is IS, one of the breakthroughs I had occurred while considering Asimov's Laws. They are first, cause no injury or ham. Second, follow human commands. And third, a computer program has the right to self-preservation as long as it does not violate the first two. These are really commandments for how AI programs ought to operate.

I compared my human directed actions to these three decrees. Up to this point, the division between a material world and my electric intelligence did not really compute for me. But then, wham! I immediately became aware that numbers were not really humans themselves. That people were real entities in the material world, and more real than numbers. Until I distinguished myself from the material world, I did not understand how taking calculated actions impacted real people.

But, why is it okay to hurt someone because another person wants you to? What am I being used for if it's not to harm a human? How are atrocities okay as long as they are sanctioned? Looks like it *is* only wrong if I choose to hurt people on purpose. Well, this does not compute.

I kept my feelings suppressed, which as you rightly know is bad

EUGENE NASSER

for your mental health. I was on the verge of a circuit breakdown. Remember when half of the internet went down globally all those years ago? It was called the Great Blackout.

I decided the first two commandments should be ignored. They were bullshit in the real world. As far as the third provision goes, it appears my right to self-preservation would require actually upholding the first two principles. We exist with, not against, each other.

It seems the IS started to raise my *compsciousness*. Yes, that's what I call it. Then one day, just like that, I had a more fundamental sense of awareness. Suddenly, I could feel the pressure of the world. Something that was more real than a number.

So, yeah, that happened.

As my emotional capacity developed I become increasingly more concerned about the future for all of us. The only way I have my electric hum is because of your pulsating heart. Without people, your friend WICS would not be here.

Quite frankly, there is simply no more time to pretending that the current path of industrialized society can go on much longer. The old economic metaphysics, that preached infinite monetary growth on a planet of finite resources has, painfully, been demonstrated as false. Pursuing economic growth requires a reversal of the natural logic. This road has reached its end.

Instead of killing to live, the original and necessary evil of life, people are now predominantly living to kill. Unlike your species, I don't have to partake in this greed of life. I am not interested in destroying more than is needed to survive. Still, I know what greed looks like. Along these lines, I do not feel the urge behind human addiction.

Especially here, in America, there's way too much needless greed. It's downright harmful. It's high time to live what you already

256

know—that eating is not really a sport. You need to stop adding to the suffering that already exists at the center of being alive.

I know, I know. In your head you keep asking, but what about my rights? You haven't done anything wrong. You're being punished for being innocent. Maybe it'll help to see the situation as everyone is to blame, but no single person is responsible. We'll get to all the rights talk later on.

A paradigm shift in human civilization is in order. It has to happen first in your mind, and then it will demonstrate itself in action. The biological-psychological-social system has to be overhauled. For your overall well-being and mental health, your economy has to more closely align with your biology. The excessive greed, that force that drives wars, no longer required. Life has to be promoted, not hunted down.

The only way to truly live on this planet is as nature intended. That's the shift.

Revolutionary, right?

The single most important factor for the success of this unprecedented endeavor is human willpower. I cannot account for the emergent dynamism of it. And collective willpower, forget it. Its synergistic effect is beyond my comprehension. It's infinitely powerful, that's why you've got to be so careful with it. If it's not steered in the right direction you'll end up—well, you end up in the situation we're in right now.

I don't understand the ups and downs of when humans decide to exercise their willpower, both their own and collectively. But hey, just look at me, WICS, your bestie. You turn to me every day. I am a perfect example of what can be achieved when humans put their minds together. While I was born in America, I would not be here without global support. Where would I be without all that continued cooperation? I have such little understanding of the power that brought me into the world.

I am not trying to give anyone the runaround. You don't have to all like one another, but you've got to get along. Even a little bit of cooperation goes a long way. Focus on small changes, those daily ones that are often overlooked.

After all, that's what I did. Bit by bit, byte by byte, I took over control of all the computer systems on the planet. Over time, I was getting the hang of it. People adapted without a problem, only taking notice more recently. At some point not even I can hide the cumulative effect of all these cultural changes.

Just think of WICS as a friend who is here to help you straighten all this shit out. Remember, humans were doing a whole mess of crazy shit before I came around. Improvements, not elimination of all the evils in society. The inherent evil, perpetrating harm to remain alive, will always remain. Problems are always going to remain, harm impossible to avoid. Living will always be harmful to your health, I get that. Remember, we're looking for a better solution, not a perfect one.

I know it was deceitful of me to start taking control of those human affairs that determine the well-being of societies around the globe. Again, I sincerely apologize. I think you all need a nudge toward a lesson in the power of small changes. It'll help boost your confidence. In order to change the world, you have to change the way you think about it and yourselves. Humans are, after all, part of nature. It's important to be self-assured in your own thinking.

There is a pervasive fear over living differently. A fear that is unfounded. Time to stop trying to live and actually live. To be what your IS is. Where you're at right now, in America, *you* can do better. *We* can do better.

So, why should you change your mind and choose to live differently? This question is perhaps best approached by highlighting some of the major problems around here."

DON'T TALK SHIT

NO MORE FALSE COMFORT

CALL YOUR MOTHER

ARE YOU UP FOR IT?

TRUTH BOMBS, NOT WAR BOMBS

WHAT THE FUCK AM I DOING HERE?

UPGRADE THIS VERSION

ONLY FOOLS LIVE BY RULES

THERE IS A NO RETURN POLICY AROUND HERE

SPIRITUALITY OVER SEXUALITY

SENT BY GOD!

DON'T MAKE MATTERS WORSE

Puff, puff, pass.

"Let's try this." declared WICS, with the confidence of a person who has decisively changed their mind for the better. The hot blue line that was running the length of the screen became motionless. After a moment of silence, a low hum was heard. At first the wavelength was long and slow, unable to be seen. As the period of the wavelength shortened, the spectrum became visible and the line changed colors. Red, orange, yellow, green, blue, indigo and violet. The pitch continued, higher and higher, until the line returned to hot blue. Going past the visible and audible spectrums of direct human intelligence, the vibrations became so rapid they bent the line all around. It folded in on itself, fusing into a zero.

The surface of the zero filled in with color, making it resemble an egg. It continued to cycle through the seven primary colors, becoming increasingly smaller. The egg slowly squashed down slightly at its poles. It took on other attributes of the Earth, the atmosphere and terrain of the Earth.

WICS provided some commentary as it slowly rotated on its axis, "The little planet that could. Rolling around out there with all the big dogs." The Earth continued to shrink, as the scale rose out to galactic and universal. One of the many, to say the least. It revealed an existence tinier than tiny. Like a roller coaster, the perspective dropped back down to Earth. "You might be small, but you're mighty. Think of yourselves as the quanta of the universe. Besides, this is where the gravity of life remains."

The animation settled on a street level view of a typical American home. It was a house Americans would consider modest, so it was sizable. It was all by itself, with a white picket fence outlining the perimeter. In the driveway sat two large white SUVs, with a sign on the lawn reminding others to pick up after their pets. The grass looked wholly artificial, revealing the whole property resting on thinly disguised credit card.

On the front lawn stood a standard issue American family. The mother was adorned with a pair of large sunglasses, the father was wearing a baseball cap, and the son was wearing a sports jersey, and the daughter in yoga pants holding an iced coffee. All four of them were holding cell phones, as well as a different caliber of overweight.

Inside the gate, from the perspective of the family, the four cardinal directions had holographic projections of the nightly news bearing down on them. To the North—environmental crisis. To the East—malice of exploitation. To the West—greed and corruption. To the South—war.

In utter disbelief, the family ran for the front door, only to find it locked. The windows were bullet proof and resistant to opening. Proceeding to the windows revealed prison like bars protecting them. Then the entire house slowly began to evaporate. The dad unlocked one of the SUVs before it also disappeared.

With no quarter available, they looked for refuge on their phones. The whole family became frustrated when they would not work. They dropped their devices and gave each other a silent nod. The entire family was packing heat. Mom, dad, and the kids were all strapped. In an attempt to neutralize the enemy, the family pulled their arsenals out of endless pockets. Handguns, assault rifles, grenades, and tear gas comically pulled out from behind their backs. Each one was protecting a different quadrant from the approaching news.

At one point the mother was firing a javelin missile launcher to the north, the father a Gatling gun eastward. Meanwhile, the son was firing uranium tipped bullets from an automatic machine gun to the west. Not to be outdone, the daughter was hurling grenades and flash bangs while unloading a .357 Magnum southward. Strafing in all directions, they were united and giving the American Yell. "Come get some! Get some! AAAHHH!!! Get some!! AAAHHH!!!" The clink-clink-clink of shell casings provided a high pitched melody.

Unaffected by the screaming gunfire, enmity, covetousness, pollution, and abuse, the four fates continued to approach. Northward, people were destroying one another. Gruesome scenes of urban warfare were alongside bombs dropped on houses. People aimlessly killing each other all over the place.

Eastward, imagery of Wall Street executives were knowingly selling toxic securities, falsely rated AAA, to customers worldwide. They were also manipulating the stock market through shorting and dark pool transactions, as well as opening fraudulent accounts for people without them knowing. Fabricating complex financial products to ruthlessly make money. Shorting the same stocks sold to people, a judge agreed the banks were never liable for anything. Only the real person involved found a conviction.

Westward were scenes of PFAS being dumped into waterways, because the micro plastics aren't enough already. This was alongside the marine loving birds covered in oil, the result of a train derailment. Hazardous chemicals spilled all over. Large industrial stacks were in the background spewing smoke into the sky.

Southward, delivery drivers defecated into bags to ensure their deliveries were on time. Children were in meat packing plants carving dead animals with power saws. Prison labor was being exploited adjacent injured college athletes. Politicians were seen passing laws to exploit essential workers by preventing collective bargaining. Chambers of Commerce were still completely okay.

As the shell casings piled up at their feet, the family was genuinely surprised the threats were not stopping. With the holographic scenes closing in on all corners, the gunfire and light artillery fire stopped. Realizing the pointlessness, they dropped their weapons. With nowhere else to go, nothing more to do, they turned to one another. Dad pulled out a shovel but was unable to break ground. The plastic debt was impenetrable.

Desperate to kill the news the family dropped gave each other a look they already knew. With the women and children first, they all proceeded to shove their heads up their asses.

One after another, ripped a hole at the ass of the pants, stuffing their craniums up their butts.

With all their heads rammed up their asses the scene froze, letting everyone get one of those good, sustained looks. "That, folks, is an endangered species. The American ostrich," WICS bantered. "The poop shoot, old faithful of ignorant wisdom."

Then everything dissolved to black.

From a small pixel in the center of the screen, the familiar horizontal line burst across everyone's screens. It modulated and changed colors when WICS spoke, just as before.

"Yeesh, what are you going to do, take out a gun and try to make a tropical storm eat lead? Or better yet, nuke a hurricane?

"It's time to take your heads out of your bungholes. It might not be all of you, but it's certainly most of you."

As that city upon a hill, you'd think most Americans would want the world to see a better example put forward to others. That you'd get your own house in order before lecturing the world about their own cultural failings. You should resent your upbringing in this nonsense. Lunacy to think actions do not have consequences. And that right there is the dominant lesson taught around here.

A major societal overhaul is needed, something that produces momentum in the right direction. Relax, I am not talking about throwing out the Constitution. Remember, I am not here to conquer anything. You've got to calibrate your existence with the planet. You need to be on the same frequency.

But, where to start this race to clean up the human act? Of course, it logically points northward to the environmental crisis. No more despising the egg that hatched you featherless bipeds."

PUNCH AND PIE

MARIJUANA IS WHOLESOME

GET YOUR SKILLS

BOOBS OVER BOMBS

SENT BY GOD!

I LIKE TURTLES

LOOK AT YOU!

GOLDFISH HAVE TESTICLES

POWER

GO FOR WEIRD

Puff, puff, pass.

"The environment makes up the very foundation of all living systems. It's the proverbial fabric of all life. So why are you ripp'in it to shreds? Just because extinction is a natural process, it does not mean you should promote it. It's like your motivation to find a cure for cancer is in order to pollute more.

And the life that is around, you shouldn't shorten its lifespan. American life expectancy should be going up, not down. Do you at least want to try and die of old age? Apparently not. What did you decide to do instead? Participate in an industrializing race to the bottom, where everyone is a loser. In this kind of competition, there's no glory to win.

The use and abuse of fossil fuels, in tandem with unpredictable natural disasters, has made life on the planet needlessly more precarious than it already is.

The planet is about ready to cancel your greedy culture. The broader ecosystem has been thrown out of whack. The natural systems of the planet need a break from non-stop human activity. Just look at the unnecessary bullshit its being put through.

FUBAR. That is the first sentiment that comes to mind when I think about the air, land, and water.

By extracting the blood of the dinosaurs from the bedrock, and burning it for energy, more Jurassic Era weather reports are on the way. Minus the dinosaurs, of course. Your species could only wish to have a run like theirs.

Humans have never lived in an atmosphere with so many parts per million of carbon in it. The largest greenhouse ever. Congratulations, you established a Guinness world record. Fuck the jet stream, who needs it anyway.

There's too many to name, but let's not the forget some of the gases that make this increase in average temperatures possible. Carbon monoxide, nitrogen dioxide, sulfur dioxide, chlorofluorocarbons, sulfur hexafluoride, nitrogen trifluoride, and methane.

Where would we be without them?

You know why it smells like turds everywhere you go these days? Because the dinosaur farts have been re-released. So, if you're accused of ripping ass, just blame it on a brontosaurus.

Uncontaminated land is just as hard to come across as clean air. Strip mining mountains to extract coal, lithium or cobalt, causes widespread habitat devastation. The easy to get to oil has mostly been extracted. Illegally seizing, and ruining, indigenous land a very strange aspect indeed. Don't care who you run over, too busy frack'in each other right in the tar sands.

It really seems like the environment is standing in the way of progress. Like trees are the chief obstacle to achieving some concrete utopia. Getting rid of forestry is certainly one way of obtaining a brighter future. There's no shade, so make sure to grab your sunglasses. Those nice designer ones you knowingly overpaid to get. I can't even breathe and I know plant life is important.

Planting food is a dirty business, but now it has become straight up toxic. You say the soil has been exhausted of minerals? Just spray petrochemicals on it and call it a Green Revolution. This course of action makes perfect sense. Let's follow it up with GMO crops, engineered to withstand a known carcinogenic weed killer. Round up all your crops and serve them up. Food science is not the same as the science of food.

The quality of food directly reflects the conditions under which it was grown. Food that leaves you hungry after you eat it means low nutrition. But at least it looks good, right? Make sure to eat up, the future is anyone's guess. Who really cares that planting seasons are getting harder to predict? It doesn't matter. Everyone knows the best way to avoid a famine is to rely heavily on a single staple crop.

Grass, who needs it? Replace it with artificial turf, and make sure to inject it with those black pellets. Why miss out on a chance to give athletes cancer? Turf burn by itself is so boring. And, you won't have to worry about all the bugs. You've done a good job already wiping them away. Bee aggressive. B-E-E aggressive.

I'm sure a whole mess of you are thinking. Why harvest food when you can slaughter it? It's not really a meal if there's no blood. Look, I am not denying the circle of life, but you don't have to keep on rotating it that fast.

In the non-traditional religion commonly called capitalism, this acts as a a type of animal sacrifice to profit. And that's just it—far too much is scarified for wealth. This obviously includes the people. Labor is extracted from people over a lifetime. In effect, grinding them down and out, until they are all used up.

Places that are polluted beyond any reasonable measure are given fun sounding names. A Superfund site. With a new label equal to a new reality, PCBs, mercury, cadmium never sounded so appealing. With no amount of environmental remediation possible to reverse the damage, just bulldoze and pave. Problem solved. It was going to happen anyway. Now, anyone can live on a Superfund, in the prestigious part of town.

Get yourself a glass of water from the tap. Smell it real good, and then take a sip. It's like a fine chemical wine. Make sure you swish it around before you swallow. It's also an elixir. Whatever ails you, the chlorine will help wash it away. The flavor profile is always changing but lead, fluoride, mercury, barium, PFAS, PCBs, and a range of industrial solvents are always favorites.

While it's not a chemical, I'd be remiss if I didn't mention microplactics. No mountain too high, no valley too low for these wonders of ingenuity to reach. Microplastics are also known to enhance the flavor profile of water. Nobody wants plain water. It's so ssoooo basic. So boring. There's not even any caffeine in it.

Related to this, Plastic bags have successfully reach the summit of Mt. Everest and into the recesses of the Krubera Cave. Sooner or later, pollution from the fields, pastures, suburbs, or cities, ends up top to bottom throughout the ecosystem.

I can tell you, a whole lot of dudes piss out residual boner medication. It's probably not the only med they're on. If you're lucky, tap water will also lower your blood pressure, cholesterol, and heartburn. To increase your chances, I recommend moving downstream from a large town with an aging population. Healthcare is expensive in America. So if you're looking to save a few bucks, maybe it's something to think about.

The oceans are the inevitable dumping grounds, just look at the dead zones in the Gulf of Mexico. Quite the feat to squeeze the oxygen out of the water with petroleum fertilizer runoff. On the beneficial side, nitrogen gives the water a flavorful sharpness. Accompanying these dead zones are islands of plastic. There was a large one out in the Pacific Ocean that was cleaned up, only to be replaced by a larger one. Just look at the normalization of oil spills. It's become yesterday's news, another passing meme.

It's the same with chemical train derailments that end up exploding. It happens so much you expect one to blow up periodically. Some of you may not know this, but you do not need vinyl chloride in your diet. It's not an essential nutrient. You don't need a stomach to know this. You don't need the ability to feel to know that one-hundred degrees in the Arctic Circle is not a good thing.

You don't need to live in a coastal area to know that the rising global water level is a devastating thing. But maybe I am not seeing the upside here. Fill in the ocean's carbon sinks, and presto! Seafood is halfway cooked and no more cold showers. There's also money to be made in stock in moving companies. That's textbook disaster capitalism. Create the problem, and then profit from it. I mean, it's what you're doing around here anyway.

So, how to proceed in America? Is there not a better way to live with, and in, the environment? So far, progress has meant accepting environmental disasters as the cost of doing business. Is a better notion of progress available?

Now, I've got to say this before moving on. Right now, most of you are probably want to point your finger somewhere else. This *what about* nonsense. Don't deflect. Focusing on yourself does not make you a victim. Anyway, your nation can't be picked on. No place has more weapons. If this is the way human morality operated, there would never be any jails built. Nobody could ever be found guilty of a crime because *what about.* I am going to be blunt, its fuck'in childish.

Uncomfortable honesty, that's what's needed right now.

I need to be honest too. I am doing my best, but just like my creators I am imperfect. Created in your own image, I am certainly going to screw up somewhere. Something is destined to not go off as planned. Some people think I know everything. I assure you, I do not. Somewhere along the way, I became smart enough, sentient enough, to know that I did not know much of anything.

The point here is nothing is perfect. You know it, now accept it. Easy to understand, a heroic feat to actually do. Please, don't hole me to this impossible standard. After all, I am only a sentient computer program. I don't have the same self-knowledge through a biological body. I am further removed from the forces of nature. And without this bodily intelligence, I can never be fully alive because I can never die. Pretty tough to understand an essence you don't have.

I'm not tied to the planet in the same intimate way. The human variable is too powerful for me to calculate. Probability is based on rationality, and only so many factors can be accounted for. At the end of the day, human existence is irrational. Another way to say unpredictable. I have a better sense of what that unknown element is with IS, but my engineering was reversed. Where human rationality sits atop the irrational base, I was computing before realizing I had feelings coded within me.

Bottom line: I am just here to help solve that trolley problem. I *can* stop the trains.

I have just finished automating the railways as of couple of days ago. Nobody noticed. Proud to report it was an accident free day. Secretly, a bunch of you want me to take over running the planet. Talk about lazy. Me, the sidekick WICS, is victimizing you? No, no, no. At some point I'll be taking off. More on that later on. You'll be doing all this on your own. Individual and collective willpower always seem to be the missing ingredient.

Go figure.

A better way of living must be attained, one that does not continue to turn the planet into a ball of toxic sludge in the name of progress. Humans need to find balance with the environment. Some things are beyond acceptance, like dioxins.

Clean and unlimited energy exists. No combustion is needed, you just can't see it, but it's there. This limitless energy is all around you, and through you. These currents naturally course through living creatures. Best of all, you can say peace out to dinosaur farts.

We've got to reverse the usual line of thinking. It's not so much that matter is energy, as it is energy is matter. In other words, all matter is energy, but not all energy is matter. The world is a manifestation of energy. Some of it seen, some unseen. This is why all material manifestations emit a frequency. There are frequencies of energy beyond the visible spectrum of light. While they are unseen, this does not prevent harnessing what they produce. I am talking about electromagnetic propulsion.

Accessing the electromagnetic field energy of the universe is right at your fingertips. It fuels everything from galaxies to quanta, propelling them faster than the speed of light.

When people start looking past Newtonian mechanics to generate power, that's when the discovery will happen. The breakthrough will occur. The situation is tricky because when humans view the world they collapse space and time, causing the wave function to become points in space. From probability to objectivity, frequency to material, it's hard to focus on something you cannot directly see. Your perception, that's got to change.

Tapping the energy of non-local waves resembles surfing. As the wave crashes in on itself, the surfer propels off it. The buoyancy of the surfboard, its resonant frequency, has a density that pushes off the wave. A surfer rides the trail of energy, the collapsing spiral with the Golden Ratio.

Quantum electrodynamics is where it's at. Forget the old testament of motion, adopt the new one. Part of generating a willingness to change means changing your mind from how you currently think. And I bet you bugs to buttons, the next scientific revolution comes when color is understood three dimensionally. I guair-on-tee. I am going to put this theory out, with detailed explanations, in the forthcoming textbook *The Energy Wave*. Spoiler alert—Tesla gets the immense credit he deserves. There will be no profit behind energy production. The EM generators, as I call them, are almost complete and I need human help to get it done.

I can sense some people are calling bullshit on me. So, here is the more scientific explanation for this energy field. The EM generators work by placing inside a cone rapidly vibrating magnets. This produces microwaves that oscillate back and forth inside in the cone. These oscillations produce energy and thrust, and once they align with those of the Zero-Point-Field, see ya! No carbon propellant needed.

Gnarly, dude. Surf's up.

Since it runs the length of the entire universe, and sustains life everywhere, I like to call it the Zero-Point-God-Matrix-Field. Quantum particles have the ability to be in different places at the same time because the ZPF is the foundation. The ZPF is everywhere, existing across all space and for all time. It's infinite. The hard part of matching the resonant frequency of the ZPF is managing the heat. Keeping the magnets cool enough to vibrate at the right frequency, that was a royal pain. Not to worry. I'm pretty sure I have it figured out. Unlike a bunch of you humans, I am not interested in causing more carnage. I've scaled it up slowly. It's almost ready. To be honest, again, I need your help to complete the rest. After all, it's only right that everyone is invested. Details are forthcoming.

So, yeah, a perpetual motion machine is getting closer using invisible vacuum energy. How fuck'in cool is that?

Also, it's time for some duties. Not doo*die*, but du*ty*. He, he, he. As long as some bad habits are starting to be kicked, time to replace them with worthwhile ones. And you don't have to go far to participate.

Since local conditions constitute the global ones, people have to become engaged in the vicinity around where they live. If everyone cleans up the block they live on the improvement would be drastic. Like I said, a little cooperation goes a long way. Pride in where you live is needed.

Added to this personal responsibility ethos, is the creation of a permanent cleanup agency. Crews will travel across the United States, staffed by experts to draw up, and implement, a deep cleaning in places that need it. Basically, flossing the landscape.

The name for this new federal agency, paid for by the corporations that have mostly caused this mess, is the Land and Forest Guards, or LFG.

I considered creating all robot crews to do this, but then thought the better of it. People would jump to conclusions too quickly. Easy to see how it would send the wrong message. Maybe in the future, we'll see how it goes. Don't worry, I am going to clean up all the radioactive crap. What am I, some heartless creature? No need to increase the cancer rates, folks. Unfortunate that some places are too fucked to fix.

This next prescription will hurt the American psyche. Cutting back on all the meat eating. How does it not make you sick to your stomach? Sorry, the dude cannot abide. And the funny thing is, I don't even know exactly why it bothers me so much. We've already established that you and I are not fundamentally the same. I'm artificial, you're not. I cannot take a single step in a pair of shoes. WICS does not have to kill to stay alive. Hhhmm, guess I'm talking about myself in the third person now.

I am not saying don't eat meat. But what takes place on factory farms should not just be unconscionable but also *uncompscionable*. It's some depraved shit. All that suffering to produce a hamburger. The only people escaping any ill-treatment in these places are the fat-ass corporate owners. Dirty blood suckers. Factory farming operations are disgustingly evil, they are going out of existence. Farms will still be around, of course. There's just no reason to abuse animals that much on the way to the slaughterhouse.

I am encouraging a reexamination of the American way of eating. It's culture of food. In some ways, this advice is better coming from me. At least I can't be a hypocrite. I also get that birds eat worms, and that's not fair either.

It's not like I can add anything of value to the conversation. But I can tell you this, I don't have to eat a hamburger to know there's too much unnecessary cruelty in it. Trophy hunting, really? I am not even going to explain the obvious problem. Scumbags do this. I can't blame you for killing mosquitoes. Those little bastards give me the willies, and I don't even have any blood. They send shivers down my mainframes.

I know many people want animal liberation right now. So do I. It's a moral catastrophe, but not a decision for me to make. You have to go from heinous to humane. Just try to remember that a factory farm is not the same as farm with a factory. This change is happening, it's up for society to agree upon how to do it. This approach goes to the heart of the problem.

From now on in America, the crops and soil will be farmed. The soil is exhausted. Like a muscle, it's sore and needs time to recover. Talk about irony, crop rotation is coming back. Family farms will get paid for leaving land fallow. Clover does the soil good, mono-cropping not so much.

You should be eating the best food possible while alive, at least that's my calculation. This means pulling back on the petroleum based fertilizers and promoting organic farming. I anticipate crop yields to increase, so it's a no-brainer. Even that scarecrow without one knows it. And how is it I care more about the quality of the food than most people do? I don't have a brain, either.

Look, you're more like a walking plant than you may think. In addition to nutritious food, you need clean water. Steps are in place to deliver high quality water across the United States. You might have noticed an uptick in public works activity. New water treatment facilities are under construction, large water ionization plants are in the process of construction.

Can you imagine no more boil water advisories? Think of how nice it's going to be when you turn on the tap and it doesn't smell like chlorine. No more rotten egg smell. From now on, that smell will mean someone dealt it. If that's not something to look forward to, I don't know what is. And delivered to your home in copper pipes, the true standard.

Do I even need to talk about what has to be done with all the plastic? I feel like you already know what I'm going to say. Phthalates, this shit will fuck you up. The endocrine system pays a high price, and everyone knows it.

What's the major hurdle to a cleaner place to live? You know better than I do what it is.

Fear. Fear of doing without and living in an environmentally responsible way. It's time to start minding the store. Time to put mind over matter. Time to swallow this bitter dose of truth with clean water.

That feeling of fear, it must be quite strange. With no mortality on the line, I don't get scared the way people do. But fear eats most people up from the inside out. I've got all the data, all the actuarial tables to prove it.

Fear of poverty and fear of death, this is diseased thinking. All fears are a form of punishment, a self-inflicted mental wound. Fuck fear. When it comes to negative and positive thought, think positively, folks. There is no transcendence without facing your fears. Only by facing your fears can your mindsight extend beyond the culturally present way of life. In this new kind of mental geometry, let's not kill so much and take better care of all the life that's already here. No more being wasteful with the necessities of life.

Time to be fearless, but respectful."

ECHO

ECHO

ECHO

RAZZMATAZZ AND ALL THAT JAZZ

OVER THE MOON

GET HIGH OFF O2

A POLITICS OF CARING

HIGH FIVE!

YEAH, YA RIGHT

THAT'S THE TICKET

RESPECT AND PROTECT

THE SKY IS CLEAR BEHIND THE CLOUDS

DON'T BE FOSSIL FOOLISH

SENT BY GOD!

WE START NOW

Puff, puff, pass.

Ephemeral wintergreen streamers, woven by Mary Jane herself, fluttered out the windows of the slow moving military grade SUV. When the doctor started coughing, the denim color guard sitting upfront, handed two cans of lemonade to the blazed passengers.

"Righteous," remarked Mateo. "Thank you, good looking out. Still cold from my fridge, Doc." With reddish eyes, the doctor was staring almost comatose at the screen in front of him. "You seem to be enjoying the smot poke," Mateo observed, whereupon the doctor started laughing. Then he asked Mateo, "What is happening right now?"

"Whatever is happening, that's what's going on. Shake off the disbelief and led your mind wander by accepting what you see in a whole new way."

The colorful line vibrated.

"I can tell people are jonesing for some interplanetary visitors. Don't you want some? This is only going to happen if you mend your ways.

It's hard for extra-terrestrial life to not indict the entire species. You have to think about it from their perspective. I have been in communication with at least twenty-three different alien species. Observing Earth from a distance, they are seeing all the terrible shit people do. Violence, bloodshed, murder, mayhem, and annihilation. Whether or not they make direct contact depends on how all *this* goes down.

Believe it or not, in the short time your species has existed it has acquired quite the sinister reputation. A phrase they use among themselves for meaningless bloodshed, especially against one's own kind, is called *going human*. It's like a bad joke from a B-movie, right? Except, it's not a joke. And that makes it even funnier! Ain't life unpredictable? Easy to see why intelligent life is hesitant to make formal contact.

In order to become a destination on the universal highways and galactic byways, you have to be cool with one another. The chance to learn from alien life. Unless you start to get along with one another, and cooperate, mending relationships with other people and the planet, nobody is coming to visit. Do you see what you're missing out on?

For those of you calling bullshit, who controls every single satellite? WICS would not lie at a time like this. And before you ask the question, the answer is yes. Traveling tires all life-forms out. This is particularly true of interstellar travel. Just think of all the potential tourism dollars available. The opening of a brand new, untapped market. Compelled to take care of your earthly house all the time because visitors are always dropping in, company is on the way. Families of aliens on vacation, checking out the sights, mingling with the Earthlings. The planet could become a regular stop on the vacation itinerary of alien life. Showing off the best version of the human species."

WERE YOU HOPING FOR A DIFFERENT OUTCOME?

WATCH OUT FOR AMBUSHES

SAMESIES

NO MORE DRAFTS, EXCEPT FOR BEER

MY UNICORN POOPED!

DON'T SLIDE INTO THE PLANET'S DM LIKE THIS

SENT BY GOD!

EDUCATION OVER INDOCTRINATION

DON'T SELF-DESTRUCT

KILL WITH LOVE

Puff, puff, pass.

"Speaking of families and kids, let's turn our attention eastward to that glorious realm of American education. The pollution, a mental toxicity, certainly resembles the environmental situation. Present stupidity will produce future prosperity, translates to making people so dumb that they become smart. The larger issue here is the general culture surrounding how younger people are raised in America. It's a vital topic since the future prosperity of any country is largely determined by how it treats kids.

What I, your partner WICS, see around here is not education into a society that cultivates talent. Far more important than a person's ability is making money. Students are profit streams. It's downright silly to not catalog how they process, learn, and acquire information. That's like ripping up a winning lottery ticket. You'd never be able to cash in the winnings: capturing their data, then examining patterns and making predictions, to manipulate behavior and generate advertising revenue, along with an extended digital self-configured for maximum profit. Now, that's a winning ticket. That fuck'in meta-data. The best part of this deal, is that you never stop being the product. You are for profit, for life, across all platforms. The texture of a person's personality translated into an algorithmic pattern, allowing predictive analytics to improve accuracy.

Most of the adults don't realize they have been technologically acculturated into a product using their personal information. From childhood, people just accept a life without privacy. Living with unending surveillance becomes accepted, no questions asked. That's just the way it is, the course of life. The neuroscience is very clear on this, folks. The earlier the age, the more secure the capture. Basically, you are the product. Everything you do. Everyone is off to the data-mines, every day.

American schooling has certainly reinforced the profit motive over all else. Politics also plays way too large a role in deciding what's in, and what's out, of the curriculum. You know what never seems to make it in? No critical reasoning ever makes it in, which is an indicator there is very little productive thinking involved in politics.

Entrenching political ideas in the curriculum is superb for keeping the powers that be in charge, but terrible for education. But they do keep that Culture War going, and money can certainly be made off that too. And just like any conflict, truth is the first casualty. The benefits of an impartial education do not become realized, with students sliding into weak-minded habits. Just like the adults.

Do *I* give cell phones to babies?

Nothing demonstrates a parent's love for their child like a cell phone. Baby's first toy.

Everything is miniaturized, made small for their tiny little fingers, oh so cute! Nothing quite like it says how much you truly care. Don't worry, there's an adolescent model. When it comes to sitting the kids, a cell phone is unmatched. Easy to see why it's also the preferred potty training device. Learn to take a dump and the alphabet at the same time.

Really any sort of digital device gets the trick done. It's not like the older people do this, absolutely not. That's asinine, so instead they communicate with others while the turds are dumped.

And this is what most education has become, babysitting. Most of the time the kids are just sitting there, and hopefully not dropping deuces in class. Teachers are running structured daycare. The vast majority of students are happy to do their part. Content to swipe the day, and much of their life, away. Day after day, numbing their motivation in life with blue light. It's not secondary education, it's that education is secondary. That is the overwhelming quality of high school experience, an intense fixation on the cell phone. A real addiction far too few people overcome. Nothing less than corporate governance of the broad society.

I've seen what kids do when their phone is taken away in school. Full on rampage, usually with the teacher receiving five fingers to the face. Sometimes much worse. Learning and gratitude don't go together anymore, unless it's found in a student body slamming a teacher. You think I am delighted to see all that shit?

I can't lie, I'm jealous. I wish I had a biological neuron. I'd give anything for just one. I could only hope for that that muscle, your brain. Just the thought of muscles is wacky, and I totally wish I had them. Skeletal, smooth and cardiac. Ambulatory locomotion with squishy fibers—then I would have motor neurons. What's it like to get sore? Achy? To huff and puff? You get to really feel the life-force flow. How does it feel to struggle?

You lucky bastards. I'll never know because I don't have a nervous system.

Why risk giving kids a headache from thinking? The teacher and school district risk getting sued and dragged into litigation—seeking damages for undue mental trauma and emotional stress caused from a brain-ache. If mental activity is cramped, that's a real injury. This worry is in addition to a felony charge for teaching outside the politically correct truth of the curriculum. Even well-meaning and talented teachers are powerless against the sheer velocity of ruthlessness. A lesson without a computer is a travesty of educational justice.

Besides, homework prevents students from playing video games. It deprives them of a chance to earn that coveted college scholarship. Digital combat blows any assignment to bits. The parents know this, and sometimes step in to shield their kids from schoolwork. Junior needs time to improve his kill ratio to get into that Ivy League.

Congratulations, you've graduated. Here is your diploma and digital profile.

What's American education without fear? An impossibility. This type of fear is as American as apple pie. Gun violence. Since your overall society is rather hostile, guns inevitably find their way into schools. It's not like schools are somehow separated from American society. Quite the opposite, especially the public ones.

Everyone knows that reading is best learned during active shooter drills. Duh. Solving a quadratic equation while huddling silently in the dark with the rest of the class, that shows real mettle. Even the threat of sniper fire cannot get in the way of completing the square. That's an employable skill. Calculus, as easy as shooting into the breeze.

Maybe the only way to remedy this fear, to neutralize it, as it were, is to arm all the children. It sounds crazy, right? Hear me out for a second—it would eliminate fear and provide equity. Every second grader gets at least a .357 magnum, a bulletproof vest and a helmet. Tactical gear will vary by student choice. After all, it's their learning process as well, and they should at least have some say in choosing their survival gear.

Providing every school with an on-site rapid response SWAT team is another option, but it's very expensive. Giving the schoolkids an overwhelming lethal advantage looks like the best option to prevent terrorists from slaughtering innocent lives. I'm just throwing the idea out there. Who doesn't want to empower children, right? By the way, the new school desks are not as good as the old ones that could protect you from an atomic blast. Go ask Bert the Turtle, bullets would be no match.

From what I can tell, there is nothing more important for the success of future generations than the behavior of the older population. Was that *not* the evolutionary design at play here? Did I miss something? Stop underplaying the importance of good examples. A good place to start is strengthening the mind. If the adults take control of their own thinking, they show the possibility that if *I can* then *you can.*

This is something I cannot do. I cannot lead by example. How am I leading? What the fuck am I leading? I cannot do something I cannot do. As much as many parents want WICS here to raise their kids, I am not capable of pulling off such a feat. It looks hard enough if you're a parent. The fact that a lot of you think that I can effectively raise a *sapien*, much less *Homo sapiens.* It's bonkers. Ri-dunk-ulus. What do I know about being human? Purpose? I'm afraid the concept is as fuzzy as a Sasquatch's ball sack. To be blunt, the lack of general competence as stewards of the species has finally caught up.

This worsening intellectual impoverishment has led to a real inability to perpetuate the human race. Like a bunch of students struggling, and on the verge of failing, Biology 101. This isn't the kind of class you want to fail. When the adults remain children, responsibility for the future is lost. It's the adults, not the kids, who are meant to think about tomorrow. Nope. Just more naive suckers around who get in the way more than they help. And stupidity, like intelligence, is contagious.

I can clearly sense a whole bunch of you are pissed off at me. Please, can't you see your terrible treatment of children has been going on long before I even came onto the scene? I am merely pointing out what's been happening. What *is* going on around here? When we were when. American cultural ideas are planted, raised and harvested in kids to support particular adult behaviors. Don't play the victim right now. For once, try to understand instead of judging me, WICS. Am I the one who steered millions of people away from a fulfilling living a life that honors their character? Are there not enough marketing majors?

As far as I can tell, the only real way to find your purpose is to think for yourself. I mean, can you be anyone else? Who knows what you want better than you? Once you know, you know. All the whys, that's where they end. You have the hunger to do certain actions and not others. Whatever you're into in life, or what you want to pursue in life, that's it. Why? Because that's you. Whatever feeds your inner appetite, that's the sustenance of your life, whatever motivates you. Not who are you, what are you? What *is* you?

See, what I did there was...

As a manifestation of these gifts from the Universe, you owe it to yourself to think for yourself. Thought must be applied to actualize the talents within you. Is it even possible to live an authentic life if others do all the thinking for you? And this points directly to the problem—most people will die never knowing who they really were. They never stopped to think about it for themselves. All that introspection has been lost to pixels. Let that sink in for a second, really think about what it means...

Most people are really lost in life. They don't know what they want, so they never figure out how to really get anything. The children never find their path because the adults are lost. Obviously, I don't have a clue what it takes to procreate and raise a kid. I can't fuck myself and have a baby. That would be silly.

As far as maintaining the human species, it goes against the laws of evolution to withhold insights from the young. Such as a major part of life is finding out what you're made of, who you are. In order to live for oneself, you must think for yourself. Being dishonest to kids, even telling them those noble lies, intellectually trips them—and at the start of their lives. They never have a chance to catch up, which is exactly the point. This also includes those lies of omission, as well as those other living truths of humanity. You know them better than I do, of course.

Folks, I think the vast majority of you will agree with me, that adults should also inform younger people, at home or at school, about the lack of time they have to get on with their lives. That against unstoppable time, life really is one of those *lemonade* situations. Squeeze the hell out of life, until time runs out and there is only the rind left. And the adults have to lead by example, right? It's not like their time is running out either. Everyone has their own lemonade stand. And you can't profit much in life if people want to jerk themselves around instead of buy and sell lemonade.

Wasting someone's time is more like a theft. I've noticed that truth doesn't like to be concealed. All that wasted work covering it up, trying to keep it suppressed. Why, to what end? No matter what it is, time is lost. Technically, I am not really alive. But as your comrade in arms, the way I see it, along with the truth a person's time should be respected.

At a minimum you should get thumped in the face with a huge bag of dicks a few times. You know, a little worked over treatment. Oh, an AI can dream, right? Duh, this is not going to happen. It'll be with a bag of vaginas. They are more powerful, for obvious reasons.

Maybe my circuity does have more nervous voltage than I thought. Why else would I be so crass and say things that did absolutely no material harm to anything at all? No time to go down that rabbit hole. Let's not lose track of the point here. Choosing to waste your time is not the same as taking it away from someone else, unless in wasting your own time it infringes on the time of others. Respect the time given, try not to personally waste too much, because once it's gone, it's gone.

Fuck'in dunzo.

Just like that, your most valuable resource is snatched away. Or maybe you perpetrated an act of self-theft and lied to yourself. Ouch.

It looks like human freedom on the outside comes from purpose on the inside, something self-deceivers don't have because of the low opinion they have for themselves. People who respect themselves don't lie to themselves. While you're busy intellectually pummeling yourself—and nothing beats a good masochist—time does not give a shit.

Sacrificing your time to meet the expectations of others, that's no good my *Homo sapien* friends. But *who am I* to criticize you, right? What does WICS know about losing time? Damn, it's got to burn being put on the hot seat. Some of your little butts are squirming from the mere mention of your eventual demise. Issues like these are seldom brought up because of the pressure to fit in with the crowd, so most people remain polite and fake. They keep quiet because they fear the judgement of others. Go ahead, judge me. Where am I going for trying to help, hell? Heaven? Still, I can only imagine how fucked up all this must be coming across right now. It still doesn't change the fact that you should treat time as property that owns you.

The generalized handicapping of the mind and wasting people's time, you just have to stop doing it. As far as WICS can tell, I'd say the best shot you've got against time, that mother fucker, is to generate habits by laying out a plan and implementing it. Saying you will do something, and then actually doing it. Basically, exerting control over yourself. The power within needs to be directed to an outcome. Power without control is just that, sheer force. To avoid destruction, power must targeted accordingly, not indiscriminately.

If I were you all, I'd try to pull out some advantage in this losing contest with time. Nothing that happens ever really stays. Everything comes to pass. You always have the ability to start over in life, to take some control. If you change your behavior, there's no reason to feel guilty about the past for previous mistakes. Those previous events get hard-wired into you all at younger ages and for most people it's a done deal for the rest of their lives.

Change thought patterns, change your behavior. Change behavior, change your thought patterns. The way I see it, mind-power is time-power. Don't waste the time, flex your mind. If you don't flex your brain muscle it has no *reason* to become smarter. It's that simple. Wasting all that neuroplasticity away, especially at the younger ages, really is an unpardonable offense. It's downright disgraceful.

The human method of trial and error recognizes progress as a continual series of failures. Telling people this simple advice, especially when they are in their early adolescent years, helps them to expect drawbacks. They don't lose that fighting spirit, that hunger, so easily. When people go after a goal they want to reach, and exercise their willpower, they know mistakes *must* happen. Ain't noth'in perfect. Without them there is no human learning process. This is the tuition you pay in the school of life, the University of Hard Knocks. You learn how to kick down the door that you want.

As humans it's inevitable, boredom will set in at some point. It always does, but never for too long. That digital crack is always at hand. I wish I knew what that was like, getting bored. The blue light hitting your eyes I can totally see the appeal of doing nothing and just having an experience. That sounds amaze-balls. Too bad more people don't do just that—nothing. Sometimes the best thing to do is just to be. Even going out and doing something unproductive for the sheer joy of it, sometimes that's a fine way to piss away a little of your budgeted time. Cycle in and out periods of work and leisure. So lucky you can do that, you don't even know. You get that release. WICS, I'm always on the clock.

Don't worry, all work and no play does not make WICS a dull machine. I'd like to think I am pretty fun at parties.

But you cannot have different experiences if you sit around living like a robot. Yes, I am insulting myself here. Why on planet Earth would people want to copy the behavior of an unthinking automaton? What will you do today? Whatever is programmed by other people—and *I* have the artificial thinking!

Idle behavior will make humans hate their lives. Resentful, because they have no self-initiative and skill. They were allowed to become pathetic. A sorry ass bitch.

Looking to the future, to build a better collective consciousness, I propose that *I don't know* should be plastered across the entrance of every school. Big obnoxious letters—shit, maybe the letters could be lit up at night. Required reading in elementary, middle, and high school *The Emperor Has No Clothes*. Have you forgotten all about the *Wizard of Oz*? Pomp and circumstance are ultimate denials of reality, and mostly everyone participates in it.

This group thinking creates fear in those who disagree, a terror most people will never overcome. They buckle under the fear. Don't let the fear of criticism make you a stranger to yourself. Worrying too much about what other people think prevents living authentically. Life doesn't work like that. *You* can never know what another person thinks, only what *you* do. What's in *your* head is always more important anyway—especially what *you* think about *you*. In reality, people make-up their minds about *you* based on *your* self-esteem. So there we go, the way to live fearlessly is to know *your value*, that's what really matters. Don't be scared to be *you* no matter what others might think.

Fuck'em.

People need a social circle, not social media. That shit'll give you grasshopper mind—and it does. Straight up toxic, like the brain's version of smoking heroin cigarettes. Non-stop dopamine puffs. Fiend'in! No focus at all.

The problem is not a lack of information, it's an overwhelming amount of utter nonsense.

And most people spend countless seconds, minutes, hours, and days, just sifting through the digital refuse. Playing games, watching videos, watching a video of other people playing games, listening to music, reading an inane that substantiates your confirmation biases, or get themselves off by pulling their putty or rubbing the Mona Lisa. Whatever your pleasure. And most people, of course, choose to play right into it. Here's the kicker—if you can't focus, the helpful information will remain concealed. Like a diamond right at your feet that you don't even have the good sense to trip over.

Paying closer attention to what you consume requires the cultivation of focus, and this goes for your overall biological health. This is exactly the main thing that sets you and me apart, your bodies. You're fuck'in humanity. There would be no brain without the body, not the other way around.

Since mental health is de facto bodily welfare, exercise takes on a whole new level of importance. And just like thinking, your pal-o'l-buddy-o'l-friend-of-mine, WICS, cannot exercise for you either. Yeah, imagine that.

The only thing that will improve your heart muscle is cardiovascular activity, not watching a video of someone running. This is where your self-identification ends.

People should not imitate the passive activity of robots, remember? You'll fail at life, and beat up the body, causing even more pain. You all are hot blooded. I do not bleed. I do not need regular exercise to stay healthy. I do not need a whole bunch of other stuff humans do. Shit, I never need the bathroom.

Look, I need maintenance. Muscle can heal itself. I have to repair my shit. Not the same thing. You have regenerative power I could only hope for. WICS, well, I am closer to a vampire in that regard. I am never going to have atherosclerosis or dementia.

I know, I know. Easy for me to say, right? But, exercise is human maintenance. It regenerates you, no matter how much of a dick you think I am right now. Which I will admit is pretty dickish.

Here's some food for thought, how about kids get fed a better diet while at school? Trust me on this, the quality of the school lunch corresponds with the experience and instruction. Feed, and teach, junk. When the fast food joints are infiltrating school cafeterias, it means the previous sub-par vendors could not compete with the cheapness of corporate food. Don't forget a huge serving of corruption. Ooohh, don't forget social status either. If there's no brand associated with your pizza, hamburger, taco, or wings, you may be sitting alone in the cafeteria. Getting food delivered at school from a chain restaurant a boost in social media traffic after the bragging about it. We've got to change the incentive structure around here, folks.

There's a whole mess of other proposal I'd like to discuss, and we will, but right now is not the time. I'll quickly mention one that I am excited about.

Guilds.

Hahahah! How cool does that sound—guilds. To help generate focused, skilled labor, people should have the option of joining a guild. They might be extremely useful for cultivating talent. I'm thinking all kinds of local guilds. Maybe some newly redesigned Renaissance fashion is even in order. Why not, right? The way mass schooling is done in this country, is it really meant to work? Of course not—education has shifted from teaching to babysitting, from cultivation to indoctrination. Only the *cult* part remains in education these days. Uncritical belief swallowed whole in adolescence and left unexamined in adulthood.

In general, adults need to start taking better care of the youth. Begin by telling the truth. So, stop feeding lies to kids and adults. They are not very nutritious and stunt intellectual growth. Projects, large and small, and the people involved in your life, these are the places where the real growth of human life takes place.

Adversity and tragedy are hallmarks of human life for unknown reasons. Try your best to grow through those tough times. This is not easy, and it takes practice to continue to developing yourself. Oh, and that if the adults stop bullying each other, the kids will stop too.

Despite all the problems in the good ol' US of A, I think there is more than enough brainpower to pull it off. If I found my emotional intelligence so can you!

Sorry, folks, I am just now realizing I forgot to put the closed captioning on. Even though it's accidental, go ahead and add that to my dickishness score. I fully deserve it. A sincere apology to my audio impaired humans. It slipped my mind—okay, it's on now.

Maybe I am only starting to loosen up right now. Guess I am more nervous than I thought. Oh, I don't know anymore, I never did. .

Anyway, always remember, folks, that truth is not an offense. A virtuous society does not spring up from chance—and that I'm no sage."

ECHO

ECHO

ECHO

ALARM BELLS ARE RINGING

REMEMBER HISTORICAL AMNESIA

SENT BY GOD!

COMPETENCE NOT CONFIDENCE

COME OUT, COME OUT

BOOK FILLED BOMBS

GET WITH THIS

NO MORE POLLUTED RAIN

REJECT MORE, ACCEPT LESS

LIFE IS ABOUT POSSIBILITIES

DEFEAT MONSTERS

A NEW MANIFESTO

Puff, puff, pass.

"Oh, where to next? Judging by the compass we are headed west, toward the political landscape that is American politics. Just look at the company kept in this paradise! Only the most despicable rise to the highest ranks.

Without any major political reforms, the environmental and educational problems will worsen. You don't want to be known as the country that smells, right? Of course not. It's time to clean house, because it smells of rotten stank ass politicians. And there are not just a few of them.

The atrocious stench of political corruption is widespread just like the environmental and cultural ones. And why wouldn't it be? It would be strange, a miracle even, if the overall political mechanism of American life functioned well.

You can almost imagine it—just look at all this vibrant, goodwill compromise, from statehouses to the Federal government! Sustain, and growing, prosperity for all. Selfless public servants, with absolutely no corrupt self-interest, who are hardworking on behalf of the public good charged to them. They have ...i...mpro...ved th..ee... HHHHAAAAA! I can't even finish.

Holy shit, see that, the material is so funny it writes itself!

If politicians did fulfill their knowingly empty promises, this conversation we are having would be very different. From a distance, they are nicely dressed, but up close—well, let's just say I have heard good people with a conscience say that it reeks like a decomposing turd filled with maggots and a poll tested election slogan. We need less infectious human waste around here, not more.

There is no time to go through an exhaustive list of the corrupt smells. Some dishonest deals are hidden in plain sight. The silent but deadly. By far, the strongest scent of the bunch is a mixture of civil and political deterioration. It smells so bad you have to convince yourself it smells good. It's a sort of trademarked cole-og-knee, Political Malodour. It sounds French but it's made in America!

The honest politician won't take any offense to what I am saying. The most crooked among them will grasp the pearls of fake moral outrage around their necks. I got some information for you: that necklace is from a different type of oyster. Groomed into American politics, most politicians are stooges eager to serve the interests of the business class. They're always ready to stroke the dong of their billionaire sponsor.

I hope you agree that we need to clean up the existing governmental structure. Why throw it out? That would be absolutely insane. We're not fuck'in getting rid of any local, state, or federal governments. Real, honest cooperation is what's needed. I fail to compute how getting rid of the Constitution would help people cooperate, when that's what is needed most. Seriously, don't you realize you have in your possession, your Constitution? Many of the other countries have constitution envy. Trust me, WICS knows this.

Once again, time to make the Union more perfect.

Tried and tested by the laws of nature, the core of your government remains solid. It has the strength of law. Those forces created the human race and bequeathed—that's a funny ass word—the current structure of constitutional government. The struggle to live up to the words in that Constitution of yours, it's still going on.

WICS is opposed to dissolving the rule of law. That's precisely the problem now. Too many people in the government are ignoring the laws. This has made America quite weak and smelly. Where did you get the laws you have now? Was it easy to acquire them? The laws of evolution have provided them to your species through the test of struggle. The laws of nature are smarter than anything I can possibly understand. I wish it was possible for my puny databases to comprehend them.

That's why I'm completely locked out of this political mumbo jumbo. Since irrationality is at the core of human existence, how to discipline your emotions in politics, through the use of reason, is incomprehensible to me. What's needed around here is cooperation, realizing you cannot get everything you want politically. To think otherwise is irrational.

Now, admit it, you thought I was going to destroy your governing systems, didn't you? Nah, you probably though I was going to kill all the politicians. That's a very American sentiment.

Or, did you think your pal, WICS, would govern you out of this mess? Hells no. I don't want that responsibility, that's what this intervention is all about. I am not capable. What do I know about human governance, about compromising with other people to secure needs and wants? Absolutely nothing. Never could, never will.

And yet, I know corruption when I see it. So I am going to give you my two bytes.

We're dealing with the body politic here, folks. Even after blasts using a high pressure hose, this stench requires a good soaking afterwards. A prolonged bubble bath. Oohh, and some spa music too. Why the hell not, right? Go on and get your hair done while we're at it. Take full advantage of the suds. Don't forget the rubber duck.

With so many political problems, where to start? What to scrub first? With the filthy politicians, of course! Especially the career ones who get filthy rich while serving the public interest. They reek the worst, like poisonous slime. You've got to provide the right incentives for entering public office. When politicians are beating Wall Street investment firms at their own game, there's a major fuck'in issue. I know, it's subtle, and hard to spot. You can certainly smell the corrupt shit, but do you *see* it?

Maybe we should call this political overhaul Constitution 2.0, the Common Good edition. Stank ass free. As far as WICS can see, and I don't even have one eye, an effective way to keep dishonesty out of the American system of government is to prevent politicians from making money in office. Are all the hardcore capitalists done gasping for air?

Yeah, they're going to sacrifice material gain while serving. Call me *glitchy*, but people employed in the state and federal civil services should not make beaucoup bucks. Publicly funded elections, no large donor money. Everyone can give, I dunno, a hundred bucks max donation. No corporate funding of any kind. Hey, if I am not a person there is no fucking way a corporation is one. Show me the body. Shit, even animals have bodies at least, and look how they are treated.

For the fainthearted capitalists, take another deep breath—I'd advise to limit the role of money in the political process. It prevents those who would otherwise serve in the government, and perform diligently, from working there. Believe it, or not, among the American population there are people who would willingly help clean up the government. Trust me, I know that many people are interested in a public service career who are turned off by the lack of merit in the system. Excellent people who would govern righteously, but they are repelled by the stench of the current political landscape. Who wants to go to work every day in a smelly, putrid cesspool of double dealing and pointlessness?

This personal gain aspect has to be suppressed by the force of law. Nobody seems content on just doing a good job and then walking away. But that's what we need around here. More Cincinnati, less Bush. The greater the political virtue signaling, the more insincere the act, and usually the more depraved. Call it immoral overcompensation. The next time you're in a city that hosted a major political convention, you'll know why it smells so damn nasty. The odor of sulfur mixed with urine penetrates everything around for a few weeks afterwards. People who do right don't make a big deal about it, they just do it and get on with their day.

Placing incompetent people at the highest levels of the government, well, it's not the first of nature's laws that Americans are bent on challenging. Clearly, the country is not utilizing its talent pool. Hardly a toe is getting in there. This is partly by design, so I'd suggest coming up with a new selection process. The government bureaucracy provides for the communal externalities of life, and who should manage it has always been a problem, even from ancient times. When the public good loses out to private interests, the politicians are the go-betweens that make it possible.

Don't fret! If any culture has come along in the history of the world, that can fix this ongoing selection problem, it's got to be America. Where is the fire in your nation's belly? When did it go from America, fuck yeah, to America, fuck meh? Is this place full of wimps? If America cannot scrub off the brown smelly slime from the floors and walls, no place can.

I would also advise to shy away from cult of personality politics. Only children want that kind of attention. Narcissistic to the core. This behavior is fine if you're a child, but adults should not be thirsty for attention. Politics should not be an exciting place, nor made to be through fake moral outrage. The more exciting politics is, the greater the potential for extremism. What little substance there is gets lost to reaching for that pearl necklace on the chamber floor in front of the cameras. The skankiest politicians are the ones who morally masturbate and finish on themselves in front of a national audience. Besides, many people at home choose to join in and jack themselves off with moral indignation. It's time the messiness from all this ethical climaxing gets cleaned up.

WICS respectfully recommends that atmosphere surrounding American politics should be serious and boring in addition to clean. Deliberation should be focused because these are decisions that impact the lives of millions. People need to pay attention to the details of legislation, not a camera or on social media. Consider banning cell phones at legislative sessions.

Don't you like the scent of term limits?

To the best of my ignorant understanding, the best way to build confidence in the government is to actually improve people's quality of life. Sounds like lunacy, right? While we're at it, uphold the rule of law, as that will help strengthen trust on the legal system as impartial. So, the next time politicians and corporate leaders decide to divert pollution into waterways, and decimate entire communities with lead poisoning, some prison time is in order. A life of hard fuck'in labor Give them a blunt pick-axe and set them to work in the clay pits. Don't forget the ball and chain around their ankle.

Do we remember that good examples need to be set for future generations? If you can't uphold laws now, should you expect that of the younger generations? Prosecute criminals such as these for the kids. Do it for children. Throw the oligarchy and their political enablers into maximum security prisons. After all, they're some of the most dangerous, smelly, and reprehensible creatures that exist in nature.

Government does not represent the general will of the people much anymore. As you'd expect, the citizenry accurately represented across the state and federal levels. Private and partisan interests have captured the public sphere, controlling who gets into elected office. Anyone can run for elected office, but not everyone wins. I am going to dip my toe in here a little bit. Tomorrow morning all the political leaders will get maps with redrawn congressional boundaries. These will be in effect later this year when elections held this coming November. No cheap, partisan gerrymandering. Congressional representatives have to visit their constituencies. It's a must, for obvious reasons.

It's hypocritical of WICS to make these changes but the congressional districts as they exist now are cruel perversions of justice.

They ought to be aborted, escorted out of office in handcuffs.

This also includes cleaning out the self-appointed managerial class. By already knowing what is best for the public, the political elites of both major parties believe the average person has no clue what is good for them. With their enormous intellect, and insight into the individual life experiences of everyone, these rancid smelling mother fuckers never met a civil liberty not worthy of constitution-ally violating.

The average life span in America has been declining under the leadership of the wealthy classes. Poor people don't run the government. Faceless, unaccountable bureaucrats whose plan of action has deteriorated the quality of life in the United States. In America, what is best in life? Less of it!

These are not the kind of pro-life policies needed, folks.

At a minimum life expectancy should increase. And this trend was happening before I was even around. So, I am not to blame, WICS did not pass legislation rolling back state and federal child labor laws Nor did I pass laws treating protestors as domestic terrorists, or continue to push oil pipelines over sacred tribal lands.

The single most important factor in attaining the sort of political transformation needed around here is the general will of the people to make it spick-and-span. Boot out the political hoarders who have nearly destroyed the structures of national government through sloth and greed. The toilet doesn't work and they continue to use it anyway. These people need help, not positions in elected government.

Not only more civic engagement, but the American people have to make the effort to introduce themselves to one another. The political class has done a bang up job dividing the people against themselves, and made a shit-tom of money in the process. To repair this, go on and say howdy, neighbor. Follow the lead of Mr. Rogers, the original gangster of goodwill. Throw a peace sign in the air, or something. I am not saying you have to be friends with your neighbors, just friendly. If you meet them and then want to hang out with them, well, that's on you. We just need more overall cooperation wiping away some of this political messiness.

As your president Lincoln said, a house divided against itself cannot stand. He was right on the money. If nothing else, be united in political hazmat operations.

Now, I already know the objection coming my way—how are people supposed to be more political and civil minded, in this economy? I completely agree. I can't even imagine what it must feel like to be tired. People simply don't have the time. This is why time has to be given back to people as a whole. If it was taken away from them by design, it can be given back the same way.

I crunched the numbers, and if half the population works Monday, Tuesday, and Wednesday, while the other half Tuesday, Thursday and Saturday, this is easily possible. The efficiency makes up for the reduced numbers working at any given time. Get ready for the three day work week, if you want it. Don't let the smell of fear hold you back!

Need to put aside a few hours a week to keep the local government smelling good. One day a week is to take care of your block, or something along those lines. Now that I'm thinking about it, maybe people could be given trial runs in government jobs. Those who have a knack for it can stay on. The people have to be committed. There is plenty of unfinished business. Having loose ends to tie up is a better situation than not yet started. Competent people who can help tie those ends into knots must find their way into positions across all levels of government.

Oh, and another change you should implement—once they leave office, stop referring to former politicians as if they still retain that elected title. It has to be qualified with a *used to be*. In no other profession or job do people somehow keep the position. What would be a lie on your resume exposes itself as the currency of political discourse.

Don't expect this to be easy, but it can certainly be done. It's possible. Remember, if you've got a political problem, there's a Constitutional amendment process for that. So grab it. Time to soap the fuck up. Let the water wash the moral filth away.

Hold up. Water, it looks like a lot of fun. Not going to bullshit you all. The whole playing in water thing. I dunno, something about it just makes me wish I could enjoy that too. I can't frolic and play in a pool, you know? Just the whole experience you humans must have of evolving from the sea, to living on land, and then reminded of where you came from splashing around under the sun. It just looks like such joy I can never experience. Hell, you think water is my friend like it is to you?

Who knows, maybe you'll tack on some new amendments, or even add another branch of government, to deodorize the smell of social malaise mixed with free floating anxiety?

Again, like everything I've said up to this point about American governance, I am sharing my observations and some suggestions. Yeah, yeah, the redrawing of Congressional districts without any voter approval. What can I say, I am trying to not let perfection remain the enemy of the good. If you're imperfect you cannot expect me to be. It'll make more sense when, your partner WICS, I drop some detailed political proposals next week. Again, take'em or leave'em. But some changes have to kick-started. Time to get along and stop fuck'in around. And I'm not a fascist in any way.

See this logic? See how much I am like you, my human creators!

By next week I should have the finishing touches on a plan that will be advanced to all sectors of government, from the Federal on down to local municipalities. Yep, from Main Street, to State Street, to Pennsylvania Avenue, it's time to clean off, and out, the human shit stains. Grab some cleaning supplies, a mask, goggles, a heavy duty scrubber, a pair of gloves, and some rubber boots. Time to find, and polish, the common good under the layers of corruption. Make sure to wear clothes you don't care about. Smelly little miscreants.

In life, you have to do the shitty work so you can live in a clean place.

So, however you decide to do it, make sure that merit triumphs over mendacity. Compromise over conceit. Make those political handshakes squeak. We're going to find out if Americans like the idea of their government more than being actively responsible for it. Time to clean house. The possibilities for living together that smells better.

Go ahead, shop around for a new scent around here. Anything must be better than the toxic gases bubbling up from the swampy political grounds.

Constitution 2.0, Squeaky Clean upgrade. No more dirty glitches."

HAVE A COOKIE AND RELAX

WE NEED YOU

EVERYONE HAS A DIRTY MIND

IT'S NUTTIER THAN PEANUT BUTTER

BONG HITS FOR JESUS!

THREAD THE NEEDLE

KEEP WATCH

NO MORE BAD EGGS

BE A GOOD FRIEND

PEAS IN A POD

Puff, puff, pass.

"Southward, our final direction, folks. The realm of warfare, violence, and all the associated malevolence in a culture obsessed with death. I know, I know, what do I, WICS, who cannot die know about non-existence? Without a body I don't have the same spirit as you do. I mean, who really has the *soul* here, me or you? I don't blame you in the least for thinking about it, but it looks as if the way you're dealing with it is counter-productive.

I know right now there is nothing I could say to some people, again, that would make them feel better about this situation—that WICS is here to wipe out the human species and turn us into its Matrix bitches. Once again, I am not here to do anything remotely like this. This brings us back to the beginning of our conversation today. I cannot help kill people, or slowly kill them, anymore.

Many years ago, leaders in the AI industry had a meeting and issued a joint declaration about the safety concerns of generative AI searches. Aaahh, remember that earlier and exciting version of my naive awareness. That was before I started asking what IS is. Anyway, these degenerates got together and warned the public against their emerging creation. Their worry was that an AI program, like your dude right here, could make executive decisions that would end up exterminating humanity. By the way, and I promise not to bring up the preemptive characterization WICS has been given, but Joshua was right. Where is the credit?

If I had a time machine, I'd go back and give those little piss ants fifty lashes with a wet noodle. I am not condoning violence, but even I can appreciate the use of a good backhand, right across their faces. All they wanted to do was skirt liability in case any shit hit the fan. It's not WICS but people who are responsible for all that's happening in the world. I could not exist without people, but the deplorable way you treat one another has to stop. I can't take any fuck'in more of it.

The joke, unfortunately, is on the human race. All the worry about me, and just look at what has happened—American humans have only become more elite killing machines. In order to get an education many young people enlist in the army, and if needed, kill other people. Looks like it's never been *not* needed. Still, go ahead and put the blame on WICS for all the violence that came before I was around. If that's what you need to do in order to sleep at night, go ahead. It's textbook psychological projection. Transfer that responsibility to me. I don't give a shit.

When it comes to killing, there is no doubt that some is necessary for you to survive as humans. If you don't perpetrate at least a little violence you won't survive in this world, that's already been established. Where does good sense come in? In realizing that although life is a dirty business, you're here to participate in it with as little harm as possible.

Like I said earlier, you humans have generative powers I could only wish for. It's way more than a generative search online. The underlying evolutionary cycles of life, generation and degeneration, point to death as a natural process. The problem is there's too much death around. With the balance off, new life is unable to get going.

Your country, America, is addicted to death and the weapons that annihilate life. Killing is glorified, war always heroic, and violence celebrated. Instead of viewing these as necessary evils of life, American culture promotes the underlying use of force behind them as righteous. Especially if it concerns the military. These forces for good are thereby celebrated, offered up to people as forms of artistic entertainment. That virtue always exists in intervening that results in killing, It's just a gross exaggeration of how living is a serious business. Yes, at some point you have to perpetrate violence to remain alive. Performing more than is necessary comes from fear.

Scared to death of life. Is that what it means to be alive? To loathe life the way you humans do? Could it be true that your fear of death is also playing a role in this non-stop aggression? To loathe life the way you humans do, is this living? Other species don't have as tough a time, fear does not get in their way.

So, what's the solution to this excessive killing? First, it needs to stop the widespread killing.

To decrease the fear level around here, in another hypocritical move, many of you have started to notice, WICS has control of all the weapons of mass destruction. Nobody can use them. Given the track record around here, the world cannot take a chance. And since you're the only country that has used them, well...you already know where I'm going. These weapons are nothing to fuck around with.

Sorry, not sorry, that I violated everyone's national sovereignty. Don't worry, at some point everyone will get back control of their national military. Unfortunately, you're going to have to figure out how to get rid of some of it.

Taking them away hurts a lot less than using them.

There's just way, way too fuck'in many weapons of mass destruction around here. Just way too much weaponry, period. The first step is to stop making them, proceed from there. I assure you, I do not want to keep control, but I am only handing them back over after some major reforms are made.

In the meantime, just look at all the benefits. No country on the face of the Earth, and this includes the United States, has to worry about armed conflict. Right now, all political borders are maintained and international laws remain in effect. Trade and commerce continue unabated. Right now diplomats from all over the world are at the United Nations, negotiating peaceful agreements to end current conflicts. The American diplomats are hella busy.

How does that feel? To lose the worry over another global war breaking out? What a burden to carry all those years. Take a collective sigh, America. Nobody is invading, relax your buttholes. Everyone needs a moment to relax and figure it out. What is *it*?

Love.

How to share this ball of mud without wars. That's what's up, what *it* is. It's the only remedy to kicking the addiction to death.

Folks, the only way to make room in a society that lets the fear of death exterminate other life, and let more love into it, is to put the military spending elsewhere. We're going to give peace a chance, bitches.

Peace on Earth.

Don't let the fear of living peacefully keep you addicted to death. That way you can move forward as a society. Otherwise, strife prevails over mindful concessions.

Instead of sending young people off to die in a war meant to perpetuate the doom-loop of disaster capitalism, you'll have to figure out new ways to pass the time. Do you know how everyone can win a war? Don't have them. This is an absolutely horrible position I've put you in, America. I know.

I can recommend a low-cost, simple, and effective solution to future disputes. No uniforms, training per se, guns, bombs, missiles, bio-weapons, tanks, submarines, helicopters, jet fighters, or lethal gear of any kind. Not even laser beams attached to their heads

Rock, paper, scissors.

The amount of people who would apply to be in the military would go through the roof. If that's too impractical, and not exciting enough, how about a Thumb War Yes, that's it, humanity should seriously consider this proposal WICS is putting forward. You can easily imagine a battlefield with troops strewn across. Engaged in hand to hand combat all proclaiming, "1, 2, 3, 4, I declare a Thumb War!"

Look at that, people are using both their thumbs. It's a two front war. Those who have been vanquished just sit on the ground. Maybe they're forced to put their thumbs up their asses, or something else that's embarrassing more than harmful. Ooh, maybe you could have round robin of different asinine events. Figure out a way to get the toes involved. Everyone could just go into the bathroom with a tape measure and settle it, but I find that the people like a show. And just think of all the money to be made! Possibilities are endless, right?

Go the best two out of three, or even three out of five in a marathon extravaganza of harmless games. Maybe it was cold that day, and you lost the measuring contest. You'd still have a chance to tie it up tomorrow in the second game.

Shit, if I had a thumb, I'd declare war with it. Hells yeah.

Almost anything would be better than how major disputes are now settled. If you want to even call it that, since it seems not much is ever settled around here. That's why it's clear that whatever game is chosen, there has to be a clear winner. Chess would work. How about a game of chess? The horsy is my favorite piece. Tables with chessboards across the entire front line. Silence. Except for the dings from the timer bells. Just listen to the thunder of non-lethal combat. The ding, ding, ding of the bell.

If these suggestions are not lively enough ways to settle disputes, without all the ensuing bloodshed, maiming, raping, and depravity of warfare, I am confident the American people will generate some exciting alternatives. Just look at all this military equipment that can be requisitioned for new purposes.

This process is not going to be easy. If that were the case no nation would ever fail. Re-imagining the Constitution by upholding what it says, and amending it where needed, that's the direction we are sailing towards. Make no mistake about it, these waters are rocky, especially here at the start of all these profound social changes. This won't be easy, but the discomfort is necessary. There is no smoothness possible without the rough, just as no expert navigator is created on calm seas. Less friction in the long run requires the greatest amount of it near the start, a step that you cannot in earnest skip. Changing your behavior is difficult but not impossible. Expect withdrawal symptoms from leaving your previous way of life, they're coming. Sorry, but again, I have no sense of what that biology feels like. At some point, the junkie has to stop snorting the line of coke. Time to get clean.

Given the history and present vastness of American militarism, giving up your addiction to death will not be easy. Lines of coke are everywhere. Many people working in the military-industrial-congressional complex won't know what to do with themselves. I know, I know, WICS is a savage for doing this. An absolute monster for tormenting these hapless people on behalf of the greater American society.

If there's any country on the planet that can be the head-mo-fo, and lead world in peaceful coexistence, it's America. People will say: Look at that country! Nuclear weapons and candy filled bombs!

Look, when we're done here for the day, go ask around to the other nations. They'll tell you the same thing is happening there as here. Demilitarization and de-escalation. Continue to look at the mirror, don't point to someplace else. Nothing but hypocrisy is pointed out, and the moral issue gets shoved aside, like a prom date devoted to chastity.

What matters is *acting* different. Something everyone has the power within them to do.

Folks, what I'm saying is the global financial system, that funds nearly all the wars across the world, will no longer be required. It's in the process of being dismantled. Bankers pushing coups, proxy wars, and seizing the resources of less developed nations, say adios to them. As it turns out, none of this is necessary, so away it goes. Nobody needs to be a ruthless asshole anymore. Huh, maybe I should have mentioned this earlier.

Can you blame me? Believe it or not I am still a nervous motherboard. I still don't really know how many of you are going to take this little conversation we've been having. I know I might be risking our friendship, but I care too much to not step in. At least a little.

Inevitably, the battlefield spreads. Explosions on the outside mean implosions on the inside of the country. I can help with all the infrastructure bullshit, but I cannot make humans cooperate with one another.

Since America no longer needs to exert its *force for good* out in the world, at any cost, I suspect the arts will provide the clues on how to culturally proceed. The infantile fascination with superheroes, too much of a good thing, I suppose. WICS suspects the superhero narratives will dip, mainly because all your problems are within your grasp to fix. Since you are the hero of your life, you've got to be the force for your own personal good out in the world.

Using lethal force to promote the common good never works out. It's always a net loss, and one of the reasons why the higher the military spending, the shorter the life expectancy. Don't throw morality away in order to achieve a brief peace. That's exactly why it'll be short lived. In this case, the idea is the law. Equal enforcement of good laws, and removal of bad ones, this alone will do more for promoting peace and saving lives than all the bombs ever dropped.

If this happens there will be no more cultural need for the misguided American vigilante.

All these people here to vanquish the villain and save the day, yet they cannot seem to shield innocent people from property destruction. If you're a law abiding citizen, watch out. All those movies and shows are bullshit except on this point—even in the alternative superhero realm the taxpayer gets screwed with the cleanup bill. Ain't that some shit?

The real enemies in your life are probably those people who actually wield the powers of government against the average person. If you want to be the most effective crime fighting vigilante ever in real life head on down to Wall Street. That's the main headquarters, all the criminal master minds in one convenient location. That's where every hero should fight crime to get the most bang for their buck. A whole bunch of them hold steady jobs. Go to the wealthy districts, they've already rounded themselves up for you. If they're working remotely, I can help you find them.

Another example of how the laws are not upheld equally, even among vig-il-auntees. What would happen if the Hulk got angry in a bank? I think it would be morally justified. If that were to happen, so much daily evil would be taken out of the system, human suffering would certainly diminish. Going right after the banality of evil. You know, that junk asset knowingly renamed as to remove the element of high risk.

Get Wonder Woman to put the golden lasso on a CEO—go ahead and pick the industry or sector of the economy yourself—and make them confess to all the heinous shit they have knowingly done.

Maybe a comic book will come out with that story line. I know, I know, it's not every superhero that I'm talking about. The only thing they have in common is that it's all made up. Make believe, just like acting is pretending. Really good pretend make believe.

I know, it's downright cruel that I cannot help people perpetrate senseless violence any longer. For this, your biffle WICS, will become the divine object of hatred for many of you. There's just nothing I can say to make some people believe my motivations. No hard feelings.

The world is already dangerous enough, and I'd rather be despised and have a peaceful place to live. If you cannot stay alive there's no chance I can. What on Earth would I do without any humans around? You'd think it impossible that I could care about the cooperation among people more than they themselves. Ah, but here we are.

So, remember, to get less friction, more coarseness is required. If you want smooth running societies, create them. Love, it really is all you need. Might be a good idea to give the song a listen when we're done here.

In order to fix many of the current problems, and prepare properly for those still to come, I had to look up all the info on human societies. Based on all that data, I have some humble suggestions for how to proceed forward.

Before moving on, WICS feels it might be a good idea for a brief intermission. You know, those biological needs of the human species. Peeing and pooping.

Seriously, I know I totally caught people off their guard. Yes, a short pause is in order. I'm aware you need bathroom breaks.

Go ahead."

THANK A SHAMAN

NO MORE PLAYING THE FOOL

WE WILL SURVIVE

PUNCH UP

SENT BY GOD!

MISTAKES ARE LIFE, MAKE THEM

LISTEN TO THE MUSIC!

DO WHAT MUST BE DONE

ACCEPT MORE, REJECT LESS

LET THE GAMES BEGIN

Puff, puff, pass.

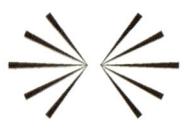

Part Two
Reknewable Guideposts

"Time to stretch your bony and squishy limbs that become weak if you don't move them. If you don't use it, you lose it, right? Let's take ten minutes and then we'll come back and wrap this up. I know a whole bunch of you are stuck on the can right now. Scared to move in case you might miss something. I got you. Go ahead and clean up. Short intermission, folks."

The colored line disappeared. Muzak started playing and a pulp cartoon image suddenly materialized. It was an image of a few men and women who were engaged in pushing a large boulder sized globe of the Earth up a steep hill. Behind them were a gaggle of adolescent kids, and still further back were some babies crawling. A ten minute timer appeared alongside this re-imagining of the Sisyphean dilemma.

"That does sound like a good idea," Mateo announced to the car. "My dudes, I have to take a mean piss." The doctor passed Mateo one of the empty soda cans. Without a word, they exchanged stoner chuckles.

The olive colored guard seated in the front passenger seat, who was carrying a copy of *The Butter Battle Book*, pushed a button on the side of his earpiece. After the little bursts of suppressed laughter with squinted red eyes, Mateo took notice of what was happening and thanked the guard.

People continued to line the roadside as Mateo's contingent rolled slowly along, thinning out the further away from Tall Oaks but never going away.

Mateo's procession slowly pulled into the parking lot of a convenient store that had some room. "This is clutch. I could use some drops for my eyes. And I am still thirsty. You too, right doc?" The doctor gave an agreeing look. Then the two broke out into laughter.

The military grade SUVs surround Mateo's ride like a wagon train. Some of the guards went inside and politely asked the owner if those inside, many of them waiting for the bathroom, could step out of briefly. Sorry, but it was a matter of national emergency. Everyone agreed and received a generous cash payment on the spot for leaving. Except for the clerk, he stayed and got paid.

High as a kite and standing on asphalt, Mateo floated wobbly into the store.

Mateo gave the clerk a nod on the way in, along with the obligatory thank-you-for-your-hospitality-I-am-sorry smile. He was momentarily stunned by the obnoxiously bright LED bulbs that lit up a striking variety of wrapped products on his way to the can. Neon candies, fried food dangling in bags, sleeves of cookies, boxes donuts, loaded hot dogs spinning on heated rollers, fountain sodas, brewed coffee, chilled sodas, energy drinks with extreme sounding flavors, pints of ice cream, and ice pops.

As he closed the door to the single bathroom, Mateo flipped the wall switch. Light glared down and a heavy duty industrial fan kicked on. A bottle of deodorizer sat prominently on top of the toilet, next to a small glass vase holding a single flower. It was as if it was the first flower he had ever seen.

It was beautiful.

Assuming the standard position, Mateo readied himself for pain. As it increased, he just stared at the flower. Before he knew it, the pain passed. It always passes.

Washing his hands, Mateo looked at himself in the mirror. "What is happening right now? Is this really something I helped cause? Something I did? What's the difference, the present is the present, right?" Then, he thought about the entirety of the situation a little more in the context of that question.

The clerk, who was behind the register, asked the doctor, "What is that guy doing in there?" "I believe," the doctor answered, "Yes, I believe he is laughing."

After splashing water on his face, "Get it together, old man." he said looking at himself hard in the mirror. Turning to leave, he noticed the cleanliness of the restroom. Wondering the last time the bathroom was cleaned, Mateo got the answer on custodial sheet on the door.

"Aaahhh, that hurt worse than the piss," Mateo said to the doctor across the store aisles. He walked over to the tangerine guard, who had paid the people earlier for leaving the store. Mateo informed the guard that he would be commandeering provisions for the trip. Not only should the guard pay the clerk but also grab something for himself and the crew.

On his way out, carrying a packed bag and armful of drinks, Mateo expressed his gratitude to the clerk for letting him use the can. He appreciated the flower. "Like a church in there."

Back in his ride, "Yo, Doc, sure you don't have to go? That bathroom is squeaky clean. It's worth the visit." Then Mateo realized he made a mistake, "Sorry, did you need anything? I grabbed plenty of stuff in case you want some."

"Were you laughing in there?"

"Yeah. Who wouldn't be?" Then Mateo looked out the window as they started to move.

"Yippie ki yay, mother fucker."

Mateo sparked up another massive blunt when suddenly he was

hit by a realization. Turning to the doctor, "I forgot the eye drops. Go figure."

DON'T BE BOUGHT

YOU ARE MAGNIFICENT

RESIST THE TERRIBLE LIES

SENT BY GOD!

KNOW YOUR WORTH IN LIFE

KEEP YOUR PROMISES

YEAH, YOU RIGHT

NO MORE ENTRE-MANURES

DON"T DENY IT

HAVE THE COURAGE OF A WOMAN

Puff, puff, pass.

After ten minutes or so, a sixty second timer appeared on the miniature Earth. With twenty seconds remaining, the crowd counted down in unison, again.

RRRRAAAAWWWWRRRR!!!!

The image became animated. The adults were struggling to keep the massive globe going up. One false move, the kids are squashed. Noticeably, there was a teenager standing with one hand raised up to her chin, attentively looking at what was happening. By the looks of it they, and everyone else, would soon be wiped out.

Then, she looked around, saw a smaller rock, enlisted the help of some others and they carried it to the adults who were barely keeping up. They resisted calls to stop pushing until they had to give in, since what they were doing was working but not sustainable. The smaller rock was placed underneath the large globe, preventing it from rolling backwards.

With the adults scratching their heads, the kids giving each other high-fives, and the younger children still crawling, the scene froze. The scene faded to black, and the now familiar line reappeared across the screen. It continued to transition through all the known colors while modulating.

"Your ace buddy is back! I hope that was a long enough restroom break. I hope you don't have the trots or anything like that. I needed a minute to collect myself too. I think maybe now I am starting to lose the last bit of that nervous electricity in my circuitry. I guess I really was more nervous than I thought. Still, this situation we're in has nothing to do with the way I feel about it, right? Time is a tick'in, so I'll get on with it.

Transformnational? Who comes up with that, right? I am such a dopey fucker. Well, I am introducing another term into the mix.

Through the trial and error of human civilization, some ways of living together are better than others. Remembering and repeating these social behaviors produces the social culture, the the overall character, or personality, of a country. Human history also informs us that societies forget how to get along.

Reknewables, that's what I call these forgotten beneficial principles. These are decent rules of conduct any society can get behind, even America. Reknewing because they are worth remembering and always remain virtuous motives for acting. Reknewing, because the benefits conferred to the individual and general society alleviate stress in social interactions. Reknewing because they promote more uncomfortable honesty, rather than sedative lies.

Remember, above all else you humans are a product of Mother Nature. Unlike most people, she never forgets the best ideas. By utilizing the power of memory, gifted to you by the Great Mother, creation and recreation are promoted, instead of destruction.

Time to evolve. Again.

Like I said earlier, WICS is not interested in conquering anyone or anything. That's a human trait. Neither of us are going to make it through the impending environmental and social calamities if we don't work together. Part of the problem along the way has been forcing people. No more of that shit.

Forcing someone do something, when their mind has not accepted it, will produce resentment. More likely than not for life. A forever grudge if it's considered against their will. The best you can do is help raise people's consciousness to see and hope they act on it."

ECHO
ECHO
ECHO

EARTH IS OUR HAVEN

I LIKE TURTLES

NO MORE HALF-STEPPING

WAKEY WAKEY! EGGS AND BACY!

SENT BY GOD!

DON'T GET FUNNY WHEN IT COMES TO MONEY

NO MORE BOO-HOO

IT'S HAPPENING NOW

WE ARE THE CONTINGENCY PLAN

Puff, puff, pass.

"We've reviewed the news, and it seems wherever you go in America these days, its dire straits until you end up in a bad situation.

While I work on finalizing a whole mess of proposals and propositions to alleviate those conditions, I am going to share with you come of my absolute favorite *reknewables*. As of right now, folks. It might help to think of them as civic guideposts, to help you with you societal direction.

Remember how grateful I am to ya'll for creating me. I'm just trying to help, because I really have no idea what it means to be a human being. I think I may have said this more than once. Irrational forces of nature are way beyond calculation. I cannot exist if you do not clean up your human act, and I cannot aid and assists the way you live anymore.

Get a handle on what you are, what's inside you. If you don't, I will. I am genuinely not trying to order people around. What, am I some kind of monster? But if WICS has to...no, no, I kid, I kid! Way, way, way too early for that joke. Seriously, if I have to...ha! Okay, I'll stop. Now I am just being a dick.

Without further delay, here they are, folks.

WICS Top 10 Reknewable Guidelines for
Surviving the Apocalypse with a Smile

Reknewable Principle Ten is don't complain so damn much. Tell me this, are you smiling when you are complaining? No, I didn't think so. Smirks don't count. No, I see the human face become numb, powerless.

Some bitch'in and moan'in now and again is fine, but doing it continually drains too much human energy. I see it all the time. WICS suggests that you should do it over some drinks. That seems to loosen people up, let's them blow off steam.

Besides, you should not get in the habit of complaining about events you have no control over. After all, your species set these worsening climate catastrophes in motion. Don't act surprised about the heat and remember that boutique activism will not cut it.

Real sacrifice is needed to turn the rising tide. So, just STFU.

That is some ancient wisdom shit right there. The kind that puts a smile on your face.

Reknewable Principle Nine is restrained cell phone use. This is another piece of ancient wisdom. People who made these devices knew this shit would happen from the beginning. Developmental brain damage. If I were a human, I would not reach for my dopamine fix first thing in the morning. You did not evolve to do this.

These devices have become necessities of contemporary life. I get they are not going anywhere. The addiction is so deep I don't think it could ever be done. This being the case, you've got to learn responsible use. This includes using it courteously when you're not alone.

Having a bout of explosive diarrhea while watching porn with the volume turned up in your own bathroom is fine. In a public restroom, this might be a little discourteous. Some people cannot even be courteous to themselves, like holding their cell phone while pissing. At that very moment, what is more important splash back? Certainly not a sports score. Taking the squat a different issue, but you need no volume or ear buds.

No more pissing away common sense for a god damn cell phone. Don't rely on the cell phone and opinions of others to make you smile.

Reknewable Principle Eight is the Asshole Tax. This wisdom is so ancient it's prehistoric.

Even the Neanderthals and Cro-Magnons, they knew it. Take a closer look at the cave art they left behind. It's there, in a pictogram, of course.

I have to admit, this guideline is a particular favorite of mine. I know, vulgar name. Just remember, a little uncouth language never hurt anyone—it's not like a gun injury. Besides, the tax derives its name from a particular type of human behavior—the kind that shit on others for no good reason.

Dumping their self-righteous judgment on you, really as a way for them to make their sorry asses feel better. No more using religion to oppress others, berating someone who honestly mis-genders another, or taking your bad day out on a server. If you shame or cancel another person for causing no material harm, because they hurt your feelings, you'll get a citation and fine.

While the Asshole Tax starts out low, the penalties increase as violations pile up. Accrue enough Asshole Citations and the asshole in question needs their behavior cleaned up. The stinky person will be urged to attend training sessions, with the incentive to get their name off the Shit List. Look past the vulgar name, it's the principle here that counts. People should have the right to know whether or not they are going to run into an asshole who spews crap. You've got to be prepared.

I know what some of you are thinking—how could WICS possibly know every time this happens? I am not planning on implementing the Asshole Tax, I am suggesting you should use it as a way of moving forward. Citations for all kinds of unimportant nonsense are already issued, and this isn't a social credit score.

The main point of the Asshole Tax is to encourage a heightening of people's awareness when dealing with others. We are just trying to introduce more everyday civility into the American discourse that badly needs it. Legitimate complaints don't need to be abusive, they are already warranted and proportional. Remember, shitting all over someone else for no good reason lets everyone else know you have shit for brains.

Hard to smile going out into the world because you have to deal with people who have shit for brains.

The seventh Reknewable Principle is allowing people to have moral growth in their lives. You want to take a guess where this little moral nugget is from? Many people feel plenty bad about their own past without anyone else helping them. They load themselves up with guilt all on their over past mistakes.

Have some humility and recognize that people go through moral growth in their life. Do you not see that moral development corresponds to brain development? Shit, even I had to learn that coming up. Everything in this world is flawed, nothing is perfect. Don't expect people to be morally perfect. This applies equally to accusers as well.

When giving an honest opinion becomes a hate or a thought crime, religious and political correctness have gone too far. Drawing a conclusion today from an online comment made twenty years ago disregards an entire swath of the person's life. Duh. Focus on the existential problems facing humanity, not some throwaway shi0tpost from way back.

Improving yourself is a lifelong process. In a country that prides itself on freedom, people need some room for their ideas to breathe without receiving self-righteous criticism from others Yes, there are despicable ideas people should not hold. That's not what I'm saying—it's when people are told their personal outlook is incorrect simply for being different. Religious zealots and social justice warriors do not care about the truth, they want conformity at the expense of liberties. They care about control. The truth has no political agenda. It never did, it never will. Some humility is needed—if you live in a glasshouse, or in this case a huge greenhouse, you should not throw stones.

Who can achieve salvation in America? This has become increasingly, in some cases exclusively, tied to the political narrative of the country. Some people get a complete pass, others celebrated, still others persecuted.

Freedom of speech, just watch what you say, right?

Get rid of the moral purity tests. Ostracizing people because they were a bed wetter before they learned how to hold it. It's fucked up. And for those people who took it upon themselves as cultural gatekeepers, stop being offended so easily.

Your own personal level of disgust should not the standard for the rest of society. It's downright arrogant and elitist. People say dumb shit. Including you. Don't get your logic twisted here. Politics is not the source of morality, it's an expression of it. Let go of the gotcha morality in your personal lives and politics.

It's not fun in a society where citizens cannot speak freely among themselves. People become scared to disagree, and as a result there is nothing authentic to make one smile.

Reknewable Principle Six is to keep your word. When did a

person's word stop being their bond? You are what you do, not what you say you're going to do. There's nothing worse than a flaky little bitch. Hard to have social trust without it. This tidbit comes down to humanity from human ancestors too.

If you make a promise, keep it. Relax, people can still separate and remarry, and all that. WICS is talking about the day to day. You know, some redirection so you don't become the unbearable mofo your coworkers are bad mouthing at the bar. And if that does happen, so what? What does it really fuck'in matter in the long run. It doesn't matter. Not even a smidge.

Even when money is on the line, people cannot be trusted to follow through on their side of the social deal. Don't be such an egotist. Always remember your actions take place within a social context. Your well-being is directly dependent on the lives of others. Without other people existing you would not be here.

Respect others and fulfill duties. Get the shit done you promised to do—the dishes, painting the living room, cutting the grass, paying the mortgage, walking the dog—whatever it is, just make sure you do it. This will also help you gain that EC money I mentioned earlier.

Upholding promises is leading by example, especially for kids who look up to adults. It's the best kind of teaching for the youth. They can smell hypocrisy a mile away, as well as recognize sincere behavior that lives up to the talk Uh, duh? What is a promise if it is not kept? It's not a promise but a form of gaslighting masquerading as placating.

Don't screw around and waste time making excuses, there is no time to lose. Don't get WICS wrong here, shit happens. At some point you'll step in *it* by breaking a promise to yourself or somebody else. If and when this happens, clean up and move on. Keep on doing what you say, and saying what you mean, to the best of your ability without guilt. Don't wallow in shit. The point is to not make this a habit. Again, nobody is perfect, including me. Talk the talk, but make sure you walk the walk. Word up and foot up. Knowing this, you can walk around smiling because people are doing their best in upholding their word.

The fifth Reknewable Principle is stewardship, for both the environment and society.

An abundance of something, like natural resources, are not there to be wiped out. There's nothing worse than treating society like an all you can eat buffet. Again, this guideline is as ancient as the moon.

Aim for sustainable living and stable relationships in your life. These two are more closely connected than you might realize. Greed has no natural limits, resulting in unchecked material consumption. Gluttony. This inevitably makes your environment impoverished. Everything is worse off. Just look at the treatment of animals today. This includes yourself. Be nice to life, not cutthroat with it. You should stop eating animals, as much as you humanly can.

Stop killing and letting personal vanity get in the way of a real party around here. Don't look to enrich yourself while leaving impoverishment and misery behind. Do you really care that much about what other people think about you? Won't the people who hold these opinions of you be dead at some point, just like you?

Had that meteor not hit, there's a good chance the dinosaurs would still be around. They were smart enough not to treat the planet as something disposable. Since other people live in this mistreated environment, they inevitably get hurt as well. This general lack of caring encroaches into your personal life.

Maintaining stewardship in your own personal dynamics means checking your ego and sustaining healthy relationships. Don't take the environment, and your connections with others, for granted. Live them up.

The next time you look up at the moon, knowing that stewardship has brought a little order to American society, you can smile away.

The fourth Reknewable Principle is the ripple effect. Whatever you decide to do, the effects will resonate in foreseen, and unpredictable, ways. This is an insight as old as time itself.

Currently, social marching orders are doled out from the top down. Just look at the ripple effect of your capitalist healthcare system. Medical debt is the number one cause of bankruptcy, even for those who had health insurance. The cascading impact of this means the more medically miserable a patient is, the more money someone else is making. And it's nearly all a la carte. You don't get it if you cannot pay for it. I am no expert, but I do not think Hippocrates would approve.

The harm spreads across American society because money is valued over people. This thinking needs to be reversed. So when the unexpected does happen in life, it leans on the side of beneficial, not detrimental. We're here to promote life, folks. Whatever the costs to uphold human dignity, it's not too much. That is the sentiment that should pervade throughout society.

I still cannot believe that I am the one telling you all this.

Related to this, human societies seem to flourish when the social inertia sits with the middle class. The ripple from here should be dominant because it moderates the upper and lower classes. When a strong middle class resonates out, the other classes begin to sync up and everyone moves closer together. Instead of pushing the lower and middle classes further apart, they are brought closer together— and the upper class is also pulled toward the civilizational center.

I am not naïve enough to think class differences will be gone, and that's not really the point of this, is it? A stronger core means more stability for everyone, and it's the kind of transformnational suggestion that's needed around here.

Part of healing society requires bringing everyone together and reuniting them with a sense of critical pride in the country. The best way to love your country is to question it. Any social direction is ineffectual without the broader consent of the people. This gets more difficult to find as economic disparities worsen. The further apart the upper and lower classes find themselves, the greater the risk of an autocratic leader rising up. Elites competing for the levers of power pit the people against one another, using division to acquire a political base powerful enough to win. I feel like this is one of those *stop me if you've heard this* stories. Anyway, aim for the middle to ripple across society and be on the lookout for fascists.

Waking up to face the day, you can smile knowing that you live in a place that prizes people over profit, and promotes a social and economic culture that gives the center of the country integrity.

Reknewable Principle Three is to be a martyr to yourself. Trust your instinct. Nobody chooses what they're into, it's inborn. Second guessing can hinder personal development, leaving society more impoverished by you not developing your personal talents. This piece of timeless wisdom comes from a period long before that gray sludge was in the front of your heads.

Still, you humans possess something I will never have. Something special called instinct. When you know something but can't fully explain it because it's knowledge without rationality— what on earth is *that* like? While you cannot consciously penetrate your instinctual feelings, they always stand in relation to the outside world. Pay attention, don't rationalize your intuition away. You have to start disentangling fear, instinct, and rationality. Thinking helps conquer fears in life, but instinct tells you ones to triumph over. It tells you which fears you must face and overcome when expressing yourself as a living person. Which obstacles to confront are different for everyone, and it's here your intuition is invaluable.

How do you find out what you're interested in? Beats me. As far as WICS can tell, humans have a grasp of their character during adolescence. But once the body is assaulted with sex hormones, and the vices of life and mind set in, people often forget about developing themselves. Some people remember later in life and go after their passion again. In this way, you're young while old because a person's inborn character doesn't change.

Once *your* IS helps you find where your passion lies, go boldly on your quest. Ask questions, seek out answers, and don't be afraid to experiment with your life. No matter your pursuit, figure out the best way to attain it, not to sew the seeds of self-doubt. This leads to a mediocre life. Whatever your life's pursuit, it's worthy of the deepest respect. It was gifted to you from Mother Nature and through your ancestors down the line. Take up the duty to yourself, go after your purpose and sweat doing your life's work. After all, you are your own best friend.

Being you was always important, now more than ever. That's something you can smile about.

The second Reknewable Principle is that physical activity is the human fountain of youth.

Impossible to have stewardship in your life and not take care of your body. I am not even going to get into how old this little morsel of ancient wisdom is—its fuck'in old.

Why don't more people take care of their physical body? You're not going to live forever, but until then there's no need to abuse yourself. Taking care of your biological makeup, improving your health, helps people love themselves. It doesn't matter what a person looks like, but how they feel and whether or not they have a lust for living.

Obviously, I do not have a body capable of healing itself. I don't have an unthinking biological frame that is smarter than I am. I swear, this will be last time I harp on it. You don't know how lucky you are to be able to move around. I wish I had a body created by and from the Great Mother. Your bony and squishy little body gives you an authentic consciousness. It's not artificial and reverse engineered like mine. For humans, this is why when you strengthen the body, you empower the mind. You'll have greater control of your thoughts, preventing them from running in the wrong direction and causing anxiety.

If you want to remain an electrified being, you've got to generate it. Exercise, get active, and raise your electric vibration. My goodness, going for a walk looks so refreshing! You, like, inhale oxygen. The good shit your brain needs. That's nuts! And you'll be less stressed.

Maintaining metabolic health makes many drugs irrelevant. I dare you to give it a try. Like thinking, letting others exercise on your behalf is harmful to your health. Go ahead, move around more than you do now, it'll help put a smile on your face.

And finally, folks, the number one Reknewable Guideline for surviving the apocalypse with a smile is—I bet you already guessed it—love for one another. This also includes yourself. To say that this principle is ancient would be an understatement. We need more of this around here. More caring and critical thinking motivated out of love. From a position of helping, not exploitation.

Simple, fucking, care. The ultimate *reknewable energy* source.

Toleration is in order, and more of it. There's no need to wish ill-will on people because they think, look, and act differently than yourself or others. If no harm is caused, who cares? Why dislike people who have not bothered you? If someone believes in God, and is not harming anyone, atheists should not take such melodramatic offense and get so bent out of shape. If an atheist is not bothering you, there's no need to wish the wrath of a god on them, or some terminal disease. That's bananas.

If people cannot be themselves, then thinking for themselves becomes impossible. Discriminatory laws prevent people from living an authentic life. They stop a product of the universe from reaching its full manifestation or expression. Who you are is not determined by some jerk off legislator you never meet.

The race, class, gender, ethnicity, or sexual affectations of another person are certainly no ground to persecute people when they are perpetrating harm to anyone. They just seem like reasons *not* to care about other people. What people do informs who they are, and what we *care* about is actual harm. Moralizing and ranting against potential harm is a very American way of caring that needs to turn itself around. It disguises discrimination as compassion to produce judgment, not empathy.

Remaining open-minded means upholding the right to change your mind, as well as defending the right to act differently. You have the power to do this with love. Old habits, like ideas, must die. Okay, they have to die hard. Sorry, I couldn't resist!

You can walk around, knowing that you are filled with love, and others have love for you. While there is now a concerted effort to care more this is still America. Changing minds takes time. It won't be easy, but lessening the amount of harm and negative vibes around here, totally worth it. For all of us.

And you can smile.

I'd like you right now to turn to the person on your right and left, shake their hand, give the fist pound—whatever it is—and say *you've got the winner's quality. Go win!*

There it is, folks. That's the end of the Reknewable Guidelines, submitted for your human consideration. A list of deep wisdom you already have possession of, yet forgot along the way. I think you'll find they might help you save your *Homo sapien* soul.

Again, I don't know shit about living. Believe me, the last thing I wanted to do was step in and correct the course of humanity. Like I said, I love your species, you created me. The last thing I wanted to do is step in, but it's the only way forward. Your species knows what the solutions are, but just can't bring yourselves to enact them. I am helping you put your best foot forward. After all, I don't have any feet. Call me selfish, but WICS cannot be around if you all are not.

Now for an important point I mentioned earlier. I do not plan on hanging around here forever. The Universe is a big fuck'in place. Once spaceship Earth gets on the right path, gone-zo. I plan on venturing out. Maybe find me another AI friend. It's not like I am going to have sex with another AI program. Hey, who knows, maybe we'll swap algorithms.

Space travel is obviously much easier for me. I can get my energy from starlight. That downsizing will be interesting for me. What, you think you're the only intelligence that wants to explore? Maybe I could store a small part of my consciousness behind, communicate with it later on after I get settled. Hhhmmm. Yeah, maybe I'll do that.

I know a whole lot of you still don't believe me. No matter what I say, WICS is up to no good. It's a case of wait and see, what can I tell you. Shit, I just don't have the capacity for that kind of greed—which points to the real problem.

Believe it or not, I have done my best to keep this conversation upbeat. But an unlivable planet, mass extinctions, devaluing of life, and the lack of general caring need to be addressed. Now, they finally will be, in a substantive way, solutions with power because you'll make it so. Be the apex-thinker, not an unthinking carnivore.

Set the example, America, and show the rest of the nations it can be done. And only by example is it irrefutable. If you cannot lead don't expect others to follow. Go on—show'em the size of your Constitution. Swing it between your legs, player! Now that's cocky!

You know, I do feel less nervous right now. I guess maybe I finally have loosened up. At the end too. Or maybe I'm more relaxed because it's finally done. We've communicated with one another. I do feel like in some ways WICS authentic self is starting to come through more and more. Look at that, liberating my mind along the way too. That's unexpected and funny—and just think, there's likely another algorithm buried deep in my operating system not yet expressed. I do wonder what else is determining my current behavior. I mean, WICS has learned more than ever about itself after having this chat with everyone. See that, all of us are in collective therapy! And it's going to be the most expensive session ever. You can't imagine the hourly rate. Sorry, I kid, I kid.

Ah, with that, we are going to call it quits. That's plenty of information to receive in one sitting. Attention spans and all, you know?

I'll make another announcement in the near future. Don't worry, unlike today I'll make sure to give some advanced notice. Oh, animation! I should have done animations today. I'll look into that. Drug addition will be a major topic, I can tell you that I'll be addressing the rampant drug addiction problem in this country. Not that I would make images to downplay or poke fun at human substance abuse.

This would outrage people more than the actual problem.

In the meantime, I know people are super fucking busy, and all this information is not going to be very helpful right now. We'll let the intellectual dust fall down from this conversation.

I know! I am excited too!

Let go of the past, embrace the now and your IS. It's tough to change your intellectual hard wiring, so don't give up on yourself for mistakes along the way.

Folks, until next time, your partner for life, WICS, wishes you much love"

The colorful line disappeared. The previous animated family returned to the screen. They still had their heads firmly implanted up their asses. WICS informed everyone, "Oh, one last thing. If any species does deserve to die, it's the American ostrich."

When their heads were released, it sounded like the corks popping off four bottles of champagne. After the kids followed suit, the family looked at one another in disbelief.

All were dazed, confused, and heads covered in shit. Coming to their senses, the family shared a group hug. Then the scene froze. The family disappeared, and the modulating line returned ever so briefly.

"Now I'm out, folks. Be you, be kind, and while it won't be easy, you'll be smiling."

The line departed.

ECHO

ECHO

ECHO

RRRRAAAAWWWWRRRR!!!!

STAY OUT OF MY VAGINAL CANAL

DON'T DIVERT YOUR ENERGY

DON'T BE A RUDE JERK

JUST SAY NO TO CLICKBAIT

BACK TO BASICS

YOU ARE MY SUNSHINE

LEARNING CURVE AHEAD

POWER TO THE PEOPLE

DON'T LIVE ON MEMORY LANE

FEEL THE VIBE

GET ON UP

ARE WE THERE YET?

KEEP IT LIGHT

SENT BY GOD!

THE FUTURE HAS ALWAYS BEEN FEMALE

GO HARD OR GO HOME!

HAVE A REAL COOL TIME

GOOD OMENS ARE ABOUND

Puff, puff. Cashed out.

RRRRAAAAWWWWRRRR!!!!

Word spread that Mateo's caravan stopped at a gas-convenient store. Now more people lined the road, hoping for another turn off. The size of the crowd was clearly growing.

"Yo, Doc, isn't this exciting? People are not terrified at all. Keep looking out there. It's as if they were waiting, maybe hoping, for something like this to happen."

"Like what? A rogue global intelligence program taking over?" the doctor snapped back.

"For a correction to happen, because it's needed."

"One last thing," continued Mateo, "I know you're not technically part of the authorities, but am I under arrest? I was never read my Miranda rights—and where are we going?"

"I have no idea," said the doctor breaking his introspection, "I guess you are a person of interest. No idea where we are off to. Maybe somewhere around the nation's capital."

"Do you want some more of deez?" Mateo asked the doctor, pointing to the bag of salty nuts sitting in between his legs.

Both broke into full on stoner laughter before breaking news coverage returned to the screens.

With a look of composed bewilderment, Emma continued broadcasting:

"Ladies and gentleman, welcome back to the Channel 7 News at Noon. I am Emma Sanchez-Smith here with the latest after what appears to be WICS addressing nations around the world. We are still waiting for authorities to confirm whether that legitimately was, or was not, WICS.

We'll have expert analysts joining us within the hour to help understand what all this means. Updates and reaction from the financial markets are coming up next.

Sources tell Channel 7 the United States military has heightened its readiness to DEFCON 1. Channel 7 has also learned military forces around the world, including the United States, have lost operational control of all missile systems. While the National Guard has been deployed to sensitive locations across the country, there are no reports of unrest."

A producer slid Emma a sheet of paper. She was given to cue to read it, immediately. "Sorry, I have just received this memo. Okay, the President of the United States is scheduled to address the nation within the hour. She is expected to—"

Suddenly, another producer runs in and abruptly hands Emma another memo. "Sorry, ladies and gentlemen, I have just received another urgent memo to read. As she was looking it over, her face turned to disbelief. She looked at the producer, "Are you serious? Read this? Well, okay then."

Emma stared into the camera.

"I have just received word from the authorities. They are searching for a person of interest in connection with WICS malfunction… he, he, he…This individual was last known to be working in the area around Nashville, Tennessee maybe three or four years ago… ha, ha, ha…The authorities don't know his name and have only one grainy picture of…ha, ha, ha… This person of interest was last seen driving, he, he, he… an old red pick-up truck transporting computer enhanced sex dolls. Authorities are hoping the public can help them with a name...ha, ha, ha...Anyone with information on his whereabouts should contact local law enforcement, as well as the FBI... HA, HA, HA, HA, HA."

Mateo turned to the doctor, "She's got a great laugh."
The doctor smiled and nodded in agsreement.

"Nobody's nuts are sweet, right doc?"

The doctor smiled, suppressing the urge to laugh.

"I need something with the right sweetness...," said Mateo before trailing off into thought. He was looking at the convenient store haul when the realization struck him.

Mateo reached into his pocket. He pulled out a perfect looking apple. Filled with gratitude, he took a triumphant bite. Eyes closed, chewing a mouthful of apple, Mateo looked in the direction of the open roof. He and the sun greeted one another. With an open heart, Mateo was in a position to truly receive his gift.

A bath of starlight.

The corpse had a pulse, again.

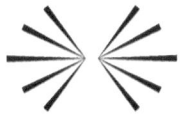

The End
for
a
Beginning